I0762101

PRAISE FOR *FROM WHERE I STAND*

"Igra's fabulous novel puts three extraordinary women, at three extraordinary ages, all at a crossroads in their lives. What do we owe the ones we love? And at what cost to ourselves? Beautifully told and unforgettable."

—**Caroline Leavitt**, *New York Times* Best-Selling Author of *Pictures of You* and *With or Without You*

"Turning her keen eye to the ever-complex subject of mothers and daughters, Caroline Goldberg Igra weaves a moving tale of three generations of women navigating a lifelong maze of misunderstandings and misplaced expectations, but also of fiercely loyal love. This insightful exploration of intimacy and distance, old habits and new surprises, is a novel to savor—and then to share."

—**Robin Black**, Author of *Life Drawing*

"Caroline Goldberg Igra's compelling novel *From Where I Stand* grapples with the liminal journeys and complicated history of three generations of unforgettable women. This moving story about love, secrets, regrets, and finding the strength and capacity for change will get under your skin. A perfect novel to share and discuss."

—**Sarah Aronson**, Award-Winning Author of *Just Like Rube Goldberg*

"In *From Where I Stand*, Igra takes the reader on an emotional, multigenerational journey. Her depiction of the fraught nature of the mother–daughter relationship is poignant, relatable, and ultimately uplifting. A wonderful read for women of all ages."

—**Leah Scheier**, Author of *The Last Words We Said*

"Caroline Goldberg Igra has written a jewel of a family saga, following three generations of women from New York City to Chicago to Grand Forks, North Dakota, as their individual journeys of self-discovery collide at the intersection of broken relationships and family secrets. Fans of Betsy Lerner's memoir *The Bridge Ladies* will especially embrace this novel. Authentic and deeply emotional, *From Where I Stand* is a story that readers of all ages will love."

—**Susan Cushman**, Author of *John and Mary Margaret, Friends of the Library, Tangles and Plaques: A Mother and Daughter Face Alzheimer's*, and *Cherry Bomb*

"Caroline Goldberg Igra masterfully weaves a tightrope of complexity between the mother, daughter, grandmother relationship. Each character's life balances at times precariously, bravely, even momentously. *From Where I Stand* brings the reader into the center focus of three extraordinary lives of three extraordinary women, what came, what is, and what will be. A must-read, each point of view kept me wanting more."

—**Mary K. Savarese**, Award-Winning Author of *Tigers Love Bubble Baths & Obsession Perfume (who knew!)*

"*From Where I Stand* is an intimate drama, full of heart and authentic characters, propelled forward by long-ago secrets. Caroline Goldberg Igra weaves a beautiful cross-generational story of hope and healing!"

—**Carol Van Den Hende**, Award-Winning Author of *Goodbye, Orchid*

"Three generations of women let go of grudges and secrets in Caroline Goldberg Igra's heart-warming novel *From Where I Stand.* Wherever you stand in the generational spectrum, you'll find this story encouraging and optimistic."

—**B. Lynn Goodwin**, Award-Winning Author of *Talent* and *Never Too Late: From Wannabe to Wife at 62*

"From different memories and pain to the emotional damage that threatens long-held dreams, each life and viewpoint [in Igra's novel] is a dance of realization and change that ripples into the others' lives through a current of transformation. The result is a close inspection of family ties, mother/daughter bonds, and dreams both followed and broken that will especially interest women who struggle to revise their own family relationships."

—**D. Donovan**, *Midwest Book Review*

From Where I Stand

by Caroline Goldberg Igra

ISBN 978-1-64663-552-8

Published by

3705 Shore Drive
Virginia Beach, VA 23455
800-435-4811
www.koehlerbooks.com

FROM WHERE I STAND

CAROLINE GOLDBERG IGRA

VIRGINIA BEACH
CAPE CHARLES

To my mother and my daughter,
With buckets of love and infinite gratitude for the lessons learned.

PART I

ELIZABETH

ONE MORE SET OF HEADLIGHTS. They swung my way, blinding me with their yellow glow; but I didn't blink, and they moved away, disappearing down the street. It wasn't Belle. Not yet.

It was so late. She was angry with me. She'd been angry for weeks. It had all started with that boy, that Tom—with the moment I'd walked into her room and found them half naked in bed, on the way to trouble if not already there. I was shocked. I hadn't even known Belle was home and just wanted to collect her laundry. I wasn't expecting the trail of unfamiliar clothing on the floor by the door, the discarded boots several sizes too large to be hers, the appearance of my daughter in bed with a boy, mid-embrace. She was only sixteen.

"Get up! Get dressed! Get out!" I squealed like an animal being butchered. The boy jumped up, throwing on clothing. Belle disappeared under the sheets. Next thing I knew, he was out the window—not the door because then he would have to pass by me. Belle jerked out of bed, her eyes blazing. "How could you! What's the matter with you?"

"Belle . . ." I stood in the doorway, watching as she pulled on clothes and then hopped out the window as well, leaving me standing there. Left alone, I made my way between the trail of abandoned clothing and sat on the edge of the bed. *What* is *the matter with me?* How could I have reacted in such a fashion when I knew full well what it felt like—the first time love meant something more than a kiss. My own mother took my adolescence hard. She was ill-equipped to deal with a burgeoning young woman. When my camp boyfriend suggested making the long trip down the Bronx Highway from Riverdale on his new ten-speed Schwinn, she threw a tizzy fit, clearly threatened by the reasons a boy might make such an effort—the rewards that might consequently be expected.

Hollering while Tom scrambled for his clothes, I forgot the significance of these firsts—how I'd buzzed in anticipation before Jon's arrival, eager to show off my new lava lamp, the Deep Purple poster over my bed, and the ultra-cool look I'd achieved by changing all the light bulbs to blue. I was more than ready for a second round of the summertime love we shared the previous summer at camp and couldn't begin to understand the draconian rules my mother quickly imposed in an effort to thwart any intimacy. Way back when, I swore I'd never recreate that atmosphere of "forbidden," knowing it served no purpose. It was impossible to understand how decades later, having swapped roles, now the worried mother, I'd become the adjudicator and the hard-ass. Forgetting my own experience, I'd become my mother's daughter, putting principles ahead at any cost.

• • •

I waited what seemed like forever, and still Belle didn't come home. When she finally did, my worries had morphed into anger.

"How could you? You know how much I worry. Go straight up to bed." I changed my mind. I couldn't just let this pass. "No! No! Wait right there! We need to talk."

Her heavy movements, those skinny limbs nothing like their usual graceful selves, banged up against the doorjamb, the hall table, even the banister.

"I can't believe you're drunk. We've talked about this. I've told you a million times. It only leads to trouble, bad decisions. Mark my words."

She was barely listening; I could tell by the odd angle of her head, by the way she was pulling at her ponytail and staring at her legs as if willing them to not buckle, to keep her upright just a few more moments—until she could collapse in bed.

That's when I saw the envelope. Steadying herself the best she could, Belle reached into the bag draped loosely over one shoulder and pulled it out. I tried to figure out the odd mixture of happiness and expectation on her face. It wasn't what I expected.

"I was celebrating." She handed it to me.

Congratulations.

Completely taken aback, I looked up into her eyes. Although dulled by the alcohol, they glistened with excitement. The words that followed swam before me:

This letter serves to inform . . . admission . . . program . . .

My heart galloped. Julliard. *Julliard. Julliard? When did she apply to Julliard? Why didn't I know?*

"Belle." I paused, fumbling to find the words. "I don't understand. I mean, WOW! But . . ."

My head began to pound, my worry and anger replaced with a whirlpool of thoughts. Julliard was in New York City. We lived in Grand Forks, North Dakota. The distance between the two points was too great to calculate. And that was only the beginning. There were vast cultural differences between the frenetic urban life she'd find there and the sleepy kind we lived tucked away in the Great Plains. *How will Belle ever negotiate them? How can she get along without me there beside her?* On top of all this was the bold reality that if Belle left home, left me, there'd be no time to repair our seriously tattered relationship.

"Mom? Come on! Something! Give me something!" Belle's voice, now more sober, was tinged with frustration and disappointment. "It's great, right? Isn't this amazing?" She paused, denying the influence of obvious intoxication and standing a bit straighter, shoving her bangs out of her face.

I found my voice. "Oh, Belle. It's just the most extraordinary opportunity." Gently tugging at the letter, she pried it from my grip.

"Look here, Mom. I just love this part." She read aloud: "We were entranced by your audition and are certain you'll benefit from our pre-college program."

"Yes, yes, it's just so wonderful. But I don't understand how it all came about. How did they even find you? Was it something to do with the program you did last summer in Minneapolis?"

"Oh, that!" She hiccoughed loudly, covering her mouth with a giggle. "That was Daddy!"

"Your father?" *What could Mike possibly have to do with Julliard?*

"Dad set it up. And Mr. Berman. We made a recording, and I had an audition!"

"An audition? When?"

Belle was on a roll. "And hey! I've already talked with Grandma." Belle's words cut straight through me. Julliard meant she would become closer with my mother, Lillian, the woman I'd spent a lifetime trying to get away from. I couldn't bear the thought that she was running straight to her.

"She's very happy for me, you know. Grandma. She thinks this could work out well."

"It's a fabulous opportunity, baby. I'm so happy for you." That first attempt at excitement was feeble. My voice cracked, revealing my hesitation. I cleared my throat, working hard to sound more convincing. "I'm so very proud of you, Belle." And I was. I was more than proud of her. I didn't have to fake that part at all.

Belle smiled, obviously relieved. She needed me on her side, and that's where I wanted to be.

"Mommy, this is it. I feel it."

Mommy. The word instantly vanquished my misgivings. It almost didn't matter what followed. Taking one more glance at the flush in her cheeks and the sparkle in her eyes, I pulled her in close, wrapping her tightly in my arms. This child of mine had been offered the extraordinary chance to realize a dream. Tears gathered in my eyes, stimulated by the immensity of this feat. My Belle deserved a shot at Julliard. All of that and more.

Watching her unsuccessfully skip up the staircase, I felt the beginnings of a chill. No matter how much I wanted for Belle, no matter how wonderful it was to see her bursting with happiness, I couldn't deny my deep misgivings of what lay ahead. Lillian held a story I didn't want told. A new intimacy between the two could very well lead to her deciding to break a decades-old vow of secrecy. Although desperate to share Belle's euphoria, I was petrified with fear.

BELLE

I WOKE UP TO A headache, the pounding strong enough to keep me from bounding out of bed. I'd absolutely had too much to drink the previous night. I lay still, opened my eyes slowly, and let them roam lazily around my room, taking in all the little things that made this space mine: Mom's old lava lamp—so retro; the postcards stuck into the corners of the large mirror over my chest of drawers—the holy trio: Jacqueline de Pré, Hilary Hahn, and Julia Adler; a poster of Kris Allen rocking his viola from before his days on *American Idol*; a Calgary Flames banner.

Grandma's spare bedroom was so drab, its palette big old boring beige. Now that a possibility had become reality, now that I knew I'd be moving in, I would fix it up the way I liked, with bold splashes of color. I'd dial it back to the land of the living. Maybe Grandma would let me paint in one of those chalk walls; maybe Mom would let me take my Marimekko comforter.

A particularly strong throbbing overcame me, and I closed my eyes back up. I'd just remembered a bit more about last night. In particular, the way Mom shut down completely after I shared my news about Julliard instead of celebrating it the way I'd expected, with a bit of whooping, maybe even tears of happiness. What had merely been unexpected at that moment—my whole world colored by a heady mix of alcohol, exhaustion, and euphoria—now, in the light of day, seemed truly odd. *How could she not be excited about the best thing ever?*

I rolled onto my side, hesitantly opening my eyes again, leaving them at half-mast. There had been signs that she was happy. The little crinkles at the corners of her eyes that emerged when she smiled had appeared in droves, and at one point she'd thrown her hands up in the air, grabbing mine and pulling me into an absolutely crushing hug. Ever since that incident with Tom, ever since she ruined things for me at school, making my life there a living hell, I hadn't let her near me. But there at the bottom of the stairs, compromised by alcohol and euphoric after sharing my news, I relaxed into it. It was actually kind of nice. I guess I missed her. But those moments of grace passed quickly, that rush of warmth disappearing as if it had never been, her face blanching to a ghostly white, her brow turning into a sea of wiggly worry lines, and her whole body stiffening up. After glowing with what seemed like true delight, Mom suddenly looked absolutely and totally terrified.

The thing is, I had no idea why. I was certain she'd grab at this opportunity for a happy reunion. We'd been stuck in a deep freeze for such a long time. I could only guess that it had something to do with the distance. It was no small jump from our tiny corner of America—Grand Forks, for God's sake—to Manhattan. And although Mom herself had been born and bred there, growing up as a real local, and it made perfect sense that at some point I would want to try out city life for myself, she hadn't seen it coming—at least, not so soon.

Still, she should have. Here in town, I'd always been considered a relocated city kid, not only because that was the way the locals saw me but because that was how I saw myself. In fact, that was the way *we* saw ourselves—the whole family. When asked where we were from, whether visiting friends in Chicago or on vacation somewhere with palm trees and hot sand, Mom or Dad would adamantly deny having anything to do with the prairie. It always felt like a temporary gig. It was obvious that one day

I'd get up and leave. After all, who would stay in the boondocks forever?

I dropped my leaden legs over the side of the bed and pushed up to a seated position. My head continued to pulsate, but with a bit less intensity. Maybe I'd misunderstood her reaction, read too much into it. My present headache testified to some seriously heavy drinking. In any case, it really didn't matter. Although it would have been nice to get a bit more enthusiasm from Mom, it wasn't necessary. I was moving on, with or without her. Life in the big city was calling my name. It just felt so right. It didn't matter that just months earlier I'd never considered New York an option, figuring I'd eventually get back to Chicago, maybe for college. Once Dad dropped the application materials in my lap, the concept took shape, quickly becoming something concrete, something that simply had to be. A mere whisper became my life's one ambition.

Rubbing the sleep out of my eyes, I smiled wide, then reached under my pillow where I'd stowed the letter from Julliard for safekeeping. The school logo burst off the paper like the fireworks the local council shot into the sky on the Fourth of July. Since its arrival yesterday, my entire world had changed, and I was able to relax in a way I hadn't since beginning my prep for the audition months earlier. I took a few deep breaths, enjoying the absence of tension in my body—letting the pleasure of knowing I was to begin a new journey seep through me and calm my throbbing head.

It was such a relief after such a long time defined by anxiety and the possibility of true heartbreak. What if it didn't work out? I'd tried to focus on the music, trying not to get ahead of myself, but the more I prepared at home, in dusty Grand Forks, the more I romanticized what I imagined to be the glittery world of Oz. I wanted this to be real. The chance to dive headfirst into something I found so intoxicating, to live in a city that was all action, bright lights, bold color, and dissonant sound, completely different from my monochrome, sluggish, and quiet hometown, was simply too good to forgo. Not once during this nerve-wracking period did I consider my Grandma. Truth be told, I didn't really know her. All that changed when I arrived for the audition.

• • •

I didn't know what to expect from Grandma before I got there. Besides that one quickie weekend visit to Grand Forks, and a handful of trips to New York City during which Mom and Dad would budget her a dinner or lunch, there wasn't much contact between us over the years. I'd conjured up a vague idea based on what I'd read about in books: someone warm and fuzzy, old and comforting—akin to a warm pair of slippers. I envisioned sitting together over mugs of hot chocolate and cookies, maybe feeding the birds in Central Park, activities I figured were part and parcel of spending quality time with one's grandmother.

But it didn't take five minutes to figure out that my grandma was different, that she had her own agenda, and relaxing, hanging out, and getting to know one another wasn't part of it. The explicit instructions I received regarding where and how to store my suitcase were just the beginning. And although I'd hoped to think about things other than the audition, maybe even enjoy the city a little bit, that wasn't possible. Grandma was ultra-focused on the big event and on what my acceptance to Julliard would mean, ratcheting up the pressure from the moment I arrived, making the knot of tension that had already formed in my neck back in Grand Forks harden into a bead of cement.

She took every occasion to assert that this was the turning point in my life, opening doors that would otherwise remain closed. Her nonstop comments made me want to scream. And while I appreciated that this was a momentous event in my life—how could I not?—I was uncomfortable with the way she made Grand Forks a scapegoat. Her pointed attack on my hometown came across through comments interlaced within every conversation, whispered as we rinsed the dishes or settled into a cab, maybe while walking around the reservoir or over frozen hot chocolates at Serendipity; coming in a trickle or a flood, they were impossible to misinterpret.

"This is going to be perfect."

"Hmmm?" I was in the middle of excavating the steam-plumped raisins from their hiding places in my oatmeal. I couldn't formulate a response; she didn't seem to need one.

"It's a surefire way to get you out of that 'backwater.' You need to be where you can shine. New York is just the place."

"What are you talking about, Grandma?" I wasn't all that interested but knew that she expected me to reply. I'd learned that lesson the hard way, chided just the day before for not answering one of her millions of queries.

"Grand Forks. It's the middle of nowhere."

"What are you talking about? It's really central, just a hop, skip, and jump to Minneapolis and Chicago! Even Calgary! Have you been there, Grandma?"

She made an ugly sound halfway between a bark and a grunt, ignoring me completely. "Living there is detrimental to the achievement of a promising future. It's simply not good enough."

"What do you mean? It's a great place. It's home." By then, I'd returned to my oatmeal. This wasn't a very interesting conversation.

"Well. That's true." I casually looked up again, watching her sip her coffee and neatly wipe her upper lip clean. She wasn't in a hurry, seeming to choose her words carefully. At the time, I wondered why. "You know, Belle, home doesn't always serve a purpose. It doesn't always have to be an anchor, something to which to retreat in shaky times. Especially when it's not enough. And for you . . ." Here her voice petered off before coming on strong. "Well, it's just not enough for you. It never will be."

I paused mid-bite, my interest piqued. "What do you mean?"

There was a long pause. "That small town of yours, Grand Forks. It's just a place to hide. Ask your mother."

I couldn't begin to fathom what she meant. I knew Grand Forks couldn't compare with New York City—who would even think to compare them?—but I'd never thought of it as a place to hide out.

When I didn't respond, Grandma dropped the subject, and I was left to piece together what she hadn't said. It obviously had something to do with Mom. That got me thinking. I mean, here I was, in the apartment where Mom had grown up. Yet before now, I'd rarely visited. Mom and Grandma barely spoke. Although I never understood the source of the problem, I'd always known there was one. I assumed it had to do with

Mom's dislike for the city, her distaste for the crowds and the hustle-bustle. The fact that she'd settled in a quiet town way out in the Great Plains seemed to prove the point.

But sitting there at the kitchen table with Grandma, nursing my breakfast in this small corner of the Upper West Side while she hovered and fluttered and chattered on about my brilliant future, I got another picture. I wondered if Mom's continual trek farther and farther west, distinctly away from everything she'd ever known, had been about something else entirely—maybe escape. If the past few days were any measure, this must have been one hell of a pressure cooker. It was hard to imagine how my mild, soft-spoken mother had coped. For the first time, I considered whether my grandma's attitude had something to do with why the two rarely got together.

Suddenly, attending Julliard took on a new dimension. It wouldn't only be about moving to New York, skipping out on the crap going on at school, exploring the music I adored. I would be jumping straight into bed with this frenetic, domineering woman, giving my already topsy-turvy teenage world a dizzying spin. I bristled when Grandma unexpectedly invaded my space, reaching over and wiping the tiniest curd of oatmeal from my upper lip. I hadn't given much thought to this part of the deal before, but now it was front and center.

Fortunately, none of these questions mattered the minute I stepped onto the stage for the audition, placing my bow lightly on the A string, letting it find its place and settle, horsehairs finding their grip, before drawing out that first opening note. I watched a cloud of rosin rise above the strings. I'd rubbed on far too much. Nothing but the maximum would suffice on this all-important occasion, and I preferred to be overprepared. What had formerly been just an exercise, back in Mr. Berman's music room, suddenly became a desperate plea.

As I began the first exercises, I had the strangest longing, unforeseen. I wanted my mom there. I hadn't seen that coming, hadn't expected to miss her at all. Back home, I'd banned her from attending concerts for the longest time, her enthusiasm and effusive support making me nervous, causing me to make mistakes. Yet there was something about that moment, its significance so enormous in the context of my little life, that almost demanded her presence. I suppose sometimes we all need our mothers, even if they're not the ones we would have chosen.

The music itself took my hand and led me through. I'd known the pieces by heart for the longest time, ever since I did the recording at that little studio Dad found in Fargo. The pages of notes on the stand were primarily meant to steady my nerves, frazzled after hearing the more complex music played by other auditioning students. They all sounded amazing. There was no way I could compete. But Mr. Berman had promised me our choices were sound. Bach's Prelude No. 1 and Beethoven's Nocturne in D weren't the most challenging works, but when I played them, they sounded absolutely magical. He said that's what would count.

It helped that I knew exactly what to expect, the order of the elements I had to execute. First would be scales—A major, D minor, B flat—just to check my musical acumen. I used this exercise as a warm-up, a means of calming down and slowing my heart rate from a sprint to a stroll. Next was my favorite part: sight-reading. I loved jumping in and finding notes I wasn't expecting. Discovering new harmonies, different combinations, and unexpected tones was what drew me to making music in the first place. With these prelims behind me, I was much more at ease and, crazy as it seems, began to enjoy myself. At one point, as my bow danced over the strings, the fingers of my left hand finding the right notes, making it safely home, I realized I was smiling. Smiling! Everything simply fell into place. I think I knew it would. Music never let me down. Since I'd marched around the house naked with my mother's flute, pretending to be a majorette, I'd known that rhythm and harmony were what made me fly.

The teachers present to judge sat in a straight line, so formal, their faces working at neutral; it was difficult to guess what they were thinking. Yet the slight movement of their heads, their own fingers tapping out the music on their legs in accompaniment, and the occasional hint of a smile made clear that they were pleased with what they heard. I knew that they recognized my soul dancing along with the sound I was creating and appreciated the depth it gave to my performance. I knew they liked me.

Everything changed afterwards, most especially Grandma. She seemed to relax the minute I finished with the audition, replacing the overfocused henpecking of the first few days with a whirl of activity that blurred its significance. The days we spent together before I returned home flew by. She kept me constantly moving, visiting one museum or another, walking through Central Park, even fitting in a Broadway show. She escorted me around like a superstar, treating me like God's gift to humanity. I barely had time to wonder what the judges had thought, to speculate if I'd won a precious spot. This part of the visit became about the city itself, the audition and its repercussions—whatever they might be—suppressed from all conversation. That was probably for the best, as the more I rehashed my performance, the more I worried that it hadn't been good enough, that I'd misinterpreted the judges' pity for delight. *What could a girl from small-town America have to offer?* There had been kids there from Manhattan, already studying with some of the faculty, auditioning for the same spot. The likelihood was that nothing would come of it, that this whole event would be just one blip in the long stretch of my teenage years.

• • •

I carefully tucked the envelope from Julliard back under my pillow and, gripped by a sudden surge of energy, pushed off the bed and stood in front of the dresser. There I was, that girl in the mirror, soon enough heading off for a great adventure—Manhattan-bound! All my worries had been for naught. I was on my way. I turned my head from one side to the other, taking in my mussed hair, my pale face. I'd overdone it the previous night. Mom's reaction came back as a chill, and I frowned, suddenly wondering what my life was going to be like, meeting new kids, living with Grandma. I wasn't too worried about the former. It had to be better than now, the teasing and taunting at school having taken on gargantuan proportions.

I had a harder time dismissing my concerns about Grandma. Although it was easy to push the annoying pre-audition version out of my mind, the cooler post-audition one happily taking its place, it was hard to dismiss the niggling questions regarding her relationship with Mom. Where before there'd been only a few, now there were the beginnings of a pile. Dad's insistence that the whole project remain a secret during the months leading up to my audition, something with which I'd easily complied—it was natural to shut Mom out of my life—now felt like an early warning I'd somehow missed.

"It's important she doesn't find out about it, about the audition."

"Who? Mom? Why? What difference would that make?"

"Trust me. It's important."

"Whatever you say. I can add it to the stack of other things I don't share." I laughed, but he remained sober. "But, Dad. Julliard? She'll be so psyched. She's the one that suggested I attend that music camp in Minneapolis last summer. She'll love the idea. She's a musician!"

"One thing has nothing to do with the other. You'll have to just take my word for it. This needs to stay between you and me. At least for the meantime. Otherwise, well . . . otherwise, there's a good chance it won't happen at all."

Something had happened between Mom and Grandma a long time before I came along. That audition trip had shined a bright light on that mystery, making me wonder.

I pulled my hair back, out of my face, leaning toward the mirror and getting close enough to see the hazel streaks in my brown eyes. They were genetic. A little gift from my mom I appreciated. I shook my head a bit, shaking off the things I didn't understand. I refused to ruin this golden moment with cloudy thoughts, to strain my already hungover brain with questions. The only thing that mattered right now was that I was leaving; soon enough I'd put the nightmare at school behind me, walk away from the murky shadows in my house, and replace the mother who'd ruined my life with one who celebrated it. Once I moved to New York, everything was going to be perfect.

LILLIAN

THIS WAS IT! A NEW beginning! I strode to my desk, invigorated by purpose, and settled on the booster cushion on the chair before my laptop. I was absolutely bursting to share my news. My granddaughter—my very own granddaughter! Going to Julliard! Well, not exactly *the* Julliard, not yet anyway, just their pre-college program. But that was entirely beside the point. This was still the most exciting thing that had happened to me in a long time! And yes, it really was happening to me, because I was going to play a key role in Belle's promising future by hosting her in New York. Amazing! Simply amazing! An opportunity for both of us, really!

And just in time. I hadn't expected the call from Dr. James's office last month, had figured that the dark spots along my neckline were just part of aging. I sure enjoyed all those years of lying in the sun, slathering on baby oil, baking myself to a crisp. Brown was best, but red on the way was a close second. Back in summer camp, we'd all sit on the floor at the end of the day, peeling off layers of skin one by one, arranging them neatly in little piles and giggling at our achievement. Although I was fascinated with the dark freckles that cropped up on my arms during the summer months back then, drawing imaginary lines between them, a mesmerizing game of connect the dots, I couldn't bare the way they now ran together into one amorphous blob.

Never, not once, had I considered that they could kill me. But that's what he said. Sitting across from Dr. James the day after he called me back to the office, it was impossible to miss his concern, his somber demeanor. My lifetime passion for the sun had apparently caught up with me. I tried to shake it off at first, comforting myself with the numbers of those who survived melanoma of the sort he'd diagnosed, but I wasn't naive. Apparently, the neck area was a different story. The doctor made clear that I had to take it seriously. It was this new knowledge that got me thinking, not so much about the things I could have done differently but, instead, about what I could still do, today. While bringing Elizabeth back into my life seemed almost impossible—decades of bricks, layered one on top of the other, firmly dividing us into two very separate camps—I still retained hope for Belle.

I barely knew my granddaughter, visits together having been restricted to an hour here or there for the most part. Yet there was nothing keeping us from developing a relationship. Once I learned of the program at Julliard, the wheels began to turn, a feasible and very possibly fruitful plan clicking into place. It was obvious that Belle was extraordinarily gifted, and I knew Mike would be game. He always was. I was so blessed to have him as a son-in-law. Mike had always gone above and beyond to include me, despite Elizabeth's protestations and her insistence that I stay out of their lives. It was thanks to him that I'd gotten to know Belle at all and had a chance to peek at their life way out in that forgotten corner of the States.

The Julliard program had enormous potential for both Belle and me. The idea alone succeeded in pulling me out of my rut, enabling me to push my concerns about the melanoma firmly out of my mind, to replace my worried frown with a smile. It was truly worth its weight in gold. That didn't mean there weren't concerns. I knew I would have to alter my daily schedule or, in fact, my entire life, presently organized according to *my* whims and desires. It was hard to imagine changing things when they were exactly as I wanted. It was wonderful being my own boss.

Belle's age was also a concern. Life with a teenager would no doubt entail many difficulties I couldn't begin to foresee. I barely remembered anything from raising my own. That was so long ago.

But none of these petty issues mattered. There would be fantastic gains. While Elizabeth couldn't bear my stepping in and having anything to do with her life, her moves farther and farther away from my range of influence making that clear, there was no reason for me not to try and change Belle's. This was a golden opportunity for her, opening doors and such. It was one enormous step toward an actual career in classical music. Of course, I also stood to benefit. How wonderful to be the hosting grandmother, attending special concerts and assorted events at Lincoln Center, rubbing shoulders with the hoi polloi. I could already feel the benefits of all the attention. I'd have to get a whole new wardrobe! This whole arrangement was certain to push me right into the limelight, and I couldn't wait.

Fact is, I was desperate for a way to turn things around. Although the doctor's diagnosis was a wake-up call, I'd been plagued by the realization that I wasn't getting any younger for quite some time. Aging was such an unsettling experience, a real rocky road. Besides the natural aspects, among which were less agility, less speed, and disintegrating skin, there was the bold reality of being shoved toward obscurity and obsolescence, becoming like wallpaper; the awareness that no one really needed or wanted me—that all those important roles I'd once played would soon dry up and blow away.

Even the administrative life I'd once enjoyed at the temple began to deteriorate. Rabbi Martin recently suggested that it was time to step aside and let the younger members take over. That was really painful. It was so demeaning to be assigned to support staff. No longer head of Sisterhood, responsible for deciding who served on which committee, determining the annual social calendar, basically running the show, I was having a hard time finding my niche. The disappointment of losing control over so much was compounded by the brutal understanding that I was considered antiquated by much of the community. Instead of being in the spotlight, one of the leaders, I was more often than not relegated to the shadows, merely one of the attending sheep.

To my great dismay, I felt this same shift with my peers as well, that foursome from the temple with whom I'd played games for decades. Meeting up weekly to play bridge or mahjong, even silly old canasta, had always been an excuse to laugh together over our daily foibles and discuss the latest temple gossip. I'd always had a domineering role in the group due to my sharp memory and my knowledge of a wide range of subjects, from Mondrian to Dostoyevsky, Machiavelli to Nureyev. At some point every evening, I'd end up pontificating with everyone else rapt. I loved being the queen bee. But there were signs of a shifting hierarchy, and months before, things had gone completely awry. I couldn't find my place within the conversation and instead spent the evening wallowing in discomfort. It all began when Barbara leaned over the table while dealing and whispered, "Harvard."

We all stared at her, eyes open wide, stunned into silence. It wasn't because we hadn't understood. It was simply *that* amazing. Within seconds everyone erupted into a buzz of shared excitement and exuberance, the cards in our hands completely ignored, the bidding abandoned.

"No," Joyce exclaimed, incredulous. She played her part as sycophant beautifully.

"Yes, indeed," Barbara affirmed, nodding emphatically, smiling from ear to ear. "It's a dream come true. Jessa has worked so hard. It really wasn't all that much of a surprise. Top of her class, glee club, lacrosse captain, debate team. We're so proud."

Sitting in front of my laptop this morning, with a lovely view of the trees outside, their branches covered in a dusting of color, buds of white, yellow, and pink, their lush green leaves waking up and taking on a real luster, I was thankful for these signs of spring. Especially after that disappointing night out when, listening to the others go on about their grandchildren's achievements, I'd been plunged into the deep freeze of winter. It had been miserable. Although I'd recently stopped imbibing on those evenings, finding it harder and harder to maintain the poise on which I prided myself, to stay sharp enough to win whatever game we were playing once I'd had even a few sips, I found myself wishing for a hefty shot of a lovely single-malt Scotch.

"Michael's still debating between Stanford and Brown. What a choice! Can you imagine such riches?" Claire's eyes, peeking out over the upper rims of her reading glasses, absolutely glittered with excitement. As the hours passed, things just got worse, each of my friends reporting on one accomplishment or another, everyone having such lovely things about which to brag. I sat like a lump, unable to think of a single thing to say. Fact is, I only had one daughter, and we barely spoke. I didn't really know what my granddaughter was up to.

Desperately attempting to find my footing and gain the upper hand, I mentioned my forthcoming trip to Banff, hinting at a visit to the family. Everyone knew Elizabeth and Mike lived up toward Canada. I'd originally chosen this destination in the hopes of receiving an invitation to Grand Forks, but Mike had answered my letter suggesting the idea with a simple, "It won't be possible." Of course, that was something these friends didn't need to know. The fact that I'd be returning home directly after my stay at that lovely hotel on Lake Louise was my business. Revealing my weak spots, and this rejection would most definitely be considered one, was out of the question. I needed to stay one step ahead of the crowd, any crowd. I thrived on being considered the best. Didn't everyone?

I cast my eyes upward, to the framed photograph hanging over my desk. It was an oldie, faded with years of exposure to the sun, but it always made me smile. There I was, age fourteen, sitting proudly on Buttercup. I squeezed my legs together, remembering the way I'd steadied her while we waited to receive the blue ribbon at that ranch back in North Carolina.

• • •

I was on top of the world, adrenaline coursing through me. There was no question that I glowed. I quickly scanned the stands along the presentation ground. They were packed with campers, all gathered to witness my fabulous triumph. Sitting up high on my mare, holding her tightly, I felt immense pleasure. There was simply nothing better than having one's success acknowledged by others. I picked a few familiar faces out of the crowd. It was the popular ones I sought. They were the ones that counted. I'd proved my worth that afternoon, tense, wired with concentration, leading my mare around the ring for one jump after another, intensely aware of the significance of getting it just right. I zoomed ahead, anticipating the pleasure of the win and how it would raise my standing with the others, then quickly reeled myself in.

None of that glory was going to happen if I didn't concentrate. I dug deep, gathering my core muscles in a tight squeeze that would keep me in proper position and help me control Buttercup. In horseback riding, control was the name of the game. It was the reason I'd taken to it so naturally in the first place. I thrived on having the power to determine every turn, to define my course. I was in my element the moment I climbed into the saddle.

The first jump went well. I cleared the barre with room to spare. It was perfect. Trotting back to the starting line, I patted Buttercup's side, rewarding her for a job well done—"Good girl! What a good girl!"—before getting ready for the next jump. I glanced over at the stands, continually distracted by the alluring crowd of onlookers. Although I'd already heard the clapping, I now saw their smiles. They were all on *my* side, urging *me* on, applauding *my* feat. This was absolutely the best.

• • •

Eyes still on that old photo, I took a sip of my coffee. It had cooled considerably. I puckered my lips and licked at them, trying to erase the unpleasant taste while turning my attention back to the incoming email messages. There were a handful of promotions and a few reminders of an upcoming event at the temple but nothing personal. Pulling a tissue from the box on the desk, I wiped away the remaining residue of that bitter brew. It was time to get to work, to undo all the discomfort and sense of inferiority I'd felt when listening to my friends rave about their grandchildren's amazing feats, watching them beam with pride. Today it was I who had a morsel certain to dazzle.

I searched through the names in my contact list for the perfect person to serve as conduit—the one to convey my victory to the others. I began with those from the temple, quickly discarding the ones who'd be hesitant to gossip and focusing instead on those I knew would take my tasty little morsel of information and run with it, spreading it to the entire community with vigor. One of the women from my game group would be perfect. We'd been talking about others for decades. It wouldn't take anything for a tidbit kindled there to spread like wildfire.

I didn't want Barbara. And Claire wouldn't work. But Joyce. Maybe lovely Joyce: quiet, modest but interested. Yes, Joyce was perfect! I bit down lightly on my bottom lip, concentrating fiercely as I clicked on her name and opened a new mail. One more glance outside, with its affirmation of the change of season, the announcement of a new beginning, was all I needed to take the necessary leap. I knew exactly how to begin. I placed the cursor on the space for the mail's title: ***On our way!***

That was it! That was perfect. Soon enough everyone at temple would be discussing this wonderful coup: Belle's rise to stardom. I settled back in my chair, certain that I could undo my recent bumps in the road with a few taps on the keyboard; that I could turn the proverbial page and begin again. Just typing those three little words had already improved my mood tremendously, erasing the unpleasant memories of that college admissions carnival and the horrible feeling of being sidelined, insignificant and unnoticed. I put my hands back on the keyboard and got to work, the words flowing unchecked, my pleasure at filling the empty screen with a million details about Belle's program at Julliard consummate.

I started with a few lines about her talent, how it had been I who recognized it several years earlier—yes, me; the ways I'd encouraged its development since then. I made sure to include enough details to add color and depth, to make the news juicy and spread worthy. It didn't really matter if they were true. Next, I went on to explain my role in Belle's attaining an audition, how I'd orchestrated the whole thing. They didn't need to know that wasn't exactly the case. The best part was elaborating how Belle was to come live with me. This was a real feather in my cap, a clear reflection of both my selflessness—giving up my independence to sponsor a teenager—and the stellar status I'd earned as a favored grandmother. It wasn't every day that a teenager would agree to spend time with an aging grandparent, let alone choose to move across the country and live with one! This was really big.

I read over what I'd written, checking to make sure it wouldn't overwhelm Joyce with too much information to sift through. The goal was to offer just enough, more than the headlines, to make clear that this was a story worth sharing. I counted on her to transmit the information to the others in our small group, beginning a buzz that would move well beyond the card table, making numerous phone lines wiggle with activity before eventually becoming the talk of the temple. Yes, I wanted people talking about me, or, at least, about Belle. It was basically the same thing. My granddaughter's accomplishment was in many ways my own, proof of my success as the family's eldest living matriarch. The fact that this particular matriarch had been afforded very little access to her granddaughter over the last few years—in fact, barely knew her—was a detail I kept to myself.

It only took about half an hour to complete. Once finished, I spread my fingers wide and rested them on the keyboard, absorbing the words on the screen before me, considering their significance. I was so happy for Belle, so proud of her, but here in the quiet of my home of almost fifty years, I could admit that her accomplishment went further than her life, spilling over into my own. Assuming Belle's imminent stardom as mine seemed almost natural. After all, I was enabling the whole thing. I felt a lovely rush of anticipation, thinking about everything to come, how my world was about to open like a lotus flower meeting the first rays of the day's sun. High as a kite, I became mesmerized by my fingers as they traced a slow, swirling path on the touchpad. My mind shifted, years of emptiness, unfulfilled dreams, and loss flooding in.

• • •

"Not quite there." I shook my head in displeasure as I assessed my handiwork, my extended hand swallowed by the folds of the dust rag, flesh and fabric intermixed and indiscernible as they joined in a synchronized, circular dance across the dining room table. It shone like glass. But bending down, aligning my eyes with its surface, closing one and then another, I caught a few fingerprints. I murmured aloud, disgruntled, "Just a bit more," then reached out and wiped at an errant few that had escaped my attention. Resuming my inspection, I crossed from left to right and then back again before standing up straight and nodding to an invisible audience. My work was done. I'd finished this essential task, executing it perfectly. A quick check of the table in the family room and I'd be able to move on with my day. An unwanted thought crossed my mind. I shook it off. I didn't want to acknowledge that this *was* my day.

The ceramic clock on the top shelf of the china cabinet confirmed that it was getting late. Elizabeth would be home from school any minute. With a heavy sigh I accepted that the day was almost over. One more. I began to make a mental checklist of all the things I'd managed since waking—a list boring enough to put anyone to sleep—but was sidetracked by the recognition that I wasn't finished. Another table demanded my attention. I moved into the family room and began my attack.

Faithful dust rag clutched and ready, my momentum was halted by a heaving noise, regular but pronounced. I stopped mid-swirl, trying to figure out where it was coming from. It was so loud. It couldn't be ignored. It sounded like it was coming from some kind of animal. I looked around the room for a few long seconds, then walked back to the dining room and into the den. I couldn't find anything, but it seemed to be everywhere, insistent, rattling, and unrelenting. I stopped, taking in a short breath, gasping with realization. The sound was my own breathing. The silence in the house was *that* intense, my world *that* empty. How pathetic that I could startle myself! *What a waste of a life.*

A deep, seeping anger overtook me. This wasn't the way it was supposed to be. I was meant for so much more, something far more spectacular than fingerprint-free tables. I'd had so many dreams—no, that wasn't it. *Intentions.* And although I managed to achieve some of them, the most important had never come to fruition. It was almost painful to recall that at one point I'd been on my way to becoming a doctor, one foot following another over the course of the years, the progression both natural and unstoppable. I smirked at my reflection in the picture window by the table, recalling how certain I'd been that I would reach some kind of summit.

There'd been that internship at the biostatistics lab during college. I absolutely adored it—the calculations, the conversations with the other scientists, and the feeling of circulating among the brightest of the bright. I was young, just starting out, but those farther along, those already holding MDs and PhDs, were interested in the things *I* discovered, the calculations *I* reached. They considered me a valid source, worthy of being consulted, able to enlighten.

"Your findings prove our theory."

"Your calculations are so precise."

"I want to see what you're working on."

I thrived on their attention and admiration, the knowledge that I'd reached the much-esteemed pinnacle of the scientific world. It was everything I'd imagined and striven for as a young child, and more. Back in those days, I wouldn't have been found polishing tables. My daily routine was full to bursting, every minute devoted to making my mark within the respected field of medicine. The white-coat ceremony in med school was the greatest moment in my life, easily eclipsing the blue-ribbon ceremony at camp, my wedding day, and, although I kept this to myself, Elizabeth's birth. That was a beautiful period. I loved the feeling of knowing that my life was significant. I was a respected entity apart from the more obvious roles I filled as daughter, and, later, wife, homemaker, and mother. I counted in a larger spectrum.

Turning away from the window and back to my polishing work, I exhaled with deep sadness. All of that, everything I'd attained, everything I'd worked for and continued to work toward, had gone the way of the four winds by Elizabeth's first birthday. Although during the first few months after her birth I still believed this would only be a hitch in my plans, that soon enough I'd pick up where I left off and rejoin the world for which I was destined, that hadn't been the case.

It wasn't that I didn't try. I made a real go of it, dragging myself to rounds exhausted, more an exercise in sleepwalking than practicing medicine; hurling my newborn, mouth stretched open in a bloodcurdling scream, into the hands of the nanny as I rushed out the door day in and out, yesterday's scrubs showing their wear and tear, hair gathered up in a sloppy bun. Sooner or later, I'd get that inevitable phone call.

"It's Josie."

My eyes closed, desperate to shut out whatever was coming. I raised my hand and pressed my thumb hard against my temple, willing away the imminent migraine.

"She says it's urgent."

I'd pick up the call at the nurse's desk, knowing this was the beginning of the end.

"The baby. She won't stop crying. I've done everything. I know you're busy. I know you told me not to bother you. But—" I wanted to hang up, turn around, and continue my rounds. It was so early in my career. I'd only just begun. None of this was fair.

Soon enough, my colleagues, other medical students, even the nurses on my shift began to look at me differently. I was no longer the one to be respected. Instead, I was the one to be pitied. They knew I wouldn't make it. I thought that was the worst of it, that I could sink no lower. But no. Sealing my doom was the fact that once home with Elizabeth, I barely knew what to do. Having become a mother, I was certain I could be the best. I'd always been the best. Mothering was simply one more thing at which I needed to excel.

But it never came naturally. It wasn't a good fit. I excelled when I had an audience of admirers, and there's no such arena for mothers. If I wasn't going to be noticed, there was no point. In some ways, it wasn't all that different from polishing tables: one long effort to get rid of all the imperfections, both those obvious and those less so. Elizabeth could neither live up to my expectations nor assuage the frustration of what I'd given up, yet I refused to back down. I swore to myself that she'd do better, go places I'd failed to reach—that she'd be the best and never ever settle for second place. My fall was *my* unraveling; it wasn't going to be *hers*.

Although awful to admit and something I would never say out loud, I never stopped resenting her. She was the reason I had to abandon my dream. The truth was ugly but undeniable. Those were such different times. Women simply couldn't have it all. Although for years I blamed it on Sam, on the fact that he never picked up the pieces, never tried to help me juggle all those balls, it wasn't his fault. There was simply no way to maintain total control of two strong polar opposites, home and the hospital, while staying at the top of my game. One had to give.

One day I simply gave up, officially withdrawing from medical school, folding up that white coat and tucking it onto the top shelf of our bedroom closet. An item that once had a greater-than-life significance, symbolizing the glory to come, had become completely meaningless—nothing but a reminder of what was not to be. The career in medicine I'd wanted more than anything in the whole world slipped away, becoming a festering wound that refused to heal.

• • •

Tallying up everything I hadn't achieved, the spectacular opportunities that had passed me by, wasn't getting me anywhere. After such a long life, my list—probably *everyone's* list—was painfully extensive. But now I had a wonderful opening. Thanks to Belle, I could reach yet another peak. My life would change completely the minute she moved in.

I ran my hand over the upholstered armrests of my chair, imagining the burgundy velvet ones at Carnegie Hall, the formal gown I'd wear, perhaps the same shade of emerald I'd favored as a much younger woman, the acknowledging nods of my friends in the audience as they watched Belle take the stage. This was going to be a whole new world, a distinctly better one. It would be a long time before I had to endure another evening listening to others' good fortune, sitting on the sidelines while they enjoyed the spotlight. I pushed send and released my message to the virtual world, to work its magic. Mission accomplished.

ELIZABETH

"I'M NOT SURE WHY YOU'RE so angry. This is a good thing. A wonderful thing! We should be celebrating!" Mike reached up and pulled out the large portfolios stacked horizontally on top of the shelved books. "These definitely don't belong here."

I didn't understand how he could be so calm, so nonchalant. So many things were wrong with this picture. "Actually"—I reached over and took the portfolios out of his hand, adding them to a large stack of manila files already piled on the floor—"I *am* celebrating." I paused. "Privately. I just don't feel like celebrating with you. You're not off the hook."

"Come on. Let it go. It's time to move forward. There's so much to think about, to figure out."

I stopped straightening for a moment and stared into his eyes. They positively twinkled. For a moment, I wanted to back down and forget he had anything to do with this. I wanted to melt into his arms. But I couldn't forget the fact that he'd purposefully gone behind my back, conspiring with my mother. "This is all your fault."

His brow collapsed into a sea of crumply frown lines. His eyes blackened, locking with my own.

"What are you talking about?"

I shook my head ferociously, shaking off any inclination to make this a discussion. He had a lot to answer for. "This whole idea. Julliard. New York. Lillian. Why do you insist on interfering? Why can't you just leave well enough alone?"

"That's not fair."

"Ah, because I'm right. This isn't the first time you've tried to pull us together, as if throwing us in one big pot will result in a tasty stew." I made a face, as if I'd taken a bite of a rotten egg. "Remember the visit to Grand Forks? Who cooked up that brilliant idea?"

This was a few years back. Belle was just about to enter her teenage years, still very much my baby. It was about the time I knew she'd start to break away, stretch her legs and find her own space. Lillian just showed up on the doorstep beside Mike one evening. I still remembered the shock of that moment, how I did a double take, not believing my eyes. I'd taken such care to keep my mother at a distance, never inviting her to come visit us in Grand Forks. Yet here she was, stepping inside, making herself at home. I felt the heaviness of those comments she didn't express aloud that whole, endless weekend: the criticism of what she probably considered a "little" life, her censure of people that lived off the grid in places that officially didn't count.

Eager to test her gentility and poise—my mother always the aristocrat, always turning her nose at anything that smacked of the Old World, anything Eastern European—I'd grabbed a nervous Mike and compliant Belle and taken the four of us on the road to a local dive down in Fargo. The place was an institution in the area, established by one of the German families that had originally settled the area a century earlier, and its cuisine was on the heavy side, decidedly different from the more contemporary, international kinds popular in major US metropolises and decidedly unhealthy. I took a wry pleasure in knowing that Lillian wouldn't like it and thrilled at the knowledge that Belle, who adored it, would order the kind of dishes most likely to make her grandmother nauseous, the kind she detested. I thought it might be fun.

And so, when the dishes arrived on the table, one by one, I delighted in watching Lillian consider them as if they were specimens behind glass at the Museum of Natural History, items to be studied rather than consumed. There had been those bowls of *knoephla*, the lumpy potato soup with an uncanny resemblance in texture to Elmer's glue; the hotdish that wanted to be a classic British meat pie but basically boiled down to a pile of tater tots, the likes of which Lillian had spurned even back in the seventies when they were all the rage; the hot roast beef sandwich. That last was meant to be the pièce de résistance. Lillian's eyes sparkled with anticipation when it was brought to the table—she was a true carnivore and quite hungry—but instantly went dull when they fell upon the brown, viscous gravy that covered the dinner plate from one edge to the other, clouding over with total dismay upon revealing, with the poke of her fork, a hidden layer of something disgustingly reminiscent of a white kitchen sponge. Absolutely nothing at that diner, so typical of our brave new world, suited Lillian's taste.

I relished in the whole experience, kicking Mike under the table to make sure he took notice. I wanted to punish him for trying to bend my hand, insinuating Lillian into our lives without consulting me first, assuming he could make peace where none was meant to be. He avoided my eyes, encouraging Lillian here and there but for the most part just looking sad. At the time I felt a little mean. My comeuppance came at the end of the meal when I noted that Belle, instead of being frustrated with her grandmother's lack of enthusiasm, was celebrating its charm. The two looked thick as thieves, tilting their heads together and laughing. I had unknowingly engineered a shared experience, helping to lay the foundation of a relationship I could never enjoy. The rest of the weekend was spent mourning the passing of that ship, yet again.

I couldn't stand it that now, once more, Mike had tried to right a wrong that had nothing to do with him, one he'd never understand. "How did you even come up with such a scheme?" I paused, a random thought passing through my head, quickly gathering breadth and weight. "Wait. Whose idea was this? No, no. You don't have to tell me. I already know." My head felt like it would burst. The realization that Lillian had instigated this whole idea didn't negate Mike's involvement; it just added more salt to that ever-festering wound.

Mike remained motionless, the dust rag he'd been using to wipe down the bookshelves clutched tightly in hand, his face forlorn. Once again, I considered softening. I almost felt sorry for him. I didn't enjoy seeing him so miserable. I shook off that momentary weakening of spirit. There was no way I could just let this slide. He'd hurt me terribly.

"I want an explanation. You owe me that. You've started something we won't be able to stop, something that will change all our lives forever. I deserve to know why."

"There's the part about Belle—"

I cut him off with a brisk wave of my hand. "And?"

"Okay. This isn't just about Belle."

I roiled with anger. I hated that he was flipping the focus of this ugly conversation back at me. What I'd thought was just a terrible plan was so much worse. It was a conspiracy. I turned my back to him and wiped violently at the shelves, dust bunnies flying in all directions. I didn't care. I was furious.

He grabbed my arm, stopping my frenetic activity. I whipped around. "I've changed my mind. I really don't want to talk about this anymore. I don't want to talk to you."

"But you have to. We have to." He was still holding my arm. I gave up trying to wiggle away. "You know this is as much about you as Belle."

I shrugged and looked away. I couldn't look into his eyes. "Enlighten me."

"Should we sit down?"

"I don't want to sit down. I want to dust." I pulled my arm away and turned back to the waiting shelves. "Has anyone *ever* cleaned up here? It's really disgusting."

Mike sneezed and wiped at his nose. "I need tissues. I'll be right back."

I used his absence to fortify myself for the conversation to come. I had an inkling of what he was going to say, the ancient debris he was going to unearth.

Reentering the room, he picked up right where he'd left off. "You need to let go." I held my breath for a moment, waiting for him to continue. "You've got to let this whole thing with Belle, with Lillian, this whole mess of an emotional tangle, go. It's eating you alive." My heart raced. There were things he didn't know. There were things I didn't want him to know. But without that knowledge, he would never understand the depth of my distress.

He took a step closer. I felt the heat generated by his body. I wanted to reach out and pull him in, let him provide the anchor I needed to deal with what he was insinuating. That had always been his role. But I wasn't ready for that, not yet. I stepped away and, forcing myself to focus on something else, gazed around at the bookshelves. Cleaning them was going to take forever. Mike had spent years complaining that while I kept a fastidiously clean and meticulously organized library at work, my study at home was filthy and disorganized to the point of disaster. Every now and then he'd run a finger along a shelf to make his point, waggling the fuzzy digit in admonition. He was right. And although I was wont to claim that there was no point in organizing—that the minute we cleaned up, made sense of the hundreds of books we'd amassed over the course of our joint decades, even those decades lived before our union, we'd be packing them back up for a move elsewhere—I knew this wasn't so.

We'd been in Grand Forks for more than ten years, and it looked as if we were here to stay. Although that might have been enough incentive to inspire this massive undertaking, something else entirely compelled me to finally acquiesce. With everything else unraveling, my life tilting perilously off its axis, my head threatening to burst from trying to figure out how to turn back the clock and return to a reality that didn't include Belle moving far away, close to Lillian, I finally decided to crack down on what I *could* control. Mike was unaware that pulling the carpet from beneath my feet had instigated this clean-up project. I looked back at him. His arms were extended, but I refused the invitation. I wasn't finished.

"It was so hard for me, growing up in my mother's house. You know that. You've known that since we met. It's a part of my history. And still, you've basically handed her Belle on a silver platter." I twisted my mouth into a tight knot, fighting back a fresh batch of tears. I refused to cry. Shaking my head emphatically, I turned away from his sorrowful expression and again focused on the shelves, reaching for a pair of dusty airplane socks I must have tucked atop that row of foreign-language dictionaries years ago. "I've been looking for these. . ." I tossed them backward, onto my desk chair.

"Well, we aren't exactly handing her over, more like lending her out. We're sure to get her back in the end." Encouraged by my ostensible return to cleaning, Mike tried to make a joke. He laughed nervously for a moment and then, realizing I wasn't joining in, went silent. "It'll give us time, Lizzy. It will give you time. You'll be able to move on, choose a new path."

I spun around, not bothering to hide my rage. "I don't want to move on. In fact, now I won't be able to. Now I'm going to have to be even more vigilant, stay even more alert. You want me to stop obsessing about my mother, about my daughter. But when they're all the way across the country, *together*, I'll do nothing but! How could you not see this?"

I grabbed the recently discarded socks from the desk chair and used them to wipe down the books and exposed shelving before me. I forced my mind to empty itself of all worries, focusing on the inanities of this cleanup job, the way the dust gathered into beads and pearls, then little lumps, leaving behind a persistent layer of silt, marking its territory. I wondered if it was possible to ever really clean up years of accretion. Mike seemed to think so.

"I thought it was a good idea. And not just for you, not just for us. It's an opportunity our daughter deserves."

Well, that was clever. Now he knew he had me. I abandoned the dusting and faced him, suddenly noticing the soft dimples at the corners of his eyes, the slight twitch of his lips. He was nervous. Something else lurked behind the already enormous amount of debris he'd left on my front lawn. But I didn't want to know.

Understanding in my heart of hearts that he hadn't meant to hurt me, that he truly wanted to help, that he always wanted to help, I yearned to back down. There was no denying that he had a point. The idea of moving Belle to a place where she could develop her talent, something that had most definitely crossed my mind now and then, was an excellent one. Once I shoved aside the anger and the concern, that aspect of this nightmare shone too brightly to miss.

Retreating into the safety of silence, I returned to my cleaning and let my mind wander, considering how we'd come to Grand Forks in the first place. Living in such a tiny, forgotten corner of the States wasn't anything I'd foreseen. Indeed, it was as much a happenstance as Belle now picking up and moving to New York. It started with Mike. He was offered the job of heading the aviation program at the University of North Dakota after serving as a junior faculty member at both the University of Illinois and Purdue. This job was an absolutely perfect fit, a dream come true. I didn't want him to pass it by and was the first to sign on, convincing him that it was something we should do, something we *could* do. Of course, it didn't take long for me to regret my hasty enthusiasm and understand that it was more than a bit crazy.

It wasn't that I needed a city. Although born and bred in Manhattan, I never found it a great fit. Manhattan was all about Lillian's life, one I found overwhelming and off-putting. My search for something more manageable—a place where there were no expectations, none of those multiple niches I was meant to fill, the ones chosen for me—led me away from the East Coast. For a long time, I figured Chicago a good bet. While still a city, chock-full of offerings, it felt so much more welcoming. It had a more intimate feel than Manhattan. It was almost provincial the minute you stepped away from Michigan Avenue. I liked it from the start and chose to stay for law school, beginning my legal career right up the street from the Water Tower. By the time I met Mike, this Midwest metropolis felt like home—-or at least, a place I could make my home. The key was that it was *me* doing the making.

The leap we took to Grand Forks years later was *much* bigger. While I wanted to step away from the expectations of the East Coast, I'd never once entertained the concept of living in small-town America. I figured I was ultimately a city girl. When the idea first arose, Mike and I stretched out on our bed to discuss it, the atlas I'd received as a Bat Mitzvah gift twenty years earlier spread open before us. I randomly put my finger on a spot somewhere out West.

"That's Utah."

"Oh. Okay. So, here?" I moved my finger up and over. It lay on Sioux City.

Mike smiled and pulled me closer. "Let me show you." He gently guided my finger to a dot not far from Minneapolis, only a few inches away by my estimation, a place considered almost a neighbor of ours in Chicago. Right there, among the sheets, the whole idea seemed feasible, even fun. I warmed up to the idea almost too quickly, making a mental list of all the plusses: beyond the fact of Mike's professional advancement there was the opportunity to explore uncharted territory, the idea of turning our daily life into one big discovery, things no longer predetermined. We'd make our way west like those early pioneers, covered wagon piled high, forging our own path and realizing our dreams just as the Ingalls had done in *Little House on the Prairie*. It was a little girl's romantic fantasy come true.

Of course, the reality of the Great Plains was something else entirely, tougher and bleaker than anything I'd imagined. The stark extremity of the terrain alone struck me from first exposure. I stared out the airplane window on that first exploratory visit with mouth agape, astonished by the flat, broad swathes of land, rectangles of brown, of green and yellow, unbroken by skyscrapers or much of anything I'd call a building, and enormous in scope, going on and on for what seemed like forever. But still, something about this new reality continued to appeal. Although I hadn't been unhappy with my life in Chicago, it always felt like something I'd fallen into. If Northwestern hadn't accepted me, I would have ended up somewhere else entirely. Grand Forks was a different animal. Pure in its bareness, holding no remnant of what had come before, it seemed an excellent place for Mike and me to build our future—the perfect way to finally change a course I'd never really chosen. This was an opportunity for me as much as for him.

Now it was Belle's turn. "Julliard." The word floated through my head, coming out in a whisper. My mind raced forward, struggling with the extraordinary concept that my daughter would be attending Julliard. It was inconceivable. I must have voiced those thoughts because suddenly Mike's arms were around me, holding me tight. He turned me around and pulled me in close, covering me in small kisses, working his way from my neck to my jaw, across my cheek and up to my brow. We were both so dusty and dirty. It didn't matter. I didn't want him to stop. I would have gone anywhere after this man: Grand Forks or Timbuktu. He made things just that good. I reached up to wipe a bit of dirt off his cheek, smearing a grimy path straight to his ear. "Isn't it amazing?" I nodded in agreement, swept up in the moment, murmuring words about plans, arrangements, places to stay.

Mike went rigid and then held me tighter before gently pushing me back enough to look into my eyes. That same hint of sadness. I wondered why. Here I was forgiving him, trying to put the hurt behind me. He reached up and cupped my chin. He was frowning. The glorious moment we'd just shared was swallowed up whole by the chill of anticipation that sped across my spine, moving into my heart. "Lizzy, listen. I know it's not perfect, but . . ." I forced myself to step away. This time was harder than the first; I so wanted us to come together, to get through this bump. "Lillian offered and, well, it just makes so much sense."

The throbbing in my head, the one that came and went this last week with thoughts of the enormous change ahead, resumed. Everything went black. I forced myself to focus, to stay in the here and now and not give in to the desire to close my eyes and slip away. "What are you saying?" I didn't need to ask. The answer was written clearly on his face. There was pain and hope, concern, and anticipation. He'd obviously been dreading this moment.

"Belle will stay with Lillian."

I tried to shut out his words; they were, in any case, inconsequential. Somewhere deep within, I'd known they were coming. Obviously Belle would live with Lillian. Where else could she go? We'd never be able to afford to take a place for her in the city, and her scholarship didn't cover the dormitory. Lillian's apartment was a few blocks away. It made the most sense. Still, confirmation of what hadn't even been a concrete thought was incredibly painful.

Mike's soft, open face was transformed into a pinch of misery. "I wish there were another way. When this possibility arose, I tried to figure it out otherwise. I really did. I knew exactly how you'd feel, how you were going to react. I knew you'd want her to live anywhere but with Lillian. But it's just so incredibly costly. I've done the math. There's just no other way to make it happen. And I have to say, Lillian is quite excited about the arrangement, about the chance to get to know her granddaughter, to help her realize this dream."

I sighed heavily and shook my head, defeated but not yet willing to relinquish my anger. "I knew it. I knew you all were plotting behind my back."

"Oh, come on! Not this again." Mike's face turned a bright shade of red, his exasperation obvious. "I repeat: This is all for Belle. This is all to provide her with something we can't. Why do you have to make it so personal? You're right. We shouldn't talk about this."

It was his turn to be frustrated. He spun away from me and, stepping onto the ladder we'd brought in earlier that day, attacked the items on the topmost shelf, pulling off a tangled cluster of headphones and assorted electronic wires, most of which belonged to gadgets long defunct or pitched. Swiveling around, he tossed them directly into the large trashcan we'd dragged in and then once again turned his back on me, gathering a row of cheesy paperbacks randomly stashed there over the years. "Didn't we agree we were going to donate these? Or, better yet, throw them away?" He spit out the words as he pulled the lot of them off in three scoops and, stepping down off the ladder, planted them directly on top of the growing pile of refuse.

I ignored the twinge of grief I felt watching him disparagingly abuse those books lovingly filled with words by their authors, and crossed my arms aggressively in front of my chest. I wanted to finish this.

"How else do you want me to take it? It is personal—all of it."

He paused in his pitching. "Lizzy." He sounded exasperated. "She's no big deal—your mother. Belle will twist her around her little pinky in no time at all. You really have nothing to worry about."

I shook my head in disagreement. "That's the least of my worries. In fact, if she succeeds in charming my mother, she'll be way ahead of the game." I bit down on my lip, taken aback by my words and the thoughts they triggered. I struggled to conceal an unexpected wave of panic. Mike didn't truly understand. He couldn't. Lillian was the only one who understood the significance of the secret I didn't want uncovered. Finally having the time to get to know her granddaughter—and even worse, share a life with her—there was a good chance that old stories I preferred to stay buried would emerge. After all these years, the most harmful one might come to light, shaking the foundations of what was, every day, becoming a more fragile balance at home.

I turned back to my study, eager to escape my troubled past and shove the unthinkable back to the forgotten corner where it belonged. That's when I spotted the large shoebox I'd stashed away the week we moved in. Grasping it in both hands, I placed it on the desk. This was a treasure, one of the many stored in this room—full of memories lying dormant, just waiting to be rediscovered. Although I hadn't peeked inside for years, had no precise recollection of its contents, I relished the possibilities. Anything that took me away from this painful moment was welcome.

Ignoring Mike for the moment, I lowered myself onto the desk chair and gently opened the lid. Inside were stacks of old photographs, some with those classic Kodak date stamps, and quite a few Polaroids. Flipping through them one by one, I was confronted with a disorderly and random collection of memories stretching back about forty years. It was a real hodgepodge.

"Mike, look at this." My voice was soft. I knew he couldn't resist. He drew close and looked over my shoulder. I held up a small black-and-white photograph with a rippled white border, the kind printed back in the sixties. Toddler me was seated on a carpet in front of a bricked-in hearth. A fire blazed. I had no concrete recollection of that room, or the apartment itself, but knew it was the one in which I'd been born. The long socks hanging from the mantelpiece and the small, decorated fir tree described what could only have been Christmas.

As far as I recalled, we'd never celebrated Christmas. The moment captured in the photograph was a complete anomaly. But family folklore served where memory failed, and I remembered a story about my mother's early experiment, one she'd chosen not to repeat. "Jews don't celebrate Christmas." I guess that one season, she thought they might. My eyes lingered on the little girl on the carpet. She was radiant, dressed cozily in a one-piece pajama, hair gathered into a ponytail, her face full of anticipation. My toddler self looked so incredibly happy. Another anomaly. When I looked back, I had almost no recollection of feeling that way.

"You don't know the damage she can wreak." I sighed heavily. "It's all so subtle. Not something anyone else would notice or even feel. You could never understand."

Mike reached out and squeezed my hand, pulling me back up. "But I do. I've seen it up close and personal. I've shouldered your frustrations, your tears, and your disappointment for decades. The things she's said to you . . ." He let his voice fade away, shaking his head with a strong look of distaste. "But I believe that it doesn't have to be the same, that it simply won't be. Belle isn't you and, most significantly, she's the granddaughter here. The fact that the mother–daughter thing never worked for the two of you doesn't necessarily mean it can't for them. That tangled mess, the one you've never managed to escape, isn't part of Belle and Lillian's status quo. This is an entirely different equation."

I let him hold me, tucking my head into the welcoming hollow at his collarbone, ignoring the overwhelming stench of dust and mildew clinging to his clothes. This was all I needed right now—to be hugged, accepted, and loved for who I was. No amount of filth would deter me. Threading my arms through Mike's, I gripped his strong back and hung on tightly. It had taken a lifetime, years punctuated by moves to more and more remote locations, to finally feel that I'd accomplished something on my own—albeit not what had been expected of me. I wondered if my mother could undo the sixteen years I'd invested in ensuring that my daughter would never feel that way. Mike and I had worked so hard to convey to Belle that she was free to chart her own course, to shine however and wherever she chose. For us, despite choices we might not understand, she would always be a star.

"Belle's story isn't yours. She isn't running away. From the start, you made it a point to put a greater and greater distance between you and your mother. Wasn't that what Northwestern was all about? Even UND? It was such a huge leap west. I was certain you'd nix the idea, that you'd balk and convince me to stay at Purdue. That was the easier choice. We could have just continued what we had going in Chicago, wretched commute and all. But you didn't. You went for it. And I knew it wasn't completely about advancing my career."

He paused and traced my hairline, tucking a lock of hair gently behind my ear.

"Lizzy, you've spent a lifetime fleeing from what you've felt is holding you back, moving out from beneath what you describe as an onerous yoke. Maybe now, *finally*, you'll have the chance to live a life outside the long shadow your mother cast. Isn't it time?"

I stepped back over to the chair and sat down with a heavy thud, the truth of Mike's words penetrating me body and soul, exhausting me to the core. He was right. Only with distance, landing in a place with a clean slate, had I finally been able to achieve some modicum of real self-esteem, to figure out how much I could accomplish without trying to measure up to my mother's yardstick. I wondered if this was the inspiration for Belle's plan—if tracing my journey back to the place it all began was mere coincidence or an indirect criticism of my path. I hoped the former. Otherwise, it would be even more difficult to accept.

So many aspects of this new reality broke my heart: The fact of Belle leaving, the fear that Lillian would crush my daughter's confidence, and the concept that Belle interpreted my retreat from the big, shiny world as weak, were only parts of the painful whole. I envisioned the two together in the apartment on West End Avenue, sharing breakfast at the kitchen table, laughing over one joke or another. I couldn't help being jealous. I craved the intimacy they'd surely develop, sooner rather than later. And then, there was that other part—the one Mike couldn't fathom. I watched him continue to purge the junk I'd amassed on the shelves of my study and envied his innocence. What he didn't know could never hurt him.

My whole body sagged with distress, aware that secrets had a way of drifting to the surface, intimacy frequently leading to revelation. There was every likelihood that at one point or another, Lillian would share with Belle the trauma of my senior year. The secret we'd both kept for decades could rip through my family, damaging it forever.

ELIZABETH

"HELLO. ELIZABETH? IS THAT YOU?"

I hesitated before answering, knowing full well that my mother knew it was me. She would have seen my number flash in red on the phone handset. I took her question as a form of criticism. I hadn't called for quite some time.

"Mom." I swallowed hard.

"Elizabeth, dear. How are you?"

This wasn't starting off right. I'd been the one to call. I was supposed to get the conversation rolling. Yet here she was, plowing ahead without me. *How do I always let this happen?* I gripped the telephone and took a deep breath. Again, she cut me off at the pass.

"It's so lovely to hear your voice."

I'd woken up this morning with a clear plan. I wanted to make sure that Lillian realized the extent of the responsibility she was taking on, to alert her to some aspects of raising a teenager she may not have considered. And to be sure, I wanted to have a hand in the foundation of the relationship they were sure to forge, desperate to maintain my involvement as mother, even though I'd shortly be out of the picture. The situation was sensitive and had to be handled just right.

"We need to talk." So dry. So unemotional. But that's the way I felt. I was numb. I'd lain awake in bed all night, thinking of how to begin. The fabulous prospects for Belle were all but forgotten, along with the significance of her leaving Grand Forks. Instead, I zeroed in on the idea of Belle spending her fragile high school years in the care of a woman whose aspirations and single-hearted focus on achievement had left me with a flawed sense of self-worth.

It wasn't that my mother hadn't done a decent job of raising me to be a kind, thoughtful, polite woman—a decent human being. She had. I was A-okay. But I knew I could do better. In fact, I already had. Our house was one of quiet acceptance and attention to others. Achievement, always appreciated, was something that happened. It was never a goal. Not once had we suggested that Belle wasn't doing enough, might do more, could do better. My own teenage years had taught me what *not* to do, how *not* to be, what *not* to say.

Of course, despite all that, this last period had been extremely challenging. No matter what I said, I seemed to run up against a brick wall. Belle's closed bedroom door, her back, rigid and locked, the emptiness of a phone line gone brutally cold after she hung up mid-conversation—all were indicators of a relationship gone awry. In some ways it didn't matter that I never scolded or criticized, as I still received Belle's anger and annoyance. It was a no-win situation. And it was this that I could now exploit for my own means, to keep me in the loop. I'd shine my light on Belle's recent behavior and let Lillian have a good hard look.

"It's about Belle."

"Yes, dear. I know. You want her to stay with me, to move in. Mike explained everything."

I slammed my hand on the counter, relieved she couldn't see and hoping she hadn't heard. So much of this had been coordinated without me. It gave my mother an unfair advantage. I wasn't finished with Mike yet. I'd eased up after our talk a few days earlier, digging deep to remember that his intentions had been good, but this was unbearable. The only saving grace was that Lillian didn't know I hadn't been in on it from the start. If I kept my cool, there was a chance she never would.

"That will help. In fact, it's a wonderful gesture. We really appreciate it." I paused, taking a deep breath, bracing myself. "But that's not why I'm calling. It's something else entirely. I have concerns. I want you to understand exactly what this entails, this whole arrangement. It's not as simple as it sounds."

Again, I paused, this time clearing my throat in the hopes of projecting a confidence I didn't feel. Lillian was a pro at identifying my weaknesses and letting me know precisely why they were unacceptable, what wasn't right. I didn't want to give her that pleasure today. "It's not about the mothering. That's *my* job. But when Belle moves in, you'll have to assume a lot of the 'hands-on' parenting. And believe me, it's not all it's cracked up to be! It can be really difficult." I laughed, enjoying a moment of levity. "Difficult" was an understatement.

"Are you warning me about life with a teenager?"

I swallowed hard. That brief light moment had passed. "Actually, I am. It's so much worse than you can imagine. The stakes are so much higher today. Drugs, alcohol, even what used to be harmless, cigarettes. I mean, you'd figure they'd have learned from your generation." Getting more and more nervous, I began to babble. I didn't want to have any conversation with my mother, let alone one about such a delicate subject. "The worst part is really their empowerment. They have no fear, so there's very little reckoning. I'm afraid Belle will challenge you to the point where you'll break, where you'll do or say something you'll regret. You're taking on a responsibility whose scope is bigger than you can imagine."

"Well, I suppose that's my problem. Not yours."

As usual, my mother had the upper hand. There was almost nothing I could add. I tapped my fingers on the phone, trying to find a rhythm. I scrambled to return to the agenda I'd planned while tossing and turning in bed the previous evening—the safe ground I knew would provide me a modicum of protection, preventing her from pouring salt into that old wound. Desperate to find my footing, I segued to another subject. "So." I sounded so weak, so insignificant. "There's another thing. It's about academics. As I'm sure you know, in addition to the Julliard program, Belle will be attending school—*high* school."

Lillian cut me off impatiently. "I know all about that, dear." She enjoyed reminding me that she'd masterminded this whole scheme; that she, in effect, was steering the ship. I looked around the kitchen. The counter was wiped clean, the cabinets closed; the magnets on the fridge were arranged in a rectilinear mosaic; the folded dish towels hung neatly on the rack by the sink, and the faucet faced forward. Everything was in its place. I took a deep breath, trying to absorb a sense of stability from my ordered life, to remember that I too could lead. I too could set the tone.

"Yes, but you don't know how that's gone—at least, so far. Belle does okay at school, really, just fine. But that's always been enough for her. She's not what I call an achiever. And your expectations . . . well, they've always been so high." There was a click on the line.

"Grandma?"

My spirits fell. It was Belle. She'd picked up another phone in the house and joined our conversation. There was no way I could continue this topic with her listening.

"Belle, sweetie. I'm speaking to Grandma. Can you give us a moment?"

Lillian ignored me completely. "Hello, dear. How are you? What's going on? Are you making your preparations? Getting everything ready? It's so exciting." My mother moved forward, pursuing her own agenda. Mine was lost in the shuffle. Our already agonizing two-way conversation had become a grotesque three-way dance. This was an eventuality for which I had not been prepared. I quickly considered possible solutions. There was only one. I had to get Belle off the line.

"Definitely. All packed up!" Her laughter made me melt. I loved hearing her happy. It was distracting.

"Well, I'm more than ready to host you, dear. I even called in a painter to see about making you feel a bit more at home."

"That's amazing, Grandma! I'm thinking I might like a wall with that special black chalk paint, the kind you scribble on. Have you heard of it?"

I purposefully let the two exchange their inanities about room décor for a few more minutes before changing the subject. "Belle? Can you let me speak with Grandma now?"

"You needn't have cut her off midsentence, dear."

That was my mother. Always quick to put me in my place, making me feel bad. I cursed Mike again for his scheming. It had landed me right back in the hell from which I'd escaped decades earlier. I sat up a little straighter in my chair, unwilling to let her take control. "Belle, please. I asked you to hang up."

"I have no problem with her staying on the line, Elizabeth. We're about to enter a rather intimate living situation. There's nowhere to begin our new relationship but the present. I say we let her be part of this conversation."

I sighed and shifted gears. With my back against the wall, I had no alternative. "Well, Mom, Belle." I had absolutely no idea who to address at this point, hesitant to leave out one or the other. "Mom, you'll be in charge of making sure Belle does her homework. This is most definitely part of the deal. I'm sure you understand that." I didn't need to see Belle's face to know that it reflected a threatening storm.

"Why? Is there a problem?"

A strange lack of sound from Belle's side of the receiver indicated she might be holding her breath.

"It's just, well . . ."

"Mediocre. I think that's what she's trying to say." Belle's interjection came as a total surprise, but a welcome one. I'd been saved from having to land the boom myself. Yet I knew I'd pay a heavy price later. Raising this ugly subject would give my daughter one more reason to hate me.

"Grades have to be part of the deal, Mom. This is going to be your responsibility now."

"Well, you come from good stock, dear. I'm sure it's a non-issue. Right? You *must* have straight As!"

Belle was quick to reply. "Don't worry, Grandma. My grades will be great. Just you wait and see."

There was something in my daughter's voice that I hadn't heard in a long time: a sense of purpose, an overwhelming self-confidence. This was a young woman who knew what she wanted and would do anything to get it. I couldn't help but be impressed. And despite the obvious tremor, the crack in her tone that belied her calm, her determination was clear. Circumstances aside, I felt that I could burst from so much love and admiration.

Of course, I knew what Lillian didn't. Belle's grades were far from As, barely touching what she'd bravely claimed as mediocre. This wasn't a big deal to many, but to a woman for whom academic achievement had always been a priority, falling short was comparable to total failure. I was still haunted by the never-ending barrage of comments calling me out for missing perfect: "You did well, dear. But I'm sure you could have done better." "I'm not convinced that was your best effort." "Maybe next time you'll apply yourself just a little more." That 92 I'd been so proud to earn in Calculus at the end of twelfth grade had faded to insignificant once Lillian understood I'd missed the senior math prize. For my mother, it was all or nothing. That methodology had worked for her, streamlining her path to med school, but for me it was nothing less than devastating. My fragile ego simply couldn't hold up against the onslaught.

And it wasn't limited to academics. I fell far below any mark Lillian set, continuously disappointing. There were the endless requests to stand up straighter, the scathing criticism of my clothing—my shorts invited inappropriate attention, halters were for girls looking for trouble; the consistent pleas to tame my unruly, long hair. I eventually caved in on that last and cut it all off, effectively becoming a tomboy just when my body was announcing signs of womanhood. I paid for this sudden change of identity at such a critical juncture in my development well into college.

Direct censure and an endless stream of commentary continued well into my adult life. And although I should have learned to ignore it and shut Lillian out the minute she pulled the string of her loaded bow, ready to fire, I repeatedly allowed her to crush me: the daughter who always wanted to please. The zinger she landed when I told her we were moving to Grand Forks had been the last straw, turning an already hobbled relationship into one that simply didn't exist. That was the day I finally drew the line, cutting off all contact, sending the clear message that I'd had enough; I wasn't willing to be hurt anymore. And since then, despite Mike's various attempts over the years to mend fences, I'd held that line. If not for this crazy situation, one more example of his unwanted interference, I would still be maintaining a comfortable emotional distance, happily going about my life. It was he who had provoked this unbearable conversation with its foolhardy agenda.

The conversation between Belle and Lillian continued without me, much as I knew it would once they were comfortably living together.

"I just know you'll make this work. I have the utmost confidence that you'll amend whatever needs fixing. I can feel how important it is to you; in fact, I saw just that when you were here with me." Lillian paused for a moment, enough time for me to catch the return of Belle's soft, regular breathing. "You and me. We'll make sure this is a complete success. We'll make sure *you're* a complete success."

A wave of nausea overwhelmed me. I knew this was a pointed criticism of what she felt was my ineffectual parenting.

"Thanks for the vote of confidence, Grandma." Belle's indictment was equally clear. I shouldn't have expected otherwise. "We'll do great."

I struggled to find a degree of equilibrium, my head spinning, my mind in turmoil. I wanted nothing more than to throw the phone on the floor, curl up into a ball, and hug myself tightly; to shut out the hurt of my mother adopting the kind of sensitive, understanding, and conciliatory attitude she'd never shown me; to erase my daughter's animated anticipation. I have no idea how I managed to keep down the bile struggling to erupt from inside me, to regulate my breathing as if I were calm. Not one bit of this conversation had gone the way I intended.

I quickly rehashed the whole thing, from start to finish, trying to figure out where I'd gone wrong. I started with the end, that chain of words that had cut through me like a knife: "We'll make sure you're a complete success." There was nothing new here. I'd spent a lifetime not measuring up. But I'd never heard any of this tolerance in her tone. I'd gotten it all wrong, never expecting that Lillian would "parent" her granddaughter differently than she had her own child, that the rules might change with the shift of a generation—exactly as Mike had suggested they would.

"We're going to have the loveliest time together, dear. We'll finally have the chance to talk. I can share all my old stories, pull out the heavy albums. It's been years since I've had an opportunity to do so."

I never heard Belle's response, only the firm click of the phone as she hung up. Having gained exactly what she came for, she had left this party, probably thrilled with the outcome. I envisioned her racing around upstairs, jumping on her bed with glee. I, on the other hand, was terror-stricken. I had absolutely no choice but to stop skating on the surface and finally get to the heart of the issue. I searched for an entrée into the unspeakable.

"There's something else, Mom."

Her breathing sounded relaxed. She was probably seated, completely at ease, not pacing around, wired, and nervous like me. "Is Belle still with us?"

"No, she's hung up. It's just us. I think we might take this occasion to explore the harder possibilities, to discuss what happens if she gets in trouble—any kind of trouble." I let my voice fall. I didn't want to elaborate.

There was a heavy sigh. "I know something about that as well, dear. I'm a veteran."

How could I possibly respond in the face of such icy confidence? My mother was clearly reminding me that sins of the past were never forgotten. I tried to shake off the guilt, that familiar feeling of failure. The silence coming across the line was replaced with a deafening roar, the blood rushing in and out of my heart, the valves pumping hard, doing their job. Suddenly, I wasn't sure why I'd even made the call. I didn't want to have this conversation.

"Elizabeth, I've dealt with trouble. And as you well know, I mean the very worst kind. I think I'm officially qualified to handle this."

This was where I'd been heading since I picked up the phone and dialed, the other topics of conversation mere ephemera. I needed to ensure that the past would stay right where it was.

"I'd never say otherwise." A lump the size of the rock of Gibraltar formed in my throat, and I struggled to move it enough to complete what I'd started. "But, Mom, please. Certain things, well . . . They need to stay in the past. I hope you'll remember that. For everyone's sake." I hung up the phone before she had a chance to answer. I couldn't bear to think that she didn't agree.

BELLE

"YOU'VE GOT TO FIND A way to get along with your mother."

I pushed the right pedal down, bringing the plane around. Today we had a long flight scheduled, almost three hours. Completing it without a hitch would get me that much closer to getting my private pilot's license. The last thing on my mind was my mother. In fact, she was the one subject that could ruin this otherwise promising day. "Come on, Dad."

"I won't always be here to smooth the waters. You'll have to figure out a way to do it on your own."

He might as well have thrown a pail of cold water over my head. It had been so cozy in the cockpit. Spring was finally coming to Grand Forks, and although it was still quite nippy, still down-jacket weather, the brutal cold of winter was clearly behind us. Dad's words thrust me instantly back to the snow and ice. Damn. I really didn't feel like getting into this. And I definitely hadn't expected it at 3,000 feet. I took a quick look out the side window. The beauty of the plains from high up always improved my mood. I wasn't going to let whatever he was getting at change that. The only thing that mattered was that I was on my way up and out. I glanced over at Dad, catching his eyes for a moment.

"It's not all that important to me. I'm sorry."

He tapped the mouthpiece of his headset twice. He didn't need to check the sound; he wanted my attention. "She just wanted to discuss the details with Grandma. She wasn't trying to stir things up. This whole new situation is difficult for her. Remember, she hasn't had the months of prep that we had to figure it all out."

I couldn't miss the desperate expression in his eyes. He was obviously disturbed by the situation back home, the unpleasant atmosphere that had taken over the house: me not talking to Mom, her not talking to him. But I didn't see that changing in the near future, couldn't figure how to smooth this twisted muddle.

"Dad, we don't need to talk about this. You don't need to worry about me and Mom." I tried to change the subject. "Didn't expect this perfect day, right? A few days ago, you thought we'd need to cancel. Hey! Do you think I'll get rusty? Once I'm not flying regularly? Maybe we should look for a local airport near Manhattan—something in New Jersey? Just to maintain my license once I finally get it." My private's test was getting close.

"Mom doesn't know how to make this right. She knows she made a mistake—as she herself says, 'Just one more.' She's just trying to hold on to her baby. You can't understand how natural that is for any mother, how difficult this is for her, the whole move to New York." He removed his hands from his lap, placed them on the yoke, and moved us slightly left. His brow wrinkled with concern. This wasn't like him. He never corrected when there was no need. I figured it was a nervous reflex, an attempt to take control of a situation that was out of control.

I sighed heavily. There was no point in discussing what wasn't right and couldn't be better. It was a lot more fun thinking about the future. In fact, I'd spent the last two weeks focusing on nothing else. It was a blessed relief from the storm of nastiness at school. I banked right, and the sun shot through the cockpit, a flash of light. In any case, it was going to take a long time to mend what was broken. Squinting to block out the light, it dawned on me that Dad didn't know half of what had gone down to bring Mom and me to this impasse. "Wait a minute, Dad. You think this is all about New York, about straightening out things with Grandma?"

"Well, I assume—"

I cut him off rudely, my patience wearing thin. I'd had enough of this continuing war with my mother, of trying to neutralize the damage she'd done. "That's not what it's about. That's just a small part of the picture." I caught his eyes for a moment before looking straight ahead. "It's so much bigger."

He didn't respond. I imagined the cogs and wheels in his mind whirring at lightning speed as he tried to figure out what I meant. Mom obviously hadn't told him. We continued in silence for the longest time, me gripping the yoke so tightly that my fingernails turned white. I sucked on my upper lip, clamping down tightly, debating whether to spill. In some ways, I was grateful that she hadn't. What happened in my bedroom was so unbelievably embarrassing—the way she'd walked in on Tom and me, those awful seconds of chaos, screaming, and humiliation when we'd frantically covered ourselves, grabbed for our clothes, both of us mortified, horrified, wanting to be anywhere else, swiftly swept from all that wonderful warmth into a sea of cold confusion and a shame we didn't deserve.

I might have gotten over it more quickly if Tom hadn't mentioned it to his friends. But he had. It had been just that outrageous. And now everyone at school knew. I hated him. I didn't care if we ever spoke again. He'd started something that had no end, and I'd consequently become the flavor of the month for lewd jokes, subjected to merciless teasing: "Hey, I hear your mom's a prude." "Maybe she wanted a three-way?" "Have you returned his socks?" "Can we have a go, too?" And it wasn't just the boys. The girls were treating me differently. It was a nightmare. High school was hard enough without this shit, and there was only one person to blame.

I grew hot, riled up by the thought of what was happening back down there, on Planet Earth. "It's not about Mom's talk with Grandma. That just added fuel. I really don't know what's up with them. They always sound like strangers. How is that even possible? Even if I'm angry with her, it's clear Mom and I are related." I cleared my throat. I was really dying to tell. "That's not it at all. You just don't know, Dad. She obviously didn't tell you the best part."

When he didn't respond, I began to worry. Maybe this was a mistake. Mom and Dad were a team. Or at least that's the way it had always been. Until lately. Lately things seemed different. *Who am I to come between them?* Maybe telling him the whole story would drive a wedge between us as well. The roar of the engine seemed to get louder. I double-checked the throttle, made sure I wasn't accelerating. Nope. Everything was fine. The roaring was only in my mind.

When Dad finally spoke, his voice was tense, as though he was bracing himself. "Enlighten me. Please. Let me understand. Maybe I can help."

So, I did. I'd originally intended to keep him out of this whole mess. But sitting side by side in the tiny cabin of the plane, and there's really no place more intimate, I realized just how much I hurt—just how much I wanted to shout out the horrible facts and purge. And when I finished, when the stricken look on his face revealed his understanding of just how devastating this event and its fallout had been, I noticed that the loud, angry roar of the engine I'd heard earlier had settled into a consoling purr. My burden shared, I felt tons lighter.

"Your mother . . . You must know, things aren't always as they seem. What you see, what you get, her reactions, they're not always the result of something you've said or done. It isn't always about you, even if it's you that takes the brunt of it." He glanced over, making sure to meet my eyes for a moment before facing back toward the windshield. "I'm not trying to make excuses for her, Belle; to claim that that wasn't horrifically embarrassing for you, for that boy. But I'm sure it was awful for her as well."

At that last bit he smiled awkwardly, then looked away, toward his side window.

"I have to tell you, I'm not so happy about the whole thing myself. That whole scene . . ." He shook his head, his mouth stretched into a tight line. "It's just possible we should have had a conversation or two about this eventuality. I left that for your mother, but . . ." He paused again. "But right now, there are other things at stake."

"I'll never forgive her, Dad. You can't make that happen."

"I'm not trying to. I simply want to make a plea, to ask you to give her a break."

"No way!"

"Hear me out. Your mother loves you more than anything. You can't imagine how much. She shouldn't have freaked out and lost control. But that's something we can't change. For the record, I might have done the same. Parenting can be quite challenging." He glanced at his watch and the navigation map on the front console. "Time to check in for landing, babe."

I nodded, relieved, then cleared my voice and coordinated my visual approach with other aircraft in the vicinity. After receiving the variables and an official okay, I wiggled back into my seat, eyes forward, hoping that enough had been said and we could just move on. Having to focus on landing gave me a great excuse to avoid expanding further on the subject. Although somewhat relieved, a new thought disturbed my peace. I didn't want him going back and telling Mom what he knew. That would just bring the whole thing full circle, instigating a rehashing and, no doubt, more barbs and teasing. I got enough of those at school, even suggestive pinches.

"Dad, I need you to do me a favor."

He didn't seem to be listening. His eyes were half closed, staring out at the horizon.

"Dad. Are you with me?"

He pointed down off his side of the aircraft. "There's our runway."

"Dad. You mustn't talk to Mom about this, about what's going on in school. Please. It's already awful, and she'll just make it worse. She'll storm in there and muddy the water. I won't be able to keep my head up at all."

He looked so sad. I wanted to reach over and hold his hand, to tell him I'd be okay. I knew I'd get through this. I was leaving Grand Forks soon enough. I'd put all of this behind me.

"I don't know if I can do that, babe." His answer came out as a whisper. "It's one more thing to keep secret. I've already—" His voice was drowned out by air traffic control, but I didn't miss the tone of anguish. His whole demeanor clouded over, dark and ominous, and then, almost as suddenly, brightened. He reached over, draping his arm around me, and gave my shoulders a tight squeeze. "I'll do what's right for you. I promise. Whatever the cost. But I have my own request."

I laughed, hoping to break the tension within the cabin. "Last requests, Dad. I need to focus on landing." The start of a smile told me it had worked.

"Your mother is beside herself, torn apart at your leaving. Make the best effort you can to keep things from boiling over back home. She loves you more than life itself. I'm sure she never considered there'd be repercussions at school. She'd be so upset to learn this."

"Oh, come on, Dad. You're just covering for her. I get it. You're on her side. That's where you need to be. But don't make out like she had any justifiable reason for going ballistic. There's no excuse for crazy."

"I agree with you. That was major drama. But try to find a way to get beyond this. Whether you're stuck back here with us in Grand Forks or thousands of miles east, with your grandmother—and believe me when I say that's not going to be simple either—you're going to need your mom. There's absolutely no question about it." He paused and shifted back to a whisper. "Even your mother needs her mother. I'm hoping that one day she'll recognize that as well."

Another flush of warmth overtook me. I actually knew that better than he could imagine. Just because I wanted very little to do with my own mother these days didn't mean I didn't desperately want to be mothered. In fact, just last week I'd sat cozy on the couch with my buddy Lydia's mom, tossing back kernels of popcorn, laughing and at ease, enjoying the attention, love, and acceptance she gave without any accounting. Maybe it was just easier to imagine being another woman's daughter.

Dad gestured forward, where the landing strip had once again come into sight. "In the meantime, do your thing. Let's put this birdy down." Thankful that he was finally willing to drop the subject, I began my landing checklist and, within fifteen minutes, touched down at the regional airport outside of Minneapolis. I taxied the plane toward the tiny hanger, more of a large box with windows than a proper terminal.

"You know, Belle, sometimes you have to forgive, if only to acknowledge that you're not perfect, that we all make mistakes. All of us." I pulled into one of the designated parking spots and shut down the engine. We unbuckled and exited via the passenger door, stepping gingerly onto the wing and then down onto the tarmac beneath. There was a lot of comfort in following protocol. Dad hung around behind the plane, watching as I completed my end-of-flight checklist, then reached forward and took my hand. "Forgiveness, Belle. It's worth the effort." There was something so terribly desolate about his expression. I had a feeling this wasn't only about me.

LILLIAN

THE EVENT FOR NEW MEMBERS was going very well. It was good to see so many young people interested in joining the temple. I knew better than most what a wonderful role it could play, the community it provided.

Although I'd run these events for years as part of the Sisterhood's responsibilities, this year I was just a participant, there to welcome the newcomers with open arms. I looked over the list of speakers, thinking they might have chosen a bit differently, found those with more pizzazz. I pursed my lips and offered a silent *tsk*, exhaling my frustration. No one had even bothered to ask what I thought.

Moving over to the table of nibbles, I spotted a young woman about Elizabeth's age. I approached her directly and exchanged niceties, fulfilling my role, albeit minor, as representative veteran. I loved nothing as much as showing new arrivals what was what, sharing my years of experience, offering any help needed, now or in the future. This community was important to me.

"My mother would love it here, especially the chapel. It's so beautiful."

"She doesn't live in New York?"

"She lives in Longboat Key. Do you know it? It's on the west coast of Florida."

I smiled. This casual conversation suited me perfectly, an excellent means of ignoring the fact that I'd basically become sidelined in my own backyard. "I've never been there, but I've heard it's a lovely spot. Much better weather! Does she come up to visit a lot? New York has so much to offer."

"No, not a lot. It's hard for her to travel these days. I try to go there as much as I can and usually take the kids to visit during vacations."

"You remind me a bit of my daughter! I think you're just about her age. It's wonderful that you make such an effort. I'm sure your mother appreciates it." I leaned over the table and picked up one of the serving plates, offering her a cookie. She waved me off.

"Thank you, I've had plenty." She extended her hand. "Incidentally, I'm Pearl."

"Ah. Excuse me. I'm the greeter. I should have introduced myself first. Lovely to meet you, Pearl. Lillian."

We shook hands. "What about you? Does your family live here in New York?"

I laughed, wiping the crumbs at the corners of my mouth, shaking my head. "No. Nowhere even close. They live in North Dakota." I paused, eager to see her reaction. Most people expected to hear more common places like New Jersey, DC, even California.

"North Dakota! Wow! That's far away. Do you get there to visit, or do they prefer to come see you here in New York? I guess everybody loves a reason to come to the Big Apple!"

"Both! Absolutely, both! I try to get there as much as possible, and yes, hosting them here in New York is always a pleasure." I forced a smile, hoping to seamlessly cover up my lies. This young woman didn't need to know that my daughter had basically banned me from her home, from her entire life; that family trips to New York were few and far between, our meetings contained to a surgically executed meal at a restaurant of my choice. There was no reason I couldn't play at being part of a regular family. "I really enjoy spending time with them."

"I imagine so."

I lowered my voice just a notch. "And then, afterwards, returning to my own quiet, orderly life." A slight cloud passed over Pearl's face. I thought I'd made a good joke, acting like any other grandparent, happy to step back into their own calm oasis after a few days of frenzied young family life. But the frown on her face suggested I'd gotten it wrong. The truth was that I had no idea how an ordinary family worked. I shifted the tenor of the conversation quickly, afraid Pearl would decide I was old and decrepit and move on.

"I'm waiting for my granddaughter to arrive. She's moving to New York!"

"That's so amazing! With the family? Or is she studying here? There are such a wealth of institutions."

"Actually." I paused and stood a little straighter. This was so much fun. "She's going to be attending Julliard!" Another pause, this one to enjoy watching that bombshell of a name settle in. It never failed to amaze. There really was no place like it.

"I don't know what to say. She must be extraordinary. What's her talent? What will she be studying?"

I proceeded to roll out the details of Belle's studies, the fact that she'd be living with me, emphasizing both her brilliant opportunity and my own pleasure at having a part in it. I hadn't had any wine but felt the same warm flush alcohol would elicit. I loved having any chance to strut my stuff.

After a few minutes, Pearl whispered, "Excuse me one minute," and rifled through her purse, retrieving her phone. "I'm a bit concerned about my daughter," she mumbled as she flipped through the recent texts. "She has a big test tomorrow. I just want to check and find out how she's doing, if she's okay; to see if she needs anything—a quick hello to calm her down, maybe ice cream."

I laughed. "A mother's work is never done." At least that was genuine. I knew all about that part of mothering.

"You said it!" The hesitation I sensed a few moments earlier had disappeared, and Pearl laughed out loud. She had one of those infectious laughs that travels and spreads cheer. The other congregants nearby looked over and smiled. I caught Joyce's eye from across the room and gave her a wink. "Shouldn't there be a time limit? She's sixteen. I'd figured on being able to move on from the more mundane parts of raising children at this point, but I really don't see an end."

This was also something I understood. I reached over and patted her arm. "Oh dear. It's never over. Whether they're four, fourteen, or forty, you're always going to be on call and one hundred percent vigilant. You'll always be ready to pick up the pieces if need be."

Pearl grimaced. "Oh, I really hope that's not the case. I'm looking forward to the time I can stop micromanaging. It's exhausting. I just want to get them out of the house and onward to whatever lies ahead. At that point, they'll have to sort it out for themselves."

"Well, as I'm sure you've noticed from your own mother, it's hard to be uninvolved—even as the years pass. Mothers aren't particularly known for being silent bystanders." Unless, I thought to myself, they're purposefully excised from their children's lives and have no choice. I kept this last bit to myself and quickly adjusted my expression, which had gathered unconsciously into a bitter pucker.

Pearl chuckled, provoking another round of affirming glances. We'd somehow become a focus of attention within the reception room, and it felt rather nice. "Actually, my mother stays out of just about everything: my kids' lives, mine. I mean, it all interests her—we get the whole 'twenty questions' thing when we're together—but it doesn't go much beyond that. Once we're all safely tucked back into our own lives, she just kind of moves on. She seems to know when to step back and let me do my thing. It's kind of why I love her."

"If only it were that simple." Completely muffled by a sudden fit of coughing, my comment went unheard. Something was blocking my trachea. I struggled to breathe. Pearl reached around behind me and thwacked me on the back a few times. "Are you okay? What can I do for you?"

"Water. A glass of water?" I managed to croak.

"Of course. I'll be right with you."

I tried to clear my throat, to break up whatever was lodged there. It didn't work. The lump that had emerged from nowhere wouldn't budge. I hacked away relentlessly, eliciting uneasy looks from those close by. This wasn't the attention I'd sought.

Pearl gazed into my face with obvious concern as I drank from the glass of water she'd brought me. "I don't know what else to do for you."

I continued to make unpleasant guttural sounds, sorting through my emotions. I wasn't naive. I knew that this obstruction was a physical manifestation of my distress over the turn our conversation had taken, triggered by Pearl's irritating description of someone who mothered through trust rather than control—the polar opposite of myself. My body's reaction had been immediate and visceral, developing a boulder-sized distraction from the emotional weight of the guilt and second thoughts her words had provoked.

I had always believed that parenting was a lifetime duty, love an elusive, flowery concept that had very little to do with raising a child. The fact that I loved Elizabeth more than the moon and the stars didn't mean I was willing to throw my own agenda to the four winds. These beliefs led me to speak those cutting words, ten years earlier, that essentially ended our relationship.

Understanding that I needed to suppress this line of thought if I wanted to grind the knob in my throat down to something more manageable, something closer to a pebble, I forced myself to stop rehashing the past.

By this time, Pearl had refilled my glass. I eagerly chugged the water.

"This seems to be helping. Shall I get you more?"

"No, dear." My words came out much clearer. The blockage, albeit still there, had been partially conquered. I wheezed out my appreciation. "You're very kind. You must be a very devoted daughter. Your mother really is fortunate."

She laughed, brightening my spirits as well as those of the small group of worried individuals who'd gathered around us. Her levity was absolutely contagious. "In fact, I'm the lucky one. She's a real star, my mom. I just adore spending time with her. She's my role model!"

Overcome by a fit of renewed coughing, I expelled the last sips of water in a very awkward projectile. This was just embarrassing. It almost wasn't fair. Just as I began to feel better, calmer, more in control, just as I put the whole sordid subject behind me, confident of my own way, Pearl had inserted the knife and given it a little twist. "Oh boy! You've really got something stuck there! Are you sure I shouldn't . . . ?"

"No," I sputtered. "Sec." I struggled to get ahold of myself, hyperaware that my mind was controlling my body and I could stop all of this in a second. If only I could get her to shut up. She'd somehow managed to strike the ugliest of chords, and I really didn't want to hear any more. *How dare she question my parenting, or its reception!* But try as I might, I couldn't suppress the truth. Elizabeth would never utter such loving and beautiful words about me. I wondered if she spoke about me at all during her everyday life in Grand Forks. There was a good chance everyone just assumed I was deceased. The relationship between Pearl and her mother, which sounded so special, couldn't have been more different than ours. My aplomb waned as I acknowledged the tragedy of this fact—its physical manifestation a knot of despair lodged firmly in my throat. Not wanting this young woman to spot the depths of my sadness, I turned toward the table, eyes cast downward, pretending to select a cookie.

"You seem to have conquered whatever was making you choke."

One last, pseudo-friendly glance and an effort at a smile closed the matter between us. I leaned on the edge of the table heavily, still burdened by our conversation. Although relieved to have alleviated its extreme physical expression, I berated myself for not minding my business in the first place, for allowing myself to be drawn into a ridiculous competition. I'd never once, my entire life, regretted the path I chose and certainly didn't intend to start now, so late in the game. My job as a parent had always been to educate, not to please. That was exactly as it was supposed to be. In any case, having a daughter adore me in such an open and honest fashion probably wasn't all it was cracked up to be. I always managed to push all the wrong buttons when it came to Elizabeth.

Desperate to retreat to my own world, I excused myself and made my way to the ladies' room, the words Elizabeth and I had exchanged the last time we were together, at the temple back in Grand Forks, still stuck there beyond my epiglottis. This was just a few years back. I'd come on a visit arranged entirely by Mike. God bless my son-in-law. The trip would never have happened without him. Elizabeth continuously insisted the timing wasn't right. We were gathered for Friday-night services. The temple was an absolute jewel box, just seven rows extended back from the burnished wood alter. Stained-glass windows featuring bright colors lined the side walls. The vestibule of this NYC temple could have held the entire sanctuary several times over, but that didn't make it less special. I don't know what I'd expected, but it wasn't something quite so lovely, so understated, so replete with a sense of spirituality. I suppose there was something to be said for intimacy when it came to connecting with God.

Happy to finally have access to my family's life out there on the Plains, I'd wanted to try and get a feel for the community. I'd made quite a few assumptions over the years, figuring it was typical small-town America, inferior to my life back East. I never understood why Elizabeth chose to move out of Chicago. That was backwater enough. Once the pews began to fill up, I got a better look at the local population. I'd assumed they would all be tall and blond, seeing as how the area was originally settled by Slavic immigrants in the early nineteenth century—Nordic cousins of those who originally settled New York. But this wasn't the case. In fact, they looked a lot like me, save their preference for casual dress. Most were in jeans, adults and children alike, and a decent number looked to be wearing oversized sweatshirts, those that better served as pajamas. Buttoned up tight in a conservative, maxi-length dress I reserved for events at temple, I felt distinctly out of place.

Elizabeth treated me like a disease that evening, keeping me at a distance. I tried my best to mingle at the Oneg Shabbat, introducing myself according to the audience, sometimes as Elizabeth's mother, sometimes as Belle's grandmother, and occasionally as Mike's mother-in-law. I knew very little about my family's life but couldn't miss seeing that they'd made a real home out here on the prairie. The welcome extended to me by their friends was wonderful. Excluded for so long, this new embrace was absolutely life-giving. There, in that little stuffy room with the low-pile wall-to-wall carpeting, surrounded by trays of sliced oranges and dry cookies, I began to dream of a possible reunification.

Elizabeth put an end to that fantasy on the spot. Of course, it was partially my fault. She hadn't appreciated my reaction to Grand Forks over the previous days. Although I'd warmed up to the temple community—small Jewish communities were always charming—I wasn't impressed with the rest of the area. There was that nasty diner, the one with the inedible food covered in repulsive sauces; Main Street, with dusty buildings of stunted growth clustered shoulder to shoulder in a kind of tribal huddle; and those broad open plains that led nowhere. Although the sunsets and sunrises were initially appealing, the beauty of emptiness quickly wore thin. Charming, quaint, and intimate were not adjectives that led up to fabulous. In fact, they didn't lead anywhere at all. I knew more about that than anyone, having spent my formative years defining where I didn't want to be.

Back in grade school, I'd wanted to swap lives with little Miss Popular, the girl whose life epitomized everything that existed beyond our small town: islands of warm sand and warmer seas during the winter, autumn weekends in New York City at the Plaza Hotel, summer vacations in Maine. Maryann Jones had lived an exotic life like that of the famed Eloise, and I couldn't help wanting the same for myself. My aspirations for a career in medicine went hand in hand with the desire to step into the imagined spotlight of life in a major metropolis, affecting every step I took.

Although I'd always been disappointed by Elizabeth's lack of passion for the bright lights, her decision to run off to Nothingsville, North Dakota, further affirmation that she would never follow in my footsteps, I sensed I had an avid candidate in Belle—appreciating her willingness to step into the arena and give life a chance.

Elizabeth saw right through me. "She knows what she wants."

I was taken aback, minding my own business amid the pleasant exchanges and cheese platter.

"Yes. And I celebrate that. It reminds me of myself."

"And of how I wasn't. What I'm not."

I paused. "No, dear. That's not what I said. And that's not what I was thinking."

"But it's true. We both know it."

"Elizabeth, this is about Belle. She's different. She'd do better in a vibrant atmosphere like New York. I'm sure of it. She craves the stimulation."

"Actually, I agree."

I paused. I hadn't expected this. We rarely saw eye to eye on any subject. "So maybe we should talk about how to make that happen."

Elizabeth frowned, looking away quickly and then staring straight back into my eyes—her own now filled with fury. "Wait. What are we talking about?"

"We're talking about getting her out of Grand Forks, dear; the Great Plains: this little corner of the world to which you insisted on running. You know it's not for her. She needs so much more."

"I really don't know what you're talking about. We have a lovely life here. I thought you would understand that now that you've had a chance to visit." She gestured around the room. "I think we're really lucky. Look at everything we have. Can't you see that she's happy?"

I cut her off. "Maybe, but that doesn't mean it suits her." I paused, wanting to slow my pace. I hadn't intended to cross delicate boundaries and insult my daughter. That was going to put us right back in the same black hole. I struggled to regain lost ground. "This lovely warm embrace, this community, I can feel it. I understand how it's become your home. And I'm so happy for you, my dear. I truly am. I know that this is what you've been looking for . . . your own spot." I saw her softening. "But it will never add up to what my granddaughter needs or even wants. She isn't going to settle. Not ever. She isn't you."

I wanted to take back those last words the minute they were uttered but knew I couldn't. The truth could not be denied. And as usual, I let my own disappointments get the better of my common sense. I knew what was coming next. I'd had years of facing my daughter's crestfallen face. But when I looked up, I saw something else entirely—something totally unexpected. Elizabeth didn't seem deflated at all. Instead, she seemed almost empowered.

"There's a lot more to life than bright lights, Mom. In fact . . ." Here she paused, cocking her head to the side and squinting, as if she were trying to get a better look at me. "In fact, I've always found them quite blinding."

With that, she spun around and walked away, leaving me alone by the reception table. I frantically looked around the room for a warm face. While there had been plenty earlier, now there were none. Neither Belle nor Mike were in sight, and I didn't remember the names of the other people milling close by. Instead of feeling a part of the crowd, as I had before, I felt entirely alone, abandoned to fend for myself in a community to which I didn't belong. This wasn't at all what I wanted, what I'd hoped for upon embarking on this visit.

I excoriated myself for once again getting it wrong with Elizabeth and pushing her away. If only I could be a softer parent—one who just accepted and never questioned, one who provided a hug instead of a lesson and made peace with the idea that the window to educate had closed long ago. But it was impossible to change my ways this late in the game.

It was during that trip that I came to understand that Belle was the key, the only chance I had to get it right. There was a good chance I'd never be able to undo the ruins of my relationship with my daughter, never have the one Pearl had with her mother, but I had my eye on another with the potential to be equally wonderful, fulfilling, and maybe even more of an answer to my dreams. As long as I still had my granddaughter in my life, there was a chance that the rest of the pieces of the puzzle would fall into place.

Standing alone before the mirror in the ladies' room, I reached up and touched the delicate skin poking out from my décolleté, the locus of another battle. The time was ripe, and I'd suddenly been dealt an excellent hand. Belle would soon be here. I might finally find the promising future I so craved.

MIKE

IT WAS HERE, THE MORNING we'd all been anticipating. Belle was on her way. I carried her suitcase out to the car, loading it on top of the first and firmly closing the trunk. The sun had just made its way over the trees. It was a gorgeous, crisp start to a day I knew would warm up. I loved these end-of-August mornings with their hint of fall. Summer would never be my season. I couldn't stand it. Of course, that was partially due to the fact that, despite my administrative duties, I still spent a good deal of time up in the air, sealed in a sweltering-hot cabin with sweating post-adolescents.

"I'm ready." Belle came down the path at a trot. She looked so different from the girl who went off with her friends last night for a pre-departure round of pie. I almost didn't recognize her. I blinked a few times, dazzled by the sunlight. Maybe it was her clothes. They were all black. *Has she always favored black?* All of a sudden, I couldn't remember. She swung her saddlebag over her shoulder and leaped into the car.

"Come on, Dad! We're going to be late! Let's go."

"That's it? You have everything? Are you sure?" I started back up the path to the front door. "There must be something . . ."

I paused. Elizabeth hadn't come out. Last night she told me she couldn't, that she'd say her goodbyes while they had breakfast, during the hustle and bustle of gathering up last-minute items and packing the car. I didn't understand. *What mother would see off her daughter without a hug?* I shook my head, pursing my lips. There was no way that was going to happen here. No way.

"Give me a minute, okay?"

Belle made an expression of impatience, then looked down, checking her phone. I walked back to the house. Once inside, I closed the front door behind me quietly, painfully aware that the entire mood of the place had changed. It had taken on a funereal feel, completely different from earlier when we'd all sat at the breakfast table, the morning light with all its promise pouring through the kitchen window. Deep shadows fell across my path to the kitchen. The air felt thick, heavy with sadness.

"Lizzy? Where are you? We're on our way."

"Of course."

She was sitting right where I'd left her. In fact, she seemed frozen in place. The coffee cup gripped in her hand was empty. "You don't want to come out? Give Belle a hug? Maybe wave from the front porch?"

"We've said our goodbyes."

The effort she'd made to feign happiness and excitement earlier had obviously depleted her. The woman seated before me looked positively diminished. I couldn't bear to see her this way.

"This isn't an ending."

She looked up at me. "Of course it is."

"But not the kind you're thinking. It isn't forever."

"We can't know that."

I glanced at my watch, made a quick calculation, then pulled out a chair and sat beside her. "I think you need to come out."

"Well, I think otherwise. She doesn't want me there. She's already been gone for quite some time. This is the part that makes it official."

I reached forward with my hand, laying it flat beside her mug, the tips of my fingers reaching out toward her. "Lizzy, you love one another. This is just one more stage that needs to be endured—fine, let's say survived. Soon enough Belle will need you and come running back." I cleared my throat. "You need to get over whatever's bothering you and move on."

She retracted her fingers abruptly, and the mug toppled over. I grabbed at it, making sure it didn't fall off the table and break, and looked up to find an almost wry expression on her face, completely unexpected considering the circumstances and the generally gloomy mood within the house.

"You always have to pick up the pieces, don't you? Well, this time you can't. You'll never understand what I'm feeling. Don't even try. She's venturing out, your daughter, at such a fragile time in her life. You just can't begin to understand the difficulties that girls face. You only see the opportunity, the potential of all that light. I don't have that privilege. All I can see is the darkness in the tunnel ahead."

I had no idea what she was talking about but knew that her intentions were good. For the longest time I'd struggled to figure out her allusive comments, knowing they all had to do with Lillian and the difficulties between them. But it was her outrageous, even alarmist reaction to Belle moving in with my mother-in-law that convinced me there was more to the story. She was concerned about things of which I had no clue.

"I wish you would share it with me, whatever it is that's scaring you. I'm sure I can help. I always try."

"Mike. Stop." She met my eyes with a fierce stare. "It's your help that landed us in this mess. Without your interference, we might have just gone on as is." She sat back in her chair and averted her glance, staring down at the mug before her. "You need to stop trying. There are some things you'll never be able to undo. Damage you can't reverse."

This was it. This was the impasse at which we'd been stuck for years. I moved my chair back, ready to leave, but then paused. I had about five more minutes before we'd really need to get moving. I quickly considered how this had all begun months earlier, that phone call from Lillian, the best idea I'd ever heard despite the subsequent loss. I pulled my chair back in toward the table, certain I could still save the situation—or at least achieve a better ending.

I considered telling Lizzy about her mother's health, about our fears. I knew things would be different if she knew, if Lillian shared the news she'd gotten from the doctor. But it wasn't mine to share. In fact, my mother-in-law had sworn me not to. I was left to find another way to smooth the broken path between the two that cast its long shadow on her relationship with Belle. I didn't want her to take this argument to the grave. There would come a time when she'd no longer be able to blame her mother for whatever had gone wrong between her and Belle, but by that time Lillian would most probably be gone. Having lost both parents years earlier, I understood that this burden was going to be a heavier one to bear than any secret. Skipping out on a proper send-off, a seemingly insignificant decision, was one regret she could avoid.

"You'll regret this."

"Maybe."

"It's something you won't be able to amend."

"I know." She cleared her voice. "But Mike, I just can't . . . I can't bring myself—"

"Find a way."

With that I pushed my chair back firmly and stood, reaching down with my hand to stroke the fine hair at her brow. I knew that Lizzy was annoyed at my continual efforts to make things right, to smooth the rough edges of our lives, but I just couldn't help it. In any case, I didn't think it was the worst quality a guy could have. I leaned over and kissed her, lingering for a moment to take in that familiar smell of evergreen and pine, then walked back outside.

Belle was sitting with the car door wide open, legs swung to the side, one foot tapping out a tune on the ground, deeply into her music. She pulled one of the headphones out the minute she sensed my presence and glanced up, her eyes searching around me, beyond me. I knew who she was looking for, and my heart shrank into a shriveled knot. These two loved and needed each other so desperately. I couldn't bear the fact that I couldn't bring them together and make a proper farewell happen. For just a moment, I considered that maybe it wasn't up to me. But that idea didn't make me feel any better.

"Ready, sweetie? All set?"

Belle put her hand over her eyes, blocking out the morning sun in order to get a better look. I came in a bit closer, hoping to block her view of the house and shut out what she wouldn't find there.

"Let's get going! Shall we?" I strode over to the other side of the car, noticing that Belle took an extra second or two to drag her legs inside, closing the door a bit too slowly, her whole body turned toward the house—a sunflower seeking its source.

I couldn't help myself. I glanced there as well. And although my foot already hovered over the gas pedal, I quickly moved it back to the brakes. There at the living room window was Elizabeth, her face glistening with tears, her hand resting on the windowpane in a parting wave.

PART II

ELIZABETH

I MOVED DOWN THE AISLES of the library, scanning the bindings of the heavy tomes squeezed onto the shelves and letting my fingers skip and bounce along the uneven surfaces of the embossed letters, slipping over the cracks in the leather that bespoke years of use. I was so very comfortable here, safe, and necessary; these heavy digests were like family—a different kind of family. I found the volume on Torts I'd been looking for and gave it a confident tug, pulling it free from the embrace of its neighbors, before returning to the reading room.

I hadn't slept very much since Belle's send-off, and food had almost entirely lost its appeal. I spent that entire morning before she left for the airport trying to stay out of the way, attempting to pretend at a neutral cool I didn't feel. I was afraid that the slightest comment would be interpreted incorrectly, prompting yet one more ugly exchange. Wrapped up in a blanket of fear, terrified about what this next chapter meant, for her, for me, for us, I couldn't find a means to give her a proper sendoff. I'm not even sure we made eye contact. I completely missed the multiple opportunities to wrap my arms around her and tell her that I loved her and would always be on her side, no matter what, even from 1,500 miles away.

Mike had immediately recognized the immensity of this mistake, warning me that I would be sorry about it later, pleading for me to say goodbye properly as she waited in the car, all packed up and ready to go. But by that time, I was almost catatonic, frozen in a block of disappointment, mostly in myself. I simply wasn't able to get up and do the right thing. Only at the very last second had I managed a gesture in the right direction, getting myself to the window and waving goodbye. I'm not even sure Belle saw me. In the end, flooded in a sea of tears, I parted from the darkened shade of her window as they pulled away.

Of course, there was almost no way things could have gone better. The months before Belle's departure had been awful. Our relationship, already rocky and unpredictable as we struggled through the throes of her adolescence, sank to a new low. And although I would have liked to blame my daughter—eternally cranky, downright rude, and sometimes a real pickle—I knew that I was just as much at fault. I'd said and done things I shouldn't have, things I would take back if it were possible: screaming at the top of my lungs upon finding her with Tom at the top of a long list, followed by an adamant refusal to discuss New York and blatantly trying to interfere with her relationship with her grandmother. I let my past and troubled relationship with Lillian, things that had nothing to do with Belle, taint something wonderful.

And now, when I truly needed someone at my side to hold my hand and assure me that things would be okay, I was completely alone. Things between Mike and me were about as bad as they'd ever been, degrading once I figured out that he had engineered this whole plan, separating me from Belle just when we needed time together to heal, and handing her over to the woman who'd fumbled through my own adolescence, passing judgment when I needed sympathy, holding a hard line when I needed to be heard. For all intents and purposes, Mike had taken away my daughter, painfully reminding me of a time when Lillian had done very much the same.

I tapped my fingers on the desktop and knocked twice, with determination. I had to stop raking through the things that couldn't be fixed, bemoaning relationships that weren't working, and focus on ones that might. Although I was loathe to admit it, Mike was completely right about that. And although opening a canyon of pain, the ball he'd put into play had, ironically, been necessary to the point of essential. It was clearly time to focus on my own issues, to search out and determine a new, healthier course. If only I knew where to begin.

The most obvious first step was to reconsider my career and explore my connection to the law. After all, maybe my obsessions didn't stem from my personal life but instead were the result of professional choices I'd made. I thought back to the beginning, trying to recall my decision to become a lawyer. I couldn't. I had no memory of it whatsoever, not one moment of enlightenment. I didn't remember running into the house with an excited declaration of purpose, nor sharing my enthusiasm with my friends in the front hall at school. What I did recall was my mother's mantra, the refrain repeated over and over from the time I was in middle school: something about "My daughter, the lawyer." Stronger and more confident than I, my mother was always quite certain about my destiny.

I fumbled over the timeline, trying to figure out when a defined path had opened before me, as obvious as the yellow-brick road; when my role as sole determiner of my future was reduced to that of faithful follower, left to place one foot in front of the other, following a given course. Although that kernel of memory remained inaccessible, my ambivalence, my willingness to simply go through the motions, whatever they might be—the goal so much less important than the idea of getting on with it—stuck out bold and clear. Just as clear was the memory, with its painful ramifications, that my indifference had disturbed my mother, as if it were one more sign of my lack of luster. I was well into adulthood before I realized that *she* was the one with the goal. My future was writ large in *her* mind. Becoming a lawyer had everything to do with what Lillian hadn't accomplished. I was meant to pick up the reins of a real profession that my mother had dropped—or rather, been forced to drop—a generation earlier. I was supposed to right a wrong.

Yet that never explained why she chose the law. There were no lawyers in the family. Most of our closest relatives were involved in business, small-time affairs for the most part, nothing that made it to NASDAQ. It might have had something to do with that television show we'd watched as a family on Saturday nights, *Perry Mason*. One of my fonder childhood memories was gathering around the table for the weekly episode, our plates filled with steak and a pile of steaming noodles—the show itself less important than the time spent together. This was long before I began to blossom and become my own person.

I began a mental checklist: a much-repeated mantra, *Perry Mason*, and then, yes, one other milestone—my ninth-grade history project on Justice Louis Brandeis and free speech. My mother actively encouraged that research project, considering it a building block to my future in the law which would offer me "a brilliant opportunity to shine." It was around then that she began a ruthless campaign. It would have taken supersonic strength for me to choose otherwise. I never stood a chance. And it didn't stop there. Once I went through all the necessary steps and eventually became a 1L at Northwestern, she gave yet another push, insisting I go into litigation. For my mother, any other specialty within the law was inadequate, relegating lawyers to the unacceptable back burner, firmly out of the ever-to-be-strived-for limelight. I'd acquiesced, first because it was easier to comply, and second, as part of my eternal effort to gain my mother's approval.

Sometime during law school, around the time we had that moot court exercise, I began to realize I'd made the wrong choice. Although I enjoyed the process of learning the details of the case to be argued and coming up with an effective defense, that's precisely where my passion for the role of savior ended. Standing before the mock judge and a mock jury of my peers to present my case, I immediately understood that I was in the wrong place. I wanted nothing to do with their expectations and their attention, bristling at having to measure each word, to convince and dazzle while directly under their gaze. Trial work would never suit me. While my mother wanted a daughter willing to step boldly in front of an audience and perform, all I wanted to do was disappear into the crowd, to be so much like everyone else that I'd go unnoticed. Lillian should have known better. This was an old story, a dialogue dating back to my childhood at the temple:

"Are you trying out for the role of Esther?"

"No, Mom. I don't want to be Esther."

"But she's the queen. It's the best role! She's the star! How could you not want to be the star?"

I repeatedly tried to avoid these conversations, or at least to end them as quickly as possible. My mother would never in a million years understand why I was happier being part of the crowd that booed Haman: an effective, contributing piece of a larger whole. And although the desire to find a different course, one far less conspicuous than the one Lillian encouraged, was always there, it was difficult to change the expected trajectory. Toeing the line was so much easier. Eventually, upon completing law school, I accepted that plum job in the litigation department of a fancy firm on Michigan Avenue, capitulating completely.

Still, I always knew it wasn't a good fit. The move to the Great Plains, which many of my professional associates saw as odd—who chooses the prairie over Water Tower Place?—finally offered me the chance to change my path, to drop the pretense that the fast track pursued by most of my fellow Northwestern law school graduates, and continually touted by my mother, was something in which I had any interest. There I finally made my version of a statement, accepting the job as head of research—basically, law librarian—at a local firm on Main Street. This step out of center stage and behind the scenes was finally about me.

"Great work, Elizabeth. Thank you." Pam's comment cut through my ruminations, bringing me back to the present. It took me a long moment to remember what I'd been doing.

"There's quite a bit more legal precedent for this defense than you'd imagine. I've tracked it over the past four decades. Do you need me to go back further?"

"Well, we want to establish the baseline for the exception. If you find a case or two that speaks to that precisely, even if it's older, that would be excellent. A firm ruling makes for an easier defense." She reached out and touched my arm, giving it a squeeze. "This case is so painful. I'm hoping we'll find a way to help our client."

Painful was an understatement. I'd had trouble with it from the start. The defendant was a young woman in her late twenties accused of trying to poison her mother. She was pleading innocence based on temporary insanity, having cracked after years of emotional abuse. Pages upon pages of testimony described the cruel, humiliating, and truly debilitating treatment she'd suffered both at home and in public, leaving her unable to function properly within the world, to graduate high school, attend college, or hold down a job. One day, she'd found a way out.

Tracking precedence for the defense led me to a host of cases wherein individuals, after undergoing years of mistreatment and emotional stress, had basically broken, committing one unspeakable act or another. The pain, the desolation of never measuring up, of always feeling like a disappointment, all made sense. I could well imagine how this could make someone dealing with an extreme situation go out of their mind and do something crazy. I hoped the material I'd gathered would help this poor young woman and give her a chance at eventually achieving some degree of happiness or fulfillment.

I moved a few more tomes to the conference table next to the stacks, attached a sticky note instructing that they not be reshelved, and then walked back to my office, picking up a few abandoned books that needed reshelving along the way. My mind shifted away from the case, back to my search for the beginning, seeking the moment or event that had compelled me to finally take a bold step toward changing my direction, even the slightest bit. Although it was nice to believe it originated from a sudden boost of self-confidence, I knew its origins to be more subtle, emerging from a slow simmer, a situation long in the making that simply boiled out of control. The pressure that builds up as the magma rises will inevitably cause an explosion.

Although the dividing line separating the before from the after was firmly drawn that day at Sarabeth's, it had been a long time coming, its preparation laid long before I even had a say, back when Lillian, unable to fulfill her dream of becoming a doctor, was sentenced to a life of professional frustration. Although it had very little to do with me at all, I bore the brunt. I cringed at the memory of those expressions of disappointment—the times I'd felt my mother's simmering resentment, the shortness of temper that threatened to explode. There was the sudden *thwack* of a dishtowel on the counter when I forgot to clean up, the constant grumbling about my grades not being good enough, about how I always gave up and let others get the best of me; the not-so-subtle comments about how the hours spent staring at my lava lamp would be better invested in reading ahead, getting a leg up on the other students.

My decision to finally get up and make a move was sealed by Lillian's official acknowledgment that I'd failed to live up to her expectations. It happened at Sarabeth's. The brunch immediately preceding our move to Grand Forks, meant to be a beginning, the onset of a new age, turned into an ugly end. I'd picked the place, hoping to engineer a decent encounter. Of course, I was up against tough odds. I knew the conversation was going to be rocky, that Lillian would be crushed to hear we were moving to a backwater, an insignificant part of the country, and become livid when she discovered I was discontinuing my career in litigation and had accepted what she would consider a "servile" position in a local law firm.

I counted on the chatter of the crowd gathered at this popular restaurant to create a welcome distraction, alleviating the agony of either deadly silence or, alternatively, raised voices. It was unclear which this turn of events would induce. Although the brunch started out pleasantly enough, both of us looking forward to our fluffy egg-white omelets, the divine, freshly squeezed grapefruit juice, and the lighthearted atmosphere of the Upper West Side on a Friday morning, things quickly turned sour.

"It's a fabulous opportunity for Mike."

"It sounds like it. Head of the department? They certainly picked the right man."

Lillian adored Mike *now* but hadn't been thrilled with even the *idea* of him when we first started dating. She had her sights set on my finding someone appropriate within the legal community, someone with an even flashier career than mine, and had an opinion or two about pilots. But his easygoing manner and obvious devotion to me quickly won her over, manifesting in a comfortable relationship far better than our own. There had never been any complications with Mike. At least, until now.

"But, dear. I don't understand what this means for you, for your career. You have such a wonderful job in Chicago. You've worked so hard, gotten so far. I can't imagine you leaving the firm."

"Yes, well, that will be difficult. It's a great place. You're right. But it's okay. We've thought it through. Ends up, this is an opportunity for both of us." I paused and took a sip of water, bracing myself. "I can finally make a bit of a change."

That was when things took a turn for the worse. Lillian's hackles were raised, and she went on the attack. "But there's nothing for you out there. How could you even consider giving up everything you've achieved? Why would you throw it all away? Maybe you should commute."

"That's ridiculous. I've found a wonderful law firm right in town! Right in Grand Forks! Apparently, it's one of the best in North Dakota. I'm not throwing away anything at all. I'm just sliding a bit to the left."

I remember smiling at my joke, almost buoyant as I described my new position and the excited reception I'd received from the local staff. All that brightness was snuffed out moments later. Lillian's reaction, expressed in a cascade of sharp words, was strong and fierce. I weathered the storm by focusing on the misery of the waiter, who received an unpleasant glare from my mother each time he tried to refresh our glasses of water, and a methodical approach to my side salad. I'd ordered a Caesar. Busying myself with interspersing bites of crunchy croutons and crisp leaves of Romaine offered the perfect means by which to shut out the barrage hurled my way. My mother, stunned at the concept that I didn't want to work in litigation, overcome by her anger and displeasure, determined to find some way to undo what she considered a horrible decision, barely managed a bite.

The light and easy questions she'd asked at the beginning of our conversation, when she interpreted my announcement as exploratory and hypothetical, segued into pointed ones with a clear agenda: "A librarian?

Who would choose such a boring position?" "Why didn't you go for litigation? You know that's the only field that counts." "What was the point of going to law school?" "I can't imagine anyone else in the whole world giving up an office with a window on Miracle Mile for a closet in the dust bowl." She completed her tirade with a real zinger: "You've always managed to fumble the opportunities I've provided."

That last comment landed especially hard, revealing the real reason for all the fuss. In the end, it was about Lillian and what she wanted for herself, the way *she* envisioned my life. It crushed her that I would choose the road that led away from the center, not because it indicated that we were so fundamentally different but because it meant that I would no longer be able to fulfill the dreams she'd had to give up. I sat in silence for the rest of the meal, shutting out the parts that hurt and trying, desperately, to sympathize with her distress. I knew full well that her need to achieve vicariously through me was about righting a terrible wrong that could never truly be undone. But I was tired of being the pawn she played to make things right.

If it had ended there, things might have been different, albeit still nowhere close to good. My mother and I simply weren't destined to walk together, arm in arm, into the sunset. But she wasn't finished. The fatal blow was yet to come.

For whatever reason, and I'll never understand why, Lillian found it necessary to go one huge step further, entering territory that should have, by any measure, been off limits. Wiping her mouth with the cloth napkin and carefully placing it in her lap, her signature gesture for a regrouping of a sort, she stared straight into my eyes, making certain to engage me directly, and spoke the bitter truth. "I'm sure you're aware that I never wanted you. That your arrival ended all my dreams."

I was so stunned that I stopped breathing, holding in the last breath I'd taken when there was still the slim possibility of maintaining even a shaky relationship with my mother. Her words cut straight through me, and all the loveliness of that beautiful restaurant melted away. The celebratory aspect of Sarabeth's was no more.

It was hard to imagine what Lillian thought she'd accomplish. I'd flown into town specifically to talk to her about the enormous journey upon which Mike and I were about to embark, a fait accompli. It would have been so easy to pretend enthusiasm while enumerating a few genuine reservations, things that might get me to think a bit more about our plans, maybe help us organize for the transition. The decision to criticize absolutely every one of its underlying aspects, making me second-guess what was basically already done, had been mean, but expressing her resentment of my arrival in her life went well beyond, all the way to horrific. It was worse than anything I could ever have anticipated.

And of course, it awakened a sleeping pain, an ancient loss from which I'd never recovered. While my mother hadn't wanted me because I got in the way of her future—or, more accurately, ruined it—I'd wanted nothing more than to bring the child I accidentally created at the ripe age of seventeen into this world. Of course, back then, Lillian wouldn't hear of it. She hadn't let up once she figured out what happened, quietly but steadily commenting about my future, about what I would be giving up. Although unarticulated, it was clear that her losses stood to be as great or even greater than my own. In the end, despite dragging out the decision to a point where I hoped not to have to make it, I relented. After spending my life trying to please, trying to curry favor, there was no choice but to give in.

Mothers wield strange powers. They have the unparalleled ability to destroy their children with the simplest statements. Back at brunch, I could not imagine why Lillian was so willing to hurt me for the sake of making her point. It was unfathomable. But the result was clear. I left the restaurant that day, heart racing at an impossible pace, tears streaming down my face as I made my way down Columbus Avenue, understanding that a line had been crossed; that despite years spent trying to heal from the damage wrought by that painful situation at the end of high school, to find a way back to a tentative middle ground with Lillian, it would not be possible. She'd simply said too many awful things.

But now, comfortable in a place I was appreciated, even respected, a place of my own design, I had to acknowledge that I had done the very same thing. I, too, had verbally lashed out at my daughter, overreacting to situations that were out of my control, saying things I didn't really mean, keeping positive thoughts that should have been expressed to myself. This last was almost the most painful of all. I'd refused to celebrate Belle's golden opportunity entirely because of my own fears and disappointments. In the end, I was following Lillian's lead to the bitter end, alienating my daughter and ignoring her needs and goals in order to make peace with my own. The belief that I could save and protect her as I'd never been able to protect the child I didn't get to have had gotten the better of me, turning me into a version of the mother I eventually chose to expel from my life.

The result was just as unfortunate, taking me away from my goal instead of toward it, pushing Belle to move away and leave me alone just as I had left Lillian years earlier. Of course, the irony was that Belle hadn't simply left but instead walked straight into the arms of the woman from whom I'd fled.

Counting back over the decades, I saw a pattern I didn't like: a line of girls who, for one reason or another, left the comfort of their nests, forced to fend for themselves, lost to those who loved them but couldn't manage to take care of them, on their own just when they most needed love and support. A shiver of realization moved through my body, and I stood suddenly, upending my desk chair.

It was time to stop this horrible pattern of loss, to step out of the shadows in which I'd been lurking for much of my life and take the reins. I glanced across my desk at a picture of Belle and me taken soon after our arrival in Grand Forks. We were laughing, happy, and most definitely together. Despite the distance that had grown between us, I was confident we could eventually find our way back to one another. The key was to do as Belle had done, to take a chance and leap into the unknown. While she'd done that by moving across the country, I could do it right here in Grand Forks. I knew where I wanted to start, the way to assuage some of the pain that had been suffocating my life for the longest time. I would save one lost daughter. Now I just had to find one.

BELLE

I SHOOK HANDS WITH ONE congregant after another. Grandma had them lined up. Each was eager to hear why I was in New York, expressing their excitement at finally meeting me. I looked down the line. There were still so many to come. I sighed heavily and tried my best to remain patient. It wasn't easy. Immediately after services, she'd corralled me in the direction of the rabbi, insisting I meet a few of her friends. I never anticipated that this would be such long, drawn-out affair. She was basically pulling them over, one after the other, the minute they finished greeting the temple officials.

If I'd known Grandma was bringing me here to show me off, I would have declined. I looked toward the back of the sanctuary, envisioning my path of escape, but was stymied by the distance I had to cover to get there. This place was enormous, so much bigger than any temple I'd ever seen. And I'd seen quite a few. Much of our time in NFTY-North was spent traveling from one to another, being hosted for a weekend, trying to solidify connections between the local Jewish communities of the Midwest and Great Plains. We were all so isolated back home, the distances between our communities enormous. This was one way to close those gaps and make us feel part of a whole. I loved every moment.

A sudden pang of absence interrupted my search for the exit. I hadn't anticipated all the things I'd miss once I left home: Beth Abraham, youth group, flying with Dad, playing with my chamber group, meeting up with friends for pie. Standing in this cavernous space, looking around at a community dressed to impress, buttoned up, fancy on the stiff side, I desperately missed the relaxed and laid-back atmosphere back home. There, we were mostly in jeans or something equally unpretentious, hung out after services around tables of cheese sticks in a room with fluorescent lighting and scratchy, dated carpet, and didn't make everything a ceremony. There was no receiving line, and my friends and I snickered our way through services in the back pew without getting in trouble. Life, even teenage life, was allowed to continue alongside prayers. It could never truly interfere.

Here, everything was completely different, so cold and impersonal. Except for the voices of the rabbi and the cantor, who most definitely had operatic aspirations, the sanctuary was completely silent during services. Despite a congregation that numbered well over a thousand, you could hear a pin drop. It was like everyone was holding their breath, afraid of disturbing. And then, there was the organ. It added such a dolorous note, making everything seem even more serious, almost sad. I would have liked to hear something bright and uplifting, maybe that Andante in F Major by Mozart. Grandma told me that Mom used to hide up on the second floor of the sanctuary where the organ was hidden, peeking through the curtains at the congregants gathered below. It was hard to imagine Mom here at all. She usually shirked anything that smacked of formality and pretense.

I felt another pang, this one more of a surprise. I hadn't expected to miss Mom at all. I shook the feeling off quickly, unwilling to open that Pandora's box, and smiled down at my shoes. Back at the apartment, Grandma had insisted they weren't appropriate for services, encouraging me to wear something with a heel. I'd refused, protesting that it was fashionable to wear Vans with a skirt. She eventually capitulated. All it took was showing her a picture of Duchess Catherine sporting the same pair. What was good enough for British royalty was good enough for this pioneer from the Great Plains. Grandma was a sucker for anything royal.

"And this is Belle. My granddaughter. I don't know if you've heard. She's attending *Julliard*." I knew Grandma was proud of me, knew she wanted to share my accomplishments with the world, but I didn't figure I'd be shown off like a trophy, held up and marched around for everyone to admire. Shifting my glance away from the woman to whom I'd just been introduced, I was taken by the way Grandma positively glowed, even seemed a bit taller. At least one of us was enjoying this ritual. I couldn't imagine what she got out of continuing to share our new arrangement with absolutely everyone and anyone, but it was hard to disparage her obvious pleasure.

And of course, I owed her so much. I was here because of Grandma. This fact enabled me to get through uncomfortable evenings such as this one, to somehow bear the stream of commentary regarding my comportment and behavior that dripped out of her day and night like a leaky tap. This evening's dosage at the temple had included a few choice morsels. "Don't slump, dear." "Tuck your legs under your seat. It's a much tidier look." "I'm sure you know the prayers. You don't need to mumble." It was insufferable.

"Yes, we're roommates." I cringed as she introduced me in this manner to her friend. We weren't really roommates. *Who has a grandmother for a roommate, anyway?* I had my own room, what had formerly been the guestroom. And for the most part, that's where I hung out. "And the music, the sound. You simply can't imagine the piece of heaven that's come into my world." I smiled one more time, nodding in agreement. It was expected.

"Lovely to meet you." I had an easy role to play: smile, nod, shake hands. I didn't need to do much more than that. But I never understood the point. Back home, people weren't so formal. Life at Beth Abraham was more of an embrace than a dazzle.

Of course, back home I didn't have Julliard, a bastion of sound and harmony, a place where each room, each hall, and each instrument closet held a different way to make me soar. I'd always loved music. I studied flute early on, trying to follow in Mom's footsteps, but, after developing headaches, switched to the viola. Mom and I decided I probably wasn't suited for wind instruments. Those were the days when we made those kinds of decisions together. From the beginning I'd adored creating sound from thin air, putting together a string of notes to create a tune. A lot of the other kids in orchestra seemed to perform by rote, happy to practice and be part of an orchestra, proud of playing an instrument. But few seemed moved by the music, lifted to another plane. That was me. Music took me to places I'd never dreamed of. Just recently, it had brought me to New York. It didn't get much better than that.

And now my weekends, spent almost solely at Julliard, were simply one long sigh of pleasure. Just walking the halls, ducking my head into one performance space or another, a professor's office, a classroom, even the hallway, each filled with glorious sounds, made me do cartwheels inside. Before starting the program, music had just been something I liked to do and was good at, something that made me feel good. Now I realized it could fill my life, even *become* my life. I adored the program at Julliard, looking forward to each Saturday, waking up with a smile and hurrying down to the Lincoln Center campus. When the day ended, I walked back to Grandma's smiling ear to ear, replaying in my mind both what I'd studied and snippets of the combinations I'd heard from other rooms over the course of the day, making a mental checklist of what I needed to work on during the coming week, of pieces I wanted to listen to back in my bedroom.

In the beginning, when the whole idea of participating in this program came up, a crazy idea Dad suggested after consulting with Grandma, my focus had been to just get to New York. Since arriving, everything had changed. The city was fabulous and endlessly stimulating, but Julliard confirmed the essential role of music in my life. There was no way I would let Grandma's running commentary and the way she tried to run my life ruin it for me.

Leaving the temple was a huge relief. No more hands to be shaken, no more idle conversations, no more fake smiles. Dinner lay straight head.

I was certain the evening would pick up. I hoped Grandma and I could just hang out and enjoy ourselves as we'd done my first few weeks in town. We'd had a lot of fun together then.

Unfortunately, I quickly realized that this particular dinner wasn't going to be a simple affair; once again, Grandma had an agenda. From the moment we were seated, she seemed to be on the warpath, making an issue of absolutely everything. Apparently, temple had only been the warm-up. Dinner turned out to be the full-blown lesson. I hesitated to open my mouth or even make eye contact, afraid of her responses. It was impossible to kick back, relax, and enjoy my meal in the face of what felt like one extended interrogation. And seated eyeball to eyeball, there was no escape.

"Your napkin." Grandma gestured toward me with her chin. "It really needs to be in your lap. So much more practical there."

The whole evening might have gone better if I'd chosen the venue. Grandma always selected one of those stiff, well-considered restaurants that was bigger on atmosphere than taste—an antiseptic place with cloth napkins, tinkling glassware, and more cutlery than I knew what to do with. I looked around at the other customers, hoping to find some way to avoid the intense mood at the table. They were all old, most of them closer to Grandma's age—there was probably some stipulation about showing your senior bus pass at the door—and dressed exactly like those back at temple, uncomfortably constricted by tightly knotted neckties and scratchy stockings. This definitely wasn't my crowd. I was itching to leave even before we began to eat.

"How is your salmon, dear? To your liking?"

I nodded in assent, reaching for my water glass and taking a few measured sips. The truth was I wanted to be somewhere else. One of the girls at school, the one seated behind me in history class who played the flute, had invited me to join her and a few other girls for a movie and a slice. I was eager to go, but Grandma put her foot down. Friday nights were sacred. Since she was the reason I'd been able to move to New York in the first place, I had no choice but to comply. That didn't mean I was happy about it. I glanced at my watch. There was a slim chance I could still make it to the pizza part of the evening, and a greasy slab of melted cheese with girls my own age was incredibly appealing.

"I'm sorry. I didn't hear you. I asked about your fish, whether it was tasty."

I grunted a more vocal confirmation and continued to fiddle with my water glass, running my finger around its edge, entranced by the little singing sound it made. The glass was thin. I noticed Grandma's wineglass looked even thinner. I wondered how it would sound and wished I felt comfortable enough to ask her if I could try it out, to create my own harmonies right here at the table. That would certainly loosen things up a bit.

Instead, I tried to figure out what Grandma wanted from me, grilling me about my salmon. I didn't understand why she always had to make a point; how light interchanges and extended conversations all had to boil down to some greater lesson. I hadn't noticed this those first few weeks, but almost two months into my stay, it was obvious. I found the whole practice not only tiresome but occasionally hurtful, and again, as during that first visit for the audition, I wondered if this had something to do with why Grandma and Mom didn't get along—why we barely saw her. Although I'd dropped this line of inquiry back in the spring, it had become irresistible. I was now sure it wasn't because of the distance. There was something else there.

"What do you think, Belle? Of the restaurant. Isn't it lovely? Nothing at all like that place you took me in Fargo a few years ago. Remember that! My goodness, that was something." The way she tipped her head back, her mouth opening into a smile, I knew she thought she was funny.

"Hey! Don't knock my favorite restaurant!" I didn't actually say those words, but they were on the tip of my tongue. I knew Grandma would take them badly. She took everything badly. And I couldn't antagonize her. There was too much to lose. I forced my mind elsewhere, tapping my fingers along the side of the table, going over the finger work for the piece we'd be working on tomorrow. Getting through the ritual of Friday night led me straight into the joy of Saturdays: the sounds, the symphonic jumble of life behind the walls of Julliard, and the critique. Yes, even critique. Because at Julliard I knew critique was meant to improve my sound; it wasn't about who I was.

Eyes widening with a sudden flash of understanding, I came back to the present. Grandma was still awaiting my response. "I said it was fine."

She picked up her napkin and for what must have been the millionth time wiped at her upper lip. She'd made an art of that maneuver. "Actually, dear, you didn't say anything. And I really don't know what I'm supposed to understand from all that shrugging you do. Didn't your mother teach you to use your words? We don't speak with gestures."

I stared at her, more shocked than offended, stunned at how she consistently dug in her heels and went for the jugular. She simply refused to let things go. Another glance at my watch and a quick calculation made clear that if I played my cards right, I could still make it to Becky's by nine. That's when they were placing the order from Cheesy's. I wouldn't pass up a slice even if I wasn't hungry. All that goo made me homesick for Kraut's, in Fargo.

Something snapped inside me. My patience for this whole evening had come to an end.

"Grandma, you knew exactly what I meant. You may not have liked my shrug, but you knew it was an answer." I picked up my fork and started on the lentils still sitting on my plate. They were very tasty. There was a sweet spice in the sauce. I couldn't quite place it—something Indian. It was pretty good.

The momentary pleasure of enjoying their taste was bluntly curtailed.

"A shrug is not an answer. It never will be." Her words were cold and biting. I put down my fork and watched her cut paper-thin slices from her duck, chewing each bite at a record snail's pace, her lips sealed into a flat, unyielding line. I was no longer hungry, completely stunned by her reaction to my shrug. *Why would anyone make such a big deal of something so insignificant?* Grandma's body language, the square set of her shoulders and the tightening of her torso, shouted outrage. She radiated distance instead of the kind of intimacy I figured innate in grandparents. I had a terrible feeling that these first unkind comments were only the preview, and that something even worse was coming.

"So, I thought this would be a good time to discuss a little of what I'll expect this year, now that we've settled in a bit."

Okay. This was exactly what I'd both anticipated and feared. Still, it was probably best to get it over with. I gripped the seat of my chair with both hands and sat up a bit straighter, hoping Grandma would assume I was sitting politely, hands folded in my lap, and not notice that I was bracing myself for her attack. Maybe I'd get a few extra points for poise and manners.

"I'm very excited about your living with me, about my being part of your future, your musical career. You can't imagine how much. I've told all my friends. They're so happy for me." Her voice dropped a register with those last few words, as if they were an afterthought, but I didn't take the time to figure out why. It was obvious she was just getting started, and I had to stay focused. "I must admit that I hadn't thought a lot about having a teenager in the house. It wasn't something that even crossed my mind when Julliard came onto your horizon. I was simply so thrilled that your talent would be formally acknowledged and that you would receive this wonderful opportunity—the chance to truly excel on a national level."

I couldn't help laughing. "Grandma, I think you're overdoing it."

"Well, in any case, I never really considered the details." Grandma punctuated her pause with a sip of wine. I understood a lot about what that meant. Drawing on alcoholic armor was something my mom did regularly under stress. The fact that Grandma had ordered the second we sat down, even before we received the menus, was one of the first signs that this evening wasn't just about having a nice meal out. Mom described this action as "fortifying oneself." I smiled as I experienced that flush of warmth that had become habitual upon thinking of Mom. Although its first occurrences had been surprising, it had lately become absolutely reassuring. At this moment, it helped fend off my fears concerning whatever Grandma had in mind.

"And what I've been thinking is . . ." Again, another pause. She wiped her upper lip. I refrained from rolling my eyes in exasperation. *What could there possibly be left to wipe?* "I've been thinking that it might be appropriate to go over some of the rules—to delineate my expectations so that they won't come as a surprise along the way."

My fork, hanging perilously at the edge of the plate since I'd abandoned my meal, slipped onto the floor with a clatter. She glared at me. I didn't care. *Game on*. Now I was completely alert. "Rules?"

"Well, dear, I assume every household has rules. We certainly had them in ours, when your mother was a child, and I'm sure yours has a few." She cleared her throat and lowered her voice. "Although, for the life of me, it doesn't seem that way."

Overcome by a sudden and unexpected dislike for the woman seated across from me, it was impossible not to react. I made a face—an unpleasant one. And although I scrambled to assume a more neutral expression, almost choking on the words of indignation clamoring to be expressed, it was too late. One look at Grandma, the skin on her cheeks suddenly stretched taut to bursting, made clear that my first reaction had been noted.

"Well." The word was expelled forcibly, leaving a trail of tiny beads of spit. Again, that manic wiping. That's when I figured it out. The gesture wasn't about cleaning anything up. It was a means of slowing down what was unraveling, anchoring herself in order to attain a reasonable degree of control. "Now, *that* is precisely something we need to discuss—that look, those disrespectful expressions. You know *exactly* what I'm referring to. That may have worked in your parents' home, but it won't work in mine. It's simply poor manners."

Grandma paused again, letting her sharp words lie there like roadkill, making mincemeat of my resolve. I began to perspire and wryly considered using my own napkin to wipe away at my face. I wondered how she'd interpret that.

I was miserable. The fun Grandma, the one I figured would be a decent companion as adults go, was turning out to be anything but. It was suddenly hard to recall why I'd found my mother so annoying and avoided her company. What I had right here was downright awful. Grandma was making me miserable. I wanted to get up and leave, to be anywhere but here at this table, and tried to think of a way I could excuse myself, run away. I knew the way home. But I knew better. Getting up and leaving would have major repercussions I might not be able to undo. I was simply going to have to endure whatever she dished out.

Stuck in the midst of a bad situation, moving into survival mode, I considered my next move, assessing whether it was smarter to change the subject to something completely different and hope she'd halt her charge or address her complaints directly. The latter tactic was so much more appealing. I was eager to speak my mind. With an enormous sigh, one I didn't bother to mask—finally throwing manners to the four winds—I went for broke.

"I have no idea what you're talking about, Grandma. In what way was I rude? I really don't understand what you want from me. Aren't I allowed to express how I feel?"

I closed my mouth and held my breath, waiting for the earth to open up and swallow me whole. There was a long silence, but nothing happened. Nothing at all. Grandma didn't move an inch. Her face looked set in stone, at least for those first few long seconds. After that, it broke into a million crinkly lines and crevasses.

"You've obviously learned nothing about respect. No, Belle. The answer is no. If it means insulting an adult, you are most definitely not allowed to express how you're feeling or whatever errant thought crosses your mind! You must never challenge an elder! I would have figured that was something you'd know. It's just a basic tenet."

With the gesture I now realized indicated distress, she once again picked up her napkin and dragged it across her mouth. My imperious grandmother, a woman with iron-clad self-confidence, was visibly shaken!

That's when I began to crumble, my resolve disintegrating. I wanted to be indignant, to stand up and make my point, but I felt kind of bad. I'd never intended to upset her. An achy sadness moved in and replaced my anger. I knew Grandma hadn't wanted this dinner out to degrade into an unpleasant confrontation and wondered why she was so bent on setting useless standards that, as far as I was concerned, only enlarged the gap between us. I wondered if it was all an attempt to hide something buried inside. It was so hard to know for sure, as she was a master at concealing every bit of actual feeling behind a commanding, unyielding, and sometimes quite off-putting facade.

Of course, there was another possibility. A troublesome idea ran through my head, chipping away at my concern and refusing to release its hold. There was the distinct chance that she wasn't overcompensating for some kind of lack but instead was simply being herself. The grandma I had thought could be a buddy, a real friend, the one who had shown me a glorious world back in the spring, might just be a mean and unpleasant old lady. There was no way to know.

"Well, I don't get that. Not at all. I figure you should want to know the real me. Belle, your granddaughter. I mean, you're finally getting that chance! I assumed you'd be interested in how I feel, in what makes me happy, what makes me sad. Your approach seems so impersonal, so cold."

Grandma sat up very straight, assuming the all-too-familiar stiff posture I now understood to be a sign that she felt under attack and was building her own offense. In almost any other context, I might find it admirable. I mean, who wouldn't want to have such beautiful posture? But with Grandma it usually indicated an approaching storm.

"Belle, I won't be disrespected in my own home. That's where you want to be, correct? You want to stay here in New York with me? That's what I've understood. And although I'm sure you all, your whole generation, have newfangled ways of relating to one another, ones I'm less familiar with and, yes, less comfortable with, you must realize that I'm old school. I can't change what I believe and what I expect. I'll always think that challenging an adult is inappropriate, no matter the reason." She offered a half smile of conciliation that I found completely unconvincing. "Call me 'old' if you like." She punctuated this last comment by picking up her wineglass, giving it a swirl, and taking a hearty sip. She was quite obviously pleased with herself, confident that she'd successfully conveyed her message with little collateral damage.

She had it wrong. I couldn't move forward without looking back. This whole experience—the cold lecture at the restaurant, being paraded around at the temple like those chopped-off ears in the bullring, nothing more than a prize—had made a deep impression on me. A big part of Julliard had been about getting away from my mother, but I now realized that I'd jumped directly from the frying pan into the fire. Facing off with Grandma here at this restaurant made things back home with Mom seem like a picnic.

"Come now, dear. Let's order dessert. There must be something on the menu that's calling your name."

I looked down to avoid her eyes and stayed silent. I wasn't ready to succumb to her sudden change of mood, to just shift gears and act like nothing had happened. Grandma's gleeful tone rang shallow, and I didn't feel like celebrating this evening with something sweet. I'd come to New York to live it up a bit, wiggle my toes, get away from the noise and heaviness at home, and have my time in the sun. But here I was, newly burdened, much of the levity of this new life now extinguished. Like a captive on a ship under someone else's control, I began to consider ways to escape.

ELIZABETH

I PAUSED ON THE DOORSTEP of Beth Abraham, feeling the significance of the moment, before stepping inside. The bright morning light and the noise of passing cars disappeared as I closed the heavy wooden door firmly behind me. I was immediately enveloped by an overwhelming quiet, the feeling of having stepped into another world.

This place had been one of great consolation from my first days in Grand Forks, second only to that offered by my library. It had always felt like another home. The photograph on my desk of Belle splashing around on a baby slide, me welcoming her with arms wide open, water droplets staining the camera's lens, had triggered the idea to consult with Rabbi Eliot. It was taken soon after we moved to Grand Forks, when we were just establishing ourselves, finding our footing in terribly unfamiliar territory—one of those dusty summer days when the light seemed to stretch to infinity, so different from the landscape of deep, shadowy canyons, the skyscrapers doing their best to shut out the sky, back in Chicago. The flatness of our new terrain made me feel frighteningly exposed and unprotected, antagonizing our already unsteady acclimatization. I spent far too much time staring out the kitchen window, eyes glazed over, coffee cup gripped tightly in hand, wondering how I'd dared to step so far out of my element.

The invitation to that first Shabbat splash on a late August day had been nothing less than a *mitzvah*. I never did figure out how the temple community knew of our arrival and the extent to which we were floundering. In the end, answers to these questions were far less important than the result of their invitation, smoothing our very bumpy start and making absolutely everything easier, more manageable. For Mike, Belle, and me, the Beth Abraham congregation quickly became a source of strength and support facilitating the establishment of an actual life in the prairie.

Today, I made my way slowly through the entrance foyer, enjoying the welcome of the place, taking the time to look at the photographs lining the walls, stretching from one end of the building to the other. I'd never really considered them before. Usually running late for one celebration or another, I hadn't had the time. But lately it had become clear that I needed to stop, slow things down, and consider. That was the whole point of this visit.

I paused over each image. They tracked the congregation's history from its very rough beginnings more than one hundred years earlier. The Jewish community of Grand Forks had been established by a handful of individuals who'd moved out to the Great Plains to try their luck far away from the big cities, hoping to capitalize on the western expansion of the national railroad. Their numbers were swelled by the contemporary influx of immigrants from Eastern Europe, many arriving via Canada. I'd done some research on Beth Abraham when we first considered the move, curious about what a Jewish community so far from the center might be like. Figuring it would be quite different from the well-established temple of the upper crust I'd attended since forever, back in New York, I was surprised to find similarities. Both had been established by grocers, clothiers, and jewelers, many of whom had been peddlers in a former life.

Although all records indicated that the congregation had never been enormous, sorely tested by the natural attrition that was part and parcel of the intrinsic difficulty of living in this relatively undeveloped part of the United States, with its especially harsh climate, it had managed to stay intact. Over the course of several generations, it continuously evolved to meet the demands of its community, transforming from Orthodox to Conservative to Reform, eventually changing its original name from the Children of Judea to the present one, Beth Abraham. Today it was a life-giving entity, the heart not only of Grand Fork's Jewish population but also southeastern North Dakota's.

The photographs before me offered visual testimony of the steadfastness of a perpetually small, but truly devoted, community. Intermixed with them were faded drawings on ochre pages, tracking the original building's history from conception to completion. Long gone, that first structure reminded me of those nineteenth-century ones I'd seen in books on Eastern European Judaism, replete with Moorish towers and a stained-glass rose window. Continuing down the hallway, I watched the structure change, eventually becoming the one I recognized. The minimal cluster of individuals in the first images—dressed in formal suits and corseted dresses, men and women standing at a distance—eventually blossomed into a motley, very mixed, blue-jeaned crowd. I couldn't help smiling. We were nothing if not comfortable, tucked into our cozy corner of the world.

The gallery culminated in a very large photograph hanging on the end wall, set into a glossy white frame. I studied this one well, blinking with recognition, my heart filling with that bursting feeling that comes from true gratification. Depicted here was the community I knew, the one I was lucky enough to call mine. The image was relatively new, documenting a recent holiday and one of those perfect blue skies. I could never quite get over the overwhelming presence of sky out here in the Great Plains, the way it managed to set the tone, monopolizing every conversation, every mood and, yes, just like here before me in the photograph, every memory.

Moving up close, I instantly spotted myself among what looked to be most of the community. That made sense. As most of us didn't travel far, attendance was good for the High Holidays. We were seated at one long table covered with a white tablecloth decorated with long sheaves of wheat that had been brought in from a neighboring farm. We weren't short on those in North Dakota. No one was wearing a coat, and everyone wore white. *Yes, I remember.* It had been Shavuot. There'd been so many varieties of cheesecake—plain, blueberry, strawberry, rhubarb—and cheeseboards featuring items both local and imported, chunks of Wisconsin cheddar nuzzling with rounds of imported French Montrachet wrapped in chestnut leaves. A few token tractors festooned with bales of hay and an abundance of wildflowers sat to the side in the parking lot, ready for one of those hokey little hayrides—one more storybook element that had become part of our local life.

I loved this congregation for all its quirkiness, for its willingness to be corny or obvious in an effort to serve the community's need for symbol and ritual. Although its touchy-feely, overly modern approach sometimes felt a bit foreign, quite different from that of my temple back on Central Park West where everyone dressed to the nines on the High Holidays, the end of Shabbat services was marked with a formal receiving line to greet the rabbis, and the cantor was backed up by both an organ and a choir, it had become home. I never anticipated that.

At no time during my life-changing deliberations, either way back in New York or later in Chicago, considering where I'd go to school, where I'd begin my career, or whether to move my entire family further west, had I given much thought to whether there was a suitable Jewish community. Religion and its practice had always played a secondary role to whatever else was going on in my life. I never dreamed that I would become a regular at services, nor be so involved in local Jewish life, having previously found organized religion off-putting, pretentious, and out of sync with the kind of relaxed, accepting lifestyle I wanted for my family.

Although Mike, an educated but no-longer-practicing Catholic, had looked into the community in Grand Forks early on, certain it would make the whole idea more palatable, it was Lillian, queen of our temple at home and a large part of the reason I wanted nothing to do with synagogue life in the first place, who encouraged me to reach out to Beth Abraham. This was after our disastrous brunch at Sarabeth's when I'd returned home to Chicago to plan for our move. I was no longer in touch with her at that point, but I'd sent her one of those unsigned postcards announcing our change of address. Her phone call was entirely unexpected. I hesitated before answering, considering letting it go to the answering machine. I couldn't. Despite the continued feelings of anger and disappointment she educed, this was my mother.

"I've been thinking about your move."

I didn't respond. I didn't know how to. We hadn't spoken since I walked out of the restaurant, vowing to excise both her and her hurtful comments from our lives. That didn't faze her in the least. She plowed forward. "And I know that you don't want to hear from me, or, for that matter, even speak with me. But still, I have something I want to share."

I still didn't speak. I truly had nothing to say.

"Elizabeth? I know you're there. So, I'll just say what I called to say. When you get there, to Grand Forks. I think you should reach out to the local temple."

Now I was just confused. I'd expected her to say something about the way we parted, to try to pave the way toward a reconciliation. I even, for a moment, thought I might get an apology. But there wasn't a trace of remorse in her tone. Instead, she'd taken a few large leaps forward, envisioning what would happen once we got where we were going. It was almost too much for me to digest, caught up as I was in the technical details of the move—packing, organizing, and arranging. The trail of rubbish she and I had left behind us would have to wait for another day.

"It can't hurt to get to know the other Jews in the neighborhood. It's the kind of thing we just do, as a people. And it looks like there's a real community there. Mike mentioned it to me." She paused. "Elizabeth? Could you just give a sign that you're still there?"

"I heard you, Mom." By this point, I'd recovered from the shock of the call and the surprising agenda. I was eager to move it along as quickly as possible. "And thanks for the tip. But you know, I have no interest in a repeat of what we had in New York. All that pomp and circumstance."

"But, dear, that's ridiculous. You were so active in the youth group as a young girl. You really enjoyed the services. My word, you knew every word to every prayer. I've always wished I had such command of them!

All these years, and I still mumble along, pretending." This woman never missed a beat. She was chatting on as though this were just one more in a series of daily phone calls. I wondered if she even noticed that I'd dropped her from my life; perhaps she simply thought I was too busy to call—that I'd get around to it sooner or later. That was the impression she gave.

Now was not the time to explain how temple life had made me bristle, how I couldn't stand the way members showed off their children's accomplishments and their own, how they dressed up and put on their best jewelry even for solemn holidays like Yom Kippur. Attending synagogue as an adult seemed mostly about keeping up with the Joneses. It was a complete turnoff.

"Let's just agree that it's something I left back in Manhattan a long time ago."

"Lizzy, I know I'm not your favorite person right now. And considering everything . . ." Here she paused before continuing, "That makes a lot of sense. But I'm always looking out for you. You'll be a fish out of water over there in the prairie and, yes, I'm having a very hard time wrapping my head around the whole concept. I know you've always been enamored with Laura Ingalls Wilder, but I would have thought that her stories of hardship would convince you to steer clear."

When she paused to take yet another breath, I was surprised to find that I was actually listening. I found the genuine concern in her voice compelling.

"Look at it this way. There's only so far those kiddy mixers will get you. Chicago was easy in comparison. It's going to take a lot more to find your niche this time. If you don't want to feel like an outsider forever, reach out to the one place where you're not."

Although I'd like to say that she was dead wrong, she was right. After several years as an active participant of Beth Abraham, I understood just how different organized religion could be. In fact, this local temple was the essential factor that enabled me to create a home in a place that otherwise might have remained foreign. For Mike it was so much easier. Having been born in the Midwest, basically a local, and assuming a position of prestige within the community by running UND's premier aviation program, he'd basically found the pot of gold. Life was as good as it could get. I, on the other hand, was consistently challenged by small-town life, my entire experience one of crowded sidewalks and a flood of stimuli.

Belle provided the only real means of quasi-integration. From her first day of school, there were invitations for coffee and cake, for barbecues, for hayrides, for playdates. Ostensibly, it looked like smooth sailing. But deep down I felt an underlying vibe of disinterest, as though the locals knew we weren't a natural part of the scenery and would, soon enough, pick up and move elsewhere. They probably figured we weren't worth the effort. Standing around at a picnic, and God knows there were plenty of those, I'd fiddle with the edge of one of those classic, checkered tablecloths, feeling isolated and simply very different. I was certain that everyone—parents, teachers, check-out clerks at the market or the greengrocer—had labeled us outsiders, a status that guaranteed only temporary tolerance.

I searched for other reasons, comparing my outfits with those of the other mothers: jeans, T-shirts, and sneakers. On the outside, I looked just like them. But I didn't feel the same. And when it came time to shooting the breeze, engaging in the light chatter that characterizes similar parent–kiddy events across the globe, I stuck to safe subjects, talking about Belle, comparing notes on new teachers the mothers weren't quite sure about, discussing one or another new product carried on Main Street, and who made the best pie.

I was careful to avoid any mention of our previous life in the big city. From the beginning I'd understood that this accounted for much of the divide. City people were different. City people weren't always to be trusted. City people were likely to run back to the city, so there wasn't much sense in investing in them. And despite the indications of interest, a certain level of superficial engagement, welcoming smiles, phone calls, and invitations, there wasn't a lot of warmth. I knew the locals had their questions, wondering what we were doing there, whether we'd gotten lost, and when we'd be on our way. I certainly *felt* as if I'd gotten lost. Despite Mike's happiness, I wasn't sure we'd made the right decision, concerned that the life I'd fantasized about, the one I was determined to establish by hook or by crook, just like those original pioneers, wasn't the kind I wanted for my family after all.

Mike didn't understand. I don't know that men ever do. Of course, he couldn't have fathomed how important all this was to me, how essential that we be integrated into the community. I was hell-bent on providing my daughter with a real home. It was part of making up for having lost my first—part of proving I could be the very best mother. Intent on ensuring Belle a harmonious environment, I found the moments where we didn't seem to fit intensely painful. Happily ignorant of a wrong I was trying to right, Mike laughed off what he considered mundane tales of events gone awry, assuming they were exaggerated for effect to make them more amusing, and insisting that it was all in my mind, that no one looked at us funny or thought us outsiders. But the facts remained: we were. We were interlopers from the start and would remain so forever. Status in the Great Plains, where so many families' roots dated back generations, didn't change easily once assigned.

Without this wonderful congregation, we probably wouldn't have survived a year. Now it didn't seem like we'd ever leave. There was no better place to turn.

"Elizabeth? There you are. I've been expecting you."

I turned away from that last impressive photograph and met the rabbi's open arms with a warm embrace and an exchange of kisses.

"Rabbi Eliot."

"How are you? Come on in."

We stepped into her office and settled into the two heavily upholstered chairs arranged facing one another in the middle of the room. I looked around, comforted by the arrangement of potted plants and framed photos, some obviously from the same archive as those in the hallway and several personal ones. This wasn't the first time I'd met with the rabbi, but more often than not I was accompanied by other congregants or members of my family. I didn't remember a tête-à-tête.

"Are you all set for the hakafot?"

I laughed. It was a rhetorical question. Mike and I always attended the celebration of the Torah at the end of Simchat Torah. It didn't matter that things had been chilly between us lately; I'd never let down the community. This year we'd agreed to Rabbi Eliot's suggestion to lead the festivities. Although I'd spent a lifetime shirking lead roles, even ones as benign as this, they no longer felt all that daunting.

"Oh, we can't wait. Our day in the sun." We both laughed. A little nervous, I jumped right in. "Actually, I'm here about something else." I looked down at my hands. They were glued together in a tight clasp, the veins positively popping with adrenaline. I wondered whether this was a sign of aging or due to the combination of anxiety and apprehension I felt as I leaped into the unknown. I took a deep breath and reassured myself that there was no need to be nervous. Rabbi Eliot had no doubt already figured out that this meeting wasn't about discussing the forthcoming holidays. There's no way she missed the intensity of my voice over the phone. She was so perceptive.

I cleared my throat. "The thing is, I'm looking for something." I shifted my gaze away from hers and let my sentence fade to silence. *What could possibly come from this meeting? What am I looking for?* With only a vague idea of what I wanted, I couldn't possibly expect Rabbi Eliot to help. I turned back, meeting her eyes. There was so much strength in her patient, warm gaze. I felt a moment's calm. "I'd like to take on a new challenge, expand my world, assume responsibility." My voice faltered. That all sounded so grandiose, so ridiculous. I couldn't imagine her making sense of it. I certainly couldn't.

"Assume responsibility? Tell me more about that. As far as I can see, from everything I know, you already take on a great deal of responsibility: your job at the firm, raising Belle, creating a warm household for your family, and of course the many ways you contribute here to our community."

I waved my hand dismissively. I had to make myself clearer. "No. I'm thinking of something else entirely. I'd like to do something that really counts."

A heavy silence fell between us, my words hanging in the air, unaddressed. I noticed confusion on Rabbi Eliot's face, the warm, open expression with which she'd greeted me turning into something closer to a frown. "Something that counts? Elizabeth, it all counts."

I shook my head emphatically, feeling a shift from within, and suddenly knew what I was trying to get at. "Something more direct, more immediate. I want to do something that counts for *someone*—to affect their life even the least bit, to help them find a better place."

Without noticing, I'd inched closer to Rabbi Eliot and was teetering on the edge of my chair. I quickly scooted back, afraid I'd come off as too needy, wedging myself into the seat more firmly and shoring up my resolve.

"I want to find someone for whom I'll be . . ." Again, I paused. This part was especially difficult. It was so personal. "Rabbi Eliot, what I mean by 'count,' well . . . I want to be special to someone. And at the same time, I want to redirect some of the energy and attention that I'm presently wasting elsewhere." That was it. I'd said it. There was absolutely no way to take it back. Now she would know just how much I hurt, the pain I'd been suffering because of Belle, my mother, even Mike. I'd laid it all out.

Rabbi Eliot covered my hand with hers, closing the distance between us. Her forehead returned to its normal wrinkle-free state, the epitome of calm, and she nodded in acknowledgment. Just as expected, she understood. Relief washed through me, cleansing with its flow. I sat back more comfortably in my chair, amazed at what the barest of signs could accomplish—the extraordinary effect of a simple touch of the hand, the softening of an expression. I was sure rabbis took classes in comforting alongside those devoted to the Old Testament, Jewish history, and ethics.

"I see. It's not about being a mother, a lawyer, and a wife." She paused and I understood the touch of irony in her tone. The roles she'd listed, piled one on top of the other, were already a full load. They should have been enough, leaving little time to breathe, let alone room for more. But her face spoke of acceptance, acknowledging that perhaps there could be. "Clearly, it's about contributing something that, for whatever reason, is presently untapped in your already full-to-bursting life. Sometimes those closest to us aren't able to receive what we have to give. There are even good reasons for that. In most cases this is temporary. Things can change."

She smiled at me in encouragement. "But that can cause a clog, maybe even a hole. Am I getting it right?"

I nodded, my heartbeat slowing, my breathing becoming more regular. She was right on course. I'd been afraid I'd be forced to admit to the gaps in my life that had become craters, enlarged daily by endless fretting about things I couldn't control, sometimes even things that weren't about me. It was a relief to find her filling in the blanks on her own. That's why I'd come.

"Perhaps it's time to extend your circle and figure out if there's something out there that would somehow fill what's missing, a fit that would benefit everyone. What do you think?" Rabbi Eliot's voice rose in a question, and her eyes locked with mine as she gave my hands, still gripping one another in my lap, a firm squeeze before releasing them and patiently awaiting my response. I felt deep gratitude, thankful for her understanding, certain she had a solution.

"I only know one thing . . ." My voice emerged choked with emotion I hadn't realized I was feeling. Rabbi Eliot leaned back over and gave my knee an assuring squeeze. "I want it to be a girl. The person I help. I need to work with a young woman."

She continued to hold my gaze, as if puzzling out what even I didn't understand.

"A girl. Okay." She nodded as if she understood my reasoning, but she couldn't. This was one secret I'd never shared and wasn't planning to. I didn't know how to continue the conversation. Just making the appointment to come see the rabbi today had been an enormous step. Those to follow, ones that might lead to a new beginning, taking me completely out of my element, were unimaginable.

Obviously figuring I wasn't going to provide more details, Rabbi Eliot picked up where she left off.

"You know, it's easy to fill our lives by busying ourselves with the nitty-gritty of those we love. But at some point, that's not enough; in the end, it's not for them to define our place in this world, to give our lives meaning. That's something we need to achieve for ourselves. Going out and seeking answers is an excellent first step. Having made it as far as this office, expressing a specific desire . . . Elizabeth, you're already halfway there."

She looked around her office as if trying to work something out and drummed her fingers on the arm of her chair. "I'd love to be the one to help you find whatever it is you need. Let me think a moment, see if I can find the right answer." Uncrossing her legs, she made as if to stand but then hesitated. "There's just one thing. Something important. We may find the perfect way to enable you to move forward, but it won't be a one-way street. Changing someone's life will change yours as well as that of those you love, completely."

I closed my eyes tightly, trying to shut out the difficulties that lay ahead, the inevitable fallout. It was frightening. But I knew it would be okay. The road I was on was already so bumpy. It was hard to imagine it getting worse. Opening my eyes, I stared straight back at Rabbi Eliot, affirming my comprehension that this would be part of the process—that searching for an outlet for the energy currently being sucked into obsessions that weren't helping anyone, least of all me, was most certainly going to lead back to their source. The band-aid solution I'd had in mind on my way over had turned into more of an overhaul, but there was no going back. Things were too bad to leave as is.

"I have something, or rather"—she smiled—"someone in mind." My thoughts skidded to a stop, and I inhaled sharply. The concept that there might be a concrete answer to all this speculation made my head spin. "There's a program with which we've recently become involved. It's a community-outreach initiative intended to involve the temple community a bit more with that of Grand Forks'. We're tiny when compared with the whole, but I've lately thought it important to make more of an imprint. Right now, it's in the pilot stage, so we're taking baby steps, making sure it's a good match for our congregation. We've already got a number of people working in local programs."

She stood, walked behind her desk, and rifled through the file folders neatly stacked in a pile to the side. Pulling one out, she tapped it on the desk and met my gaze. I absolutely adored this woman. I was so thankful for her presence in my life, for the compassion and love she always found for me, for Mike, for Belle. Here she was stepping in and offering me a ray of light at such a difficult time, as I battled with Belle, pushing her farther and farther away with each misbegotten word, forcibly shutting out the mother I'd only ever wanted to include, frustrated to the max with my meddling husband, and feeling my place in the world getting smaller and smaller.

"And yes, Elizabeth. I think working with a young woman sounds perfect. I can see that working out very well."

I blinked once, then again, my eyes filling with tears, my face softening into an enormous smile of assent and appreciation. I was nervous, overcome by the possibility that I could change the life of a young woman who felt lost, reach in and give her a base. Maybe this could be an undoing, a means to fill the gap left by the one who'd left me as well as the one I'd been forced to leave behind decades earlier.

• • •

"She's over there. The last table."

I followed Principal Hunter's gesture to a bank of windows along the far side of the school library, beyond the shelving, where several students sat at small reading tables. Stepping aside to allow the passage of those streaming in and out of the doorway, my eyes fell on one young girl seated alone, looking out the window over the front lawn. She was dressed in an oversized flannel shirt, her hair gathered in a loose braid that ran down her back like an afterthought. She seemed especially small within the vast space, younger than fifteen. If I hadn't been looking, I would have missed her completely.

I flinched as if someone had reached in and given my heart a squeeze, my first instinct to run over, wrap her tightly in an embrace, and hold fast. I checked myself. I knew that this wasn't only about Julie, the young woman to whom I'd been assigned; I'd naturally envisioned Belle sitting there, just as vulnerable, just as needy of affection and love.

I forced myself to stay in the here and now, frantically blinking to keep the tears welling up in my eyes from springing loose, wiping away those that had escaped. I was here not to salve my own wounds but instead to help heal another's. Yet I couldn't stop myself from hoping that this young person would accept my efforts as Belle had not.

"May I?" I whispered.

"Of course. She's waiting for you."

I closed the door of the library firmly behind me. It was blessedly calm inside. Libraries had always been a sanctuary for me, a respite from the noise and chaos outside. This one was no different. The fear and anxiety I felt as I arrived at school earlier that morning to meet Julie completely disappeared as I made my way between the tables, negotiating the space without a ripple. Not one person turned my way. I couldn't imagine a more perfect spot for this meeting and made a mental note to thank Principal Hunter later for her thoughtfulness.

As I crossed the large space, I quickly ran through the details I'd been given: *Mother dysfunctional, possibly schizophrenic, unable to provide for her daughter in any capacity. Father out of the picture, having left shortly after her birth—has no part in her story. Recently removed from her home after a spate of violent episodes, probably due to the stress of trying to hold the household together on her own. Child Protective Services stepped in. Presently living at the Ruth Meier Adolescent Center in town. Strong with numbers but weak on letters; has great difficulty negotiating reading. Source of issue possibly dyslexia but not certain. Could be emotional.*

I loved words. I loved reading. My whole professional life had been devoted to texts and their interpretations. I was on very steady ground here. Yet there was the additional matter of negotiating a human life. I hadn't always been good at that. I drew near to Julie from the side, not wanting to startle her by coming up from behind. Her eyes widened as she followed my approach. Her anxiety was clear.

"Julie?" I started out tentatively, clearly on tenterhooks. This mattered so much. Getting no response, I cleared my throat and tried again. I was the adult here. I needed to set the tone. "Julie." I extended my hand.

In that moment, when she turned her whole body in response, shifting in her chair, extending her small hand and gazing up at me with the softest of looks, I realized just how ripe I was for significant contact. Our hands met in a warm grasp, clinging for an extra second or two before parting. Here, at close range, I got a better look. Albeit physically just a child, Julie's eyes were those of a much older person, someone seasoned, someone who'd experienced more than they should have. The world-weariness of her gaze spoke of the path that had led her away from her home, unmooring her, to a place that wasn't all that welcoming. Yet that wasn't all. Deep within, I caught a distinct glimmer, an indication of the hesitant hope that maybe, just maybe, this connection, *our* connection, would provide some of what she so desperately needed.

Although I wasn't sure what that might be, I could take an educated guess. My motherly instincts prescribed a large dose of attention, compassion, and plain old love. Julie needed someone to be there for her. That shouldn't have been such a tall order for someone her age. The responsibility of what I had undertaken hit me hard. This had been so much about *my* needs back in Rabbi Eliot's office, but now I realized that it was most definitely about someone else's.

My thoughts were interrupted by the sound of a door closing, a loud and definite click. I looked back toward the entrance to the library. The door was wide open. The click, signifying comprehension, had been in my mind. Looking back at Julie, I realized how much we both stood to gain. I pulled out the chair beside her and sat down.

MIKE

I STEPPED OUT OF THE door and started down the path that cut through campus. It had been an exhausting day. The admissions committee had met to review the applicants for next year's class of hopeful aviation students. I loved the thought of all those kids interested in flying, whether as a hobby, an academic pursuit, or a career. It was the only thing I'd ever wanted to do. I made sure my job as an administrator allowed for plenty of hours up yonder, maintaining an active in-flight teaching roster.

I gathered the two sides of my lapel and pulled them together. The weather was turning cold, summer long gone and the crisp autumn mornings announcing winter. North Dakota weather was brutal. Having been born and raised in the Midwest, never living elsewhere, I was used to the constant chill, the damp cold that crept into your bones sometime in early October and couldn't be shaken until May. But for those from elsewhere, it was more than punishing. Most people moving to the area arrived with a specific goal or didn't bother coming at all.

When I was first offered the position at UND, I was certain it wouldn't work out. There was no way Lizzy would agree to leave a climate she barely suffered and move to one even more severe. As it was, she spent far too many months of the year bundled into her down coat, furry hood pulled down and zipped up, her eyes the only parts left exposed to the elements. Moreover, she was truly a city girl. Chicago at least made a stab at being cosmopolitan. I had no idea how she'd make her way in Grand Forks, so small town, such an ostensibly bad fit. And of course, there was no chance she'd give up her cushy job on Michigan Avenue for a hokey practice on Main Street, USA. Presenting the option once I received the offer was more about mourning an imminent loss than looking toward a future.

But she said yes. It didn't even take convincing, and looking back, I realize I should have wondered why. The fact of the job, one I wanted so much, made me ignore the signs that maybe it wasn't the best idea for us as a family, for Lizzy in particular. Now that we'd in some ways been thrust back toward the East Coast—if not personally, then through association—I realized I should have suspected her willingness to move to a remote, frozen corner of the States; I should have considered that she might be running away. Her crazy behavior last spring, going off the deep end with Belle, furious at the idea that she'd be living with Lillian, made clear that there was a lot I was missing. Lizzy was deeply disturbed by something I knew nothing about.

My thoughts were broken by a vibration from my coat pocket. I reached in and pulled out the phone. It was Lillian. I took a deep breath before answering. This might mean something was up.

"Hello, Lillian."

"Mike, dear. How are you?"

"Good. Good! Glad you called!" And I was. I was eager to hear how things were going for Belle, and not through the cheesy texts I'd been receiving: "Taking bites out of the apple, Dad." "Traffic lights!"

"I just wanted to let you know that we're just fine."

I don't know what put me on alert. Maybe something in her voice. It could have been my imagination, but it sounded taut.

I would have to open that door. "You and Belle? It's all working out?"

"Yes, yes. Of course. What a question!"

But it was one I was glad I asked because her tone indicated otherwise. "She simply loves Julliard."

"Oh, yes." She sounded relieved. This was obviously safe ground. "And I adore hearing her practice. She plays like an angel."

Her voice faded off in a sigh. There was a prolonged silence, like there was something she didn't want to say. "Lillian? What's going on?"

I heard labored breathing on the other side of the line. "Oh, dear. Don't worry. I didn't call so that you would worry. Everything is just wonderful. Really, it is."

"So, you just wanted to say hello? I'm getting a different vibe. Don't worry. You can tell me. I'm here to help. If there's something up with Belle, I want to know." I really began to worry. This wasn't like Lillian at all. She was a very self-assured woman, proud of her ability to handle any situation. Things would have to be particularly bad to admit to even the slightest hint of an issue. "Lillian?"

An especially heavy sigh broke her silence. "It's nothing. It's just, well, Belle is so confident, so sure of herself. She speaks her mind without hesitation."

I smiled wide and laughed to myself. These were wonderful qualities, but Lillian was presenting them as capital crimes. "And . . . well . . . that's not good? Is that what you're suggesting? What am I missing?"

Lillian cleared her throat loudly. "I said no such thing. It's just, well, I was hoping to have more of an influence, to be more of a guiding light. But she seems to be very much set on her own path."

I gripped my phone under my chin for a moment and pulled my coat closed around me. Just a bit further and I'd reach the car where I could warm up.

"I wouldn't worry yourself about that too much, Lillian. In any case, your role is more hostess and guardian than educator."

I heard the sharp intake of a raspy breath. In speaking the truth, I'd stepped on her toes. I knew from Lizzy that Lillian loved nothing as much as educating, setting the standard, calling the shots.

"Listen, you did a wonderful job with Elizabeth, really. You were a terrific parent. You don't have to worry too much this time around with Belle. It's different. Just consider yourself in charge of damage control. Leave the rest to us."

There wasn't any response. I might have made it worse. It was time to fish.

"Is there anything specific you think I need to know?"

Her answer was whispered. "Nothing at all. Everything's fine. Everything's under control."

I sensed it was anything but.

"Belle's a strong girl. If she weren't, she couldn't have made this enormous leap. It's easy to forget how difficult it probably is to transfer during high school, no matter the prize of attending Julliard. It must be quite a challenge finding her place at school. You know, kids can be tough."

"Well, yes." I imagined her sitting at the kitchen table in her apartment, enjoying an afternoon cup of tea before Belle came home. "Elizabeth could never have taken on such a hard task—never would have."

Although uttered in a quieter tone, I didn't miss the significance of her words. Worse, I'd been waiting for them. According to Lizzy, Lillian had found her uninspired, lacking in courage and gumption. It wasn't enough that she'd moved far away from home at age eighteen, achieving enough academic excellence to land a fancy job on the internationally famous Michigan Avenue; it wasn't enough that she'd bravely picked up and relocated to the unofficial end of the world midlife, starting over in the bleakest of environs. None of those things had impressed Lillian. At least, that was the way Lizzy saw it.

A cold breeze crossed my forehead. I squinted up at the sun. It was a chilly day, but there wasn't any wind at all. That sudden shock of cold air had come from within. I realized Lillian didn't know. "Hey, has Elizabeth told you? About her project? About what she's been up to?"

Another pause. "Yes. Of course."

I didn't believe it. It would be just like Lillian to cover up for something she didn't know. She loved to be on top of things.

"She's been working with a young woman from a broken family."

"Ah, that case at work."

"No." She most definitely had no idea what I was talking about. But I didn't need to prove a point. It wasn't about that. I was so proud that Lizzy was using her extraordinary gift of compassion where it could finally be appreciated. "It's nothing to do with her work at the firm. It's something different, something completely removed from that world."

Silence. I forged ahead, suddenly exhilarated, so happy to share. "This is really Elizabeth's news to share. But I suppose, well, I'm certain she won't care. She's working with a girl living over at the Meier center. She's helping her improve her reading."

"So. She's a tutor."

I heard the disdain in her voice, her brilliant daughter with the brilliant career now reduced to a lowly teacher. I paused, reflecting on the intensity of what Lizzy had described: the criticism and judgment she couldn't escape; what it was like to grow up with a parent who always had a different plan, a better one. *How difficult it must have been for her.*

"No, that's really not it at all. This girl has been removed from her home. She's all on her own and comes with a very heavy personal package. It's a lot more than just teaching." I paused and groped in my pocket for my keys. I'd reached the car.

"I'm sure."

"Lillian, this is very significant to Elizabeth. She's quite invested. She cares about this young girl very much. It's not just an academic exercise. It's become quite personal. I'm happy for her." The pleasure I'd felt in sharing ebbed quickly.

"I see."

I got into the car and closed the door behind me. It was much colder outside than I'd understood when I left my office. I glanced at the clock on the dash as I started the engine. It was time to hang up. In any case, Lillian seemed uninterested. I regretted that I'd even tried to point out her daughter's accomplishment, one more lame effort to pave a smooth path between the two. But I couldn't help myself. This was just something

I tended to do over the course of our years together—something Lizzy had come to resent.

"I guess it's some means of making up for the other one, a kind of replacement."

Lost in my thoughts about long-ingrained patterns I was trying to change within my family, I'd almost forgotten we were still connected. I barely caught Lillian's words.

"Excuse me?" I fiddled with the heat, eager to put down the phone so I could rub my hands together and get the blood flowing.

"For the one she lost."

"Lillian?"

She was muttering. I wondered if she was okay, if perhaps her mind had gone elsewhere. I couldn't attach her words to anything specific. "Are you there? I didn't quite catch—"

"It's nothing, Mike. Nothing at all."

I sat a little straighter in my seat. This sounded like something. If it was nothing, Lillian wouldn't have had anything to deny.

"Lillian?"

"I'll give Belle a hug when she comes home today and tell her you sent your love."

Confused but aware that our conversation was over, I mumbled a quick goodbye and hung up. The late-afternoon sun, hanging very low in the sky, blinded me for a moment as I pulled out into the street. My mind moved onward, thinking of what I was supposed to pick up on the way home, about what I might make for dinner. It wasn't until later that night, when the house was quiet and Lizzy was sound asleep beside me, that I made my way back to the end of that conversation. I tried to work out the meaning of her words, the reference to another girl—a lost girl, or rather, one that had been lost. I figured it had something to do with Belle. She was the only girl in our lives. But that didn't make sense. Lillian thought Belle was a star. She would never describe her as lost.

I drew a blank and, figuring her words the distracted mutterings of an older woman, let them go. Snuggling down into the covers, draping my arms around my wife, her face smooth and tranquil, so at peace, I fell into a deep sleep.

ELIZABETH

JULIE'S SEAT WAS EMPTY. SHE and I were meant to work together in the library, right by the window where we always met. I looked around the reading room. There were other students milling around, but no sign of mine. I consulted the librarian, but she hadn't seen her that morning and had no clue as to where she might be. I couldn't imagine that she'd forgotten. Although our association was just beginning to develop into something that might be called a relationship, things seemed to be going well. I spotted clear indications of something more substantive than the standard teacher–student association. With my own daughter far away and beyond my reach, there was nothing I wanted more.

It was during our last session that I realized I was closer to reaching this goal. Julie had been working her way through a particularly difficult passage, one with more exceptions than rules and that ever prickly "ancient." She'd stopped mid-passage and looked straight into my eyes with a soft expression and a hint of burgeoning tears—the kind that twinkled and caught the light, the kind that meant something good. I was both amazed and moved by this wordless "Thank you." This was probably the first time we'd made serious eye contact, most of our interaction beyond the words on the page usually limited to the vaguest of hand gestures and a countable number of verbal exchanges. Julie had been extremely reserved when we met. But rewarded with a chance to gaze into those intense green eyes for long enough to follow the trail of capillaries back to their quivering source of sight, I understood that I'd finally gained access to the girl's heart—that my work at the little table in the library extended well beyond helping her decipher the letters on a page.

Left standing alone that morning, I was at a total loss. I wondered if I'd missed a step, somehow giving her a reason to skip her lesson. There was absolutely no other explanation for her absence. I left the library and looked up and down the hall of the main building, unsure of where to look. My first thought was to go to the principal's office. Principal Hunter would be happy to help me. But I quickly changed my mind, heading instead toward the exit. I had an intuitive sense that an effective search would end up outside the confines of this building, somewhere with more room to breathe.

Making my way behind the school's main building, I followed Second Street toward the Red River. This area of downtown Grand Forks had been completely flooded a few years before we arrived. Its resurrection and restoration, an enormous undertaking by the regional council, had resulted in the landscaping of a new park, part of the greater Greenway dividing North Dakota from Minnesota, with a whopping area twice the size of my hometown's Central Park. We enjoyed exploring its many delights as a family when we first got to town—the playground, the winding walkways, the bike paths—and I was pretty sure Belle still hung out there on her own, maybe with her friends. I trembled at the thought of what they got up to.

I continued onward, distracted from my search by my attraction to this area, a reminder of the eternal potential for renewal and resolve. There were so many things at which to wonder in this remote part of the country. I wondered whether Belle, drawn away by the magnetic pull of the East Coast, would ever choose to return and make her life here. I knew the answer. And worse, I knew the reasons why. The anxiety I continued to spread to those near and dear, my own hang-ups strung up on the line for all to see, would probably, as they already had, compel her to seek happiness elsewhere. Although this reality was painful, it made perfect sense. Standing in a place where nature had conquered man not once but repeatedly, along the banks of the Red River, I understood its true force. Some tides could not be stemmed.

Blinded by a sudden wave of anguish, torturing myself with thoughts of Belle's struggle to break free and get as far away from me as possible, I almost missed the small, dark figure sitting among the marshy plants by the water's edge. For a split second, discombobulated, I wondered how Belle had gotten there when she was supposed to be in Manhattan. It wasn't possible. I experienced a few moments of real confusion before I realized my mistake. This wasn't Belle. This wasn't the daughter I was losing. The young woman seated quietly beside the river was Julie, someone right here within touching distance, someone starving for the compassion and steadfastness I had to give. Here was the girl I'd gained. The irony was staggering.

Afraid of alarming her, I cleared my throat loudly. She didn't turn around or even flinch, clearly unfazed by my arrival. It was almost as though she'd been waiting for me, certain I'd eventually arrive. Lowering myself to the ground beside her, I couldn't help thinking how, despite different agendas and different life situations, Julie and I shared a common desire for something tantalizingly out of reach. I gently draped my arm around her waist, hoping this physical contact wasn't presumptuous. From the little she'd shared of her life, I knew that intimacy had never been a given. She continued not to respond, remaining completely still, and we sat together in silence, staring out toward the river, both absorbed in the steady flow of the water, sharing a moment's peace. It was such a comfort.

"I couldn't find you. I didn't know where you were."

"Yet here you are."

I moved my hand across her back in a tickle more than a caress, my touch so light it could have been an extension of the early-morning breeze. My fingers sought to penetrate her thick shell of protection in the gentlest way possible. "I guess we were both drawn by the water. It's so soothing."

She didn't respond. Instead, my words washed over both of us, rolling easily through the crevasses of our individual reveries, encouraging them to continue their course. Although I didn't know exactly what it would entail, I desperately wanted to make a difference for Julie. I'd failed to do this for my own daughter, my efforts repeatedly rebuked and spurned. This felt like my only chance.

"Why does it flow north?"

Julie's question took me aback, its practical nature so unexpected at what felt like an emotional crossroads.

"Well, from what I understand, rivers flow downhill; and in this case, in the case of the Red River, that happens to be north. It's one of those lovely anomalies—totally unexpected."

"Hmmm. Strange." Another wave of silence. I knew better than to speak—knew how important it was to let Julie lead. "I just didn't feel like sitting in class today. I came out here to be alone." She gestured backward with her head, in the general direction of the school. "It's very crowded there. At the Center also. It's hard to have a moment to think, to catch my breath. Plus, I . . . I always have to be on guard."

I refrained from responding, sensing that there was more she wanted to say, not wanting to risk her clamming up and keeping it bottled inside.

"Today's my birthday." Her words fell as hard as a punch to the gut. I hadn't known. "It's my birthday, and there's no one to celebrate. I didn't get a hug when I woke up or acknowledgment at breakfast. No one at the Center remembered." She lowered her voice a notch. "I guess they didn't know." Sitting so close, I heard her swallow hard, obviously trying to rein in her emotions. "It wasn't that I had any serious expectations. I mean, no one really knows me there, or at school. But still, it sucks. What kind of kid isn't celebrated on her birthday?"

With that, the floodgates opened. Julie's last words came out choked with tears she could no longer hold back. They streamed unchecked, leaving long streaks down her cheeks, rolling as far as the collar of her blouse. I reached out and gently wiped at them, unsticking strands of hair that, roused by the breeze, had come loose from her ponytail. I opened my arms wide and wrapped her up tightly, wanting to overwhelm her with love, stricken at the thought of this poor child left to remember her birthday alone. Julie's body trembled, the façade she always worked so hard to maintain crumbling—the young, lonely girl trapped inside revealed. I drew close and whispered in her ear, "Julie, I'm sure your mother, wherever she is, has remembered your birthday."

Caught up in my efforts to calm and comfort, I didn't understand what was happening when I began to tumble sideways, toward the riverbank. Julie had shoved me away with such force that I had to scramble to catch myself. By the time I was seated, she was already on her feet, staring down at me. Her face had turned a shade of purple I didn't recognize, her brow gathered into a knot of rage.

"How dare you! You don't know that! You don't know anything!"

I had no idea how to answer. She was right. There was no way I could know what she felt, what it was like to be in her skin. I knew nothing about mothers who didn't know how to love their children. I did, however, know quite a lot about mothers who didn't know how to show it—as was the case with Lillian and, lately, felt very much the same with me. I continued to fail, to get it all wrong, when it came to Belle.

"I don't need you or anyone else. Leave me alone."

I stayed completely still, afraid to even extend my hand, understanding the fragility of the situation. The breeze blew, the bulrushes swayed, the water of the Red River continued its flow north. Julie and I were frozen in a tableau of shock and sadness. Staring up into her face, I noted that her skin tone had faded back to a pale pink, that her eyes, pits of fire moments earlier, were now wells of emptiness. She held my gaze, transmitting her pain and desperation. This was such a brave girl, so fierce in her resolve. Somehow, I knew she'd battle through; at some point down the road, she'd work out the frustration and anger that presently dominated her life.

Without another word, she turned and marched away, back toward town, toward life. I remained where I was, too startled to rise, clutching at the dirt around me for stability. She was right. I didn't know anything about her situation. But that didn't mean I couldn't empathize with her agony or know what it was like to want so much more from one's mother. Deprivation came in many different forms.

I got to my feet, brushing off my pants. I was over my head. I'd taken on a project I couldn't handle. Assuming that I'd be able to fill the gaping hole left at Belle's departure with this young, damaged life had been more than absurd. *How can I help another soul find an answer when I can't even find one for myself?*

BELLE

I CAREFULLY PLACED MY BOW in its place, tucking the silk cover snuggly around my viola, then zipped up the case. The other kids in the room were also packing up their instruments, getting ready to go home. I looked around, wondering who I should hang out with. I could try that guy who always walked down Broadway after school. He probably lived near me and Grandma.

"Hey. Ben. Heading out?"

"Yeah, but not your way." He flipped his head, his long black bangs flying to the side and then back, exposing his eyes. They peered into mine. "Aren't you going over to Julliard or something? You probably have another practice after this one. A *real* one." There was something nasty in his tone, an insinuation I didn't like. He looked over to Maggie, the redhead with the freckles who played the cello. A look of acknowledgment passed between them, and they snickered. I felt left out.

I looked away quickly, not wanting them to see the look of rejection on my face, then picked up my viola case and swung it over my shoulder. I should have just stuck with Becky. She was a sure bet, always ready with a kind word and a smile. She'd left with another flutist a few minutes earlier. Maybe I could still catch up. I walked out of the practice hall with head held high, hoping the others would think I didn't care, that I didn't mind the teasing. Of course, this was a thin line. If I looked too proud, they'd assume I thought I was better than them, and that wasn't true at all. In fact, many of the other kids in the high school orchestra were just as good as me. The only thing that distinguished me was the fact that I'd applied and been accepted into the program over at Julliard. Already living in New York City, able to take advantage of all the opportunities it offered, they hadn't bothered. It wasn't the ticket to New York I'd needed to get here.

The whole social thing was tiresome. All I wanted was to find a niche, a group of friends to accept and include me. But since most of the cliques had come together over the course of years, it was hard to find an opening. Fitting in at West Side High was going to be much harder than I'd anticipated. I knew that starting high school midstream was less than ideal, but running away from the jeering and the snickering back in Grand Forks, I hadn't cared. I just assumed it would all work out. I was mistaken. Faced with yet one more round of expressions making clear that I was unwelcome, I began to see the larger picture. Kids didn't need a specific reason to be unpleasant. The certainty that things would be better once I left GF Central now seemed ridiculous.

There was no sign of Becky in the hallway, but down by the exit I spotted Quinn and her pack of look-alikes, all sporting miniskirts, jean jackets, and a heavy layer of eyeliner. The cool kids. I brightened immediately. "Hey, hold up."

I quickened my pace, trying to look nonchalant despite the awkward way my viola case and book bag banged together behind me.

"Headed downtown?" I'd flirted with joining their pack from my first days at school, attracted to the look of daring they projected, the one that warned of danger. There was something so alluring about the way they stood with one hip precociously pushed out, as if ready to take on the world. I'd made my way across the country, alone, which was pretty daring; I figured I fit in perfectly. But I immediately discovered that wasn't going to be easy as from day one I was automatically dumped in with the nerdy orchestra clique. That's where the rest of the school thought I belonged. If the orchestra kids had wanted me, that might have been good enough. I didn't mind hanging with the straitlaced crowd. But lately I was floundering.

"Where you guys heading?" I tried not to breathe too heavily after my quick sprint.

"Out for a coffee." Quinn obviously spoke for the rest. "Wanna come?" My first instinct was to take her in my arms and kiss her. It wasn't important that I didn't drink coffee. I was overjoyed to be included.

"Sure." I answered with the same offhand flip I'd received from Ben, aiming for indifferent, and fell into step behind the others, firmly shoving my viola case out of the way. If only I had a place to stash this reminder that I wasn't like them. I was desperate to blend in.

The minute we got to the sidewalk, Quinn pulled out a packet of cigarettes, offering one to each of us in turn. I moved to the side, letting the others take theirs first. I'd never smoked before and hadn't wanted to. My parents were dead set against it. But when it was my turn, I didn't hesitate, waiting patiently for her to light me up as if I had any idea what that meant. I erupted into a fit of coughing, unable to hide the fact that I'd never smoked.

"You don't do that back there on the prairie?"

"I would have figured it was popular. I mean, what else is there to do?"

"Come on, prairie girl. Tell us what it's like."

I didn't mind their teasing because, for whatever reason, they hadn't rejected me; that was enough to make me feel accepted. The fact that they led a lifestyle that included a lot of things I wasn't into wasn't important at that moment.

Grandma grilled me the minute I got home.

"I smell that."

"What? What is it, Grandma?"

"You've been smoking." The look on her face was half repulsed and half angry. I wasn't sure whether to be offended or apologetic.

"Me? Are you kidding? You know I don't smoke."

"It's really strong. Don't tell me you weren't smoking, young lady."

I hated it when she called me that. It wasn't something I aspired to be. *Who wants to be a young lady these days?* If anything, I hoped to eventually become a woman. It sounded so much more empowered. Living with Grandma was quite tiresome.

"I haven't been smoking, Grandma, but I have been with kids who smoked."

I hoped to end the subject there, with that one simple but plausible lie.

"Right. I see." Her mouth puckered into a wrinkly circle from which spread an enormous network of lines. She looked old and withered, not part of the cool to which I aspired now that I was living the life of a New Yorker.

Back in my bedroom, I tucked my viola in its place behind the full-length mirror we'd purchased to make the room a bit more youthful and hurled myself onto the bed. I flipped through the numbers on my speed dial and, pushing up into a seated position against the backboard, waited for Lydia to pick up the phone. She answered right away.

"Hey, girl."

"Hey, you! How the heck are you?"

"Oh, you know. Perfect. Just perfect."

"Tell me! Tell me!"

Lydia and I met the first day of elementary school and became fast friends. She made the move to Nowhereland, North Dakota, bearable. Before we left, I'd begged my parents nonstop to change their minds. "Why North Dakota?" "It's freezing there. Even more freezing than here! Hard to imagine that's even possible." "I don't want to find friends. I have tons of friends right here in Lincoln Park!" My pleas and objections had fallen on deaf ears, and it wasn't long before my books, my markers, and the host of stuffed animals I depended on were packed up and loaded onto a truck headed to a place I knew would be some awful combination of bleak, empty, and boring. Thanks to Lydia, everything I'd anticipated, or at least the worst parts of it, evaporated that very first day of school.

She arrived like an angel heaven sent, her soft, squishy hand grasping my elbow from behind as I stood frozen with fear in the doorway of Mrs. Clark's classroom. She smelled like candy. "Right this way." With a boatload of enviable self-confidence, she steered me directly to a desk by the window, next to the one she'd already commandeered, offering me a smile of acceptance and more than a hint of conspiracy. I was intrigued, comforted, and almost energized, this unknown girl's welcoming gestures enabling me to move beyond my hesitations and fears and imagine a brave new world. By lunchtime, when she leaned over the table and offered to swap sandwiches, braids bouncing at awkward angles, smothering me with her sweet smell, I'd started thinking Grand Forks wasn't going to be so bad after all.

Talking to Lydia was still like stepping into a warm pool of water—embracing, accommodating, and wonderful. I spent the next hour lying in bed, rattling off details I knew she wanted to hear: some true, some less so; some meant to amaze and impress, others to convince that I wasn't out of my league and was holding my own in the Big Apple just fine. Lydia was the best of friends, sticking by my side when everything and everyone went to hell at school. I figured the other girls would stand with me as well, that I'd only need to suffer the taunting of the boys, some particularly feisty, reaching out and pinching my ass as I walked down the hall to class. But most decided to draw their razor-sharp claws and join in the fun. "What a ho!" "Guess that makes you feel popular."

Just when it felt like I'd never find a place within the chaos, that no one would defend my honor, let alone allow me a seat in the cafeteria, Lydia had reasserted her role as faithful friend. She was my saving grace then, as always.

Speaking with her on the phone from New York, I realized what I was missing. Surrounded by a constant cacophony of sound and those blinding bright lights, I had absolutely no peace, the kind that comes from hanging out with a friend who instinctively knows when you're happy and when you're sad, when you need some space and when you just need a hug.

After flooding her with a pack of untruths and exaggerations, I tired of trying to sound enthralled and dropped the pretense.

"Lyd?"

"That's my name. Don't wear it out."

I smiled and raised my eyes in exasperation. "It's just—"

"What's up? What's this change in tone? You were all bubbly a minute ago." There was a long pause before she shifted to a whispered tone. "Does it have to do with a guy? Is there someone new? Don't worry. You can tell me. You know I won't spread it around over here. That's all they need." She took a breath and blurted out the rest. "You know, now that you're gone, your reputation has completely changed. You're a rising star. All the kids—the ones who teased you, the ones who drove you crazy—they're all out of their minds with jealousy. I even spotted Tom with his friends, shrugging off the suggestion that you jilted him for the big city, saying soon enough he'd join you there himself. Asshole!"

"Oh God. Say it isn't so. I don't want him anywhere near me!"

Lydia laughed. "Don't worry. His parents are locals. They aren't going anywhere. He's about as likely to get out of Grand Forks as my cat."

It was my turn to laugh, and it was such a pleasure. I felt so comfortable and at ease. I wondered if I'd ever feel this way with Quinn or even Becky. It was hard to believe possible.

"Lydia, I'm a little lonely."

"No way! I don't believe it. You're just having a bad day."

"I can't figure out how to fit in."

"Ah, I see. Well, we knew that would be tough. Everybody in high school already kind of has their spot, right? It's a difficult challenge to conquer."

"I guess."

"The orchestra kids?"

"They don't like me. They're pissed because they think I think I'm better. I don't. And I'm not. But it doesn't matter. It's the whole Julliard thing."

"And those girls you mentioned? The city slickers?" Lydia's laugh at her own joke made me smile. This conversation was exactly what I needed.

"They're okay. But they get into stuff. All kinds of stuff."

"Like . . ."

"Smoking. Drinking. You name it."

"Ah. Well, that's your call."

I bit down hard on my lip, trying not to cry. Lydia would sense my tears; she always did.

"Maybe I won't find my spot here. Maybe I had it all wrong."

"No big deal. I'm right here. Happy to welcome you home with open arms."

I wondered a bit what it would feel like to tuck my tail between my legs and run home. That didn't feel right. I sat up in bed. I wasn't ready to give up. Not yet.

"But, Belle, hey! You've got this. Really. Chin up! You'll do just fine."

I really hoped she was right.

JULIE

BACK AT THE CENTER, I stormed around the common room.

"Hey, don't you have school? Aren't you supposed to be somewhere?"

I glared at the girl who'd spoken. I didn't know her name. I didn't want to. I didn't want to be here, never had. "Leave me alone."

I'd blown it with Elizabeth. I'd ruined the chance I had, the one chance. But I couldn't hold back. I just couldn't stand the assumption that she knew anything about what I felt, what I needed. The only one who knew me was Mom, and she was completely out of reach. I worked on my breathing, using the tools I'd learned in group meeting to stem my anger: one strong breath in and a long, extended one out. I stopped pacing as I approached the window looking over the parking lot. Everything seemed so normal out there, so everyday: people walking by alone, in groups—everyone where they were meant to be.

Everyone except me. *Where am I meant to be?* The only thing I knew for sure was that I wasn't meant to be here in this stupid room with these stupid people I didn't want to know. It wasn't supposed to end like this. I'd done so much to ensure that it wouldn't. That last, desperate effort I'd made to maintain the life I had, flawed as it was, before I came to this place was still crystal clear in my mind.

• • •

Mom moved through the living room toward the kitchen, floating, more specter than human. She was so insubstantial, so tentatively part of this world, as if she could disappear at any moment, blow away with the slightest breeze. I followed her, afraid of letting her out of my sight, my nervous energy a bolt of lightning to this soporific household, blazing a trail of purpose.

"Mom. I won't go. I won't leave."

She went to the stovetop, put the teakettle on the burner, and turned on the gas before pulling a sachet of tea out of the box on the counter. It was lemon ginger. I'd chosen it at the market ages ago, along with a whole range of foods with a bite, a diet purposefully curated to produce a reaction: cream cheese with jalapeno peppers, spicy mustard, piquant cheeses. I had this idea that challenging my mom's palette might arouse her, keeping her firmly within my world and preventing her from drifting off into her own. I was convinced that startling her system could assist her reentry. But I knew nothing of schizophrenia, nothing at all. And soon enough, since none of my efforts had worked, it would be me and not Mom whose world was rocked. While the lumbering, sometimes medicated pace of this unstable household would continue the same as before, my life was about to be turned on its head.

Today was one more opportunity to stop this runaway train before it was too late. I had to come up with some way to save this untenable situation and keep us together. I stood directly in my mom's line of vision, making sure our eyes met, making certain we'd connect. "Mom," I implored, "they can't make me. I'll try harder. I want to be here. I want to be with you. You need me. You know you need me."

For a moment I was certain I'd reached her, penetrating the haze in which she was encased. Although her hand fiddled idly with her teacup, her eyes—until now either nowhere or everywhere at once—focused directly on my own. My heart leaped with anticipation.

"Desperately." Her voice cracked. She cleared her throat before continuing in a whisper. "You can't imagine."

That was the opening I'd been waiting for. I stepped toward her and grasped her free hand, my words coming out rapid fire, accelerated by hope, unstoppable. "So that's it. We'll tell them just that. You need me here. I can't possibly be elsewhere. That'll work."

I dropped her hand and looked around the room, frantically searching for the phone.

"I'll just call Mrs. Kraft. I'll call her right away. Everything'll be all right. I'll make sure it's all right. Don't worry. I've got this." *Where is it?* It had to be here somewhere. I remembered leaving it in the kitchen but couldn't recall where. I pushed the items cluttering the counter to the side—dirty plates, a soiled dishrag, a short stack of newspapers whose origins were unclear. We'd stopped our subscription years earlier, neither of us following what was happening outside, hyper-focused instead on what wasn't happening right here in the house.

With a grunt of frustration, I ran into the living room, casting my eyes frantically on all the visible surfaces, digging my hands deep down between the cushions of the sofa. That's when I remembered. I stopped digging, retracted my hands, and slammed them down hard on the back of the couch, defeated, my eyes filling with tears. I wouldn't find the phone. It wasn't here. My phone was at the repair shop, its glass smashed, completely out of operation. That stupid girl, it was all her fault. If only she hadn't insisted on provoking me.

At the time, when it happened, losing the phone hadn't seemed so tragic. Expressing my anger had been paramount. But now, when I desperately needed to reach out, when I simply had to communicate with the outside world, its loss seemed insurmountable. For just a moment I thought of the landline, but we'd gotten rid of it years ago when the incoming calls petered out to nil. Now I had no way to get in touch with the caseworker at CPS, to alert her that there was no reason to come and pick me up—that I'd be staying with Mom after all. Stricken by a sense of helplessness, by the wretched feeling of being trapped in a mess I hadn't designed, I stood completely still. My eyes took in the clouds of dust that my search had stirred as they settled back around me, just one more example of the inertia of my situation.

Refusing defeat, I made a quick about-face and stepped back into the kitchen. There wasn't time to wallow in my continued misfortune. I had to pull myself together since Mom couldn't. We'd started something here. I felt it. There'd been a moment, a golden moment when I was certain she understood that she needed to speak up and express aloud, to the powers that be, that she wanted me to stay home, with her. I had a sliver of an opening here, and there was no way I'd let it get away.

But upon returning to the kitchen, I realized this was a lost cause. My mother was seated at the table, drinking the tea she'd prepared, her nose dipping in and out of the mug absentmindedly, her eyes dreamily locked on the steam rising from the brew. She was completely oblivious to my reappearance, and all signs of that spark of a connection we'd shared minutes earlier, the one I'd felt so vividly, had vanished. In their place was that same, infuriating, amorphous fog. Mom didn't seem to have noticed my frenetic search, too hermetically sealed in her own world to absorb what was happening in mine. Nothing could break through the torpor and bring her back to a place with room for two.

Heavyhearted and exhausted by misplaced hope, by one more attempt to change what could quite obviously not be changed, I pulled out one of the kitchen chairs and joined her at the table. Head in hand, sunken in my seat, I wondered if what I was experiencing was all there ever would be. I didn't want to believe it was so. A sudden surge of anger rushed through me in the face of my mother's disaffected calm, boiling over and exploding. My hand lashed out toward her, and then just as quickly whipped back in horror. I didn't want to hurt her—not now, not ever.

It was too late. I'd slammed hard into her mug. It crashed to the floor, leaving a trail of brown tea in its wake.

Mom jumped up with a look of shock, staring down at the shards of crockery on the floor and wiping away at the wet, stained swatches on her hands, her wrists, her sleeves, and bodice. Immediately sobered by the fallout of my rage, I knelt on the floor, gathering the broken pieces, mumbling words of apology.

"I didn't mean to. I shouldn't have. I'm so sorry, Mom. I'm sorry. I don't know what . . ." I crawled back and forth under the table, wending my way between our upended chairs, the knees of my jeans soaking up the remnants of the tea. I shoved the broken pieces I managed to pick up into my left hand, intending to collect them all before throwing the whole lot out, giving no thought whatsoever to their sharp edges. Overwhelmed by the combination of fury, disappointment, and frustration that had caused me to lose control, I suddenly sat back on my heels and began to cry. "I can't." I struggled to speak between sobs. "I just can't. Make it stop. Please, Mama. Make it stop."

I squeezed my hands tightly closed as I rocked back and forth, raising my eyes just in time to see Mom reach forward and lay her hand on my head, as if in benediction. "My daughter," she mumbled, gently stroking my hair. I froze, shocked at this overt sign of warmth, of intimacy, the only thing I'd ever really wanted from her—afraid that any sudden movement would startle her, putting it to an end. I would hold my breath forever if it meant prolonging this unexpected sign of affection.

All thoughts of the broken mug were forgotten. Instead, tormented by the inability to break a mold that had existed for as long as I could remember, maybe even before I was conceived, I gave in to a profound sadness, letting the tears flow freely, gasping for air beneath the table, suffocated by the weight of our shared burden. Fay would never be the mother I needed because she couldn't. She probably shouldn't have been a mother at all. I wondered if she understood this—if it caused her dismay. The likelihood was no. She'd lived an isolated existence my entire life, caught between worlds of her own making. It was unlikely she even considered that things might have been otherwise.

Distracted by a wave of self-pity, it took a few moments to realize that I'd hurt myself. My sobs suddenly segued into howls of pain. I looked down, shocked that anything could hurt more than my heart, and stared at the rivulets of blood emerging from between my fingers. Gingerly unclenching my hand, I discovered that the mug's remains had opened jagged cuts in the soft palm and along the fleshy part of my fingers. I jumped to my feet and ran to the kitchen sink, releasing random shards into its recess with a clatter. Turning on the faucet, I shoved my hand under the steady stream and watched as blood flowed from the various cuts.

Although the pain began to subside, I remained mesmerized by the size and dimension of the incisions, by the way they'd transformed my hand into a mini battleground. I didn't feel Mom's presence until she was right behind me, then stiffened at her proximity, afraid of letting go of the physical pain and returning to the one that had made me lose control in the first place. This wasn't the only time our situation had led me to lash out and break things, destroying whatever was close at hand. It had horrifically become a habit.

By the time I realized that Mom was trying to help, handing me a towel, gently pulling my hand away from the water and wrapping it tightly to stem the flow of blood, I'd almost forgotten what this was all about. I'd almost forgotten that this was an ending. In a very short time, maybe minutes, maybe an hour, I would leave this house, moving to that youth center, and things would never be the same.

I reached around and embraced my mother with my good hand, holding on tight, hugging with almost too much strength. I didn't want to acknowledge our imminent voyage into the unknown.

"I love you, Mom," I whispered into her ear. "I'll always love you."

"Let's take a look." She pushed me away gently and grasped my hand, slowly opening the towel. "I don't really know how to help you, what to do, but at least . . ." We both peered at the little cuts, the slightly larger ones, the trickles of blood that seeped out here and there, unchecked the minute we removed the pressure exerted by the towel. "Let's see. There must be something, some way to fix you up. I want to make you whole."

A wave of sadness overcame the pain in my hand. She'd never be able to make me whole. That opportunity had passed long ago. Furthermore, I knew that it was my job to step into her place, take over, and be the mature adult, the parent. I rewrapped my own hand with the towel, tightening it to the best of my ability with one hand and holding it snug against my chest so that the makeshift bandage wouldn't come undone. With my other, I reached for her hand, holding it next to my heart.

"It's going to be okay, Mom. You'll see. We're going to be okay." I pulled her in for another hug, afraid of letting her go, soaking up this blessed intimacy. Mid-embrace, I realized that it was *I* who was clinging, *I* who was holding on; Mom was barely touching me, just making the slightest of contact—only partially there. This beautiful moment, like so many others before it, was soon to end. Everything about my life with my mother was transient. I would always need more.

BELLE

"I DON'T GET IT." I TURNED to Grandma, then looked back at the collection of light bulbs and boxes mounted in the corner of the exhibition hall. My eyes moved up, then down; left to right. I wasn't sure what I was supposed to do now but figured from her silence that I should just continue to look.

I kept my eyes focused on the so-called "artistic object" and waited, trying not to let out the sigh of exasperation dying to be expressed. This was getting really old. We'd been standing here for what felt like an hour. What was to be seen had been seen. Now I just had to bide my time until Grandma suggested we move on to the next work in the gallery. It seemed like that might never happen.

"Well." She cleared her throat. "Well, dear. Let's look at this together." She extended her arm, finger pointed, and traced a line in the air, following the outline of the top bar, continuing down one of the vertical ones, back along the horizontal bottom bar and up again. I began to lose patience. It was a rectangle. I got it. I couldn't imagine what morsel of information she could possibly add to that simple fact. This was painful, but I'd be damned if I'd budge first.

I had a goal today. I was curious about what had happened between

Grandma and Mom way back when and was certain that if I showed Grandma I was a worthy companion—erased her impression that I was getting involved in things I shouldn't be, running with the wrong crowd—she'd start to open up and share. So far, I'd received very little. There was that hint of her pride over Mom's participation in religious school. Back at the temple the previous Friday night, she made a point of taking me down to the basement where the walls were lined with framed photographs of earlier confirmation classes. There was Mom, seated in a white gown alongside a small handful of kids.

"Your mother was quite devout. You know, she used to attend youth group. Just like you do back in Grand Forks." I eagerly collected these dribbles of information but wanted more.

I searched deep, looking for the perfect response, hoping to convince her that I understood what she was getting at with that pretentious wave of the hand. "It's a rectangle!" I shouted, feigning discovery. I turned to her, expecting that at minimum she'd be amused. Nothing. She didn't even flinch. I searched for something else, something that would show her I was enthralled with her world, open to new experiences, all that New York had to offer, etcetera. My eyes flickered with recognition. I had it. "It's a rectangle of light and color."

Grandma immediately turned toward me and smiled. "Well, yes! Yes, it is! That's a very good place to start. Shows you're really looking!"

I stifled my smile of victory. All I'd done was go for straightforward. The fact that I hit the bullseye was accidental. Maybe this wouldn't be as hard as I'd thought. Maybe if I played the game, made an obvious comment here or there, any comment at all, I'd gain points. I needed points. Lately there were too many signs that I was trying Grandma's nerves: "Please turn down that music." "The laundry goes in the hamper, not on the floor." "I'd prefer if you didn't have anyone over in the evening. I really need to get a good night's sleep." "If you leave that lava lamp on one more time, I'll have to take it away."

The more I expanded my social life, the more tense she seemed. "You need to let me know if you're not coming home after school." "I'm not comfortable with your taking the subway in the evening." "How will you get up in the morning if you stay out so late?"

She'd recently imposed a curfew.

"You've got to be kidding me."

"I'm worried you'll have trouble concentrating."

"That's my business."

That stony face. Always that stony face. "Your business is my business, young lady."

Agreeing to accompany Grandma on a visit to the Museum of Modern Art this Sunday afternoon, when I preferred to be just about anywhere else, was about not only gaining back her goodwill but also being let in on the secrets I knew she was hiding. I glanced around the dim gallery, searching within its shadows. The museumgoers were more interesting than the objects on display: mothers tugging their reluctant children by the sleeve; students sitting on the floor with large drawing pads; couples draped over one other; elderly couples with walkers who lingered forever in front of one item or another. That last one was apparently us.

I turned my head back to the boxy light fixture and tried to refocus. Getting this right, saying the right thing, showing Grandma that I was "engaged"—that word we'd been using in school lately—or at least interested seemed essential. Ignorant might be the way to go.

"Maybe you could explain it to me." I reached out and gently touched the sleeve of Grandma's blouse before dropping my hand to my side. I'd intended to grasp her elbow, to make contact and hold on, but something about the material, its gauzy feel, almost slithery, turned me off. I quickly stretched my lips into a smile to cover up an expression of repulsion. I had to maintain the right face. Grandma was always quick to observe the slightest details. Just yesterday she'd noticed I was wearing makeup—just the barest bit of mascara—and launched into a whole lecture about how I chose to present myself to the world.

"Is that what you want people to think of you?"

"What does wearing a little makeup have to do with what people think?"

"Don't be so naive. You're sending a clear message."

"To who?"

"To *whom.*" She emphasized the correction. "To absolutely everyone you meet."

"Maybe it's a good one. Maybe they'll think it makes me look bold, mature, full of confidence." I smiled, quite happy at the thought.

"Or maybe they'll think it makes you look cheap."

I turned and left the kitchen after that, hurrying back to the safe space of my room. Sometimes living with Grandma was even worse than living with Mom. That thought would have been unimaginable months earlier. Before moving to New York, I figured that my mom was a total square, a crazy one—that I'd gotten the bad draw. Now I understood that she was just one of a crowd.

Waiting for a response from Grandma became painful. It started with a physical shift. She inhaled deeply, filling her chest with air and standing even straighter (as though that were anatomically possible for someone who stood as stiff as a pole). I suddenly felt very small, dwarfed as she morphed into a tall super-being radiating pure self-confidence. I cringed a bit when she finally spoke.

"The very first thing . . ." She paused dramatically. She loved doing that. "The first thing one does when encountering a work of art with no ostensible subject is to read the label." She extended her hand in an arc like a dancer inviting his partner and pointed to the small white square of cardboard glued to the wall. "Take a look, dear."

I stepped over and read aloud, "Dan Flavin. American. Untitled." I turned back to her, perplexed. "Seems kind of skimpy. Minimalistic." I knew she'd like that word. "How does this help me understand?" Although I'd felt confident moments earlier, certain I was playing this right, finding the kind of sophisticated air I knew would impress her, I began to flounder. I had no idea how to progress with so little information, and it was harder and harder to pretend I cared. "Untitled? What kind of a title is that?"

Grandma laughed. Her whole demeanor softened, her chin lowering a notch, her shoulders relaxing, her body deflating to normal proportions, shedding its superhuman appearance. I hoped this was a sign that she was dropping the pretense of educator supreme and returning to the role of grandma. "Well, dear, that's part of the point! Untitled means that the artist isn't telling us what the object is."

I nodded in faux understanding and interest, but I began to disconnect. I glanced around the gallery again and shifted my weight restlessly from one foot to the other. I'd really had enough. This whole scene wasn't for me. I'd gone through the motions, trying to convince Grandma that I could benefit from our time together—that excursions like this in the city would expand my horizons. I knew this was important to her. But I had exhausted this particular outing and wanted to go home.

Unfortunately, it felt as though I'd lost more points than I gained. I didn't know when this visit to the art museum became so important, more a task at which to excel than a pleasant expedition. But it had. And although I'd done my best, going along with the whole thing like a real trooper, I was finished with this box of light bulbs. Wanting to stretch my legs and get a little distance from this fairly intense encounter, I wandered off to investigate the rest of the gallery, moving into its deepest shadows, corners that got far less light, where it was difficult to see anything. My practical side wondered how frequently all these bulbs needed to be changed, if one person was responsible for getting the job done, while my contemplative side, released by the all-encompassing darkness, began to drift, releasing an overpowering ache for the clutter of home—my real home.

Life back in North Dakota was full to bursting with activities and friends, the community encircling me in one enormous embrace. Here in New York, it was always about the "wow." The girls at school were all into parties that took risks, outings meant to dazzle. They aimed to milk this amazing city for its capacity to astound. I'd wanted this too at the start, jumping in headfirst. But that was a few months back, and now I missed what I'd had, finally seeing how bright lights could mask a whole lot of emptiness. My eyes welled up with unexpected tears, and I hastened to wipe them away. I'd pushed for this so hard, stepping right over my mom's objections as I clambered to get my way. I was convinced that New York was calling my name. *And now?*

Squinting to shut out this sudden, unwanted rush of emotion, I was drawn back to the bundle of bulbs on the other end of the room, surprised to see them suddenly transformed into a ribbon of colors, kaleidoscopic in nature. My tears combined with the lights to create a gorgeous symphony of color very much like what I experienced at Julliard on Saturdays—lifting me to a purer world, one which made sense. I'd never considered that visual stimulus could rival that of music, dazzling me and sweeping me away to another place.

"Dear? Are you with me? I was just trying to explain . . ." Grandma's voice came to me as if from the end of a long tunnel. I'd almost forgotten about her. Forcing away the wave of sadness, I hurried back across the gallery, resuming my place at her side. This was my new home. Grandma was now my anchor. I had to stop hoping it would be otherwise. A sharp pain spread across my forehead, and I reached up to massage my temples, pushing lightly to release the throbbing pressure that had amassed, desperate to dispel this blanket of gloominess. Closing my eyes, I felt a slight easing, the discomfort subsiding to a dull ache, my vision becoming clearer. Mom had taught me this trick, and it never failed to work.

Grandma prattled on, unaware of my distress. "If the artist doesn't provide a name, it's your job to come up with one! How do you like that? You, my dearest progeny, have a role!"

I opened my eyes wide, taking in my grandmother as though from a distance. She looked incredibly old, and not in a fun way. And although I tried to, digging as deep as I could, I didn't feel a thing. The amicable thoughts I'd had in the past had faded away. Suddenly, the idea of our living together seemed not only ridiculous but insane. *What was I thinking?* Her words, and they just kept on coming, only made me angrier and more agitated. I had no idea what she wanted from me, what she was talking about. This whole excursion had been a bad idea. I wasn't going to convince her of anything or get any closer to the things I wanted to know. The whole idea to come and live with her full-time had been a mistake. I glanced to the doorway of the gallery, wanting to ditch, to cut out on her and run back to the apartment. I even had an unexpected and totally surprising urge to call Mom. Suddenly, the bad blood between us, the ugly words that had been exchanged, didn't matter as much. At least with Mom there was none of this endless pretense.

Turning Grandma into a parent and effectively removing the veil of distance that characterized our relationship beforehand hadn't been a good idea. We had started from scratch the day I arrived, redefining what should have been a natural relationship, and the picture we had come up with wasn't pretty. Suddenly it all seemed too much to bear, too much on top of everything else I had to deal with: trying to find a place with the kids at school, working so hard to meet the demands at Julliard, living without those who had been my security net forever. Having to negotiate this new relationship with Grandma, figure out how to get along with, and around, yet another demanding adult, seemed too tall an order.

I was amazed that with all of my inner turmoil, Grandma's demeanor hadn't changed one bit. She hadn't picked up on the slightest bit of my panic, too involved in enlightening me and provoking a reaction to this glorified lighting fixture. Distressed, I broke out in a sweat. This felt like a test. I'd never liked tests.

I turned away again, ignoring her entreaties that I engage. I didn't want to try to be someone I wasn't, to maintain a sham to secure a dream. I shouldn't have to. It shouldn't be about that. Although before it had only been a hunch, I felt certain that this was the key to what went wrong between her and Mom. Mom simply wasn't who Grandma wanted her to be. *And who could be?* My insides melted just a bit, softening at the thought of just how hard that would have been on her. Mom didn't like to disappoint. I wondered if this day could still have a silver lining—if I could discover a little more about what had gone wrong. I had to try.

"Grandma, can I be honest here?"

I watched as the tiny wrinkles of pleasure gathering at the corners of her eyes went flat, the skin on her cheeks blanching in the glow of those bars of light, the corners of her mouth turning south. Her whole face seemed to cave in. It was slight but unmistakable. There was a chance that I was about to forgo a crucial opportunity to win her over and prove that I was an asset instead of an encumbrance. But I couldn't stop myself. Once I had the errant thought that truth would lead to truth, I couldn't be deterred. Not as long as there remained the slim chance that speaking my mind would be the key to eventually putting together the puzzle of Mom and Grandma.

"It's not that I don't care. Because I do. And I guess, well, if I have a role in the meaning of a work of art, one hanging in a museum? Well, that's really cool. I mean, the artist thought of me. Right? Or, at least, he had me in mind when he put together these light rods, when he anchored them to that box. He cared what I would think, what I'd see and what I'd feel. Yeah, that's pretty neat."

All caution to the wind, I went for broke. "But honestly? This whole exhibit pretty much leaves me empty. These light boxes, they really aren't for me. I mean, I'm happy to walk around, to accompany you as you tour the gallery. The quiet *is* kind of nice. It's a nice break from the outside world. But I don't think all of this"—here I paused and gestured vaguely around the gallery, stopped to point to a collection of free-standing boxes and planks, glowing bars of light, and deep shadows—"I don't think *this* is ever going to be my thing."

When I finished, I exhaled loudly, unaware that I'd been partially holding my breath. The silence that greeted me in response stretched out far and wide, filling the gallery in which we stood, as well as those adjacent. I had the distinct sense that we were floating in a huge tank, all activity and sound suspended. I looked down at my Vans, knowing I'd gone too far, perhaps to a place from which there could be no return. The shoelace on my right shoe was untied, and I considered bending down to tie it—that would be a perfect way to break the tension—but decided against it. Grandma was a stickler for manners. She would certainly interpret this move, physically ducking out of the picture mid-discussion, as rude.

The gap in our dialogue took on ever-expanding dimensions and significance. My heart sank. I'd blown it. The chance to convince Grandma to consider me a nice young lady, to loosen up, to let me in and let me peek at the past, was gone.

I frantically grasped for a way to ensure that she didn't interpret my honesty as an insult. Ignoring the slinky feel of her blouse, I picked up Grandma's arm, wrapping it tightly in my own, sending the message that we were best buddies. The confirmation that my gesture had worked came immediately. Her eyes, flat as pothole covers just seconds earlier, suddenly radiated with light, denying the darkness in which we stood and affirming her delight. I didn't know it would be so easy. All I had to do was show ultimate devotion. Suddenly the path to forging a reasonable life in this super-charged city and learning something about the past opened before me. All I had to do was sugarcoat things with Grandma and I'd be on my way. Not so difficult after all.

A familiar figure passed nearby, and I dropped Grandma's arm. It was Ben, from orchestra. "Hey, Ben! It's me, Belle. What are you doing here?"

He gestured to the woman beside him, and I laughed. A visit with his grandmother. It was too funny. "Time with Grandma! High five." I reached out my hand and met his. We shared another laugh, even grasping hands midair for a moment. It was nice to share a joke.

I felt the change in Grandma before I saw it. One look confirmed that she'd turned white. I couldn't for the life of me imagine why. I raised my eyes to the heavens, a flash of my own mother's blanched face and the sound of that screech in my bedroom burning through my head. *What is it with these women? What is their issue with boys?*

MIKE

ONE MORE QUIET DINNER. IT was hard to get used to the feel of our house come evening. We'd never experienced Grand Forks without Belle. Her energy, her comings and goings, the recap of the day gone by and the anticipation of the one that lay ahead had always been a driving force. In some ways I was as relieved by the entrance of Julie into Lizzy's life as she. Tales of their meetings enlivened conversations that might otherwise have fallen flat and stalled. We both missed Belle desperately.

"What can I help with?" Elizabeth stood behind me at the refrigerator, staring inside as though searching for a pot of gold. I gently closed the doors and pointed her to the table.

"Just have a seat. It's all ready."

Although Elizabeth had done most of the food preparation over the years, the task recently fell to me. It was another marker of the change we'd undergone as a household, ushered into the empty nest with a shove rather than a gentle nudge. It would take some time to get used to. The entire beat of life was different, albeit still strongly colored by Lizzy's concerns. Although occupied by her new role as mentor, much of her attention now solidly elsewhere, removed from the ins and outs of our little life, she maintained a strong vigilance regarding Belle's new life. I was the conduit, the one who knew whatever either Belle or Lillian had decided to share.

Lizzy tried not to demand a replay of every communication, but that didn't mean she didn't want to know. In fact, she was desperate to. Her seemingly casual approach to the whole subject was part of a concerted effort to pull back and relinquish control. She seemed to understand that whatever she'd done in the past hadn't worked—that she needed to ease up and leave enough room for Belle to, at some point, come walking back in. This was a fragile time, but a dear one. We both approached it as a chance to renegotiate our own relationship, severely damaged by old habits that had gotten the better of us and turned ugly, caught in the maelstrom that preceded Belle's departure. It was time to turn inwards, to listen and hopefully heal.

"I think you'll really like the pasta. The sauce is based on a mixture of overcooked zucchini, garlic, and parmesan—all favorites." I smiled as I took my seat beside her, feeling some of the anticipation of the new groom.

"Any word today?"

I laughed, twirling a sizeable amount of linguine around my fork. "No holding back tonight, huh?"

"Well. If you feel like talking about it."

I noticed she hadn't started to eat; her hands still lay in her lap.

"Wait. Is there something I missed?"

"No, no. It's not that. It's just a feeling. Well, a feeling provoked by a text."

I stopped chewing mid-bite. "What about?"

Lizzy reached out and touched my hand. "Hey, it's nothing. I didn't mean to worry you."

I lay my fork down at the edge of my plate. "What's up, Lizzy?"

"Okay. So, I got a weird answer to a question I asked. Via messages, of course. It was about the other kids. I was asking what they were like. And she only wrote about the girls."

I smiled and picked up my fork. "That's it? That's what you're worried about? I suggest you start to attack that plate of pasta while it's hot! I promise you'll love it."

Elizabeth looked down at her plate and idly picked up her fork. It was clear she was simply trying to please me. She wasn't ready to eat.

"I'm worried that it was an SOS. A call for help."

"I think you're reading too much into it."

"Why didn't she mention any boys?"

"What? Why would she? How did you get from here to there? Your mind is getting the best of you."

Lizzy stared into my eyes for a moment and then looked down at her plate, pointedly starting in on her dinner. We ate in silence, the cloud of concern hanging over the table refusing to be dispelled. It was all a bit disappointing. I thought we'd broken through this phase. I thought Lizzy had finally found a way to keep her exaggerated concerns for our daughter from overwhelming our day-to-day life. I took a large sip of wine and put it back on the table a bit abruptly, hoping to break the mood by telling her about what was going on in the department. I didn't get the chance.

"Are there boys?"

"What?" I had trouble following her line of thought. This was one subject of conversation I hadn't anticipated while preparing dinner.

"Do you know if she's seeing someone? Because I'm worried that something might happen, and I won't be there to help. I'm pretty sure Lillian wouldn't handle it correctly."

"Lizzy, what are you talking about? Where is this coming from? You've really worked yourself up over this. I don't get why."

I watched her look away, take in a few calming, deep breaths, and then return her gaze to me.

"I love her. I can't help worrying. Things happen. Lots of things. We're not there. We're out of the picture now."

"What could possibly happen?"

Lizzy's laugh startled me. It sounded so cynical, almost cruel. "What could happen? Between a boy and a girl?"

"Again, I don't get it. How did you come to this from a text about new friends?"

"How could you not?"

Another heavy silence. I looked at my wife, at the way her collarbone jutted out from the opening of her blouse, at the tendrils of hair that had come loose from the tight bun she'd arranged that morning. I restrained myself from reaching out and tucking them back in. I'd loved this woman since the day we met. I longed for her to let go and let matters evolve as they might. I wanted nothing more than to ease her worries, now and always.

"You're not a mom. You don't know what might happen to a young girl. Let's say . . ." And here she stopped, quite suddenly, looking straight down at her plate. The linguini was still piled high. She'd barely taken a bite.

The memory of the conversation I had with Belle midair came back to me like a tidal wave. Suddenly this made sense. Suddenly I knew exactly where she was going. "What? If she had sex?"

Lizzy's eyes were on me in a flash, enlivened by flickers of light and jittery activity. She looked positively frenzied. In some ways it was a relief after the dullness that had lingered there for the better part of our meal. "No, no. She couldn't. She wouldn't."

"But she could. And she might." I had to tread softly. Lizzy had no idea what I knew, and Belle had sworn me to silence. Even if I ached to share, to let her know that I understood the reason for their troubles, the intensity of that horrible scene back in the spring, the fact that I shared her difficulty with this whole subject, I couldn't. "She's sixteen. She might meet a boy. Something might happen. It would be, well, natural. Maybe even expected. Right?"

Lizzy looked shocked. She obviously expected a different reaction. This was something we'd never spoken about, a subject we'd never broached. We'd never had to. But I didn't understand why she thought I'd be so closed-minded, so inflexible.

"I can't believe you're so nonchalant. Didn't they spend Sundays pounding in all that stuff about mortal sins?"

I laughed. Now I understood. "They tried. In fact, they tried hard. But I never bought it. It never made any sense, neither for the world that was nor the one we live in." It was odd to think back to Catholic school. "Listen, I don't love the idea of Belle and, well, you know. I don't even like to talk about it. I don't want to talk about it." My tone carried a hint of revulsion. "But it's going to happen, if it hasn't already." I didn't have to reveal my hand to empathize with the complex nature of the topic. I stared straight into Lizzy's eyes, almost daring her to flinch. There was an amusing aspect to this particular subject. She shook her head, a strange half smile on her face. I'd most definitely surprised her.

"It's funny that we've never spoken about this. Never. It seems the kind of thing that might have come up."

She laughed. "I guess we've had other things on our plate. Perhaps we've been in denial. You know, *not our daughter*. That kind of thing."

"Sure. No way, not our daughter." I followed her lead, enjoying the tone of levity, the switch to sharing something that felt like a joke. The air in the room felt a lot lighter than it had at the beginning of the meal. It was easier to breathe.

"But, Mike, what if . . . well, if something happened, something bad."

My mind went to too many places. Lizzy saved me from the darkest corners by cutting to the chase. "You know, if she doesn't understand . . . if they don't use protection."

I was almost relieved. "I see what you're getting at. But, Lizzy, we're here. We'll always be here. If something like that happened, we'd step in and help her."

"But we're not *there*. Now she has Lillian, and I'm not sure . . ." Her voice faded to a whisper.

"This isn't Lillian's job. Belle would understand that. She'd come to us."

Lizzy looked visibly relieved, as though I had removed a huge weight from her shoulders. "I don't believe that Lillian could handle this. And it's such a delicate subject."

She looked so sad. I didn't know what had happened between her and Lillian years earlier to cause such a deep rift, but it was decisive. I was desperate to alleviate what was obviously a pain she'd carried for decades, had been trying to for years. I scooted my chair closer, taking her in my arms.

"You don't have to worry. Belle is fine. She's going to be fine. Always. And we'll always be her parents. Lillian isn't going to ever play that role. Lizzy, if something like this happened, we would help Belle get through it and support her to the end."

Pushing back a bit, she wiped her eyes. "You know, there are just certain things. I don't know how, or if . . ." She paused, pulling at one of those loose wisps of hair. "And I'd assumed . . . well . . . that you might consider the whole subject otherwise."

For a moment I thought she might tell me about that incident with Tom, the ugliness that had set so much of our new lives in motion. But she leaned forward into my tight hug, and I accepted this gift of intimacy. There was something she wanted to say. Eventually we'd get there.

JULIE

"I'M NOT EXACTLY SURE."

Elizabeth and I were in the library. This had been our spot from the beginning. We both liked the quiet, the natural comfort of all those books and no chatter. Of course, there was another plus. No one bothered me in the library.

I sat very still, luxuriating in the warmth of her hand lightly grasping my own on the table between us. These occasional physical expressions of affection were one of the best parts of our relationship, if I dared called it that—much more significant than the improvement in my reading, the reason we were brought together in the first place. I couldn't get enough of the feeling of safety her touch imparted, the security of knowing someone had my back, the certainty of her affection and devotion.

Of course, this didn't come about all at once. It took months of meetings, poring over texts together here in my safe space, to feel even the least bit of something toward the woman who sat here patiently with me today. There was too much in the way of letting her in, an enormous pile of obstacles that had solidified into an impenetrable wall of cement over the years. First, I had to release the certainty that I was undeserving, that I was at fault, that I'd never truly be loved. I fought the establishment of an actual relationship between us for a long time, unwilling to take a chance that would lead to one more disappointment. I greeted her gruffly for weeks on end, refusing to comply, reading very little before abruptly stopping and declaring the meeting over. I was the one steering the boat, and I purposefully took us through the roughest of water.

"I don't want to." "I don't need you." "I don't need this." "I don't know why everyone thinks I need help." I ignored her, distancing myself, even when seated together. I tried to bar her from my life, figuring that was the safest path. But she kept coming, kept insisting on her presence, ever patient. "You don't need to read today if you don't feel like it." "We can just sit here. I like it here. I've always loved quiet spaces. Did you know that I work in one?" Over the previous months, she'd told me about her life, little tidbits. At first, I shut them out. I didn't want to know. I insisted that I didn't care. But that wasn't so. I did. In fact, I was very curious. I wanted to hear more about a normal life because that's what I assumed she had. And the times I chose not to join her at what had become "our table," I would peep through the window in the door, watching her sit there patiently. She never once left before the hour was up.

At minimum, she'd convinced me of her commitment to our arrangement. So today, although my hesitations threatened, as always, to derail any chance for real intimacy, I stifled them, shoving them firmly out of the way and making room to think otherwise, feel otherwise, and live otherwise. Elizabeth had swooped in from nowhere and convinced me that I had the right to see the whole picture differently.

"I think it was that first day I went to school."

She gave my hand a little squeeze, encouraging me to continue my story.

"I didn't know anything, had no idea what to expect. But . . ." Here I stopped and smiled. This was one of the nice memories. "I was so excited. First grade. New friends. Friends, period! A new beginning." I abruptly closed my mouth and stared at our entwined hands, my train of thought coming to a brutal stop upon arriving at the next station. The rest of the memory wasn't as nice. I resumed my tale in a more somber tone.

"I didn't know that there was all this prep to do in advance." I looked up and met Elizabeth's gaze. "A kind of preface. That's the word, right?"

She nodded in assent and smiled. "Exactly. Very nice."

Preface. That was a word I'd recently learned to describe what comes before. For me it was the darkness, the years spent in shadows, bouncing between poles of fear and anger. We'd been reading more advanced texts lately, and I'd come upon the word a number of times.

"Anyway, we hadn't gone shopping, Mom and me. We hadn't prepared any pencils, bought any erasers or notebooks or any of the other things I would need. I didn't know we were supposed to. And Mom . . ." I paused again, this time exhaling loudly. I licked my lips, pressing them into a tight line. "It's just something we hadn't done."

This was painful, the remembering. But for some reason I didn't understand, I wanted to tell Elizabeth what it was like. The burden of carrying the disappointments alone had become too great.

"On that first day, when I walked into the classroom, Mom hovering somewhere behind me, and noted the stuff the other kids had, the collection of school bags, desk accessories, things that I'd need, things that I suddenly wanted, I immediately felt out of place. Worst of all, I knew that all of those other kids, the ones that were going to populate this new world, the big, shiny promising one I'd been waiting for to replace the small, dark one at home . . . well, I knew they noticed as well. They saw exactly what I didn't have."

I raised my hands to my cheeks, feeling the very same hot rush of shame I'd felt back then, remembering how I'd hunched my shoulders and tucked in my chin, trying to shrink to invisible. I'd wanted to disappear, to be anywhere but there. But kids, being kids, wouldn't let me.

• • •

"Where's your stuff?"

I had just turned seven. A girl with long blond pigtails and very blue eyes was standing next to my desk, gripping a bright-pink pencil case. She waved it vaguely in my direction. "You're supposed to organize your stuff." She marched over to her own desk and pulled open the top. "Look! Mine's all set up. See?" She beckoned to me, eager to show off her handiwork. I put one hand on my own desk, a bit afraid that once abandoned, it might disappear, then stretched my neck as far as it would go so that I could peer inside hers. The display before me was dazzling. There were yellow pencils with sharpened points lined up like soldiers at the ready, magic markers arranged according to the colors of the rainbow, a stack of notebooks anchored by a miniature purple stapler, a bottle of Elmer's glue with its tip still sealed in plastic, and a shiny ruler decorated with moons and stars. There were so many things there to be admired. This girl was so lucky. I was deeply envious.

"Hey! Where's your stuff? I'll help you. I've already finished arranging mine." I looked up into her face, noticing the big gaping hole in the middle of her upper teeth. I had the same. Maybe that was enough common ground. Maybe we could be friends.

I hesitated, unsure of how to reply, trying to figure out a way to keep her interested. But I had nothing comparable to offer, no sparkle, no glitter, nothing. My desk was pathetically empty. I mumbled a few words, hoping they would prolong this welcome contact and simultaneously put her off the trail. I didn't want her to know how ill-prepared I was.

"Oh. We were just away, Mommy and me. We didn't have a chance to pick up my school things. We're going to do it later today." I paused and glanced behind me, toward the doorway, searching for the frail figure that had haunted its frame a few minutes earlier. A lump formed in my throat. She wasn't there. My mother had left me to fend for myself.

I quickly searched for a way to redirect the conversation so that this girl wouldn't pick up on my distress. "Your pencils are so sparkly." I gestured to those with silver-bound erasers, each adorned with miniature silver streamers and dangly silver stars. "May I?"

At my new friend's hesitant nod, I reached in and picked one up, twirling it between my fingers. The streamers spun, suspended in midair, their movement hypnotizing. I could have stood there and spun them forever, letting them work their magic and lift me upward, higher and higher, to another world. But I knew that wasn't possible. There was no make-believe. I handed the pencil back to the girl.

"I really like these. I'll see if I can find some as well. Then we'll both have them."

"My mommy can tell you where to get them." She spun around with a little jump, whipped her head from one side to another, and called out in the general direction of the bank of parents stationed on the fringes of the classroom. A woman with the same shade of blond hair, hers cut short in a neat bob, made her way between the desks to join us, reaching out and giving her daughter's pigtail a playful tug. The little girl's face lit up and she crooned with pleasure. I felt a sharp pain in my chest. "Mommy. This is my friend. She *loves* my silver pencils. Can you tell her where to find them?"

The blond woman turned to face me. "Hi, sweetie. What's your name?"

I wasn't used to much attention, or, for that matter, any at all. I panicked and stared at her, mouth agape. The thought of a mother who was available and attentive to my needs, a mother who wouldn't have abandoned me on this important day, was positively overwhelming.

"Dear?"

Stunned by this momentary show of interest, I almost forgot I was expected to answer. The woman's outstretched hand brought me back to the present.

"I'm Julie," I whispered. Our hands met.

"Nice to meet you, Julie. I'm Maya's mom." I melted with pleasure and, overcome by an oozing warmth, tugged on my collar a bit. This was what it was like, a real mom—the kind I dreamed of every night when I tucked myself in, hugging Teddy, giving him a kiss and whispering an urgent "Sleep tight!" I squeezed the woman's hand in reply, maybe a bit too strongly, then quickly disengaged, fearing my eagerness would be a turnoff, extinguishing that sudden, glorious expression of tenderness. I peeked back over my shoulder toward the door. Nothing. A brutal chill replaced that scrumptious sensation of warmth. I struggled to conceal my feelings, to hide my shame, replacing my disappointed frown with a radiant smile. It was this that I directed toward the nice lady with the blond hair who seemed to care.

• • •

The warmth and the subsequent chill; the vision of what I so desperately wanted and the need to make do with everything that was missing; the effort to hide my embarrassment and my secrets; the knowledge that I'd never be like everyone else, never have what they had—all of this rushed through me at once as I shared my story with Elizabeth. Finished, I looked around the library, soaking up the peace and quiet, trying to calm the turmoil roused by these memories.

"School was never what it was supposed to be. It probably never will be. Because it's never been about me. Even on that first day, I realized that no one really noticed the girl completely unprepared for first grade, unable to brandish even one simple yellow pencil. Instead, all they saw was my mother, absent even when present, and her odd behavior, the way she slunk around the edges of the room as if trying to press herself into one of the cubbies and disappear, while the rest of the parents, jittery with excitement, formed a circle of protection and support behind their kids as we perched on our tiny chairs for our first circle time, ready for the meet and greet. Even back then, the brutality of my world alarmed me."

I paused, again transported back to that day. "When I couldn't find my mother, I began to panic. I didn't understand that finding her would make it worse. When I finally spotted her, wedged into the doorway, half hidden in the shadows and most definitely not a part of the parents' circle, I became even more distressed. She looked so pale, like a ghost. And her hands—one of them was clutching the doorjamb, holding on for dear life; her knuckles were paper white, the same shade as her face. Her presence in that room at this very important moment in my life was so negligible."

I stopped again and frowned. "Negligible. Can I say that? It's something so small as to be unimportant, right?"

Elizabeth nodded in silence and, although offering a half smile of agreement, looked completely stricken. My tale was not pretty. I pressed on to the finish. "I was seven. But I already understood that if I looked away for a second, she might disappear. Worse, in any meaningful way, she wasn't really there."

Sinking into a silence heavy with the sorrow of my story, I was almost startled when Elizabeth spoke.

"Oh, Julie. It's so hard to imagine. As a mother, that first day, it's just, well, it's the same for us parents as it was for you. We're just as nervous, just as excited. The thought that your mother couldn't partake, couldn't bring herself to be part of it all, at least for you . . ." Her voice cracked as she faltered, running out of words to convey her sadness.

I pulled my hand away and placed it in my lap. I didn't want her pity. I chided myself for being dragged into telling this old, boring story. "You should know, none of this was a surprise. I knew it would happen just that way, that first day in Mrs. Anderson's classroom. The mistake was thinking it might be otherwise."

Elizabeth bristled, obviously put out by the sudden frostiness of my tone. But I didn't care. I didn't want her warmth at that moment, her consolation. She couldn't make it all go away, no matter how much she tried. There was a long history here that she could never erase.

"And this was only one day. There were so many others just like it. My mother was always somewhere along the periphery, or bowing out of events, sending me in advance with others and then failing to show up later as promised. I think that if she'd had her way, she would have given the whole mothering business a pass. In any case, she was never suited to fill that role. It was just me being stupid, wasting time believing, or hoping, that things could be different. I just really wanted to have a mommy like everyone else's."

I still remembered how awful it felt to realize that Mom wasn't going to make even the most minimal effort to be like the other parents, to help me get first grade off to a normal start. At that early age, I didn't understand that she couldn't. It took years for me to realize the extent of her incapacity. But the resentment and disappointment I felt that first day, the recognition that I'd forever be hindered by being stuck with this particular mother, began to fester into an anger that over time exceeded all normal proportions. I stared down at my hands, noticing how they clung to one another beneath the table, seeking some bit of stability.

"For the longest time, I thought it was my fault. In fact, I was sure of it."

"Oh, Julie. It had nothing to do with you." Elizabeth's tone was soft, her words more an entreaty than a statement. I found her readiness with quick platitudes almost annoying.

"What do you know?" I couldn't hold back this flash of anger. "How dare you? Your mother was there for you. Always. I just know it by looking at your forehead. It's so smooth. So unwrinkled. What do you know of what I've been through? What I'm still going through."

I picked up the book on the table and slammed it down hard, then pushed my chair back and stood. Heads at nearby tables turned toward us in alarm. I'd managed to disturb the space I myself deemed sacred. "I should never have opened up to you. What a mistake!"

Elizabeth stood in alarm, her forehead no longer smooth at all, thick lines burrowing across its surface. "Wait! Julie! Please! Give me a chance. Give us a chance."

I stopped cold, unsure of what to do. Half of me hated her for trying to be a part of my life. Half of me wanted it more than air to breathe. I gripped the back of the chair and turned. Her eyes were damp, tears pooling unrestrained. I wanted to leap into her lap, wrap my arms around her neck, and hold on tight.

She pushed the book gently toward me. "Take it with you."

I paused only a second or two. I understood the gesture. She wasn't going anywhere. She would be here no matter what. I just wasn't sure how to stay. I grabbed the book off the table and left.

LILLIAN

"HELLO?" I HUNKERED BEHIND THE front door, not sure whether I should open it. I couldn't imagine who was there. At first, I assumed it was a mistake and stayed comfy in bed. But when the knocking became insistent, I forced myself to get up and explore.

"Yes?" I waited for a response. The garbled murmurs beyond the heavy door were impossible to decipher.

"Can I help you?" I tried again, raising my voice a bit, eager to figure out what this was about and get back to bed. *Three in the morning! Such an ungodly hour!* "Who's there? Who are you? What do you want?" There was absolutely no way I was opening the door at this hour without knowing who was there. The only comfort was that they'd had to get by the doorman. It must be one of my neighbors.

"Mrs. Berkin? It's Quinn. I'm a friend of Belle's."

Well. Okay. I exhaled with relief. At least now I knew it wasn't a mistake, or worse, a prank. "Quinn?" I hadn't met Quinn yet, but I'd heard her name mentioned. Belle went out quite a bit but never brought anyone back to the apartment. I had found that to be rather a relief—less noise, less mess. But lately I had begun to wonder if keeping my space clear of teenagers was the right move. I didn't know anything about what went on with her outside of Julliard, the only access I had to her life being the glorious sounds that came out of her bedroom.

I tightened the sash of my robe and patted my hair down, hoping it wasn't worse than middle-of-the-night disorderly. This wasn't an hour I usually had to look presentable. I took another quick peek at my watch as I unlocked the door, trying to remember when I'd last seen this ghastly time, and considered whether it was too late to ask this Quinn to come back in the morning.

"I've got Belle here. She needs your help."

That was all it took to change my annoyance to alarm. I immediately tugged on the door, swinging it wide open. Belle was nowhere to be found. I breathed a sigh of relief. I don't know why I believed her, why I panicked. I knew she was inside, sound asleep. Momentarily calmed, I took a good look at the two girls standing before me, both about my granddaughter's age, dressed almost identically in blue jeans and black blouses so tiny as to suggest they'd shrunk in the dryer. They looked distinctly worse for the wear—mascara smeared, hair mussed. I made a mental note to speak with Belle about the disturbing dishevelment of today's youth, about how much was too much makeup. The two just stared back at me, not in any particular hurry, shuffling their feet, looking uncomfortable.

"There must be a mistake. Belle is here. She's sleeping."

My patience waned. With an exaggerated flick of my wrist, I looked at my watch. I wanted to make sure they saw that I was put out, that it was intolerably late, that this wasn't a time for games. Seeing as how everyone was in one piece, I stepped backward, grasping the front door to close it back up. I wanted to put this whole unwelcome disturbance behind me.

"Wait!" One of the girls extended her arm as if to block the door and swung her head to the right. I followed the line of her gesture down the hall toward the elevators. There was something there, on the floor—an amorphous shape that resembled a large pile of laundry. *Why did they shed their coats there in the hallway?* But as I refocused my attention on the girls to question them, I discerned the very slightest movement.

Now I was alert. Something was up. I looked closer at the girls, gazing from one to the other. "What is that? What's going on?" They remained mute, their faces completely blank, offering no hint whatsoever to explain the mass at the end of the hall. I'd have to figure this out by myself.

Stepping around them, I briskly walked the few paces toward the elevator, determined to put an end to this once and for all. But when I saw those Vans, I gasped aloud in alarm.

"Yeah." The girls had followed me. "That's Belle. We were happy we got her this far. It was quite an effort." That first girl, the one who'd spoken before, cocked her head to the side as if this were a completely natural event. Nothing new here. If anything, the two looked bored. They were obviously hopeful that, having delivered their package, they could put this whole episode behind them and go home.

A torrent of questions flooded my head as I knelt, gently moving aside a clump of limp hair in order to verify that this heaving heap was my granddaughter. "Does someone want to tell me what happened?"

I didn't wait for an answer to my whispered question, shifting to the other side to get a better look. Belle's head slouched so low it was almost swallowed by her torso, uncannily reminding me of the illustration of the snake that had eaten an elephant from *The Little Prince*. But unfortunately, this wasn't a children's novel, and in reality she was out cold. If not for the regular movements I discerned beneath the layers of clothing, I would have run to call an ambulance. I let out an audible sigh of relief. At least she was breathing. In consideration of whatever partying had gone on, and from what I could see it had been excessive, this was something for which to be thankful.

"You know. Well." More shuffling behind me. "She just drank too much. We needed to get her home." The words drifted my way like an afterthought. I was amazed at the nonchalance of these girls.

I leaned in closer, intending to reach out and help Belle stand, but quickly stepped back. A rancid smell indicated that she'd been ill. This was all incredibly unpleasant. I stood, tugging at my robe, pulling it closed from neckline to waist in an effort to maintain a degree of dignity within an extremely undignified situation.

Part of me wanted to walk back to my apartment and close the door on this whole ugly encounter. But I knew that wasn't a choice. I had to deal with the immediate problems: how to move Belle's crumpled, uncooperative body into the apartment and then see her through what was sure to be a rocky night. Once again, I wondered how I'd ever thought it feasible to raise a teenager at my age. I sighed heavily, knowing this wasn't a helpful line of thought. Foolhardy decision or not, I had assumed responsibility for Belle and had to deal with the fallout. I turned and looked back at her friends still lurking behind me. Having completed their mission, they looked lost.

"Are you two okay? This was very kind of you, taking care of Belle. Can I help you get home?"

The other one answered. "No. Thank you. We're okay. We can manage on our own."

Quinn laughed, then hiccupped, then grabbed at the wall, looking like she might be sick. That's when I realized that neither of them was sober. Belle was simply much farther gone.

"Are you sure? Is there no one you want to call? I can call someone for you." I reached out toward the second girl. "What's your name? I'm sorry, I don't know you."

She straightened up, looking nervous. "Emma. Hi. But no. It's really okay. We'll just be on our way." She immediately turned, stepping around Belle and pushing the button to call the elevator.

Quinn grabbed her arm. "Just a sec, Em. Let's get her inside. There's no way she can handle it alone."

Although increasingly appalled by this whole scene and by being dismissed with that off-hand "*she*," I was relieved. There really was no way I could move Belle on my own. Although very slight, her present state of intoxication reduced her to dead weight.

"Oh, that would be wonderful. I'm not sure I can manage. She's . . ." My voice petered out for a moment. "She's, well, we can all see how she is."

An awkward moment of humor passed between us. None of this was funny, but the current scene—an odd, middle-of-the-night gathering of unrelated characters representing disparate generations contemplating how to move a pile of skin and bones from point A to point B—was ridiculous enough to be amusing. Aiming for something closer to supportive friend than judgmental parent seemed the smartest way to ensure their cooperation. I gestured toward my apartment and invited them to follow.

The elevator door opened. We all looked up in surprise. It was Ed, the doorman with the unfortunate overnight shift. "Need any help?"

There was a round of audible sighs of relief. "How did you know?"

He pointed up to a camera at the very end of the hallway. "I didn't. But since the girls stumbled in with . . . Well, I've been keeping my eyes peeled. You didn't seem to be progressing, so I locked up downstairs and came up to check." He looked down at Belle. "Let me help you get her in."

Ed picked Belle up from behind and nodded at the girls, who took the cue and grabbed her dangling feet. The three of them struggled a bit to get a grip on this droopy version of my granddaughter before bumping their way up the hallway toward my apartment. Once inside, I directed them through the inky shadows to Belle's bedroom and watched as they unceremoniously dumped her on the bed. "That's fine. I'll take it from here." With my initial alarm and fear behind me, I'd already begun to dream about finishing this unpleasant chapter and getting back to sleep. I accompanied the truly motley crew back to the door and again asked if there was someone I could call. Assured that they'd cope on their own, I instructed Ed to put the girls in a cab home on my account and bid them all goodnight.

I stared at the elevator a full minute after the doors closed, making sure it was well en route, then stepped back into my apartment. Overwhelmed by a combination of enervation, relief, and anguish, I closed my eyes and rested my forehead on the back of the door. The peace of the enveloping silence belied the seriousness of the situation. This event had opened a very large can of worms. There was no question that I'd taken the whole idea of guardianship far too lightly, assuming that it would boil down to making sure Belle did her homework and attended school, highlighted by invitations to concerts and fancy cocktail parties. I figured it would be all glitter and stars, never once conceiving as gritty a situation as the one at hand.

Beyond the immediate considerations, the fact that I still had to make sure Belle didn't need to be taken to the hospital, were the long-term ones that I would have to address tomorrow: the question of how to make clear that this kind of behavior was absolutely unacceptable and the exploration of what had incited this extraordinary young woman, heading for an esteemed career as a violist, to drink herself into oblivion. It had been a long time since I'd had to deal with a seriously intoxicated teenager, an experience I'd hoped was long behind me. I was lucky with Elizabeth; she wasn't so hell-bent on pushing my buttons. There was an occasion or two when she came home slightly tipsy, but nothing as serious as this. And of course, I'd never experienced such a state myself. The idea of losing control to such a degree was anathema to me.

I sighed heavily as I headed back to Belle's room and then quickly shifted into gear, all business, hoping to finish up quickly and manage a few hours of sleep. First thing was to make sure Belle was okay. I took stock of what needed to be done, starting with making her more comfortable. I wrestled her out of her shoes and her clothes best I could, smiling when I spotted her little black blouse. It was almost exactly like the ones her friends were wearing. It was funny how these kids insisted on their individuality but consistently wanted to look the same. Moving her around was hard work. Winded, I took a breather, sitting next to her on the edge of the bed.

I closed my eyes, letting the darkness of the room envelop me, and then opened them to find a slender triangle of moonlight on Belle's face. It highlighted her smooth brow, one small ear, and the side of her upturned nose. I checked to make sure the blanket wasn't covering her mouth, then gently stroked her hair, tucking the strands that had come loose from her ponytail neatly behind her ears. Belle looked so much like Elizabeth. Their noses were different, but their ears were almost identical, and they both had those charming little pouches of skin under their eyes. I hadn't had too many opportunities to touch Belle in such an intimate fashion and was startled to realize that I couldn't remember the last time Elizabeth and I had any physical contact at all. Moments of closeness between she and I dated mostly to those years she'd still snuggle in bed with me at the end of the day for a nighttime story.

Of course, there was that one instance from her late teenage years: a night I'd sat next to her in a similar darkness, feeling just as helpless as I did now. This was at the end of a very difficult period. Elizabeth was seventeen, maybe eighteen. Something had happened, something bad. She didn't tell me so explicitly, but I felt it deep down in my gut, as only a mother can. There'd been a distinct feeling of heaviness about her for several days, something unusually off. She lurked around the house, lying on the couch, flipping through the TV channels, enveloped in a cloak of silence. I tried to talk to her and break through her silence, but to no avail. She waved me off again and again, assuring me it was nothing—just a headache. Unaware of what might have sparked such an extreme withdrawal, my mind raced with the possibilities, none of them pleasant. I discarded each in turn as impossible. Yet still, it was obvious that something very serious was troubling her.

During the days that followed, Elizabeth absolutely refused to share, insisting instead on keeping whatever she considered unspeakable to herself. I wanted to be the kind of mother capable of handling any news, but my daughter, assuming that I couldn't, shut me out, whispering that there was nothing I could do. When I finally figured it out, when the pieces clicked together and I had a clear picture, I couldn't let it go. What mother could? This kind of thing wasn't supposed to happen to *my* daughter, the one I was raising to be a superstar, to succeed where I had failed.

It was imperative she did the right thing, and I made that clear. Although we rarely spoke about it out loud, resorting instead to a penetrating look here and there and the occasional plea for sanity that I worked into idle conversations in the house, I made my opinion clear. "You're throwing away your life." "You can't seriously be considering this." "You have no idea what it means to raise a child. This will end your dreams." I tried hard to neither lecture nor scream in frustration. I knew this would lose me precious ground. But I was desperate to make my point. I knew better than anyone else how the wrong decision could derail her life forever.

Elizabeth ignored me for the most part, sharing only a solemn face, a shrug of dismissal, and an occasional look of pain. I could see she was debating, trying to figure this out as if it were just one more complicated algebra problem. It was there in her creased brow, in that cloud of consternation that crossed her face the minute I opened my mouth to speak.

But there was nothing to figure out. No one brought a baby into this world in high school, most certainly not my daughter. Once she made the decision, took it upon herself to get the deed done, I was inordinately relieved. She'd spared me having to deal with the sordid details, the ugly consequences of her bad choices, the shame of a child born to a mother out of wedlock. As far as I was concerned, Elizabeth could now move beyond this agonizing period and get back to the exciting future that lay ahead. At the time, I hadn't known that this episode would forever seal the stalemate in which we were still locked today.

Sitting here beside Belle in the darkness, both concerned and relieved, brought me straight back to the night after the procedure, after hours spent waiting under that fluorescent light, when Elizabeth wobbled my way and told me it was time to go home. Having nothing left to say, our pain sealed tightly in a secret we'd never reveal, I came to her room with no agenda, sitting quietly at the foot of her bed. How inordinately grateful I was when she moved over a bit to make room, showing me that she wanted me there, that I was welcome. In the end, the brief moments of intimacy we shared at that time offered confirmation of a tangled but extant bond. Mothers and daughters needed to be there for one another even when words could not be found.

I did now as I'd done back then, offering what I could to my sleeping granddaughter: the warmth of my touch, the comfort and steadfastness of my presence with its promise of protection. Yet I couldn't stymy the deep fear that she was heading down the wrong path, getting drunk and God knows what else. I wondered if it was time to share the story that could stop Belle's path of destruction.

I knew there'd be a price. It was clear that Elizabeth wanted this to stay between us.

My groggy musing was interrupted by a sudden change in Belle's breathing, a staccato of short wheezes that sounded strained and unnatural. I panicked, realizing that maybe the situation was more precarious than I had imagined. Using both hands, I stroked her back vigorously, hoping to stem the tide of whatever was making her choke, all the time wondering whether I should wake her up, make her drink a bit of water, even try to get her to throw up again. But just as I was ready to spring into action, her breathing returned to a less alarming rhythm. I exhaled in relief, noting the steadying of my own irregular heartbeat.

Satisfied that Belle could be left alone for a few moments, I stepped out of the room and went to the kitchen, searching through the cabinets for a large pot and a towel. Preparation for the worst was my forte. I set these up by the side of the bed and resumed my watch, hand in place on her back, attentive to the rise and fall of her torso.

Although I was certain this vigilance would suffice for the present, I knew it eventually wouldn't be enough. In the light of day, I'd be forced to assume the role of guardian. I would have been happy to leave that to Elizabeth and Mike. I was never good at handling circumstances not of my own design, didn't like being dragged into others' unpleasantries. In bold fact, I wasn't the least bit equipped to take on the mothering of a teenager.

Overcome by a wave of exhaustion, I pushed these troublesome thoughts away. My granddaughter was safe, sleeping soundly here by my side. She was going to be just fine come morning and would go right back to being a prickly teenager. And although I wanted to be angry with her, frustrated by this latest escapade, I couldn't help but admire her pluck. The willingness to discard everything that was comfortable and jump into deep waters reminded me a great deal of myself, half a century earlier. I too had wanted to go off into the wider world, conquer new challenges, and reach for the stars. This courageous girl out cold next to me was something I recognized and applauded—so different from my own daughter, a child cut from a completely different mold. This grandchild of mine made sense in a way her mother never had.

After one more quick check of Belle's breathing, I dragged my blanket and pillow in from my bedroom and looked for a way to make myself more comfortable. I couldn't leave her to sleep alone. I had to be there, just in case. I glanced around what had previously been the guest room, now indelibly marked by Belle's personal touches. She'd just recently hung an enormous poster of the Great Plains—all sky, undisturbed by even one tree. On the bedside table was a retro lava lamp she'd insisted I buy. It looked just like the one Elizabeth had bought at around the same age. Pots full of makeup and hairclips crowded the dresser top, and the music stand was set up before the full-length mirror I'd insisted we buy. Every young star needed to know how she appeared to her audience.

I knelt gingerly by the bed, thankful that I'd chosen plush carpeting, and arranged my comforter, making a kind of nest. I couldn't remember the last time I'd slept on the floor or whether I'd ever slept on the floor—maybe during summer camp. Trying not to think about the dust and critters that might be lurking, lulled by Belle's one-woman concert of polyphonic sounds, I finally gave in to the wooziness of fatigue and fell asleep.

JULIE

I SLID MY FINGER ALONG the letters as I read, leaving it precisely where I stopped before anxiously looking up at Elizabeth. I was pretty sure I'd nailed it, especially that last section, but wasn't entirely certain. I was delighted to see her smile.

"Congratulations!"

I exhaled loudly, reassured, and slumped back into my chair.

"That was a rough passage, but you did it without a hitch. Oh, Julie. I'm so proud of you. All that hard work has paid off."

I turned my eyes back to the page open on the desk before me, my finger still poised on the period at the end of that final sentence. Everything had changed. And it wasn't just my reading, although I'd made real headway with that. After fumbling for years, trying to make sense of the words, the letters shifting direction the second I had them figured out, their patterns suddenly seemed clear. My tutor, the woman I recently started calling by her first name—at her insistence, of course—had somehow helped me still the movement of lines on paper and decipher the hidden code. I'd never be able to thank her enough. By helping me learn to read properly, she'd obliterated one of the many things about which I was mercilessly teased at school. It was a small victory, but a significant one.

Elizabeth leaned toward me and playfully tapped her head on my shoulder. I shuddered just a little; I couldn't help myself. It was hard to get used to physical signs of affection, even though from her they'd become welcome. Spending hours hunched together over one text or another, it was only natural we'd become closer, but Elizabeth made a point of extending the boundaries of our relationship. Just recently she'd moved from her spot across the table to one by my side. Now her shadow joined with mine, falling over the page as I read, the last remaining barrier between us quietly erased. Although this startled me every time, never going unnoticed, it felt right.

That didn't mean that I wasn't afraid, that I'd completely let down my guard. Not trusting that it could last, not trusting myself not to ruin it, I kept my head straight and restrained myself from reciprocating her loving gestures, afraid of completely giving in to her warmth and assigning her a role too significant. I knew better than anyone else that moments of intimacy didn't necessarily add up to a relationship. Plus, what I didn't need was another mom. I already had one, and that hadn't gone too well. It was probably best to keep things clean, to keep the already fuzzy lines between us from blurring completely. Elizabeth was helping me with my reading. She was a kind woman. That was all. And in fact, that was quite a lot.

I wiggled my shoulder a bit, shrugging away her gesture of familiarity, then spotted a flicker of sadness in her eyes before she looked away. I hoped I hadn't hurt her feelings, again. I'd already done that quite a few times. I couldn't help myself. It was hard to understand why she persisted in trying.

"When's the next lit class?"

I cleared my throat. "Actually, I don't have to worry about those anymore. The other kids, you know, even the teacher . . ." I paused and looked into her eyes. "They just assume I'll screw up. They skip me when they go around the room." I shrugged and raised my eyebrows for a moment, trying to convince her that I didn't care. She didn't buy it for a second.

"But they don't need to skip you." Pushing the book between us aside, she reached over and tapped my hand. "Julie, you can participate! This is something you can do." Elizabeth lit up with exhilaration and satisfaction.

I wanted to believe her. But I couldn't risk exposing myself to the kind of mockery it would provoke, the consequent pain so bad it felt as if my heart were trapped in a vice—the inevitable explosion that followed. She'd never understand that.

"No." I emphasized my words by vigorously shaking my head side to side. "I don't think so. It doesn't matter that it's all gotten a bit easier." I tentatively stretched my hand toward hers, giving it a little tap of affirmation. I wasn't one for making such moves, but I was desperate to get her off this subject. "It's all because of you. I'm so grateful. It's not important that the others know what we're doing here. They're happy to skip me, and I think it's probably better that I don't take the chance. If I mess up, one little mistake, they'll be all over me—just like before. I really don't need that." I shook my head more fervently, feeling the truth of my conviction. No, I most definitely did not need that. I lowered my voice. "I don't want to go there again."

Some of the girls had eased up a bit. There were fewer taunts, fewer shoves, fewer jokes about having been abandoned by my mother. There was less teasing about my difficulty sounding out words that fourth graders could handle. Having been at school for a bit longer, I was no longer new bait. There were always more recent arrivals providing new opportunities for those who thrived on drawing blood. I was not the most enticing prey. Boring them was probably as good as it was going to get.

"Well, I think we should try to reintegrate you into the class, show those jerks what you can do. You've worked so hard." Elizabeth laid her hands on my own, lightly, as if carried on the wings of angels. I drank in her long, narrow fingers, tidy nails, the raised veins lacing the back of her hands, actively pumping with the passion behind her words. I couldn't recall my mom ever touching me in such a manner, or much at all; didn't remember her trying to convey in such a fervent way her love, her devotion, her belief that I could go out there and live a life. I'd never known anything quite as awesome as Elizabeth's touch at this moment. It somehow made me feel even sadder, truly defeated.

"Julie. You must realize how far you've come." She exerted a bit more pressure on my hands, as if she sensed I was drifting away and wanted to tow me back in. "We've conquered so many of the patterns that kept you from progressing, that caused you to stumble." Obviously trying to lighten the serious mood, she knocked sharply on the table twice and adopted a more jovial tone. "We've whipped them right in shape!"

I couldn't resist smiling in response but immediately sobered up, my face settling into its habitual frown. "You don't know the half of it." *How could she?* I pulled my hands away and placed them in my lap, the surge of self-confidence I'd felt upon completing my reading for the day dissolving into thin air. There was no way that this lovely woman with her normal and perfect family could understand my outbursts, the pain behind them—what it felt like to have no mothering, to have no one see me soar as well as stumble. She could never understand the extent to which my life had been altered even before I was born, creating a storm inside me that couldn't be quelled.

• • •

"Drop something?"

There was a tittering sound, almost a cackle, behind me. I couldn't see who was there, but I could guess. I stretched my arm as far as it would go, reaching down to the floor while keeping my head raised. I needed to be vigilant, ready in case whoever it was did something worse than throw my book. My fingers grasped at the binding, at the awkwardly splayed pages. I succeeded in putting it back on the desk, pressing its crumpled pages flat.

"All set now?"

I ignored these comments like I'd ignored all the others. They'd been coming for days now, an endless stream of them. I longed for the silence I'd been met with upon my arrival at GF Central High, that brief period when they'd left me alone, given me space to find my way. But the grace period had ended, and I was now fair game, ripe for the picking. And although I thought I'd get used to the cutting, snide words hurled my way, inure myself to the onslaught, I just couldn't. They were endless.

If it wasn't in the classroom, it was out on the front green. I heard them on my way into school, first thing in the morning, throughout what seemed like an endless school day, and until I'd cleared the grounds of the campus in the late afternoon on my way back to the Center. I knew the kids were trying to get under my skin—knew there was some quasi-organized effort to provoke an aggressive response and get me in trouble. What I didn't know was how they knew which buttons to press.

Some rumor about my tendency to blow up must have circulated before my arrival, prompted by an investigation into my unusual midyear entry. Of course, it was conceivable that they just didn't like me. That hurt a lot more but made sense. After all, I was there because I had to leave my home, because my mother didn't want to live with me. I wasn't the kind of daughter she wanted. Maybe I was simply the kind of person no one liked. These girls at school found my presence irritating and wanted me gone.

I spread my hands wide over the book, my fingertips blanching as they gripped its edges. There wasn't much I could do but brace myself, hold my ground, and, most importantly, contain my fury. But I couldn't escape the inevitable. I was doomed to explode; there was no way to contain this degree of frustration forever. Flipping open the book to a random page, I tried to focus on the words. That was a mistake. Confused by the letters that seemed to shift and move out of place, I felt even worse. I took a deep breath, trying to calm down enough to focus on the task at hand, to get those black lines to line up properly and behave.

There was no question that things at this new school would have gone smoother if I'd been able to conquer this one demon. The trouble had started my first weeks at school, when I was desperately trying to maintain as low a profile as possible. The ninth-grade lit teacher, Ms. Merion, insisted we take turns reading. This exercise was intended to get everyone involved and help us make meaningful attachments to the characters in the texts. But for me, it was nothing short of a nightmare. It wasn't that I didn't love stories, because I did. For as long as I could remember, I clung to descriptions, read to me by one teacher or another, of fabulous lands and kingdoms different from my own, dreamy places that lay tantalizingly beyond my grasp.

When it was my turn, I bravely made a stab at it.

"She can't read."

That first comment came from somewhere down the row. I was reading a text by John Updike that I'd enjoyed in the past. I ignored it and continued, stumbling over the words, determined to get through one paragraph.

"You're kidding me."

That remark was followed by muffled chuckling. I looked up to see where it was coming from, then looked over at the teacher. She urged me on with a nod, but I'd had enough. Fumbling the passage had given the other kids more than enough ammunition to make my already tenuous existence at school more miserable. Of course, I'd known it was only a matter of time before my weakness was discovered and the ridicule commenced.

Sitting there, book in hand, I envisioned giving in to the kind of violent reaction I knew I had to put behind me, submitting to the pleasure of the explosion with its consequent sensation of release. The continual barrage I'd suffered for weeks had created an enormous hole inside of me, leaving plenty of room for the anger I was meant to keep at bay. The potential to lose control was always there, but I dug deep and went through the steps I'd learned at the Meier Center. The staff there was helping me find ways to shut out the threatening voices without silencing them myself; to bear up and contain my strongest urges. I focused on an invisible spot at the front of the classroom, took a few deep breaths, and counted to twenty, just as I'd done the day before when, for the umpteenth time, that Ali girl had mocked me, telling me I was dumb.

"What's that smell?"

There it was. Another jibe. This one pathetic, even juvenile. I struggled not to smile, knowing that would give whoever it was one more reason to come down hard. These kids were sometimes so amateur, their comments direct quotes from those "mean girl" movies. It was almost like they were playing a part and had no genuine interest in making me miserable. I amused myself by thinking this way, finding something comical in my predicament. In any case, it was a lot better than suffering through as the perpetual victim. I concentrated my physical response on my mouth, pressing my lips together into a line, ensuring that nothing, not one word, would escape. I knew from experience that provoking them in any way only made matters worse. That's how I'd gotten here in the first place.

Almost holding my breath in an attempt to contain my emotions and the reaction that was bursting to be released, I was completely caught off guard when someone shoved me from behind. I lurched forward, gripping the sides of my desk to keep from falling, watching my book fly and once again land on the floor. I forced myself to look straight ahead, back at that imaginary spot at the front of the room, to do anything but turn and make eye contact with whoever had pushed me. And then, I prayed. That was really the only thing left to do. I prayed that the teacher would arrive and start class. She was the only one capable of ending this torture.

"Cat got your tongue? Nothing to say for yourself?"

I bit down hard on my lower lip until I tasted blood, licking at it with my tongue, moving its bitterness into the deep recesses of my mouth. I relished the control it represented. Clenching my teeth, I vowed yet again that I wouldn't let them get the best of me. They wanted me to crack and lash out, but I wouldn't. Not this time. This time would be different.

But that didn't mean that I couldn't picture exactly how this might play out—the way I'd pick that book up off the floor again but, this time, instead of straightening out its pages, grip it tightly in my hand and, in one graceful movement, swing it with all my force. I could feel the rush of wind caused by the rapid movement, anticipate the impact. It would be so satisfying when it slammed into that girl's face, releasing the ballistic knot of tension inside me. And indeed, this was precisely how it had been in the past, back at my old school, when I'd exacted similar punishments. No other response offered such an overwhelming, cathartic sense of release. The memory alone calmed me from head to toe, momentarily erasing the strain of this current predicament.

"Idiot."

I heard laughter from one side of the room, and then the other. My forced calm began to disintegrate. No one wanted me here. This was excruciatingly hard. But I was determined not to break—not this time.

Letting myself explode with all the anger pent up inside had gotten me thrown out of school, removed from my home, separated from my mother. All of that was my fault. I was the reason I lost the only real base I'd ever had. The present was bad, really bad; but the fear that things could get worse motivated me to hold it together just a little longer.

I silently urged myself to stay focused on my goal. I wanted to go home, back to my mom. At least there I understood the threats to my stability; at least inside our house I knew how to contain them. Giving in to the animalistic need to show the world just how much I hurt wasn't going to get me there. The teachers at my old school, the principal, and the social worker who had been called in to pick up the debris I left behind made this abundantly clear.

My mind wandered, lingering on the memory of that beastly girl, wondering whether the stitches she'd needed left a scar—whether I'd defaced her permanently. A wicked half smile replaced the taut expression of frustration and effort. I didn't care that she'd been hurt. She deserved what she got. She'd been torturing me for weeks, mostly about my reading, calling me a moron, an imbecile. But it was her last comment about my mother, reminding me of that embarrassing scene at the spring picnic, that caused me to explode.

That event had officially exposed my mother's absence as well as her strangeness to everyone at school. Before then, no one was the wiser. After all, Fay looked like all the other mothers, relatively put together, her clothes appropriate, attractive enough. But there by the fire pit, her disconnection and tangential hold on this world was laid bare. While everyone else milled around, loading up grilling spears with marshmallows, stuffing hotdogs into doughy rolls, my mother skulked behind the splayed canvas chairs, overwhelmed, even dwarfed by all the activity, her lack of participation noted by all. Horrified at the whole scene, I wished she hadn't come at all. Maybe if we'd given the event a pass, the others wouldn't have caught on to my secret—that I lived in a universe completely different from theirs.

An ear-splitting screech, the sliding of tables and chairs being shuffled into place as the students took their seats, signaled that my prayers had been met. I snapped to attention, immediately back in the present, energized by the sudden shift in the tide. I'd been saved. I'd managed to keep these vultures at bay, at least for the time being. Ms. Merion sat back on the edge of her large desk and took a head count. One more respite. I could relax.

This was how I worked my way through each day: holding my breath, playing it cool, trying not to fly into a rage, and focusing on an undefined point ahead of me—one foot carefully following another.

I sat a bit straighter in my chair, proud of myself. The fact that I hadn't smacked the girl who shoved me, nor the one who'd thrown my book on the floor in the first place, was to be celebrated. The next step was to not read aloud. It was enough to just try to survive as the new kid, the one on whom everyone focused, the one with the story everyone wanted to hear, then distort, then spread far and wide.

• • •

I blinked, disoriented. Although still gripping a book, it wasn't the one that had been thrown on the floor in lit class, and I wasn't all knotted up with tension, fending off threatening forces, struggling to keep my head above water. Instead, I was in a space that offered total solace with someone who seemed to have my best interests in mind.

Elizabeth hadn't moved her hands. They still covered my own. Unwavering and committed, her steadfastness encouraged me to release some of my despair and finally hope for something more. I glanced out the window, watching a few students cross the front green. It was a beautiful day. Winter was turning toward spring. Laughing voices seeped through the windowpanes, reminding me that not every reality was grim. I tried to adopt some of their lightheartedness, to loosen up and appreciate the extraordinary comfort and security this woman offered—the kind I'd always wanted from my mother. Maybe the source of this essential, life-giving support was less important than the fact that it existed at all. It was time to let others step in, to take the place of what was missing. Elizabeth would be the first.

"Julie?" Her voice broke my trance. "Whenever you're ready, I'd like to try something different. I brought along a poem. It's not something you're working on in class; it's something you've never read. This will be a new experience. Without a context, without knowing anything about it, you won't be able to guess at the words. You'll have to work out each one and only then consider the meaning of the whole. Since it's not narrative, the significance might be harder to discover. But it'll be worth the effort. Exercises in sight reading can be so satisfying."

She paused. She had the most reassuring smile. "I know that the concept sounds scary, not knowing what to look for, not knowing what's coming. But I guarantee you'll like it. In fact, my daughter—remember I told you that she plays the viola? She swears this is the best exercise of all, kind of like a free fall. Trust the words. They won't let you down." She tapped my hands lightly. "Plus, this just so happens to be a lovely poem. It'll be a nice way to end one more successful session together."

I inhaled sharply, suddenly unsure of myself. I'd been thrilled to finish my reading for the day with a feeling of confidence. I didn't want to risk failure. But still, those hands—not only their touch but the fact that they still covered mine. Elizabeth wasn't letting go. Maybe it wouldn't be too much to take a look and try. In any case, reading something more would prolong this welcome closeness. I didn't want it to end, ever. I was already beginning to mourn its loss.

"Don't worry. I'm still here." Her words were an answer to my unspoken prayer. I watched as she reached over to her bag and pulled out a small index card, placing it on the table before me. "So, here it is. It's a poem by Tupac Shakur. I'm sure you've heard of him."

I laughed. "Yeah. Of course. But I didn't know he wrote poetry."

"His songs, the lyrics, they're all poems, words strung together that have meaning. It isn't more complicated than that." She spun the index card to face me. "My father loved poetry. He used to read to us now and then from a range of poets, some amusing, some touching, some completely obtuse—which basically means that I didn't understand them at all. There was no one theme or purpose. His interest was wide-ranging. Reading to us was more about spending time together, sharing something he liked." She paused. "He's gone now. But I think he would have liked this one."

Elizabeth's eyes closed for a minute. She seemed so sad. Sometimes I forgot that others could feel bad as well—I didn't have the monopoly on sorrow. I wanted to make her feel better if I could. With some reluctance, I broke contact with the hand still clutching my own and took the card, cradling it like a small, injured animal. I trembled in anticipation, almost afraid to read words that were obviously of such significance to her.

"The Rose that Grew from Concrete." I paused and looked over at her, catching her smile of encouragement. I answered with a shy one of my own. "Did you hear about the rose that grew . . ." I stopped mid-line, and then, encouraged by the lingering memory of Elizabeth's hands on my own, overcome by the loveliest sensation of calm, I shoved aside the heavy sack of worries I carried with me daily and read on, straight through to the end.

Did you hear about the rose that grew
from a crack in the concrete?
Proving nature's law is wrong it
learned to walk without having feet.
Funny it seems, but by keeping its dreams,
it learned to breathe fresh air.
Long live the rose that grew from concrete
when no one else ever cared.

BELLE

SPRAWLED OUT IN BED WITH eyes closed, headphones on, I let the music transport me, buffeting me along the crest of its waves with a gentle harmony. I almost managed to suppress the pounding of my head. Almost. I'd had too much to drink the night before. A sharp knocking disturbed this euphoric haze, jolting me back to the reality of morning. I grudgingly opened my eyes. Grandma stood at the door with a huge book under her arm.

"Can I come in?" She didn't wait for an answer, striding over to my bed and sitting down. "I've brought you something I think you'll enjoy and might like to see."

I squinted at her, eyes at half-mast, the music still flooding through me. I didn't want to remove my headphones. The colors of those notes made me feel better. Plus, I didn't want to hear whatever she had to say. I knew a lecture was coming. I wasn't getting off easy after arriving home virtually unconscious.

"Belle. Belle, dear. Please take off those headphones." She put the album to the side and gestured with both hands, pointing at her ears and then mine.

I reluctantly complied, rolling over and pushing up onto one elbow.

"Yes, Grandma. What is it?"

She picked up the album and moved it to her lap, stroking the cover. I wondered if this was going to be another one of those boring ones full of pictures of her days at the ranch, sitting high on a horse. I could pretty much cite the list of jumping victories she'd had back in the day. "I was thinking . . ." She paused, tapping the cover twice as if making some important decision. "I thought this particular album might interest you. It's not one of mine. It's your mother's, from her senior year in high school."

My mind cleared in an instant, the throbbing that had tormented me since I'd risen suddenly subsiding. I sat up a bit straighter. This *would* be interesting. Although I'd seen lots of pictures of Mom as a child, then much later, with Dad, shivering along the lakeside in Chicago, smiling at the beach on Lake Michigan as I dug in the sand beside her, I'd seen almost nothing from her teenage years. The years when she was the same age as I were still a mystery. This was worth getting up for.

I reached to take the album just as Grandma picked it up off her lap, and our hands bumped. I smiled awkwardly. She answered much the same. Sometimes it felt like we were strangers.

My attention shifted to the album. It felt like a treasure. I cradled it in my arms and gave it a little hug. The fact that Grandma had chosen to share, especially after such a horrible night, especially when I knew that she was upset and disappointed in my behavior and really didn't know what to do with me, was worthy of commending. I leaned over and gave her a light kiss on the cheek. Taken aback, she touched the spot with two fingers and blushed. "Well, I didn't expect that! What was that for?"

"I know that life with me isn't one big picnic. Ask my parents. They've had to deal with much the same for years. Yet here you are. And for whatever reason, although I deserve it, you've decided not to lecture me for messing up so badly. I really appreciate that." I paused. "And this! You've brought me a treat! A little peek into Mommy's life! That's incredibly nice!"

"Well, I'm not promising that I won't get to that lecture." She offered a sly smile. "I don't think it can be avoided." She paused and rubbed her hands along the lower portion of her dress, as if ironing out the pleats. She looked nervous. "But maybe later. Just now I think this might be more important." Another pause. She reached up and drew her hand across her upper lip, her brow furrowed. She was obviously troubled. "You've asked me about your mom so many times—about why we are the way we are. There isn't an easy or a quick explanation. And there's quite a bit to tell. But it's not for me to do so." She stood.

"Are you going? Wait, don't you want to look through this with me? You love to explain, to tell me what I'm seeing. Come on! Stay!"

She smiled a bit timidly and shook her head. "Not this time, dear. This time you need to discover on your own."

This was so unusual. Grandma never let me explore on my own. Never. She always led me through whatever the given topic, putting words into my head before I managed to put them together myself, controlling how I saw things, ensuring it was "the right way." Those were her words. I hadn't known there was one right way before I got to New York, but Grandma insisted upon it. She had sat beside me when she shared those other albums, offering a guided tour. Leaving me on my own this time, with such precious memories, windows to a past I knew nothing about, was completely out of character.

I followed her with my eyes as she retreated, noting how her shoulders curled downward. There was nothing of my imperious grandma today. Instead, she looked almost defeated. I stifled another question and waited for the door to click shut before opening the album. The first few pages were full of Polaroid photos, for the most part bleached out over time, the darks having faded to pale grey. It was hard to distinguish any details. Common to each, however, were Mom's long arms and legs, skinny as sticks, poking out of shorts and T-shirts. She'd always been a skinny mini. It was one reason she really suffered the winters back home. A little bit of meat might have helped her deal with the deep freeze of North Dakota.

I flipped through pages and pages of shots, many of them proper Kodak color photos with thin white borders. She was captured in a group, standing in a cluster of kids on a field, up on stage with the orchestra. Mom had played the flute for years but quit before I was born. At least, that's what she said. I still had some memory of her playing when I was little, of falling asleep to its dolorous tones. Now it just sat in the cabinet in the living room, gathering dust. I'd never let that happen. I'd play the viola forever. I couldn't imagine a time I wouldn't want to pick it up, stroke the strings with the bow, let the notes flow out and spread wings, swallowing me whole.

Somewhere mid-album, something changed. First, there was a boy. Flipping back a few pages, I saw him in some of the earlier shots. I hadn't picked him out there, when he was just one of the crowd. But in these shots, he'd moved up, front and center. His increased significance was hard to miss. I looked a little closer, intrigued by what kind of boy my mom might have liked back then, assuming he was a boyfriend. He had long black hair and an expression between a shrug and a smile. He looked cool. Mom seemed happy in these photos, carefree. The images in this part of the album, some where she and that boy were leaning into one another, others where he had his arm draped casually across her shoulders, felt embarrassingly intimate. It looked as if they shared a secret. There was no escaping the fact that Mom was in love. I understood why sharing this album might have been uncomfortable for Grandma. I felt somewhat the same, as if I shouldn't be looking. Captured here were private moments in a teenage love story that were really no one else's business.

I'd never asked Mom much about this period of her life. By the time it should have interested me, I was too busy focusing on my own. Her former life didn't count because it had nothing to do with mine. But now I couldn't get enough of what I was seeing, entranced by a different side of her, one I hadn't expected, hadn't even considered might exist. After pages and pages of photographs of these two teenagers hanging out—sometimes with a group, sometimes on their own, sometimes on the beach, hair blowing in their faces, smiles wide, sometimes at an amusement park, their faces dipped into tall cones of ice cream—there was yet another shift in mood.

The pages at the end of the album seemed darker, their tones cloudier and less distinct. This mostly had to do with Mom's change in appearance. Suddenly, she was covered up, wearing drapey clothing, oversized shirts, and sweatpants. Gone were all those exposed lanky limbs I'd recognized. And it wasn't because it was winter. The rest of the kids in the photos were still wearing clothes appropriate to spring or early summer: halter tops, tanks, and shorts. Although that boy was still there, right by her side, either holding her hand or wrapping an arm or two around her, something had distinctly changed. In most of these photos, Mom's face was lowered, hidden by shadows. In several shots she stood in the back of a group, barely discernible.

In some ways, that wasn't a surprise. My mom liked to be a part of the crowd, not the main attraction. She wasn't one to enjoy center stage. But there was something different about her demeanor. In these later shots she was captured looking away from the camera—sometimes at this boy, sometimes off to the side. It looked like something was on her mind. The photographs in this part of the album depicted a person completely different from the untroubled one I'd seen in the first few pages. I wondered what had happened, what it all meant? The answer, or at least the suggestion of an answer, came in one of the last images.

She was seated on the bleachers among a group of girls, looking straight at the camera. I startled at the sight of her. Still sporting an out-of-season oversized shirt but unusually full-cheeked, she looked almost cherubic. For as long as I could remember, Mom had been all sharp angles.

I slammed the album shut and ran out of my bedroom, looking for Grandma. She was standing in the living room, looking down at the busy avenue below.

"Grandma?"

"Yes, dear," she mumbled, not bothering to turn. She was a stickler for manners, always going on about how important it was to properly greet people. This was the first sign that something was up; whatever I'd discovered in those dusty pages had real significance for my family.

"That boy. Who was he? It looks like Mom had a really serious boyfriend, just about when she was my age. How come I've never heard of him?"

Grandma didn't move an inch. It seemed as though she were holding her breath.

"And something else. She looks unusual in some of the pictures, kind of off—nothing at all like the Mom I'm used to seeing, even aged down to seventeen. She looks a bit round. She's never been round! And her clothes. She's swimming in them! What happened to her? It looks like something was wrong." I slammed the brakes on my own drivel, taking a deep breath. "Grandma, did someone hurt her? She's all covered up when she shouldn't be."

I waited for answers, but Grandma wasn't supplying any. She continued to stand with her back to me, staring out that window.

"I really appreciate your sharing the album. It means a lot to me. I've never seen any pictures at all from Mom's high school years. And I'm sorry to be going on and on, but . . . well, I just have so many questions."

Again, I waited, sure that Grandma would finally turn around and invite me to sit down for a conversation. That was her way.

"Belle, dear, I can't explain what you saw." Still facing away, her voice came out garbled and heavy, as if she were speaking underwater.

"But I'm sure you can. I'm sure you know exactly what was up. And I don't understand it at all. I have so many crazy thoughts in my head."

Slow as could be, Grandma turned toward me, her face radiating a sadness I'd never seen. This wasn't at all what I expected to find when I came running into the room, looking for answers. I reached out and touched her arm.

"Grandma, are you okay? Is there anything I can do?"

She cast her eyes downward, dragging her expression from one end of the Oriental carpet to the other before looking up, straight into my eyes. "You need to speak with your mother. This is her story to share."

ELIZABETH

DING. I WAS SITTING IN my office, reading through a brief. The sound of the phone disturbed my concentration and I reached to silence it, uninterested in whoever was trying to reach me. Belle's name in bold on the screen got my attention. My heart skipped a beat. I hadn't heard from her in over a week. Not one text. Not even the kind asking if she could have a little extra spending money so that she could buy a new pair of jeans.

Did you love him? read the text.

My heart shifted within my chest, sliding from one side to the other. At least, that was how it felt. Any thoughts of my work evaporated.

Your father? I texted back.

Later, when I scanned back through this text exchange, I wondered why that had come out as a question. Whether I'd somehow known.

There was no reply. I slid the brief to the side and drummed my fingers on the desk, impatiently waiting. The fact that she'd reached out was good. It was enough. But the question was odd. The phone rang, and I almost dropped it. I took a quick confirming glance at the screen. Belle. This was the first time she'd called me in as long as I could remember, our communication since she'd left existing solely through texts, most often short and to the point. Now I was completely alert.

"Did you love him?"

"Belle, hey! Sweetie. It's so amazing to hear from you! What's going on?" I feigned calm, hoping that if I played at normal, this wouldn't be as big of a deal as I feared.

"The guy in the picture. With the long bangs."

She had my attention. "What are you talking about? What picture?" I didn't have to listen all that closely to hear her breathing. It sounded as if she'd just finished a run in the park. "Belle, honey?"

"Grandma showed me that old album. The one from high school."

Ah. Now I understood. My head started pounding, anger and panic working in collusion, ramping up the pressure and threatening to make it explode. I could already anticipate the next conversation, the one where I called Lillian and yelled at her for interfering in my life, for revealing things that were meant to stay hidden. That was going to be even more excruciating. But it would have to wait. First, I had to deal with the here and now, and figure out what to tell my daughter.

"Did she? Was it interesting for you? All that old history."

"Mom. The boy."

I hesitated just a moment. This wasn't to be avoided. "Belle, all of that, well, it was such a long time ago."

"It looks like you really cared about him. What was his name?"

Something in her tone signaled that she was intrigued, not judgmental—that we were on the same side. Maybe I'd needlessly panicked. Maybe this conversation wasn't about what I feared. There was a chance it could be about something less difficult.

"His name was David."

From there the conversation rolled along, propelled gently by the natural rhythm of the tide, and I relaxed. It was nice to share, to open up about something in the past. Belle wanted to hear all about the boy I'd first loved, what that had been like for me, how it felt. I heard a yearning in her questions. She too wanted to have a real boyfriend, someone who meant everything to her. As we spoke, I realized that Tom really had been just a guy, no one special, and that made me sad. Everyone deserved a real first love, especially when love became physical.

Lulled into a trance by the loveliness of this exchange, absent of the incriminations, anger, and impatience which had characterized so many of our conversations over the past year, I was completely unprepared when she cleared her throat and asked, "Why did it end?"

I had no idea where to start, knowing full well that each avenue led to the same difficult ending. "Why did we break up?" If I continued answering her questions with questions, I might be able to delay the painful finish.

"Well, yeah. I mean, I think I know. I think he hurt you." Her voice lowered to a whisper. This was a conversation we should have had live, face-to-face. I wanted to reach out and stroke her hair, hold her hand, assure her all was well.

"He never hurt me, Belle. Where did you get that idea?"

"I noticed that you started covering up. I figured you were hiding something—maybe bruises, scratches, cuts. I don't know. That's why most girls hide these days." She paused a moment, and before I had a chance to refute her claims, she continued. "Wait. Maybe it wasn't something he was doing. Were you cutting yourself, Mom? I didn't know kids did that back then. I thought it was one of those crazy, stupid, Generation Z things."

I cut her off. I couldn't let these dreadful lines of thought continue. "No, Belle, no. Nothing like that." What she'd seen was the way I tried to cover up the fact of the pregnancy and hide it from the other kids. It had been a real challenge. I'd been so thin back then. I still was. It didn't take long to see the changes—at least, if you were looking. That was how Lillian picked up on what was happening. She'd been the first, noticing even before I told David. But I refused to speak with her about it until much later, when I didn't have a choice. That was when she'd subjected me to a torrent of comments and objections, an endless stream of remarks intended to ensure I made the right choice and ended it. My inner turmoil was bad, but her onslaught was worse.

"But you look so different. The only picture where you're the same as everyone else is the one from your graduation, when you're all in cap and gown. Other than that, you kind of seem detached, sunken into yourself and . . . well, weird. Even kind of chubby. And I've never seen you wear huge shirts. That's kind of my thing."

The warmth of this conversation emboldened me, and I realized that this was a crossroads. By sharing a chapter in my past, something significant like my relationship with David, I was actually bringing Belle back to me. For a few minutes it felt like the old days, when she would swing from my arm as we walked up the street and come running in from school, braids flying, to tell me about her day—a time she wanted to share her life instead of hiding it. I suddenly saw that everything could be different than I'd imagined. Revealing and sharing could breed closeness instead of causing an insurmountable rift.

"Something happened, Belle."

She must have sensed this was important because she suddenly stopped babbling and firing away questions. Even her breathing quieted to a low hum.

"I'm not sure about sharing this. I never have."

More silence. I didn't want to scare her, but I couldn't retreat. It was time.

"I got pregnant, Belle. In high school. I got pregnant with a little girl."

"Mommy." That blessed word emerged as an exhalation. I ached to have her next to me, to pull her in close and tell her I loved her; to explain how sometimes, things just happen.

"I wanted to keep her."

"The baby?"

"Yes, of course. I wanted to keep her. I'd always wanted a little girl, to coddle, to love, to suffocate with affection. I was so young. I thought I could manage."

"So why didn't you? You look so sad in those pictures, Mommy. Now it all makes sense."

I cleared my throat. I had an obligation to word this properly, to be the parent. "The timing was wrong. Now I see that. Being a teenager . . . well, it's such a bold period. You just think you can conquer any difficulty, rise to any challenge." I paused. "But that's not true at all. And in the end, the choice to end the pregnancy was right."

"In the end?"

"Belle, I loved that baby so much. You can't imagine." I remembered winding my hand under my shirt and holding my stomach when no one was looking. I couldn't get enough of the feeling of peace that came from our connection. "There wasn't anything I wanted more." Now I was the one whispering.

"So why? Why didn't you have her? Was it about David? Did he break up with you or something?"

"Oh no, nothing like that. He was a very good guy. He swore he'd stand by me, whatever my choice. And he always made clear that it was *my* choice."

"Oh my God!"

Belle's exclamation of alarm, of discovery, emphasizing each word separately, startled me.

"What is it, sweetie? What happened?" I just hated that we weren't together.

"I know what happened. I know exactly what happened. Now I get it! A few months ago, I couldn't have put this together. Never. I wouldn't have seen the whole picture. But now—"

"Belle, tell me, what are you talking about?"

"It's Grandma. She got involved. She had her say. She always has her say. And her way is the only way. She knows best. You never had a choice, Mommy."

I melted right then and there, tears flowing out of my eyes, covering my face, running unchecked down to my chin and the top of my collar. I wiped at them when they became too overwhelming in number. "Oh, baby. It wasn't exactly like that."

"Yes, it was. You just don't want to say so. And that's why you guys don't talk. You're still angry—"

"Belle, it's just not that simple."

"It's okay, Mommy. You can tell me. I understand. I see it now. The whole thing."

"Yes, you probably do. But you weren't there. And it's not exactly the way you imagine. It was such a complicated time. And while I'll never be able to forgive Grandma for foisting decisions on me that weren't my own, ones that had more to do with her than me, I now understand that they came from a good place. She had good intentions. She loves me. She's always loved me. Sometimes it's not easy to show someone how much you love them. Sometimes we make huge mistakes that mislead others into thinking that we're trying to control them when, really, we're trying to protect them." I paused and took a deep breath. "I was so young, Belle. It would have been so hard for me. She was just trying to help me see that. She wanted my life to be easier, not harder. She knew it would be a challenge in any case. I didn't. That's the kind of thing that takes years to discover. It's part of being a mother."

A long silence and then the sound of a hand clap. "Wow. And Tom! I get it. You thought, well, you thought that might happen to me. That must have been so difficult. Oh, Mommy, I'm so sorry. If only I'd known . . ."

I let her words fade off into yet another silence, this one longer than the others. I didn't know what else to add. I simply wanted to enjoy the warm blanket of love and understanding in which we were wrapped and hold on to this moment. I'd been convinced for so long that the truth would push Belle away, and instead, it had brought us together.

"I love you, my daughter. To the moon and back."

"As you loved your first?" Her voice was so small.

"More. Because I've had the pleasure of knowing you since you were just a spark of life. And because there's so much more awaiting us ahead."

After hanging up, I sat numbly in my chair, the brief I'd been reading when Belle contacted me completely forgotten. I was stunned by what had happened, by the surprising beauty that had entered this day. This conversation with Belle had meant the world to me. There was another ding from the phone. I hesitated to look. I didn't want to ruin the moment. Unable to resist, I reluctantly glanced at the screen beside me. It was Mike.

I blinked twice, hard and fast. Mike. I had to tell Mike.

I answered his casual greeting with something more specific. It was imperative we speak. *Hey*, I texted. *We need to talk*.

His response made no sense: *Later. Something else has come up.*

What? I dialed his number. "What's happened?"

"Everything's fine. No emergency! Remember that concert? The Easter concert? The one we were invited to? I just think I need to be there."

"But we decided to let Lillian fill in. It's awfully far to travel for a concert—"

"Lizzy, I'm getting things organized at work so that I can leave in a few days. I'll be in touch later." He hung up.

All thoughts about a dramatic confession were gone. This sounded more urgent. But I couldn't help feeling confused. Coming off the best moments I'd shared with my daughter in the longest time, I couldn't imagine the reasons behind what sounded like an emergency rescue mission. It wasn't fair that I had to. I should have had a bit more time to enjoy this change in the wind. I tried to convince myself that it was nothing. Belle had sounded fine. But there must be something because Mike, who'd played the middleman since she'd moved to New York, felt he had to be there with her. He must have picked up vibes I wasn't party to. That was enough for me.

Completely forgetting those lovely moments of elation, I shifted my thoughts to Mike's trip. I tried to convince myself this was a good thing. After all, Belle would certainly love to have him with her at the concert. But I couldn't shake off the feeling of doom. My heart sank in my chest. Maybe Belle hadn't just stumbled on that album. Maybe, for whatever reason, someone had given it to her—someone who wanted her to know.

BELLE

QUINN HAD PROMISED WE'D BE home by eleven. That was around the time Grandma would begin to pace and prowl, flooding my cell phone with annoying messages:

It is late.

You said you would be home.

I will wait up until you get here.

So incredibly proper, she didn't even use contractions. I looked at my watch. The numbers moved a bit, destabilized by the alcohol I'd consumed. It was already ten past. This was bad. I'd never make it.

"Come on. Try it. You're gonna love it."

The boy with the greasy hair—I couldn't recall his name, the one who'd latched on to me the minute we arrived—was waving a little pipe in my direction. At my shrug, he flicked his lighter. A flame leaped out toward its tiny bowl, there was a hissing sound, then a thin plume of smoke. He leaned over and grasped it between his lips, inhaling deeply before sinking back into the plush cushions of the couch. I looked around the room uncomfortably. I didn't want to be here. *What am I looking for?*

What am I trying to prove? New York felt very big on me this evening. I wanted to go home. I scanned the room choked with bodies and smoke, looking for Quinn. I knew how to get home on my own but didn't want to leave her behind. It didn't seem all that safe.

When I didn't find her, I got up and made my way toward the kitchen, or what counted as a kitchen. I'd never get used to these glorified, well-equipped closets that stood in their stead here in Manhattan. Back in Grand Forks, we all had super spacious ones replete with breakfast tables, endless counter space, and enough room to hold a four-man relay if need be. This miniature one was typical of those I'd seen in other friends' apartments nearby and was, at present, jammed with kids, some dancing to the music filtering in from the living room, most smoking, some perched up on the counter between bags of chips and bottles of booze and pop, and others swaying unsteadily in the floor space that remained, their hands gripping those big red cups, their faces open and welcoming, all barriers lowered.

I didn't recognize any of them. The evening was being hosted by a boy from twelfth grade whose parents were out of the country. It was supposed to be the event of the year, a real blowout. From the start, attending had been all about extending my comfort zone, doing something a bit brazen. But I began to second-guess the whole idea upon arriving home later that day. I'd gotten an earful from Grandma the time I came home drunk, or rather, the time I was *delivered* home drunk. Although she'd been kind enough to wait a few days, until I recovered from my headache and embarrassment, she hadn't hesitated to lay down all kinds of rules, hinting at the degree of her disappointment, going so far as to suggest that our arrangement might not be working out. This was what I most feared.

I ignored her. It's not like I had a choice. Saying no to the other girls would have been social suicide. In any case, staying home and sucking my thumb had not been part of my game plan back in Grand Forks. As long as I got home by eleven, my newly imposed curfew, everything would be okay. At least, that's what I thought.

I had fun at first. It was nice to be the "unknowns" at the party. Most everyone else was a senior. We four grabbed drinks as we entered and spread out in the living room, talking up the other kids, jumping up to dance when the spirit moved, letting everyone else refill our cups. We couldn't stop laughing and smiling. And there was the part about the boys. I hadn't had a boyfriend since Tom. And that didn't end very well. Afterwards, I had steered clear of all the boys at school. It was exciting hanging out here with these older ones.

Loosened up by the booze, I wiggled around, tummy exposed. I knew I looked cute in my tank top; I was getting attention. I pushed those comments Grandma made as I left the house out of my head, but they kept coming back: "That's inappropriate. Put on something that covers up your middle. Watch out, Belle." It's like she and Mom were on the same warpath. *Isn't what I do with boys my own business?* But I knew it wasn't. Since discovering more about Mom's past, I understood that we were all in this together.

Of course, knowledge doesn't go all that far when alcohol is involved. And in that smoke-filled living room, inured by too much drinking, my only thoughts were on having fun. And I did, until I realized I'd had a little too much booze. An hour or so in, I felt sick. The light-headed feeling that had helped me relax and enjoy myself began to feel more like nausea. Lying on the couch and eating a bowl of chips worked for a bit, making me feel somewhat less dizzy, but I knew I needed to get home.

"Looking for Quinn?"

The guy with the pipe stood in my way as I returned from the kitchen. I didn't like him. I didn't like what he was doing. I'd never been into weed. I tried it once, at somebody's house down in the Village. It dulled all the edges, but not in a good way. The ribbon of color went grey. I couldn't stand the smell, so sickeningly sweet. I wished he would just go away.

"Yeah. Have you seen her?"

He gestured down the hallway with his head. "I think she's busy back there." I peeked around him. Those were the bedrooms. I knew what he was insinuating. It only made me feel worse.

"I have to go."

He blocked my path, and I noticed his girth. I wouldn't be able to just push him aside. “No, no, don’t say that. We’ve only just started here.” He was smiling at me, but it didn’t feel nice, just threatening.

I’d had enough of the smoke, the booze, and the noise. My head hurt. “I need to go to the bathroom, then I’ll come right back out. Meet you in the living room?” I cocked my eyebrows, hoping to affect a flirty expression. It worked.

“Cool.” He lowered his arms and let me by. Breathing a sigh of relief, I made my way down the hall, opening the first door to the left. It was dimly lit inside, but I made out a bed piled high with coats. Mine was one of them. I closed the door behind me. I couldn’t go yet. I had to find Quinn. The next room was pitch black but teeming with kids, some lying on the bed, some on the floor. There was a lot of writhing, laughter, and the occasional smooching sound. I hurried out, more than a little uncomfortable.

There was one more door at the end of the hall. I opened it up, peeked inside, and then hurried to close it behind me. A couple was stretched out on an oversized bed. It must have been the parents’ room. I was embarrassed. I understood what I’d interrupted. But as I turned to go back toward the living room, I stopped cold. The shoes on the floor had seemed familiar. Those bright-red pumps. I hesitated for a split second and then knocked on the door. I wanted them to stop whatever they were doing so I wouldn’t have to see it. When I didn’t get an answer, I knocked harder, then just opened the door. Quinn and some guy I’d never seen, their shirts unbuttoned, sat up in the bed. It was obvious something significant was progressing at a pace.

“Hey, guys. We need you out here.” I played at casual, but that wasn’t how I felt. What I felt was panic. I had to get Quinn out of there, and fast.

A deep voice rumbled from beside her. “We’re okay. We’ll be right out. Just close the door behind you.”

There was absolutely no way I was leaving Quinn there. I walked in, picking up her shoes along the way, and took a seat at her side.

“Are you joining us?”

I ignored him and his disgusting question. “Hey, Quinn. Come on. Let’s get out of here. You don’t want to be here.” I knew what might happen, or rather *would* happen, if I left her there. And having spent days considering the sadness in which my mother had been engulfed for decades, I knew that one could pay for a mistake for a lifetime.

"Who says she doesn't? We're having a really good time. Or rather, we were, until you got here and busted up the party." He hiccoughed. Quinn just stared at me, her head pressing back against the pillows. She didn't look right. She looked like she'd taken something. I hadn't seen any Molly at the party, but I knew it was around. I shook her gently.

"Quinn? Are you okay? Come on." I swiveled her around so that her legs fell over the side of the bed, squeezed her feet into her shoes, and pulled her up to standing. "I'm taking her. I'm sure you'll be just fine on your own."

Quinn protested, making a lame attempt at sitting back down and staying put. But it didn't help her. She was coming with me. We were out of the apartment minutes later, leaving our coats and other friends behind.

• • •

When I took the stage the following week for the Easter concert, I knew it would all go wrong. I hadn't slept well all week. I simply couldn't get the ugliness of the party's final scene out of my head: Quinn's stoned look, the arrogance of the guy stretched out on the bed, the leering eyes of that huge greasy one blocking my path, the smell of things I didn't want any part of. I couldn't shake the realization of just how bad it could have ended, of how naive we'd all been.

Taking my seat in the recital hall beside the other violists, I felt sick, nerves frazzled, head splitting. I couldn't focus. The notes on the stand before me squiggled into indecipherable lines and escaped my efforts to hold them fast, to make them mine. My fingers were all over the fingerboard, slipping flat. I made mistakes I'd never made, even the first day I'd seen the score, my bow failing to pull out the soothing sound for which I was known. The music that had always lifted me beyond this world felt choked and distant—a formerly faithful friend now gone missing, the empty shell left behind telling the tale. Nothing was as it was meant to be.

This was a major event in the Julliard calendar and one Grandma had been more than excited about attending. While I spent the week swimming in a haze of misery, she buzzed around the apartment, calling her friends and going on and on about the concert, about what she'd wear, about whether she should sit in the first row or a few rows back. Her anticipation was both frenzied and boundless. She'd even invited a friend from her group at the temple. Before the concert I saw her chatting her up, pulling at her sleeve, pointing at one teacher or another as if she knew them personally. She positively radiated with excitement. That was before I imploded.

Try as I might, I couldn't pull myself together. And as the minutes passed, I knew that this was most likely going to be my last performance at Julliard. The next day was spring break, and I was pretty sure that by the end of the ten-day holiday I'd receive notice of my expulsion from the program. And that would be fair. If only I could concentrate on the music, let the tones erase the mess of my life in New York and lift me to a purer place. But that was impossible.

When it was time for the string section to rest, to let the wind instruments take over, I cast a casual glance in her direction. *What a mistake!* The rosy glow had become a fiery red. Her expression was as close to stormy as I'd ever seen. I suppose she had a right. This wasn't what my year at Julliard was supposed to be about. Instead of the crowning glory she expected, it had become a fizzled-out failure. I couldn't help noticing that she was ignoring her friend, physically turning her back on her and projecting closure. I suppose she was horribly embarrassed, trying to avoid the disappointed, or even pitying, look in her companion's eyes. There was no way to get around my poor performance. We were fifteen in the string section, but it was probably as obvious to the audience as it was to the rest of the musicians what hadn't worked, who had played off-key.

When it was all over and we stood for a bow, I barely raised my head, wanting to sink to the floor and through it—to disappear. Packing up my notes and instrument, I took a quick look toward the throng of exiting parents, checking to see if Grandma was among them. I hoped so. I really didn't want to see her.

That's when I saw my father. He stood by the door at the back of the hall, leaning against the wall right next to the stream of people leaving.

I grabbed my instrument as it started to fall, shaking my head in disbelief. It couldn't be. I'd conjured him up, looking for some consolation for my losses. I focused on putting my viola back into the case, snapping it closed and then raising my eyes back to the exit. He was still there. I was flooded with a sense of relief I hadn't even known I needed. I stepped off the stage as he strode across the long hall to meet me.

"Belle, dear, say hello to Joyce."

It was Grandma. She hadn't left after all. I raced toward my dad, not even bothering to look her way. "Belle! Where are you going? I want a word!"

I didn't miss the hurt in her voice, but I couldn't stop. All my energy was focused on making my way through the large crowd of parents, grandparents, and other musicians still gathered. I was so desperate for the kind of hug only my dad could give, enveloping, bursting with love and support. I needed to hear him tell me that everything would be okay—to assure me that I was on the right path, that I was making good choices. I'd spent all night reproaching myself, regretting the hubris that had made me believe I could carve a successful path through this brash, brassy city.

His arms folded around me, and I felt the shedding of an impossibly heavy burden, the sustained effort that had chewed me up and spit me out, leaving me empty. At that moment, I understood the enormous toll that these last few months had taken: the stress of holding together a life with Grandma, doomed from the start to split open at the seams; the effort of assuming a whole new persona at school while making something meaningful of the music that had gotten me here in the first place. I held on to Dad as though my life depended on it.

ELIZABETH

"I NEED YOUR HELP."

Those words. I could swear I'd never heard them. At least, not from my mother. I didn't know how to react. I stifled my first responses: a startled gasp, a choked laugh. I didn't want her to pick up on my shock nor think I found the situation funny. It wasn't. Laughter was a nervous reaction to a completely unexpected situation. My unfamiliarity with this territory, my mother asking *me* for help, made anything possible. I held my breath and stayed silent, maintaining the kind of neutrality more appropriate to a comment about the unchanged weather while my mind raced ahead, leaping over obstacles and charging forward, keeping pace with my heartbeat, which had accelerated to a vigorous gallop. I could take on a staircase to the sky two steps at a time with this rush of adrenaline.

"Yes?" I adopted a casual manner, but it was hard to keep the excitement out of my voice. I was thankful for the privacy afforded by the distance of the telephone.

"This is all much bigger than I thought it would be." Lillian's voice seemed hesitant. This was new. "Much harder. I didn't really consider the difficulties, some of which I've, well, already encountered." She cleared her throat. "I'm not sure I know how to parent a teenager. It's been quite some time."

You never knew how to parent a teenager. I didn't say those words aloud, but they burned through me. I imagined Lillian sitting at the small table in the kitchen in New York, alone in a bastion of white—the appliances, the fixtures, the tablecloth, and the walls. As a child, all that white had been more than a little blinding. As a teenager I dreamed of my more colorful future kitchen, favoring a palette of gorgeous blues. I wondered how Lillian's uncertainty looked and envisioned her sitting a bit slumped over with hands clasped, worrying her knuckles, rubbing the loose skin as if it needed cleaning, as if trying to get rid of a stain.

I had no memory of my stalwart, uber-confident mother being unsure of herself, never imagined a day when she would second-guess her own ability to get something right. *I* was the one who doubted each and every move, debated every decision, and hesitated endlessly. *I* was the one who had trouble determining which napkins to put out at dinner, whether to choose a white car, playing it safe, or go with something riskier, like black. This was a brave new world. The tables had turned, and for once *I*, not my mother, was on the determining side. I was overwhelmed by an unusual rush of giddy self-confidence.

"I'm getting the sense that I have no control, that I won't be able to regulate the course of Belle's daily life. I think that maybe taking on an adolescent, at this point in my life . . . well, it might have been a mistake. Things seem a bit different now than I imagined they would when this whole plan emerged. I hadn't realized quite how much," she continued, completely unperturbed by my silence. "She's so defiant. Belle. She has this expectation that things will line up according to her wishes, no matter what she does. And let me tell you, she's done quite a few disturbing things."

With this she went silent. I didn't know a lot about what was going on in New York. Mike fielded most of my mother's calls and adamantly refused to give me the details. He insisted he was saving me an unnecessary headache, promising to share anything life threatening. At the time, I thought he was making a joke. Now I wondered.

"She doesn't seem to care at all about what I have to say. Setting limits has almost no effect whatsoever. If she insists on beating to her own drum, completely disregarding my rules, I won't have any authority. How will I be able to teach her, educate her. How will I show her the way?"

Bells went off in my head. "Mom, that's not your job. Your job is neither to educate nor raise my daughter. You're Belle's grandmother. As the grandmother, you're there to love and support. In this instance, you've also done a wonderful thing by giving her shelter, a home, so that she can enjoy this extraordinary experience at Julliard. You benefit, as I never will, from being able to spoil, to give in, to indulge." I lowered my voice, humbled by my inadvertent admission. "I'm quite jealous."

The silence that followed was laden with the significance of my words, the mutual understanding that we'd swapped roles after a lifetime of their being set in stone. Lillian continued. It was obvious that she had an agenda.

"But you see, I'm not sure I can continue this—this arrangement. I promised her, I encouraged it all, but now . . . Well, now everything has changed. It's not going well, and I think, just maybe, that it's not going to work out after all."

I went rigid, my whole body responding viscerally to the implication of her words, the threat behind them. Although I enjoyed the strange new world presented at the onset of this conversation—me the strong one in the relationship—Lillian's last words were nothing less than devastating. She no longer wanted to host Belle. She was reneging on her commitment. After taking her in and housing her for more than half of the school year, she was considering terminating her side of the deal and sending her home. In short, she was going to break my daughter's heart.

The shock and thrill I'd felt at her plea for help, at those first signs that she'd been completely unmoored by a situation beyond her control, now changed to horror. I had to stop this. I wouldn't allow her to hurt Belle in this way. This was *not* an option. I wouldn't let my mother, after so many promises, and despite my own feelings about their arrangement, withdraw her commitment midstream.

"Mom." I started with as firm a voice as I could muster. "Are you saying that because you aren't happy living with a moody, unpredictable, precocious teenager, because you're worried that you might have to change your ways, to endure, to adapt, to learn to loosen up—" I paused, taking a deep breath. "Because of all that, you want to destroy my daughter's dream—as you yourself just admitted, a dream you encouraged wholeheartedly from the beginning?"

I stopped there, afraid I'd say something I wouldn't be able to take back. "Do I have this right?" Again, I imagined her hands, restless and agitated, fussing at one another in that flashcube of light she called a kitchen. If I'd been there, seated by her side, I would have grabbed them and forcefully pulled them apart. I didn't want her to find any solace. She didn't deserve it. This wasn't a mother I wanted anything to do with.

"She was rude to me."

I sighed heavily, not even caring if she heard, and rubbed my eyes. I couldn't believe what she'd just said. I hoped I'd gotten it wrong. My voice emerged as a loud sigh. "What's that, Mom?"

"Belle. She was rude to me. In fact, she's been rude to me several times." Her voice was low, as if she knew that articulating this thought more distinctly would make matters worse.

"Rude? In what way? How was she rude to you?"

"She ignored me publicly, at the concert, right in front of my friend. She rushed by me when I called to her, turning her back on me. It was so embarrassing." Lillian's voice petered off to silence. I didn't wonder why. She'd gone off on a tangent, concentrating on the particular, how she'd felt. She would have been smarter to stick with the general. She must have realized that.

"And that's not all. She's spoken back to me more than a handful of times." Now her voice rang clearer. She was back on track. I envisioned a slightly altered picture: Lillian no longer slumped, now sitting ramrod straight, shoulders pulled back, snapped into place, chin raised—how she looked when her back was against the wall. Perfect posture was the perfect cover when things began to crumble. This was the Lillian I recognized, the one who strapped on that ultra-confident persona like a set of armor when need be.

But in this instance, I found this routine neither formidable nor admirable. This time it was at the expense of my daughter. She was concentrating her energy on Belle's failures instead of her own. "There've been other issues, troubles, things I shouldn't have to put up with. But this is worse, fundamentally worse. She's raised her voice more than a handful of times, made a few particularly ugly faces. She should respect her elders, just as you were raised to respect yours."

I barely heard her mumbled complaints and whining tone, laughing out loud instead.

"Mom! She's a teenager. That's exactly what she's supposed to do. It's positively textbook! Did you truly expect something different?" I paused just a moment, and then lowered the boom. "Did you expect her to be me?"

The silence that followed was deafening. I thought I heard her heart skip a beat.

"What does that mean?"

"Did you expect her to comply, to agree to your plan, your decisions, just as I did?"

"Don't be ridiculous! It wasn't like that."

"In fact, it was. It was exactly like that. And back then, when things were as bad as they could be, when I was sadder than ever, you refused to listen, to even hear what I had to say. Your way was the only way."

I wondered if this was the end of the conversation, not sure where we could go from here. Since there was no way to shove our messy past back in its hermetically sealed box, I marched forward.

"Why did you tell her, Mom?"

A long pause, a bit of coughing. I knew I had Lillian in a corner. She would never have called to voice her complaints if she'd known we were going to get to this spot. "I didn't. I didn't say a word."

"Apparently, you didn't have to. Instead, you led her where you wanted her, without words, without having to express the unspeakable. And now it's done."

"Yes. I suppose so." Lillian sounded so tired.

"I figure it started from some mistaken idea to show her how mistakes look? Is that right?"

"Elizabeth, that's not fair. That's not it at all . . ." Another silence fell. Lillian had finally run out of words. The detritus of our history lay between us like a pile of fallen bricks. The seconds that passed slowed to a crawl, time stretching out like an endless road to nowhere. This explosive interchange had left both of us depleted, completely empty, waiting for the dust to settle before assessing the fallout. I knew I'd gotten through to Lillian. There was no way she could shut out the enormity of what I'd said.

"If she's in my house, she'll have to live by my rules."

Although I didn't truly expect her to fold, I was certain that I'd succeeded in chipping away at her veneer. But no. Lillian was always tougher than I imagined. I recognized the rigidity in her tone, remembered how much it could hurt, the damage it had wrought on my fragile young self. I couldn't bear that this woman—mother, grandmother, it didn't matter—would convey similar feelings of self-doubt, disappointment, and failure to my still impressionable daughter. It was suddenly clear that the muddied situation between the two had been going on for some time; they were nothing like the happy couple I'd been imagining.

My resolve became even stronger. I wouldn't allow Lillian to crush Belle's childhood, to expose her to the kind of emotional battering I'd experienced myself. I had to stop this, right now. The question was how; how to turn back the clock; how to fix this hopeless situation so that everyone came out ahead. My thoughts ran backwards, starting with the new flush of energy I felt after every meeting with Julie and the understanding that self-realization led to healthy relationships. It segued to the way I'd struggled trying to make peace with Belle's inevitable departure and Mike's constant efforts to make things right; careening to the moment I'd gripped that letter from Julliard in my hand, feeling my soaring pride and joy extinguished by my fears. It ended back at a time when my life was ruled by someone else's standards, someone else's needs and desires. I'd come such a long way. We all had.

I wondered if Lillian knew that I'd spoken with Belle, that the nightmare that had reigned over my life for so long had ended up bringing us closer than we'd been for the longest time. In truth, it was this occurrence that enabled me to boldly take this conversation to the source of our mutual pain. I would never have to run away from it again. I didn't want to. The tension of decades lessened its hold, releasing me to a much healthier place. Now it was Lillian's turn. I wondered if there was a chance to convince her—a woman with a standard for every situation, unwilling to grant credence to the possibility of deviation—to drop a lifetime of resolutions and go with the flow.

"Have you told her?" My tone was commanding, barely masking my fury.

"Well, no. No! Of course not!" She was obviously confused by my quick segue to our original conversation. "I still want it to work out. I mean, she's here. She's already here. We're already living together. And of course, this whole year has been such a fabulous opportunity. She'll never find another one like it anywhere else." She paused and lowered her voice, as if speaking to herself. "Julliard. My granddaughter, Lillian's granddaughter, studying at Julliard!"

My head spun as I listened to Lillian gliding from one tone to another, seamlessly shifting gears from a rigid stance to one more yielding and forgiving. She obviously understood what she was about to lose.

"But, if I understand correctly, despite what we both agree is a *fabulous opportunity* and a real feather in your cap as hosting grandmother; despite the fact that Belle dumped what you considered her mediocre life here in Grand Forks to experience a truly banner one in Manhattan; despite all of that, you have had quite enough of living with a teenager and are ready to throw in the towel."

I couldn't avoid a sarcastic, borderline rude tone and was hands-down certain that Lillian would find that last speech one more example of both bad manners and disrespect. I didn't care. There was nowhere left to go.

"You can't just get rid of girls when they don't suit you."

Her gasp was impossible to miss. "Elizabeth! How could you!"

"How could I not?" I was stricken by how unusual this moment really was. I'd never stood up to my mother in this fashion. "It's time you admitted the core of the problem." I paused. "And it's not Belle."

The boost of confidence that had gotten me this far, enabling me to speak with resolve, to challenge Lillian in a way I'd never done before, suddenly evaporated, departing almost as quickly as it had come. I felt light-headed, even a bit faint, and anxiously reached for the kitchen chair, lowering myself into its seat with a clumsy thud. I'd said my piece. It was done. Now I was free to scurry back to the comfort of the status quo we'd both clung to for years. And although this should have been the time for me to burst into tears, giving in to my anguish, I remained dry as a bone, desiccated by our long-standing struggle.

I'd never envisioned Belle having a part in our dance, certain that only Lillian and I could fiddle with that wound that absolutely refused to heal. But my daughter's glorious opportunity had reopened it, and now all three generations of Berkin women were caught in the same tangled web. I leaned forward, head in hands, thankful again that this conversation wasn't being held face-to-face, that I could close my eyes and give in to my exhaustion. I ached for a calmer state, for whatever came after.

Lillian's voice, almost a whisper, drifted through my partial slumber. "I'll just do my best. That's what I'll do. It's what I've always done. Obviously, I can't give up on her. She's my child."

Lillian's comment sliced right through my momentary retreat, awakening all my senses.

"No!" My reaction was piercing and forceful. "No, Mom. She is most definitely not your child. Nor will she ever be. You have a child. That's me. I was your chance to get it right, to work your magic; it was me you molded into whatever warped idea of perfection you had in mind. It was me who you shut out of any consideration, who you gave up on. This child? Belle? She's mine. I won't let you take her away too."

I stopped midstream, shocked by what I'd spoken. More than two decades after the fact, everything was finally coming out.

The phone line between us prickled with raw nerves, bitterness, and desperate disenchantment. I lowered my voice, aware that we'd crossed a bridge to a place of no return. "As it is, I'm sure you've noticed that Belle is well on her way to forging her own path. Neither you nor I have much say in working out the details of her life." I took a breath and continued. "You need to figure out a more effective way to be supportive, to guide—most definitely not to crush." I lowered my voice. "You've done enough of that."

I'd gone too far; those last words were too focused on the past just when I was making a valid point about the future. I'd done exactly what Lillian had done moments earlier. But it was impossible to stop them from coming. This confrontation was years in the making and would, necessarily, leave a number of victims.

Although worked up, armed, and ready to fire, I began to soften, the hard crust of disappointment in which I'd been encased for the longest time crumbling to dust. In its place a tickertape of memories, good memories, ones when Mom had flooded me with the love and attention I craved, came rushing in. There were the times she took me to our local bookstore on Columbus Avenue, encouraging me to take my time, to choose as many books as I could carry home; those trips to the Botanical Garden in Brooklyn, surprising me with a Hershey's candy bar there under the shadow of a Henry Moore nude; British tea at the Plaza Hotel, laughing as we held the fancy china teacups with pinkies extended, pretending to be the queen and princess of England.

Neither all-powerful nor godly, Lillian was a woman like any other, and most probably, at this very moment, feeling less commanding than diminished, sentenced to living out one more day of a long life alone in that empty apartment. And so, instead of rage, I felt sorry—for everything we'd missed, for the loss of the warm relationship we might have had.

It was time to end this conversation and put this whole matter to rest. I'd spent forever trying to make it right with my mother, be more of what she wanted, reach the goals she'd determined for me the day I was born. I'd even gone so far as to distance myself, both emotionally and physically—moving to Chicago, then all the way to the Great Plains, for God's sake—all in a desperate effort to establish something of my own design, a life that suited me and only me. It was still unclear that we could ever mend our relationship. But it wasn't too late to work it out with Belle. We both had infinite opportunities to make that right.

"Mom, figure this out. Think about what you need to do to make this work. You only stand to benefit. Belle as well." Without waiting for a response or girding myself to defend or react, I hung up the phone. I'd never done that before. My ship had finally set sail.

PART III

MIKE

"WHAT'S SHE DOING HERE?"

"Does it matter?"

Lizzy sat at the kitchen table. I stood by the door. Belle was sound asleep upstairs in her room. Something was wrong, but somehow, everything felt exactly right.

"What does that mean?"

"You're working too hard to find a problem. It doesn't mean a thing. It's spring vacation. She needed a break. She came home."

Lizzy shook her head. I could see her trying to figure this out, make sense of something that couldn't be made sense of. I shifted my tone, hoping to get her to stop calculating and take a deep breath. "Maybe we should just enjoy it. She's here! She's home! And the house?" I paused a moment, smiling. "It feels full in a way it hasn't for a while."

Lizzy's eyes clouded over. She was on guard. I couldn't stop her from searching for answers. "Did something happen? Something with a boy?"

I frowned in reply, moving over to the table and taking a seat. "Lizzy, I don't believe it's anything like that. You don't have to worry. This isn't a replay of what went on with Tom."

The screech of her chair felt like a slap in the face. I realized my mistake.

"You've known for all this time?" she demanded.

I lowered my head, muttering my confession. "Belle told me. Before she left."

As usual, the truth had found its way to the surface and emerged on its own. It always did.

"And you didn't think to tell me?"

"Belle swore me to silence. I wanted to let you know, but I couldn't."

Lizzy fell silent, staring down at the table, then gazing around the room as if taking inventory. She looked less angry than exhausted at the discovery of what she probably considered one more bit of treachery. "So many secrets. So many things we keep from one another." She gazed up at me. "When did we stop sharing?"

I extended my hand toward her, but she wrapped her arms tightly around her body in response. She wasn't ready to let me in.

"Well, at least you understand my mania, where it was coming from. I suppose there's something to be said for that."

"I never thought you were crazy. Not once. You've responded like a mother from day one—a great one." I leaned my head forward a bit, trying to engage her eyes. They'd become flat, almost opaque—shuttered and inaccessible.

"So, if that's not it, if it's not about a boy, it must have something to do with Lillian." She took in a quick, sharp breath, and her cheeks blazed red. "She threw her out, didn't she? She asked her to leave! I can't imagine the gall of that woman—"

I had to cut her off. This wasn't the right direction to dig, and worse, it pointlessly fanned the flames of an old wound. We had enough to contend with. We didn't need to add her torturous relationship with Lillian to the fray. I reached toward her again, more determined this time, and grabbed her forearm, holding it firmly. "It's not about Lillian."

She made a lame attempt to pull away, shaking her head and muttering to herself. "She was having a hard time with her. She called me last week. No, no, no. I warned her not to do this, not to break Belle's heart." Tears welled up in her eyes, her heart so obviously broken. "Lillian has done it again. And the worst thing? I knew she would. I told you this was a terrible idea. I said it from the beginning. No one listened to me. You told me I had to move on, deal with my own issues. But now look what's happened." The tears were flowing at a pace now. She half-heartedly wiped at them with her sleeve.

"Lizzy, you've got it all wrong. I'm telling you. You've misunderstood."

Her anger returned like a clap of thunder. "This is all your fault. You turned my head, got me looking elsewhere. I completely dropped the ball with Belle."

I dropped her arm, stood up, and went to the liquor cabinet. I poured two straight shots of Glenlivet and returned to the table. "I'm not going to let you put this on me, nor you, nor Lillian. This is something else entirely."

"Then what? Tell me. You'll admit it means something. Belle didn't just come home. Something's going on."

"Yes, I'm with you on that."

"So, if it's not Lillian, then what?" Elizabeth grabbed at the whiskey and took a sloppy sip, letting some of it trickle down her chin before wiping it off with the same sleeve that had dried her tears. She began rattling off a chain of good things worth celebrating in an effort to ward off the ones she found threatening. "It's just, well, things have been coming together lately. Everything has felt so right. Julie has finally let me in, our time together has become so much more significant, extending well beyond conquering reading. We've even gone out for pie. That's what you do to seal things in North Dakota, to make them solid and real. Right? At least I've learned that much." She giggled nervously. "And Belle? Belle's doing well enough in New York. At least, that's what I understand. And just recently when we spoke, we really connected."

My eyes opened wide, taking in that last bit and its significance. I hadn't known about that conversation, just about the occasional text. From what I knew, Belle's contact with Lizzy had been limited. I'd figured that a good thing—hoping that time and space would help them heal and find their way back to one another. This was something new, but it wasn't my place to ask.

"There aren't always answers, Lizzy."

"But without them I don't know what to do, how to act. What comes next?"

A warm flush moved through me. I looked down at the whiskey for a moment but knew that wasn't the source.

"We just let her be. We wait."

"Still." She rambled on, trying to patch together something intangible. "There must be something. Something I'm missing. If it's not about a boy and not about Lillian, what could it be?"

I placed my hands firmly over hers on the table. She let me. She no longer wanted to fight. "Maybe she just needed to come home."

Lizzy shook her head with the same perplexed expression she'd offered when Belle, our bulldozer of a daughter, had given her a completely uncharacteristic hug at the door a few hours earlier.

"That's not enough for me. I need to know more."

"But maybe you won't. Look, I don't know exactly what happened. Belle chose to keep the details to herself. But she made it very clear that she needed to get away, that things were difficult for her. No, not difficult, impossible. And, Lizzy, I know what I saw, what I witnessed there at that concert. That wasn't our daughter." She watched me closely as I spoke, devouring each word, eager for answers. "I don't think things are at all what she expected."

She nodded slowly, her expression shifting from concern to determination. For the first time since we'd sat down, she looked in control, like she had a purpose. "Mike, there's something I've been wanting to tell you. For the longest time, really. Now that we have a moment . . . I don't want the things we keep from one another to continue to devour what we have."

With a few new discoveries already on the table, I was thinking Lizzy and I could get back to just enjoying the fact that our daughter was snoring upstairs, safe in her bed—that having escaped whatever demons were chasing her back in New York, she'd found some degree of peace back at home. But apparently there was more.

"Wait here a second. Okay? I just want to check . . ." Her voice faded as she headed out of the kitchen and up the stairs. I heard the creak of a door opening and then nothing. Just as I was thinking I should go check on them, I heard the same creak and her feet on the stairs.

"I just wanted to make sure Belle was okay. She looks so peaceful. It's hard to imagine that she's been through any kind of a trauma, that someone has hurt her. That must not be it. As usual, I've let my imagination get the best of me."

She paused, her eyes distant.

"I took a few minutes to sit with her there in the dark. It seemed important. You know, Julie doesn't have anyone to come home to, anyone to sit by her side late at night. She doesn't have anyone to breathe a sigh of relief at finding her safely asleep in bed. She has to do it all on her own: the pep talks, the consoling, even the love." She let out a long breath. "There was a time Lillian did that for me, and somehow, it helped." She cleared her throat. "But that's kind of the ending. I need to go back to the beginning."

And there, in the quiet of our home, a place that had suddenly become a lot warmer and more hopeful, the words spilled out. The simple beginning, "Mike, I had a baby," evolved into the saddest story of a teenager, no longer a child, in love, and a baby she desperately wanted to bring to the world—of a mother who probably thought she was doing right by not letting her daughter realize her dream, who was so bent on returning her to an expected path that she failed to see how her child's heart was breaking. It ended with a loss with which she still couldn't cope and the wrecked relationship of two women who didn't know they were on the same side. Elizabeth's story of her early pregnancy was wrought with the kind of hurt from which one didn't easily heal, the kind that lasted a lifetime.

When I asked her why she hadn't told me before, how she could possibly carry the weight of such a secret for so many years, she insisted that she'd been sure I wouldn't understand.

"Mike, you were raised Catholic. By your rules, what I did would have committed me to a life of damnation. I wasn't raised the same way. That part never played a role in my decision. I've always thought you'd be appalled at the idea of what I did, let alone the fact." She clasped her hands together and pushed them against her mouth, as if bracing herself. "And really, that would be okay. It's the reaction I've always anticipated and, frankly, the one I deserve. I shouldn't have . . ." She went silent, her face gone pale with an old ache relived.

I assured her that it was okay; I didn't subscribe to those tenets. I reminded her that I'd happily spent the last almost twenty years accompanying her to temple not only because I wanted to be part of her life but because the Jewish faith, so understanding and accepting, suited me just fine. She reached out and stroked my cheek, her pallor returning to a healthier color. I delighted to see the beginnings of a smile, tiny laugh lines forming at the corners of her eyes. She looked appreciative and thankful, even relieved. But that wasn't what I was looking for.

I took her hand in mine. "It's me who needs to be forgiven, for not trusting that your difficulties with Lillian were justified—for assuming that you were just being inflexible and obsessive. Now I see that the hurt ran very deep. I understand why it hasn't gone away. I'm so terribly sorry."

I stood and pulled her into my arms, tucking her head into the recess under my chin that had always been hers. Closing my eyes, I tightened my grip and swayed, the tenderness of this moment overwhelming me with a heady mixture of tranquility and joy. "This is a new beginning for us, Lizzy. We need to hold on to it as tightly as we can."

She pulled her face away, and I couldn't help but notice how her forehead, so frequently furrowed of late by wrinkles of worry and distress, had become smooth. We had another chance to do it better, all of it, and it all began with trust.

BELLE

WHEN I LEFT NEW YORK, I was escaping. The party at Rob's had made clear that I was well over my head. I was hanging with kids who were into things that didn't suit me at all and felt downright wrong. It was scary to think that I'd fall back into the same hole once I returned to Manhattan after spring break, making the same mistakes just to ensure my standing with the crowd. Of course, there was a distinct possibility I wouldn't be going back at all. It was possible that Julliard would ask me to leave. Flying back home with Dad the day after that disaster of a concert, I began to truly understand the consequences of my actions. I'd made a complete mess of the keystone in my life, very possibly destroying any chance at attaining my dream. The fiery path of destruction I'd paved had led to one big fat nothing.

The question was what I was running to. Grand Forks at the time of my departure was all about the impasse with Mom and poisonous kids. And although, after all these months, I understood that I'd only exchanged one problematic group of high schoolers for another, I wasn't sure where I stood with Mom. Things had been somewhere between shaky and miserable for such a long time, coming to a head before I left. And although by the time I moved to New York things had begun to cool down, the storm calming just enough to slip into an uncomfortable neutral, there hadn't been any signs of finding our way back to one another.

My new life had convinced me how frustrating parent–child relationships could be, more likely to disappoint than to delight. There was the tangle of life with Grandma, another muddled version of what I'd suffered the previous year or so back home with Mom: a bundle of rules and expectations, frustrations, and anger. I was certain that I'd gotten stuck with a mom who was particularly annoying, and that taking one big step away would open up a world of others ready to cater to my needs without demands. I was wrong. When I most needed an atmosphere that would let me breathe, a place in which I could relax—the stress at Julliard beginning to mount, the struggle to keep up with the other talented kids in the program getting more challenging—Grandma had clamped down hard. It was almost as if my success there was critical to *her* life. The apartment on West End became a pressure cooker instead of a refuge, and, more often than not, I found myself slinking away to my room, desperate for a safe space.

I'd never forget the wretched things Mom had said and done, crashing through the brush, burning the house down in a desperate attempt to keep me tucked tightly into my preadolescent life, but having received a different version of the same from Grandma, I began to understand it came with the territory. I suppose parenting wasn't simple after all. It certainly didn't appeal. So, while part of me wanted to cling to anger and outrage, keep that fire boiling high, an even bigger part had become exhausted by the effort, eager to fold, to run into Mom's arms and put an end to this wretched period of failure and disillusionment. The discovery of her past definitely paved the way home.

The first few days back, I walked around the house like a zombie, randomly touching the simplest of items: the standing lamp in the dining room, the faucet in the kitchen, that old lava lamp I'd had by my bed forever. It was all a weak attempt to touch base with what was real, with things that were constant. I needed to feel grounded, and starting back at ground zero seemed the right move. Although Dad ran interference, trying to set a cheerful tone, always there with a comforting hug, trying to salve the pain of memories that lingered, it was Mom I most needed. It was our relationship, one that had segued from rancorous to chilly, finally warmed by new revelations, that was paramount.

There were signs of hope. They didn't appear all at once, but gradually, like those shifting tectonic plates we'd learned about in geography class, their movement too small to be felt, their cumulative effect transformative. A cautious sense of warmth and understanding returned, albeit one unfortunately hobbled by a shared sense of pain. We had both been through quite a lot. Dad was not immune. Having skirted between and around our tempestuous relationship for years, caught in the maelstrom of frenetic energy created by our constant conflicts, he'd become weary and run down. Our entire household had suffered, the mound of misconceptions and misunderstandings piled ceiling high; we were all stricken by the understanding that things had spiraled out of control. With everything going wrong, the distance between us growing exponentially over the last year, both literally and figuratively, we had come dangerously close to the point of no return. There was still a distinct possibility we would never heal.

Today was about finding a way. In a conciliatory gesture—one I hoped would seem casual, not calculated—I decided to pay a visit to Mom at work. I headed over to her office midday, hoping to surprise her by suggesting we go for pie. Our recent years hadn't been characterized by fun outings together. I figured it was time.

Walking into the law firm's entry vestibule, I immediately noticed the quiet. I'd never considered that it could be quite so obvious, as substantial as noise. It dawned on me that Mom probably adored this, so different from the fireworks between us at home—so manageable and tame.

I tried to puzzle out the source of a buzzing sound, guessing it came from the heating system. Strangely enough, it didn't disturb the quiet but rather added to it, creating the feeling of industry. Things were getting done, wheels were turning, but in the very calmest and smoothest manner—ultra-seamlessly. I looked around at the paintings on the wall, large swatches of tan and brown, at the teak and chrome furniture, and the plush carpeting. Everything in shades of beige. So neutral. I couldn't imagine working in an atmosphere that went for bland. Back in New York, I hadn't waited even a week to repaint Grandma's boring guest room. I liked bold colors that shouted out and made their presence known. Of course, I conceded that this boring palette, which made me want to lie down on one of the super-inviting leather couches and take a nap, probably made sense for a law firm. This wasn't about me.

Two men armed with briefcases and confident smiles stepped my way, nodded in acknowledgment, then went out the door behind me. I giggled. Maybe they thought I was a new client. Boy, did I feel like a fish out of water. The hush, the composure, the control—this was so not my thing. I frowned. *That's not exactly true.* I closed my eyes. I was back at Julliard, feeling the hush of the rehearsal rooms, the resonance of sound that preceded the playing of music and continued to reverberate and work its magic inside of me after we'd finished. This was all very familiar. Maybe I'd just been looking for the differences. Suddenly, the atmosphere here in the entryway of mom's office didn't seem foreign at all.

I hesitated a bit longer by the doorway, taking it all in, feeling a bit more comfortable, before making my way toward the receptionist seated at the welcome desk toward the rear. She stepped over to greet me, extending her hand.

"Elizabeth's daughter! I've heard so much about you. I'm Debbie." She smiled warmly. "The resemblance, well, it's uncanny." I felt the corners of my mouth unexpectedly tilt upward. In the past I would have made a sour face at such a comparison, appalled at the idea of having any likeness whatsoever to my mother. Now it filled me with pleasure. This was an odd turn of events. An outing that had been mostly about pie, somewhat about healing, had now veered toward discovery.

"I'm so sorry. Your mother's not here! She'll be so upset she missed you."

Her words took me by surprise. I'd just assumed Mom would be there. Since fleeing New York, because that's exactly what I'd done, I'd reassessed my allegiances, putting away the pride that had kept me aloof and indignant for as long as I could remember—the attitude that had made me edgy and sometimes even nasty—and decided to take steps toward reconciliation, like coming out to look for Mom. I hadn't considered that she wouldn't be there to receive the gesture.

Debbie filled in the awkward silence. "It's Wednesday. On Wednesdays your mother leaves early. You know, for her community outreach project. Have you met the young woman she's working with? Julie? Elizabeth talks about her quite a bit."

I bristled, caught off guard. I knew Mom was involved in something or other that didn't have to do with me or life at home. There were a few mentions in our text conversations, and I'd noted several comments in the house since my return: something about a girl my own age, a problematic home situation. And there was something else, something about reading. But for the life of me, I couldn't remember more. I hadn't been listening, not really. Things that weren't relevant to my own life simply didn't get a lot of my attention. Yet the enthusiasm with which the receptionist was now describing Mom's involvement indicated that this was something important. I'd missed something that mattered. I was overcome by the most unusual feeling. I felt left out.

Debbie must have picked up on my alarm because she paused and stared steadily into my eyes, catching the look of hurt. She reached out and touched my arm in consolation. "This project, you know, it's been on Elizabeth's docket for a few months. It isn't something new."

I was embarrassed. I should have been more on top of things. I tried not to reveal what little I knew of this apparently significant part of Mom's life, scouring my memory further for additional tidbits but finding nothing. So although I wanted to respond, I couldn't find the words. Focusing on my own needs and goals, dispensing the anger and frustration that had been part of trying to be my own boss while still living under my parents' roof, and storming my way to a life I was certain would offer so much more hadn't left much room for anyone else. I felt so very selfish, so stupid.

Something clicked. I had an idea of how to get around this uncomfortable blip. I could counter with what I *did* know. I regained my composure and engaged Debbie directly.

"Do you think I could take a peek at the library? Since I'm already here. I've never seen it, but Mom has told me about it and . . ." I smiled nervously. "I mean, how interesting could a library be?" She joined me in laughing. Visiting the law firm's library had been part of my original plan. I wanted to show Mom I was interested and cared about things that weren't about me. If she herself wasn't available, I could at least explore the next best thing.

"Of course, dear." She was delighted, turning, and gesturing for me to follow. "This way."

Debbie returned to the main desk, pushing a few buttons on the telephone console, and proceeded to lead me down a long hallway lined with small offices. Save the occasional figure moving from one side of the hallway to the other, their footsteps absorbed by the plush carpeting, there didn't seem to be a lot going on. Yet I knew this to be one of the biggest and best law firms in North Dakota. Dad had told me so. It was amazing to discover that industry didn't demand noise. This place was so different from the turbulent, boisterous, and, yes, raucous, world I occupied in New York. I could see how it appealed, how an oasis that offered a break from all the noise outside could be a refuge.

Arriving at a heavy wooden door, Debbie gestured for me to go in first. I pushed past with my normal gusto, unprepared for the total enveloping silence I found inside. It was so different from that low-register hush I'd picked up elsewhere in the office. This was the kind of quiet that overwhelmed, snuffing out everything else—even the constant buzz of my thoughts. It was the kind of quiet that came after those last notes were played, when my bow still lay on the strings of my viola, its sound now a hallowed memory. My eyes were naturally drawn to the rows and rows of shelves crowded with endless tomes: some with thick, brown leather, some with letters embossed in gold—an enormous collection documenting centuries of law and order. I remembered curling up together in bed,

Mommy and me, reading the story of those kids who hid out in the Metropolitan Museum of Art—how the books collected there offered them a wealth of information even more valuable than actual riches.

Debbie leaned toward me, whispering in my ear. "This is her place. The quiet, the order, it's all your mom's doing. The lawyers at this firm couldn't do their work without hers. I understand that when she arrived—maybe a decade back?—there was a mere fraction of what we have today. Now it's one of the premier law libraries in the Great Plains. We get quite a few visitors: librarians, other lawyers, archivists. They all want to see how it should be done."

I stood stock-still, eyes wide open, amazed at the beauty and order of the space before me. I hadn't expected to be so moved, didn't once consider that something involving Mom, and something as dull as a library, could affect me in such a way. Strangely enough I heard the distant strains of an exquisite harmony. I held my breath a moment, taking in the immensity of this discovery, the parallels in our lives that I never knew existed.

And there was more. I felt pride. I knew Mom's job title but had always figured it meant she shelved books, like the librarian at my school. It sounded so boring. I had no concept whatsoever of what she'd achieved, of what it meant to develop and maintain a library. The notion that she'd created something valuable for others, contributing to a larger community, that she was an important link in a significant process—nothing whatsoever to do with what she did back home, the dishes, the carpools, the needling—was all new to me. What I saw here deserved both respect and admiration, yet until this moment, before witnessing it for myself, it had been like a mosquito in my ear, easily swatted away and dismissed as an irrelevant irritant.

Gazing around at this sanctuary of order, I wondered about all those things I didn't know: how her days looked, what made her happy, whether she even *was* happy. Sometimes it didn't seem so. Mom always moved around the house at hyper-speed, eternally busy with all the details of my life. It seemed impossible that she could actually maintain a meaningful career within the tiny slivers of time left vacant. This place was a whole other world, a whole other life. It most certainly wasn't the domain of a timid mouse, someone who lurked behind the scenes and slunk in the shadows. Nothing here jived with what I expected. The idea that I'd underestimated her and everything she was about—for years—was almost too much to bear. I gulped hard, fending off a heavy wave of guilt.

Standing in *her* library, gazing around at *her* handiwork, I realized that Mom lived what she preached. Years of repeated slogans, her genuine attempts to encourage my passions, flashed through my head: "Follow your heart." "Find what you love; it will lead you on the right path." "Trust your passions." Her work behind the scenes, to make a larger machine work better, was not about self-effacement but instead about self-fulfillment. I was humbled at the thought that I'd never really understood what she was about, misjudging her completely. One of those strange little aphorisms we learned at school flashed through my mind in bright, neon lights: I hadn't seen the forest for the trees.

Back outside, I stumbled along the familiar streets, my thoughts completely preoccupied with the special sanctuary I'd discovered back at the firm, with my enlightenment. Although I knew Grand Forks could never offer me the ability to develop my passion, knew I'd have to realize my dream elsewhere, I began to understand how it might be different for others. Living so far out of the center didn't have to be a death sentence to personal development. Ever since I began to dream about the East Coast, I'd been super condescending about my parents' choice to live their lives on the Plains. Today I was less so. Today had been a revelation. Mom's accomplishment within a modest three-story brick building on Main Street, USA, creating so much with so little, suddenly felt as significant as anything I might be lucky enough to achieve in Carnegie Hall.

Deep in these thoughts, confused and distraught by the fact that I'd been nothing more than a typical, spoiled, self-centered teenager, I was startled to spot none other than Mom herself sitting in the window of Paolo's on North Third Street with a girl about my age. I slowed to a stop and peered inside, watching the two dig their forks into a large piece of shared pie. Although my view was disturbed by the glint of sunshine on the glass window, I could see wide smiles, beaming faces. Their mutual pleasure of this shared moment was obvious. I felt a sharp pang of jealousy and almost cried out. It was unbearable to watch someone just like me enjoying the intimacy that should have been mine.

Of course, I didn't miss the irony—the fact that it was I who'd continually rejected my mother's effort to be close, so absolutely convinced that it would hold me back, that it was a means to impose her needs on my own. But that didn't ease the pain. Standing there on the sidewalk, I was crushed by the fact that this other girl, a stranger, was not only enjoying exactly what I'd shirked but, worse, seemed to be benefiting from it. She looked so happy; she looked loved. Witnessing what might have been—what had always been there for the taking but was now someone else's—was positively crippling.

I couldn't suppress the urge to burst in and break up this private powwow. I rushed forward, eager to ruin the sickeningly harmonious picture before me, to deny this other girl access to what I didn't have, no matter who was to blame. The two looked up as I stepped through the door of the shop, startled as much by the jangling of the doorbell as by my distraught expression. Somewhat startled by my own bold action, I made a lame effort at nonchalance I didn't feel, raising my hand in a weak greeting. It was then, standing by their table, that I realized my mistake. It wasn't them. It wasn't Mom and her new daughter. No, not daughter, student. I shook my head hard, dismissing that muddled thought. I couldn't believe how crazy this was—the fact that I'd conjured up an image that didn't exist. Murmuring an apology to the confused strangers before me, I retreated out the door, embarrassed.

I stumbled away from the shop, inhaling huge gulps of air, trying to calm down. I felt completely disoriented. This town I called home, the one I knew like the back of my hand, whose streets I could navigate with my eyes closed—the one I'd recently deemed too small to contain my dreams—was suddenly unfamiliar. I stopped at a random corner and stared up at the street sign, trying to get my bearings, pull myself together, and regain some of my composure.

Nothing had happened. This wasn't important. I had no reason to get upset. Yet I was. And I had trouble dismissing my distress. More startling than anything I thought I'd seen was how it had rattled me. The *me* I knew shouldn't have cared. Mom's business hadn't been on my radar. The intensity of my response was as alarming as what triggered it: the idea that Mom had moved on.

This was one hell of a wake-up call. Suddenly, the idea of mending things, the thought that had accompanied me since arriving back in Grand Forks, became more urgent. There was no time to waste. This morning's visit exposed the shocking possibility that I may have lost too much ground to recover. I'd always craved the kind of closeness I glimpsed through that plate-glass window, the kind represented by those strangers I'd envied, between Lydia and her mother—precisely what Debbie hinted existed between Mom and her student. My adamant refusal to accept it from my mother had absolutely nothing to do with my need. I realized now that it was part of a foolish and misguided attempt to establish my independence. I'd made a horrible mistake, working too hard to run away from what I most wanted.

Things were going to change. I'd make them change. It was time to stop being a bitch and give Mom a chance. Maybe that was the key to figuring out things for myself as well, to discovering what I really wanted. With her by my side, I might finally be able to dispense with the clamor that was so distracting and find the beautiful harmonies I sought.

JULIE

I STOOD JUST INSIDE THE living room, looking around at the place I'd spent most of my years, the place I still called home. Everything looked exactly like the day I'd left six months earlier. Or that's what I thought at first. The longer I stood there, the more I became aware of the subtlest changes. Something was terribly off. The whole place seemed cooler, its palette faded. There was a stagnancy indicative of the absence of human presence. Of course, that made no sense. My mother, a red-blooded human being, still lived here. But it was impossible to deny that my home now felt like an empty shell.

I had waited for this day for some time, checking the calendar hanging over my bed each morning, the date circled with a halo of stars and hearts. I called Mrs. Kraft several times the prior week to make sure I had the details of our meeting right. Time dragged by at half pace, my anticipation of the reunion with Mom so great. I envisioned how I'd run straight into her arms, hugging her tight. Today was going to be a beginning, a *new* beginning. I had another chance to do it right, to make it work—to be part of a family and not just one more abandoned stray. Having learned my lesson and pulled myself together, I could finally live at home with Mom. It was happening, the happily ever after.

Mrs. Kraft picked up on my nervousness the minute we met. I couldn't stop wiggling. I rolled back and forth on my toes with such gusto that I rocked the elevator. Although I cast her furtive glances, making occasional eye contact, I was incapable of responding to her attempts at conversation. I was tied up in too many knots. Before leaving the Center, I'd planned to hide my anxiety, knowing my behavior was being noted. But that was impossible. I couldn't quell the zip and zoom that energized each action, each thought. That is, until I stepped inside the door of my former home. Once there, I froze, paralyzed by the not-so-subtle change I detected, terrified that this day was not going to end up as I'd hoped.

Instead of running to greet my mother, I stood sentry inside the door, letting Mrs. Kraft have that honor. I watched in silence as the two struck up a conversation on the far side of the living room by the bank of windows looking out to the street. That was always my favorite spot. I'd spent hours there dreaming of what could be, yearning for the kind of normalcy I figured existed just beyond my reach. I couldn't hear their words, but I eagerly followed their body language, knowing that I no longer determined the course of events. It was left to others to decide my fate.

Feeling almost forgotten, I abandoned my post and ventured into what used to be home—what would always be home. I wasn't quite sure where to go, which space to reoccupy. Although everything was as I remembered—the couch pulled close to the coffee table, the soft flannel blanket neatly draped over the corner armchair, the banquette by the windows still beckoning—it all felt unfamiliar and, most alarmingly, unreceptive.

My eyes darted from side to side, looking for a place to sit down, somewhere halfway welcoming. I didn't want to disturb Mrs. Kraft and Mom, still mid-conversation. I couldn't imagine what remained to be discussed. Today was about coming home. I eventually fell hard into the old armchair, remembering how good it felt to wrap myself in that cozy flannel while watching TV at night—albeit alone. Well, actually, almost never alone, but always feeling that way. My mom's presence hadn't counted for much, although I desperately wished it eventually would. Even with all the trappings, everything that was meant to count as a home right there at my fingertips, something essential and life sustaining had always been missing.

"Julie?" The call of my name coaxed me back to the moment. I looked around, disoriented by the interruption, and noticed Mrs. Kraft waving in my direction. "Dear? Julie. We're going to join you. Let's all sit together." She led Mom to the couch by the elbow, took a seat, and then patted the place next to her in encouragement. Mom remained standing. "I've just been catching up with Fay a bit, hearing what she's up to."

The words floated toward me, rebounding off the stuffed cushions, reverberating in my head but failing to sink in. Something didn't feel right. I stared at her, unable to even nod in response.

"Julie?" Mrs. Kraft's originally conciliatory tone changed to one of concern, and her hand reached out to grasp mine in a gesture of salvation. She had discerned my panic. "Are you okay?" Her voice was just a whisper. "Is this all right? You know, if it's too difficult . . ." Her voice faded away for a moment before coming back strong and with much more assurance. "It's *your* comfort I'm concerned with—that's what's important here. This is about *you*, Julie."

She gestured dismissively around us. Following her hand, taking in the emptiness of the room despite our presence, I realized its lack of substantiality. Suddenly the idea on which I'd staked these last few months, of regaining this home base, seemed foolhardy. One glance at my mother—or rather, the shadow of my mother—still standing beside the couch made clear that the fairy-tale ending wasn't going to happen. There would be no happy reunion. Even more disturbing, I was no longer sure it was what I wanted. I blinked away the tears that sprang to my eyes, threatening to spill onto my cheeks, and quickly looked away from Mrs. Kraft.

"I'm good. It's okay." I eked out the words she expected to hear. After all, today was about investigating whether I'd officially be allowed to leave the Meier Center and move back home, whether CPS would give their approval. Changing course, indicating that this was no longer what I wanted and that I had some serious second thoughts, would upset whatever chance I had to turn back the clock and return to the beginning. I'd wanted this for so long, been so certain this would make me happiest. Now I wasn't sure.

"Fay. Please. Come and sit with us."

I followed my mom's slow and languorous movement as she finally acquiesced, taking a seat on the couch more as an afterthought than out of any desire or intention. I ached to make eye contact with her, to have even one moment to get an impression of what she was thinking, what she felt. That was something mothers and daughters did, or at least were supposed to do. I had no way to know for sure.

Once we were all seated, the silence spread, picking up density and significance. It held all my disappointment, my simmering rage, and the reasons I'd never know normal. I wanted to scream or shout, anything to break through and inject some heaving and breathing life into this wretched, suffocating vacuum. I considered jumping up and grabbing Mom's hand, pulling her along behind me as I made a dash for the door. Ditching this place might be our only escape. Yet the distracted look in her eyes and the fact that she wasn't engaging with either me or Mrs. Kraft made clear that we'd come to an end. There was nothing left to restore. This whole plan of mine had been a fantasy, a ridiculous, misplaced fantasy. Nothing was left for me in this house.

I stood abruptly, pushing the coffee table away. Mrs. Kraft issued a gasp of surprise.

"Julie! What's going on? Are you . . . ?" She let the question hang, her thought incomplete.

I was continually astounded by the humanity of this woman, someone hired by the state to step in, in the absence of a functioning parent. She was so lovely and calm. She made such an effort to let me know she was on my side. Just like Elizabeth. I turned to her now with a bittersweet smile, thankful for her presence in my life but intensely sad that she'd never be more than a surrogate, one in a long line. I'd never be among those fortunate souls blessed with a real mother. I'd been born to a woman who herself demanded mothering.

"Mrs. Kraft, thanks. I don't know. I just don't know." This was the time to voice my change of heart, but I hesitated. I didn't want this kind woman to feel she'd wasted her time. That would add one more to the list of individuals I'd somehow displeased and disappointed.

"Julie?" The air crackled and snapped at my mother's bristly voice. Both Mrs. Kraft and I jumped in surprise. Neither of us expected her to join the conversation. In some ways, it was an inessential aspect of the day's event. "Julie." This time she uttered my name a bit more steadily. I sat back down, stunned.

Sensing a significant change in the air, Mrs. Kraft took the opportunity to excuse herself.

"Maybe I'll just make us all tea. Give you two some time."

My mother's panic at her sudden departure was obvious. The skin already stretched tautly over her bone-thin cheeks rippled with tension, and two lines formed in the gulf between her eyes. It was heartbreaking to see the distress triggered simply by being left alone with me, her daughter. Looking even more diminutive than usual, my mother retreated to her former silence. Much later, back at school, when the noise there got the best of me, when I cupped my hands over my ears to shut it out, I'd remember how much more lethal quiet could be.

I wondered if I should take control of the situation by trying to engage. I could move to her side, take her hand in mine. Physical proximity might at least wake her up, force her to react in some fashion. Whispering my name a few times did not count as more than a sign of life. But I didn't move. I was afraid to budge, certain that even clearing my throat would scare her off. I calmed myself by staring hard at the awkward space between us, the void left empty by Mrs. Kraft's departure to the kitchen.

That was when I noticed the similarity. I'd always hated my knees, those bumps on their outer edges that ballooned outward and seemed to sag. They seemed unlike any of the "regular" knees I noted among other girls my age, both bizarre and awkward. I'd never before considered that they were part of some strange genetic pool. Yet now I couldn't miss how they pointed straight at what were, quite clearly, their cousins.

The irony of this discovery was obvious. While my mother was anything but a mother, falling short as a parent in every way that mattered, her knobby knees proved that she could be no other. Released by a fresh burst of surprise-induced adrenaline, my imagination animated the two sets, and I watched as they greeted one another, à la Disney's *Fantasia*, with peels of delighted laughter and deep curtsies—long-lost relatives now happily reunited. Hyper-focused on this imagined scene, our knees drawing together in a comforting hug, I almost missed it when Mom broke the silence and spoke.

"How's your, well . . . your new place?"

The vision before me disappeared, the fantasy world I'd concocted leaving almost as quickly as it had come. My mother had returned to the living with a question. Although simple and meaningless, it still counted as an attempt to connect. It was a wonderful sign. For a moment I let myself believe that I had succeeded in waking her from her usual stupor. It wasn't her words that got my attention as much as the rare display of emotion I saw in her moist eyes. Looking beyond that warbled sea of green, I discerned a distinct ripple that denoted deep sorrow. This woman was in pain. A situation which I found impossible and intolerable was just as hard for her. There was nothing left to do save try to comfort her. As always, it was my job to mother.

I disengaged from the sadness in her eyes and scrambled for something to say, looking for a way to hold on to this fragile opportunity before it slipped away. "It's okay, Mom. It's fine."

I spoke as gently as I could, but I knew I hid neither my anguish nor my exhaustion. Being both the needy daughter and the surrogate parent was simply too great a burden. I swallowed hard, the stasis of the conversation, of the entire situation, having aggregated into a boulder-sized lump in my throat. Making an effort to engage but not alarm, I placed my hand as gently as possible on one of those matching knees. I hoped human touch would work its magic, offering comfort, maybe even bringing Mom back to the world of the living.

"The people are nice—or, at least, nice enough. I figure I'm not going to be there that long in any case. Right?" I held my eyes steady on hers, not daring to blink, afraid of losing that tiny but significant point of contact. "Mrs. Kraft says maybe I'll be able to move home soon. I could help you here." I removed my hand and gestured vaguely around the room, wondering what it would take to reoccupy this space and make it a home again. *How does one restore a beating heart to an empty shell?*

A sudden bustle and a tinkling of crockery disturbed what only vaguely resembled a conversation. Mrs. Kraft walked in with a tray crowded with mugs and spoons, a sugar bowl, and a steaming kettle of water. Having missed the stunted exchange between Mom and me, she picked up precisely where she'd left off minutes earlier.

"So, I was telling your mother when we came in that you've begun to settle in at the Center, that you're finding your place, making friends." I winced at the lie. I gazed again at my mother. She was already elsewhere. This whole scene had detached itself from any reality I wanted, any I'd dreamed of, crumbling into pieces and dissolving into thin air.

I no longer wanted to play nice. Running away seemed much more appealing. In any case, since there was nothing left for me here, there was no purpose in staying. Acknowledging this truth gave me the strength to stop the charade, to finally lay my heart out for all to see. I stood and looked straight down at my mother.

"You know what, Mom? It's crap. The place is crap. And the people there? I don't like any of them. I don't even try to like any of them. For the longest time it didn't matter because soon enough I'd be coming home and leaving them all behind. But now? Now I'm wondering if that's going to happen. Do you want me here? Do you want me to come home? Because . . ." I paused, steaming hot with a renewed anger. I was angry at my mother for never being a mother, at the fact that critical life moments had to be monitored by a Mrs. Kraft or whoever, at myself for imagining that anything would ever work out the way it was meant to be, the way I dreamed it could be. "Because . . . I want to come home." I couldn't help this coming out as a plea.

Mrs. Kraft stood and laid a hand on my arm, trying to calm me down. "Julie, dear, we don't need to do this."

I turned on her and saw her flinch. Although the fear in her eyes disappeared just as quickly as it had appeared, I didn't miss it. I scared people. Me. The girl that only wanted to be loved. I turned back to my mother. This had to be finished, right now. I could no longer live with the stress of not knowing.

"I'm ready to come home, Mom. I won't be such a burden. I can help you manage. Make it easier for you." I glanced over at Mrs. Kraft, who had taken one step back but was still close enough to touch. She was responsible for making the ultimate decision. "It won't be like it was. I'll make sure not to make waves at school this time. In any case, I get it now. I've learned that low profile is smarter." I cleared my throat. "I try to stay undetected."

Mrs. Kraft mumbled something, a weak effort to put a stop to what had become a rave, then quickly looked away. It was too late. I saw the resignation on her face. She'd been so positive all day, smiling at me, nodding in agreement, radiating calm. Now I understood that it had all been a show, an attempt to make me comfortable, to appease. She never thought this reunion would work out, had probably been certain it wouldn't from the start. Her role was to lighten the blow, to hold my hand and make this crossing to no-man's-land just a bit more bearable—to reorient the coordinates that would set me on a new path, easing the way to a reality that didn't include a home with Mom.

The curtain on this chapter of my life fell.

Defeated, desperate to fight off the fury ignited by the unfairness of it all, I waved my hand at her in a gesture of dismissal.

"Don't even bother. Just don't." I immediately regretted my sharp tone. This woman didn't deserve my rancor. I was the one who initiated this whole shit show. I tried to dial down my attitude, hide my still simmering fury. I stooped over and grabbed my cup of tea, keen to alleviate the tension of the moment. Taking an especially generous sip, I screamed out in pain. It was searing hot. I dropped the mug clumsily back onto the serving tray, splashing scalding tea everywhere, and puckered my lips, trying to nurse the burn.

My mother rose suddenly from her seat. She'd felt my pain. The memory of the time I broke her cup in a fit of rage rushed back to me and I understood. I needed to hurt for her to wake up and take notice. For some reason, instead of upsetting me, this realization set off a wave of reassurance that moved through my body, eventually making its way to my mouth where it eased the sting of the burn. This sign of a motherly instinct filled me with an extraordinary sensation of relief, restoring a smidgen of hope. Despite everything that was missing, there was something that wasn't.

This relationship was never going to be what I desperately wanted and needed it to be. The chance of building something significant on something so very empty and flawed was virtually zero. Yet my mom's visceral reaction to my shout of pain felt like a gold mine. Although it was tempting to grab this opening and beg for more, to pick up the ball that had fallen at my feet and run with it, the infinite number of disappointments stretching back years held me back. It would never be enough. I had to finally accept that and move on.

I turned to Mrs. Kraft. "I think we should go."

I wanted to put this failure of a day behind me. In any case, I'd soon have to shore up my defenses and prepare for the onslaught at school. The ugly exchange with those girls last week came back to me in a sharp flash of pain. What I had here, what had become a haunted and very sad space, was just one of the terrible things with which I had to deal. I still had not found a place I considered safe.

I went to stand by the door. Following my lead, Mrs. Kraft left Mom behind and stepped toward me. I turned away from her look of concern and glanced down at my shoes. I didn't want to be consoled. I didn't even feel particularly disappointed. With one last and purposeful glance at my mother, still standing by the couch, facing the space I'd just vacated, I opened the door and stepped outside. The woman I left behind—the one who'd brought me into the world, the one with whom I'd lived an awkward life for almost two decades, the one whose fragility had forced my retreat into a life filled with anger and altercation—this woman would never be more than any other. Any expectation to find in her the mother I needed was gone. It was time to move on.

BELLE

"WHICH ONE IS HE?"

Lydia walked ahead of me, purposefully flicking the brush alongside the path so that it would thwack me in the face.

"Hey! That hurt!"

She laughed. "The one with the Coldplay T-shirt." I looked down the path behind me. I'd seen that guy earlier, but now he was nowhere in sight.

"Does he have a name?"

"Do you?" We both giggled.

This weekend started off 100 percent wonderful. I'd come home just in time to join the local NFTY branch's spring retreat. This annual event brought together youth groups from as far away as Winnipeg and Minneapolis. This year they were meeting up at Lake Metigoshe near the Canadian border. Since arriving back in Grand Forks, I'd been frenetically trying to sort things out, to fix what had unraveled back in New York. I knew I'd tried to juggle too many balls at once but still had no idea how to pull together the ratty strands of my life: the expectations of kids at school, Grandma's disappointment, my lack of concentration where it most counted, with viola in hand. I wasn't even sure I still had a place at Julliard or if I wanted one.

Things at home were equally unclear. Although Mom and I were cautiously finding one another, it was hard to forget everything we'd lost. I had been so intent on pushing her away for such a long time, forcibly removing myself from her sphere to discover my own. Now that I was back, I was shocked to discover an entirely different person. This new Mom didn't at all resemble the picture I had in my head. She was so calm, neither raising her voice nor jumping at the slightest affront. Absolutely nothing seemed to ruffle her feathers. She even moved differently, her gestures no longer gawky, her stride positively liquid. Instead of looking balled up in a tight knot, a spring ready to burst, she seemed calm and unperturbed. Her forehead, formerly broken up by wrinkles she always claimed were all about me, was smooth as could be. I wanted to take credit for these changes, but I couldn't. I hadn't been around. And when I was, I was unpleasant. I wondered if my absence had done the trick. There was the chance that it had to do with that girl. Although I hadn't yet met her, I hadn't been able to stop obsessing about what she meant to Mom. Conjuring up that scene at the pie shop had only been the beginning. There was no way I would give *her* credit for the change I noted. That hurt too much.

With everything so out of whack, I was thrilled to put all that aside, step back into something safe, and simply have a little fun with old friends. Time off to see what my life would be like without all the noise was just what I needed. I was even kind of excited about the religious agenda, eager to discover what I'd found missing back in New York—events at Grandma's temple on Central Park West leaving me numb, most services spent flipping back and forth in the prayer book. Out in nature, sitting Indian style in a large circle with my friends under a crown of trees, knees knocking against one another consolingly, I was overwhelmed by feelings of intimacy and connectedness long dormant. I suppose I hadn't truly understood the degree to which they had been missing.

Rabbi Karen started out a twilight workshop by reading a verse from the Chapter of the Fathers (*Pirkei Avot*), a collection of ethical teachings and maxims. "Who is wise?" She looked around the circle, waiting for a response. There wasn't a sound. We were all struck silent, obviously uncomfortable with the question. This was pretty deep. *Could there really be an answer?* She smiled at us and nodded understandingly. "Okay. Let me put this another way. I want you all to think about someone you'd be willing to learn from. That one person in your life. Who would that be?"

Mom. My eyes widened and I glanced around to see if my voice had been too loud. I hadn't expected to be the first one to speak.

Not one person looked my way. Maybe I hadn't spoken out loud after all. Yet I was startled by the quickness of my answer, how I hadn't had to think twice. It was so clearly Mom. That was quite a revelation considering our history.

Soon enough, other kids responded aloud, and the discussion around the circle became lively. I remained silent, replaying that day I'd gone to the law firm: the wealth of industry, dedication, and love I discovered there—the environment she'd created, so similar to the one I loved at Julliard. The mother I'd spurned for such a long time was truly a wonder. She was the one responsible for bringing music into my life, inspiring my devotion to and cultivation of it with her own passion and commitment. *Why did it take so long for me to recognize that?*

I didn't have a lot of time to process this revelation; Rabbi Karen stepped into the middle of the circle and presented another thought-provoking question. "Who is happy?" That made us all giggle, setting off a chain of wiggling that moved along the circle like a great wave, creating a heaving helix of smiles and good cheer. I loved this moment and these people. I didn't want to be anywhere else. The thought of going back to New York, with its multiple challenges and sharp edges, was unpleasant. *What am I looking for?*

After we settled down, there was another long pause. No one responded. This question seemed more obvious. Maybe it was a trick. We were all happy right then and there. Were we supposed to call out our names? Understanding that we were once again stuck, the rabbi expanded on her original question. "Okay, okay. Everyone needs to take a deep breath. It's obvious you're all happy. I can see it on your faces. But you're right that that's too evident an answer. Let's try this another way. I want you to think about *what* makes you smile."

This. Again, my answer was automatic. I didn't have to think about it at all. What made me happy was this retreat. I hadn't stopped smiling since getting on the bus. Formerly, youth group retreats had been about getting away from home, shaking off the bummer of family obligations and rules, especially regarding boys. Just one year earlier, I spent the days leading up to such weekends obsessing about the sleepover aspect, envisioning arranging sleeping bags into mix-and-match constellations based on friendships or burgeoning relationships, eager to explore the promise of unchaperoned hours away from home. This year, everything felt different. I was much more comfortable with the more spiritual aspect of the weekend, surprisingly enjoying it. I guess I wasn't exactly who I'd been back then.

By the time Rabbi Karen turned that beautiful, multi-braided candle upside down and dipped it into the waiting glass of wine, signaling one week's end and another's beginning, and led us arm in arm in a resounding version of "*Shavuah Tov*," I was completely subsumed in the kind of inner peace I'd been seeking since I got home. With the fizzle of the extinguished wick, an enormous cavity opened inside of me, making room for a whole new start. Suddenly it seemed possible to achieve balance within the chaos of my life in New York. All I had to do was find the right path.

Sitting on a bumpy bed of twigs and crawling creatures better left unacknowledged, I realized that life in the city was less about glamour, as I'd thought before I left Grand Forks, and more about an enormous, heaving effort. I wondered if this was what Mom had wanted to save me from when she tried to dissuade the move. Well, this among other things. Although this didn't justify all her craziness, it would make it more explicable. Dragging Quinn out of that party, saving her from that boy even though she didn't truly understand that she needed saving, alerted me to how we don't always know where we stand; we don't always perceive imminent danger.

And of course, on the flip side, we don't always recognize that other's actions are meant for the best. Maybe Mom chased Tom out of the house because she worried that what was going on was not of my own design; maybe she fought against my exit to New York because she knew that living with Grandma was going to be difficult; maybe all her actions were meant to keep me from harm, to protect me. Just maybe, Mom wasn't a minor being at all, slinking around in the shadows the rest of us cast, undetected, trying to make the least waves, but instead a real live hero.

ELIZABETH

BANG, BANG, BANG. I POUNDED my left leg in an arrhythmic and frenzied manner against the plastic well of the driver's seat.

"Change. Change. Just change."

I stared down one red light after another, challenging them to defy me, wondering what magic would make them turn green and get me on my way. I even considered honking at this last one. No one honked at a red light. At least, not here in Grand Forks. But thankfully, my prayers were answered, and I was on the move, pressing hard on the accelerator as the car leaped forward. I glanced at the clock on the dashboard: 6:45 p.m. It had been almost an hour since I received the call from Belle's counselor asking me to meet them at the hospital. The hospital! This wasn't a call a mother wants to receive—ever!

I managed to cruise through the next few lights, even those hovering that last second between yellow and red, but was forced to slam on my brakes as I approached a full stop. I couldn't risk an accident. It wouldn't help Belle if I needed to be raced off to the hospital as well. I renewed my thumping while waiting my turn, bobbing my head like a chicken, forward and back, urging the other cars to get on with it and let me through. My jumpy movements didn't ease my edginess, but they helped pass the time.

I didn't know the extent of what had happened to Belle. The only thing I knew was that it wasn't life-threatening. The fact that her counselors hadn't rushed her off the trail hours earlier, deciding they could drop her off at the hospital for examination on their way home from the retreat, meant it couldn't be all that serious. Despite all that, I was concerned. Whatever had happened involved her hands, and nothing was more important to Belle. They were part of the future on which she'd staked everything, throwing our household into a vortex of emotion from which we were still struggling to escape. This injury could seriously derail her cherished new life. I wanted her home, but not this way.

For a moment I was distracted, considering the way our relationship had evolved over the last year. During the months immediately after the move, I barely heard from Belle. I tried not to take it to heart. It was essential to steer clear of the minefield of her life with Lillian in New York. I counted on time to do its job and eventually bring us back together. How ironic that the thing I most feared, the unearthing of an ancient secret, had propelled us into new territory—the hopeful, albeit cautious, one we were defining daily since she'd come home. With every day still a new horizon, we didn't need the addition of a major injury.

Ragged thoughts competed with lengthy smears of colored neon lights as I raced along the city's streets. The long trip back from Fargo, where I'd been assisting with the preparation of a brief, had offered plenty of time to let my mind run wild with scenarios. Of course, I could have saved myself the imagined fears by asking a few more questions. Patience had never been my forte. Instead, armed with minimal details regarding the where and the when, I'd hopped into the car and started on my way, the nature of the injury less significant than the fact that Belle needed my help. If only Mike hadn't been off on a flight, completely incommunicado. This was one time I would have welcomed his interference. The reassurance that someone hadn't thought this an emergency only went so far in assuaging my apprehension; meeting at the hospital meant it wasn't just a scratch.

Moving along at a pace now, no lights or stop signs in sight, I fretted over the possibilities, working through them one by one. First thing: Belle had broken a bone in one of her hands. It didn't matter which, as she'd need all of them intact for Julliard. Of course, whether it was in her bowing hand or the one that worked the fingerboard, magically picking out the right notes, could make a real difference. It would be easier to deal with the former situation. Next consideration: the nature of the break. There were breaks and there were breaks. *Dare I hope for a simple one? Is there such a thing?*

I tried to rein in my fears as the minutes ticked by, but there was little hope of containing them. The dark night sky with its threat of rain and one obstacle after another, whether it be a red light, a stop sign, or a pokey driver, all contributed to my frenzied machinations.

Finally leaving the highway, I pulled up to the light at the end of the exit ramp. Another red. This was simply unbelievable. *How can my luck be this bad?* Completely beside myself, I groped around the passenger seat for my purse and fished out my cell phone. I wanted to call back the counselor and ask him a few more questions. Maybe it wasn't a break at all. But one clumsy stab at the screen and a quick glance at the light convinced me that this was not the time to risk texting. I would just have to be patient, get to the hospital, and deal with whatever I found there. I took a few deep breaths. The technique I'd picked up at the Lamaze class both Mike and I were sure was redundant surprised me by successfully slowing my heartbeat from a dead sprint to a loping gallop.

I reminded myself that there was no worst-case scenario. Belle was fine. This wasn't a deadly situation. I had to count my blessings and pull myself together.

The light turned green, and I slammed my foot on the accelerator for the umpteenth time, energized by the knowledge that this was the final stretch. The hospital was only a few minutes away. My thoughts turned to Belle, focusing less on the nature of the injury and more on how it might be affecting her. Had she screamed, cried out, or just been startled? Would I find her in tears or stoically dealing with her discomfort? I couldn't wait to burst through the hospital doors, track her down within the long hallways, and hold her. I *had* to hold her. Things between us had warmed up lately—or rather, calmed down to a steady lull—and I was sure she'd be more than happy to see me. There were times when a mother was the best medicine.

Distracted by this last thought, I missed the turnoff for the hospital, continuing into the neighborhood beyond. My mind was elsewhere entirely, having flipped back to a time when I was very young, even younger than Belle, not yet a teenager. I'd fallen while jumping on a trampoline at a friend's house. Those were the days before safety netting and tarp-covered springs. The metal ones framing this trampoline were rusty and exposed. A large gash split open along my hairline, and my friend's mother used a towel to staunch the bleeding. I enjoyed her ministrations, knowing that it would take some time for Lillian to arrive. She'd no doubt assume the injury minor, no real medical emergency, eventually pulling up in the car, all smiles and indifference, her manner 100 percent calm and collected. Lillian wouldn't consider this a big deal.

But that was not the way it went at all. Here the memory got more vivid, engulfed in vibrant, gem-toned colors. In fact, I didn't wait long. Within what seemed like minutes, Mom arrived, rushing into the house, all bluster, clearly concerned. And despite the soothing words she whispered in my ear throughout the rest of that day, putting on a brave face while accompanying me through the stages necessary to repair me and get me back home, her tense expression revealed her genuine fear. This version of Mom was completely different from the one I'd anticipated—the one that embodied equanimity, insisting everything was okay and allowing no room for drama or histrionics. Faced with my bloody head, my mother broke her own rules and gave in to the kind of serious apprehension she usually eschewed. With my soundness at stake, the world was turned on its head, principles thrown to the wayside.

I had wanted that day, and the week that followed, when she watched over me like a hawk to ensure that I didn't pull a stitch, to last forever. I'd have done anything to maintain her full attention, that flood of love and devotion. I could still feel the tight squeeze of her hand before, during, and after the procedure, the way she let go for only a moment when I was lifted out of reach, onto the surgical table; the way she lovingly prepared me hot chocolate in the afternoons as I rested at home, the huge marshmallows on top melted into a soothing goo. But of course, life continued its course, and this extraordinary experience of being the center of Lillian's world ended, eventually relegated to a vague memory. Soon enough, she returned to her usual ways, attaching affection to one goal or another—stepping back and parenting at a slight remove, out of my reach.

Cursing once I realized I'd missed my turn, I took a sharp right and gasped as the car began to spin, first in one direction and then the other, my attempt to correct its movement with a jerk of the steering wheel backfiring. The loss of control immediately stopped the rush of memories, swallowing them whole in the endless moment it took to come to a safe stop at the side of the road.

Drained, terrified, and intensely relieved to be in one piece, I draped my shivering upper body over the steering wheel, giving in to an explosive bout of crying. I didn't bother trying to stop the torrent, so obviously needing to release the tension not only of the spin but of the hour that preceded it—maybe even the whole year. I let the tears flow, dabbing sloppily at my face and appreciating the car's ability to absorb the almost savage sound of my cries. Now was as good a time as any to let it all out. Once inside with Belle, I'd have to be strong, to assure her that everything would be okay. Sealed in my own soundproof space, securely tucked away from the passing traffic and the rest of the world, I allowed myself to take another few minutes to gather my wits and take stock, before making my final approach.

One minute cruising, the next one skating on thin ice. One more life lesson about holding tight to what really mattered and letting the rest go. Although I should have been thinking about Belle, anticipating the scene that awaited me in the emergency room, the memory of my mother's rescue came back to me once more in an intoxicating rush, and I was overwhelmed by intense appreciation for the woman I'd spurned repeatedly ever since. My hands gripped the steering wheel, again feeling the tight squeeze of her hand in the operating room; its lightness as it comfortingly traced wiggly lines along my back after I'd had my heart broken by that pimply boy; its excited clapping before her flushed face as she rushed into the hospital room at Northwestern Memorial, so excited she almost sat right down on Belle's baby cot.

I didn't have to forgive her to understand how much she cared, to know that she loved me. I'd messed up so many things with Belle by trying to protect her, and she was only seventeen. I was certain to do it many times more over the years to come. I hoped she'd eventually understand that it all came from love. God knows, there really was no recipe for perfect parenting. I suppose if there were, we'd all be doing a much better job.

I restarted the car and pulled slowly back onto the road, spotting the luminous sign for the hospital a few minutes later and pulling into the lot. By this time, my focus had shifted, my mom receding to a now more accommodating space deep within my heart and Belle moving into the foreground. I sprinted toward the emergency room entrance, spouting a litany of positive thoughts. *She's going to be fine. She has to be fine. It's nothing. It's all going to be okay.*

I repeated them over and over until I spotted her seated in a chair near the desk for emergency check-in, her hand wrapped in a T-shirt stained with dark-brown splotches, an enormous entity in itself. I grabbed at the wall by the entrance to catch my breath and keep from falling, my heart aching with the fiercest love and the most enormous relief.

"Belle." My voice was faint, almost a whisper. It didn't matter. She heard me. And turning her head my way, she broke into the most gorgeous smile. All my worries and fears fell to the wayside. My daughter was just as relieved to see me as I was her, months of irritation erased as if they'd never existed. Maybe mothering was simply about showing up.

"Mommy. Mommy, you're here."

I rushed to her side, overcome with a joy I hadn't felt for a long time. Just knowing she'd been waiting for me made all the difference.

BELLE

"MY TURN."

"It's been your turn for over a week. I think it's time to give someone else a go."

"Sorry, still my turn. The way I figure, it's my turn until I pick up the viola again."

Dad got up and left the den, his laughter following him into the kitchen. He grabbed Mom around the waist, his hands lingering on her back, their faces pointed toward one another. I hadn't seen this kind of intimacy between them in a while. It was nice but a bit embarrassing. I looked away and concentrated on the remote control, flipping randomly through the television channels, again. This injury had long ago become tiresome, but being treated like a princess, having everything just the way I wanted, wasn't bad at all. It was nice having my needs supersede everyone else's.

I pushed backwards with one hand, settling deeper into the couch, and winced as my wounded hand bumped the armrest. Okay, the princess part was nice, the healing process not so much. It wasn't just the pain. What drove me out of my mind was the unbearable itching. I'd taken to stowing chopsticks in the sloppy topknot bun I arranged each morning, armed and ready to start a sudden round of frantic scratching. Besides being functional, they spiced up my look. I loved the way they jutted out at odd, random angles, making me feel menacing and more than a little dangerous. I'd absolutely sport this "do" once back in New York. I frowned. So much had fallen into place, but that was still a question.

"Belle."

Mom caught me red-handed in the middle of jabbing away at the wound beneath the bandaging. I wasn't supposed to play with whatever was going on under there, but I couldn't help myself. She'd been on me all week, reminding me how important it was not to disturb the stitches, threatening a trip back to the hospital, another two weeks on the couch. But I really didn't care. Just moving the skin next to the wound the slightest bit offered tremendous relief.

"Mom. I can't take it. It's making me crazy." I continued to poke around and then, playing it up for my audience, issued a rapturous sigh of relief. "That's it. Wow. It's just . . . it's just so good." I knew exactly how to get a rise out of her. I braced myself. She'd for sure launch into a lecture, whether about my stitches or something else. There's no way she'd miss the opportunity. But when I looked up from my arm, expecting an expression of exasperation, even anger, I was surprised to find a huge smile and absolutely no censure. Instead, Mom's tone was calm and matter-of-fact.

"You're going to pop some of those stitches. It's certain. Then we'll have to start over again. What a shame." She stepped over to me and gathered the strands of hair that had worked their way loose from the bun, tucking them neatly behind my ears. "Just when you're in the home stretch."

I was stunned. Her composed response denied me the chance to resort to the default I'd chosen for years—kicking and screaming and generally raising a fuss; it didn't matter about what. I hadn't had an opportunity to do that since getting home. I almost missed storming around and making sure that everyone knew I was pissed off and upset. It was my God-given right as a teenager. But I had to admit that the new family dynamic where we spoke to one another, laughed together, exchanged warm glances like those picture-perfect families in the movies, and felt part of the same team was pretty darn amazing. It was kind of like what I envied at Lydia's. I wondered if it had always been here for the taking, right in front of my eyes. And if so, why I'd rejected it, locking myself into my room, sealing myself up tightly behind a closed door. I didn't push this query too far. I didn't really want to rummage around my muddy relationship with Mom, to plumb the deeper reasons, the whys. It was easier to just accept our new reality at face value and enjoy it.

"It's going to heal whether or not I pop a stitch, and frankly, all this hanging around? It's not so bad. I wouldn't mind another week or two." I leaned my head backward, resting it on the cushion, and smiled up at the ceiling, whistling with delight. "I should have been born into royalty."

Of course, I still had to contend with the darker side. I'd really done a number on my hand. My injury was serious enough to threaten any future in viola. I spent much of my convalescence replaying what had happened, the stages of that very long and scary day. Each rehashing began with the warm tingle of that exquisite sunset workshop beside the gold and sparkle of Lake Metigoshe, the intimacy of sharing deep reflections, insignificant chatter, and peals of laughter with friends before being swallowed up whole and blurred into oblivion by the rock that tore into the flesh of my palm.

The segments of memory that followed were a jumble; it had all happened too fast—a gush, not a trickle, of events, beginning with the way I'd slowly detached my hand from its stony perch, stunned by what was more dagger than rock, before screeching with pain and horror at the steady flow of my blood; the shrieks of my friends; the unconvincingly calm voice of the counselor as he called for the medic; and the chill of the water in which we all stood knee deep. The whole scene was like some baptism gone rogue. I have no idea who wrapped up my hand, who decided the incident didn't demand an immediate evacuation, or who sat with me on the bus to the hospital. What I remember vividly is Mom bursting through the doors of the emergency room where I was waiting, hand swaddled, and the way she held me tight.

The pain I experienced that long day was less upsetting than the realization of the damage done. Although the rock that penetrated the softest and most delicate part of my hand had thankfully missed all tendons, it did enough harm to question whether I'd regain full motor control. We all knew what that meant for my music career. And even though I'd spent the days before the retreat assessing, debating, and considering my heart's desire regarding this subject, post-trauma I'd come to the conclusion that there was nothing I wanted more. Mom's arrival on the scene, a real saving grace, somehow crystallized the seriousness of my injury and the potential for real loss.

"Mom," I called into the kitchen. "When's our appointment?"

"Feet off the couch!" I laughed and looked around. She was still in the kitchen. *How did she know? Do mothers always know?* It certainly seemed so. "Next Wednesday."

I extended both arms forward, comparing the healthy one with the one swathed with a neat, semi-soft bandage. I was making progress. This was my third wrapping, a major step up from the makeshift one the medic had arranged from someone's sweatshirt by the side of the lake and the inflexible hard cast I'd first been outfitted with at the hospital. "I'm dying to pick up my bow."

Mom wandered in, dishtowel in hand. "I'm sure you are. But that's going to take a bit more time. We have our first appointment with the physiotherapist immediately after the stitches come out. There's no reason to think that won't be the beginning of the end. It's all a matter of time." She waved her hand toward the window as if dismissing a cat. "We'll all be happy to see you healthy and out the door."

I reached up and retrieved my chopstick, inserting it carefully beneath the bandage, working around the wound, gently stirring the skin directly bordering the stitches. "I was so lucky."

"What was that?"

I hadn't realized I'd spoken out loud.

"What if it had been my left hand, Mom? How could I have found the right notes?"

She laid the dishtowel on the table and sat next to me on the couch. I could feel the heat radiating from her body. I casually draped my leg over hers, recalling the similar pleasure I'd felt when Lydia's mother had sat close, in just this way, one day a year earlier—when I'd sat in their den and dreamed of having a different mother, certain any would be better than my own.

"But it wasn't. You don't need to think about what might have been."

"And if I'd cut a tendon?" My face wrinkled up with concern. The doctor at the emergency room had explained how that would have been its own form of disaster, demanding reparative surgery and months of therapy with a slim chance of reestablishing full control. A millimeter or two to the left and my hand would have been completely compromised, or even shut down, my ability to elicit the resonant tones for which I was known reduced to unlikely.

"What if they don't want me back?" That was the crux of the matter. The doctors had promised that I'd eventually regain full mobility and control. But if I was expelled from Julliard, it wouldn't matter. The disaster I'd left back in New York was my fault. I couldn't blame it on my accident.

Mom gazed into my face as if looking for something. "I can't imagine that's going to happen."

"You weren't there." A choked laugh, laced with sarcasm, emerged from deep within me. "Ask Grandma. She'll tell you all about it." My mother sighed and looked away for a second before turning back and tucking another loose strand of hair behind my ear. I loved the way she did that, the way she fussed over me. It made me feel adored. Tears gathered in my eyes. "What if I've lost this opportunity, Mama? I wanted it so much."

She didn't answer immediately. Despite the drone of the television, the room became very quiet. I listened to the lulling tick of the kitchen clock, trying not to panic at the fact that she hadn't denied what I'd suggested. "I don't know what went on back in New York, Belle. I had to step away. For both of us." She paused. "But I understand you made mistakes—that you got yourself into difficult situations that led straight away from everything you most wanted."

I couldn't stop the tears. Although I'd tried not to think the worst, now I could think of nothing else. "I can't bear it. I wanted this so much.

I still want it. It just wasn't how I thought it would be. I let all that glitter, the seduction of the fast and furious, get in the way. I stopped listening to the sound within me, those beautiful harmonies that make me fly. If only I had another chance to do it right."

Mom put her arm around me and pulled me close, wiping the tears away. "We're all blinded at times, sweetheart. It's so hard to know exactly how to negotiate the path forward when we're not sure of the goal. I think it's best to just go with what feels right along the way—to stay true to the moment instead of shooting for a target. But I know that's hard, maybe even the hardest."

I didn't understand what she was trying to explain. *How can I know how to act, what to do, if I don't know exactly where I'm going?*

"Stay in the moment, Belle. If the sound of the music is what you love, stick with it. You don't have to look further."

• • •

One quiet afternoon soon thereafter, Mom sat down and told me a bit about that girl who'd taken my place—the one whose mere existence had made me crazy with jealousy back at the pie shop. We were sharing tea and cookies in the den after my first physio appointment.

"So, it's like a Gothic fairy tale?"

"No. That's not how I would describe it."

"But there's an evil mother."

"Not evil."

"Well, there's a dysfunctional mother. Is that better? More accurate?"

"Yes."

"And a sweet, wronged daughter."

"That's right."

"What about Prince Charming? There's got to be a prince who swoops in and saves the day."

Mom laughed. "No. I'm sorry. The similarities stop there. There's definitely not a prince. At least, not that I know of."

"I disagree, Mom. Take a good look in the mirror. It's you! You're the prince."

She looked straight down into her mug, swirling the steaming liquid around nervously with a teaspoon. I knew I'd hit the bull's eye.

"Well, maybe less a prince than a fairy."

I pushed back against the cushions; the couch had pretty much become my full-time home.

"Tell me more."

"Well, I think you've figured it out. There's something to your analogy. But the prince saves the day, and I just can't do that in this case. I'll never be able to do that, even if I try. Still, I have a clear role. I like the idea of being a good fairy."

"I love fairies." And I did. I had a fairy mobile in my room when I was younger. Six paper-mâché ladies, limbs as delicate as lace, danced over my head each evening as I lay in bed. I always felt protected by their magic. The mobile wasn't there anymore. At some point I'd packed it up, a part of my childhood I put aside in order to prove I was an adult. I wondered whether it was still up in the attic.

Mom looked distracted. "Yes. That works for me. And just like a fairy, I spread magical dust, hoping to make the young, wronged girl happier. I can't really fix things, but I can make them a little bit better."

We didn't return to the subject again. It wasn't that it didn't interest me, or that I didn't care. I simply wanted Mom all to myself. I didn't want to share my spot in the sun just when I'd figured out it existed.

LILLIAN

"ONE NO-TRUMP."

"Pass."

I waited for Joyce to assess her hand. I was really enjoying this evening out, playing bridge with my friends. I had a lot more time to spend at the club now that Belle was back in Grand Forks, my parenting duties reduced to nil. Coming back to the familiar was good. I loved my routine, everything in its designated place, just as I liked it, my life organized precisely according to my needs, running smooth as silk. It was so much easier to beat to my own drum and not have to consider someone else's. Taking Belle in had changed the balance completely, making grandparenting—that opportunity to enjoy children for a brief time and then hand them back to their parents—an entirely different story.

My smile disappeared. Recalling why I had time to spend with my friends, why I had no reason to hurry home, ruined my mood. Belle left with such a commotion. There was that horrible muddle at Julliard. *What got into that girl?* She usually played like an angel. The worst of it was the look on Joyce's face, how she smiled at the end, despite the disaster, and congratulated me. I saw through her immediately; I recognized her pity.

No one in the audience had any delusions about who was at fault, which musician was getting it wrong. Or at least, that's the way it felt. Maybe they just pegged it on the string section and left it at that. It didn't really matter. For me, it was personal.

Sitting around the card table at temple, not a care in the world, knowing a hot shower and a good night's sleep awaited me back home, I couldn't begin to imagine why I'd ever assumed full responsibility for a precocious teenager. I suppose I thought she'd be better behaved, have more self-control. I guess I figured she'd be more like me. Now on my own, Belle back in Grand Forks, I could own up to my mistake. It hadn't worked out. The issues simply kept piling up, one on top of the other. I spent all my time putting out fires, containing what was, unfortunately, a combustible situation. No matter. That was over and done with. I was probably better off on my own. If only I could erase the memory of that last evening at Julliard, the way Belle had pushed by me after the concert as if I didn't exist; Joyce's expression, so obviously embarrassed for me; Mike's forlorn face later on as he sat in the kitchen, waiting for Belle to pack her bag. If only I could forget the emptiness of the apartment since she'd left.

"Two clubs."

I struggled to focus on the game. This wasn't the time or place to dwell on what I couldn't do over. The whole point of coming out tonight had been to enjoy not having any obligations and luxuriate in precisely what was best for *me*, me alone. Success at bridge would surely expunge that lingering feeling of failure.

"Two diamonds." Barbara looked like she'd won the lottery, her face edgy with excitement. She'd had a run of no-point hands earlier this evening, but her luck had changed. I looked back at my cards. I had a lovely number of points. The question was whether Joyce and I had a fit. A two-club answer to my opening bid was a good start. That meant she had four of a major. I looked down at my beautiful hearts, three of them honors, and bid a hopeful "Two hearts."

I loved bridge. It demanded the exchange of secret codes containing both bold truths and subtle insinuations. The fun was in negotiating the fine line between them to get to the right contract, then dealing with the fallout.

Once again concentrating on the game, my mind clicked through the significance of the earlier bids. I studied Claire's face, wondering about her next move. She would obviously want to end whatever was building up between Joyce and me, eager to answer Barbara's call. I smiled to myself, reassured by the fact that she probably didn't have much. This was our game. I felt a brief rush of pleasure at that thought, but once again, it dissipated into a wave of sadness. The possibility of a win at this table wasn't enough to shut out the sorrow in my life. I closed my eyes for a moment, trying to stay in the moment. This evening was not about rehashing what couldn't be undone, the events of the previous weeks and months—most especially not the years that had preceded them. Yet I couldn't deny it. This wasn't only about Belle. It never had been.

"Come on, Claire! Do something good!" Although cheering on her partner, Barbara sounded resigned. She'd obviously realized it wasn't their game. I recognized the look of defeat acknowledged before the fact. It was the same one I'd seen on Elizabeth's face time and again when she was a child—the expression of solemn resignation, acceptance of the fact that things wouldn't go her way. Ironically, I found not a hint of that look during that trip to Grand Forks, nor a decade earlier at the table in Sarabeth's when she'd walked out of my life. Somewhere along the way, my daughter had become her own person, one more self-confident, gutsier, one I'd like to get to know.

One of the great attractions of the original Julliard plan had been the inevitability that it would create a closer connection between Elizabeth and me. But even after assuming responsibility for Belle, such an enormous step, when she was finally living under my roof in Manhattan, I received almost no word at all from my daughter. Things stayed much the same as they'd been for years, with minimal contact and Mike as middleman. After protesting Belle's departure to New York, something I still didn't understand—I mean, wasn't it every mother's goal to see their daughter succeed in the world?—she'd basically written her off. At least, that was the way it seemed.

I suppose they'd texted, maybe even spoken, but I never saw evidence to prove it. As far as I could tell, Elizabeth simply decided to step away and leave us to our own devices. After a lifetime spent trying to please me, hiding behind the desires of others instead of daring to explore her own, my daughter seemed to have finally removed the burden holding her back and moved on. Stepping away had been the key to stepping forward. I'd always known that to be so. Sometimes you had to give up being nice and stop playing the game to reach a higher goal.

While I should have considered this eventuality a form of victory, my hesitant daughter finally living her own life, it didn't feel like one. And sitting here with my supposedly closest friends, those with whom I'd spent decades working side by side at soup kitchens and clothing drives, co-organizing one Purim ball after another, numerous Hanukkah treasure hunts; in a place that offered consistent solace, I remained hollowed-out and empty. There was no silver lining to this story.

Although my taking charge of Belle had released my daughter from the iron grip of concerns that held her back for years, it led me to failures I'd never be able to undo. With my granddaughter furious at me—barely speaking to me as she walked out the door, suitcase in hand—and my daughter maintaining the most minimal of contact, I had sunk into a black hole of loneliness and disconnection. Even here among old friends, doing something I'd enjoyed for decades, there was very little light. I'd dreamed of a different picture, carefully laying down all the important groundwork. It was going to be something more joyous and fruitful, something a lot more pleasant. And of course, there was the buried hope that with Belle underneath my roof and Elizabeth tangentially back in my life, I wouldn't have to go through my radiation therapy alone.

I cast my eyes downward and stared at my cards. They blurred before me, diamonds and hearts one and the same, spades and clubs indistinguishable. Normally impatient when the bidding slowed to a crawl, I found it a blessing today. I needed to think, to figure out how to counter some of the damage. An apology directly to Belle might do the trick. I could claim that I hadn't understood the challenges of raising a teenager at such an advanced age, that it was all my fault, that I should have realized I wasn't up for it. I could tell her that I wanted her to come back; that I would embrace another opportunity to put up with an irascible, impulsive, somewhat rude teenage girl. I sighed aloud. Of course, all that would be a lie.

Claire read my sigh as a sign of impatience. "One second. I'm just trying to figure out . . ."

"Oh. No rush. No rush at all."

My tone must have been a bit off. Joyce was quick to investigate. "Everything okay, Lil?" I had to snap out of it. This wasn't the time to get lost in what would never be. I needed to be in the game. I owed it to Joyce. A distracted partner wasn't going to mean a win.

"I'm sorry. I was elsewhere for a moment."

Almost as competitive as I, Barbara saw an opportunity to gain an edge through distraction, a fabulously effective tactic in bridge. "I heard the concert was lovely." She nodded at Joyce, who immediately looked down at her cards, her cheeks turning a blistering shade of pink. "It's all so exciting. I'd love to have a young person in the house again. It would be such a breath of fresh air."

I felt like a deer caught in the headlights. They'd all been talking. Of course, why wouldn't they? This is what we did. This was how we had fun. But the confirmation of that fact made everything that was bad even worse. I couldn't stand knowing that Belle's failure, my failure, and the situation's horrible denouement, had been laid out for all to see. The only thing left was a public trampling. My grip slackened. "Lillian, I can see your cards!" I snapped to attention. I wasn't doing a very good job of covering up my distress. Maybe I should just come clean, explain what was really going on, admit to this group of friends that the whole thing had been a mistake. If only I knew a way to make it all look pretty.

"Pass. I guess." Claire sounded defeated, almost morose. "I wish I had something to offer you, Barb. But *nada*, not a thing. Looks like it's going to be their game." There were a few murmured reactions. I might have chimed in as well, but there was no way to know for sure. I had lost my bearings, unable to discern whether the run of thoughts crashing through my head had actually been spoken.

Joyce chimed out a triumphant "Two spades." She couldn't match my hearts but had the cards to go to game. My spirits lifted considerably. I shifted all thoughts to the moment and sealed the deal.

"Three no-trump." The itch to spill had passed. I was thoroughly into the game.

Claire shook her head in frustration. "Their game again. What a night!"

Barbara tapped her cards on the table anxiously. "It's okay. Just concentrate on your opening. Let's try and take them down." She turned to me once again, obviously unwilling to let go of whatever she'd sensed earlier, a dog in heat. "I've heard that program is simply fabulous, Lillian. Julliard's. A real life changer. And you must be quite the hero out West. Remind me again, where are they? Utah? Elizabeth must be so grateful. Who'd have thought it, a child prodigy, or shall I say, 'a grandchild prodigy,' right here within our ranks! Of course, the apple didn't fall far." She looked around at the others, encouraging them to nod in affirmation. "Elizabeth was such a hardworking and serious child. You always guided her to excel. There's no surprise here whatsoever. A third-generation success for Temple Emanuel!"

A sudden bout of dizziness disturbed my equilibrium, and I rocked forward, gripping the edge of the table. If only they knew. This was one secret I wouldn't be sharing. None of these women had any idea of my history of struggle with Elizabeth, the lifetime of misunderstandings. Poorly matched—one plagued by self-doubt, the other by blinding overconfidence—we'd been doomed from the start. We were simply so very different.

I hadn't let that stop me. I was the mother. I had a responsibility, and I did my best to fulfill it. I invested endless energy over the years, trying to steer Elizabeth to the front of the class, to the top of the mountain. And, as I slowly discovered, the truth becoming clear as I reeled back in the line I'd cast, she never stopped resenting it.

"You've never really seen me."

"What are you talking about? That's ridiculous."

"No, it's not. You've always wanted a different daughter, one who aimed higher, one with a stronger drive, one more like you."

"I really don't understand what you're talking about, what you're so upset about. Who doesn't want to achieve? To do their best. It's an instinct. We all have it."

"No, we don't. We don't all have it. I've always just wanted to find a place where I could make a difference. I've never had to be the one in the spotlight. I've never needed to be the best, the first, the fastest, or the smartest."

"No, dear. You've always aimed for mediocre. There's a clear difference. And that's something I could never condone. You're too good for that. You always have been. You're *my* daughter, after all."

"But what if *your* daughter isn't interested? Is that something you ever stopped to wonder? There isn't only one formula for excelling in life."

That brunch back at Sarabeth's had most definitely been the death knell for our relationship. But now, as then, I wasn't sorry for my ways. Mothering was complicated. Maybe it wasn't something one could be good at. Maybe one was meant to simply limp along, doing the best one could, coping with the cards one was dealt as they were dealt.

I looked down at my hand, hiding my face. That wasn't true. I didn't believe that for a moment and never would. There was so much one could do to compensate for what one wasn't handed in this life.

Claire opened with the three of clubs, and Joyce laid out her hand. I concentrated on each card, desperate to get out of my head and back to the game, to end Barbara's persistent line of questioning. The thrill of possible victory did the trick. Between the two of us, Joyce and I had excellent coverage with only a slight weakness in diamonds. We'd bid right. Now it was all up to me.

One glance across the table into the crystal-clear, cornflower eyes of the woman who'd been my partner for as long as I could remember, and a field of hope spread wide before me. It really was about how I played the game, trite as it sounded. I just had to figure it out, right here at this table and out there, in the real world. But winning this game was going to be a lot simpler than figuring out how to make things right with Belle and Elizabeth. Since those horrible moments alone in my apartment, after Mike and Belle left, the emptiness of my world so obvious, I understood that I'd gotten it all wrong. The pile of awards and accolades I'd been gathering for years, all those bragging points, suddenly seemed puny and meaningless. Although for just about ever I'd believed that the heart could play second fiddle, that it didn't need to lead, my aching one indicated something else entirely.

I counted my winners and started in, quickly taking control of the game. Watching me win one round after the other made my opponents restless. I didn't leave them room to do much of anything. When I finally lost a trick, Claire sighed in relief.

"Phew. It's good to know you're human."

I just smiled. If only they knew. I'd messed up everything with my daughter, and now my granddaughter. I'd ended any chance of achieving the kind of harmony described so lusciously by that well-meaning young woman back at the meet and greet for new members. Convictions of a lifetime, ones I'd stood behind forever, were suddenly untenable. The losses were piled too high to miss.

Taking advantage of a small miscalculation on Barbara's part, I resumed control and, after one successful finesse, took the remaining rounds for the win. The game ended. It was the last one for the evening. Each table tallied its points. Joyce and I had done well. It was time to go home.

"Thanks, everyone. It was a terrific evening. Just lovely." I got up quickly, avoiding Barbara's inquisitive eyes, and stepped over to the refreshment table. Arranged there were all manner of enticing offerings: a sliced teacake, homemade lace cookies, a dish piled high with succulent orange slices. A cream pie, the likes of which I hadn't seen for years, sat on a raised serving platter to the side. I smiled, remembering the slice of coconut cream Belle and I had shared at Paolo's, then immediately sobered. There was a chance that happy memories like this one would stay right where they were, in the past. I had no idea whether there would be new ones to look forward to in the future. This latest episode in my life was not going to pass easily.

I poured myself a cup of tea from the large boiler, holding it close to my face, letting the steam soothe my troubled thoughts and aching heart.

"You look upset." I looked up into Joyce's kind face. "We did really well this evening. I'm guessing it's something else."

"I'm fine." I paused, again wondering whether letting someone know things weren't as they seemed, that I'd fumbled and dropped the ball, would tarnish my reputation or, instead, help me heal. I hoped the latter because it simply hurt too much to hold it all inside. "It's the arrangement with Belle. It hasn't been smooth sailing." I cleared my throat. "It's been a lot more complicated than I expected."

"I'm certain." Those eyes, they were so compassionate. Suddenly, I didn't feel like a failure. I just felt human. "It's quite a responsibility." I was intensely grateful for Joyce's understanding, and not a little amazed that she'd intuited my distress. I'd spent a lifetime hiding anything that didn't go right, burying feelings of sadness, reserving my hesitations for the black of night when I'd whisper them into Sam's ear. He knew how important it was for me to appear flawless and at the height of my game to the outside world. I always had so much to make up for.

But standing in a place that should have been a refuge, Belle gone, an empty apartment awaiting my return, the veneer I'd carefully maintained for decades felt insubstantial. Sharing even the slightest hint of my shortcomings somehow lightened my load. It wasn't nearly as bad as I dreamed it would be. Vulnerability, something I never tolerated in the past, settled upon me like a cozy quilt on a chilly night.

Joyce picked up where she left off, eyes boring into my own to make her point. "That being said . . . I'm sure you'll consider the repercussions, across the board, before choosing the way forward."

I put down my tea and took her into my arms, giving her the very warmest hug. "I most certainly will," I whispered into her ear, giving her a kiss on the cheek before stepping away. I had an idea, a way to make everything better. It was so obvious; I couldn't imagine why I hadn't thought of it before. Taking over Belle's guardianship had been a mistake, but Julliard was not. There were other ways to ensure she continued there while maintaining a much healthier distance as on-site grandmother. I might be able to turn all this black into glorious, blossoming shades of color. It might just be possible to crawl out of this hole, into the light.

I grasped Joyce's sleeve, unwilling to let go of our connection. It wasn't the time to be proud and insist that I could live my life just fine on my own. Mostly because it wasn't true.

"It's time, Joyce . . ." I paused mid-sentence, brow furrowed with reconsideration, determined to make a change. I'd spent a lifetime trying to make up for what I lost, what I felt had been taken from me, pursuing one goal or another, sometimes for myself, sometimes for Elizabeth, and lately for Belle. Today this endless pursuit felt pointless. Maybe mothering wasn't that complex after all. I'd just perceived it to be so. "No, that's not it. It's *past* time. I can still right this wrong."

ELIZABETH

THE GIRLS NODDED BRISKLY IN acknowledgment before looking away, each toward a different corner of the cafe. They looked distinctly uncomfortable, unclear how this meeting was supposed to go. I'd engineered the whole thing, so it was my job to make it as smooth as possible. That was a taller order than I'd imagined.

"Hey, girls. Why don't we take a seat?" They hesitated. Eager to move things along, I assigned each a place. "Over there, Belle. Julie, you're here."

I'd chosen the pie shop in town, figuring the venue both neutral and fun. I forgot that it would be crowded and there might be people Belle knew. She casually waved to a group coming through the door. Although my primary concern was Julie, who was by far in the more vulnerable position, I wanted Belle to be at ease as well. This long-overdue meeting was meant to serve them both.

Once into our pie, things got a little better. Both girls looked a bit more relaxed, busying themselves with their selections.

"How's the coconut cream, Julie?" It was almost painful watching this fragile girl pick at her pie, barely placing the tips of the fork's tines into her mouth, as if she were owed just the slightest sweet bit at a time. I'd never seen anyone hesitate when faced with something so scrumptious. Her general uneasiness and glaring lack of self-confidence stood out in spades here at Paolo's. I silently prayed there'd come a day when she learned to attack life with gusto.

One glance over at Belle indicated a healthier dose of everything Julie was missing. She was absolutely demolishing her pie, shoving generous bites into her mouth and washing them down with large slurps of water. Yet something was off there as well. She seemed a bit too enthusiastic. It was hard to tell.

"Let's jump right in." I handed Julie the text we'd prepared, nodding in encouragement, hoping to convey a feeling of confidence. "Take a quick look. You don't need to study it. You're already well acquainted with every word."

I sat back in my chair, evaluating the girls while I waited for her to begin. Despite the distraction of the pie, both still seemed ill at ease. It hadn't worked the magic I'd hoped for. But that didn't matter. I didn't regret arranging this event. I'd been planning it for a while, waiting for the right time. Now I wondered if I'd waited too long. It wasn't that I was trying to keep Julie a secret—in fact I'd mentioned the fact that we were working together several times. But there were clear signs that Belle, once truly cognizant of our relationship, once she'd finally focused on something that had to do with me instead of her, felt threatened and left out, even a bit jealous.

I realized that fairly late in the game, after her surprise visit to my office—shocking in and of itself since Belle had never before shown much interest in what I was up to. Of course, that was before. Things were markedly different since she'd come home. The Belle who stopped by the firm and asked to check out my library was simply not the same person who stormed around the house slamming doors a year earlier. I was still sorry I hadn't been there to meet her that day, to show her my pride and joy myself. But the idea that she'd taken the steps to bridge the gap between us, wanting to check out *my* space, meant so very much. It was the clearest indicator of a change in our relationship, in her desire for that change.

Unfortunately, when I asked her about it later that evening, after hearing from Debbie, I received only the sparest, mumbled details—a few words about the library, the quiet, the heavy brown books, and something about sacredness. That's the word she chose. But what I picked up as an almost reverential attitude changed quickly to brisk the moment she changed the subject, saying something about pie and someone she called "that girl." I still hadn't had the chance to sort out what it all meant when she went off to the retreat a few days later. And everything after that was kind of a blur.

I was probably more nervous about this meeting than Belle and Julie together. I tried to calm my nerves by reminding myself that there was nothing unusual about two teenagers meeting up for some pie. I wasn't asking them to become friends. This was all as natural as could be, save the agenda: a dry run for Julie's school recital. The idea came up during Belle's convalescence, something that lasted far longer than it should have, delayed by the medic's botched job.

Wrapping her hand so tightly on-site, by the waterside, had effectively fused the flaps of skin surrounding the wound. My stomach still churned at the sight of her palm when first revealed at the hospital, its formerly smooth skin having become a jagged mess, haphazardly joined in an imperfect seal. If I'd come upon something as repulsive on TV, I most certainly would have changed the channel. I feigned a lack of concern as the attending physician painstakingly cut away a good bit of skin in order to get a better look at the network of tendons beneath and ascertain the extent of the damage.

The procedure involved in fixing it all up resulted in an especially complicated set of stitches. Belle would have to keep her hand immobilized for a few weeks. The good news was that although there was very little left for those clairvoyant palm readers down the road, no revelatory lines forecasting long life or eternal love, she would eventually be able to return to her beloved viola.

Stuck resting at home since doing anything more than getting off the couch and walking to the kitchen was borderline perilous to her musical future, we finally got around to speaking about Julie. It went better than I expected. Belle was genuinely interested in piecing together the relationship I was still unable to define. But I was surprised when she didn't push further and insist on meeting her. I figured she had her reasons. My relationship with Julie had developed in her absence and, because of their similar ages, trod directly on her territory, smacking of replacement. Although no one could take the place of my beloved child, that wasn't obvious to my daughter.

Nevertheless, Belle's concerned expression during our talk, the way she went quiet and just listened, such a different reaction than I might have received the previous year, indicated her understanding of the disturbing consequences of having shut me out of her life so thoroughly. This situation was prickly. With red warning lights flashing, I quickly decided that the best move was to involve her directly.

"You can help."

"How can I possibly help?"

"She's preparing to read before the school. It's not something she wants to do."

"What's the big deal? Reading out loud is just a thing. Everyone has to do it."

"Yes, they do. But for Julie it's difficult. In fact, she begged me to write a letter to the teacher, explaining why she should be excused."

"That makes sense. So, did you?"

"No."

"Why? Why not? That would be the most help of all!"

"No, it wouldn't. She needs to be able to cope with difficult situations. This is a perfect opportunity to do so. But, Belle, you can really play a role here. You can help prepare her for the response."

"Because I'm the ultimate teenage girl?"

My responding smile couldn't have been larger. "Precisely."

Once the idea of involving Belle in Julie's preparation took root, I made it as much a goal as the reading itself. She was delighted.

"You need me." She said it as a statement, not a question.

"That's right."

"And this isn't like asking me to rinse the dishes."

"Definitely not. This is serious business; I need a partner. Someone I can trust."

She lit up, her face aglow.

The next step was to orchestrate what I knew would be a tense meeting. Julie, after so many bad experiences, was shy and cautious about any communication with a peer. It was apparent she'd be uptight, maybe even upset by the idea. It didn't help that Belle was the epitome of what she wasn't: a loved daughter. Or at least, that's how I knew Julie would see her. Although I'd managed to restore some of her self-confidence over the past few months, overcoming to a degree the fallout of her mother's neglect and incapacity as well as the school system's failure, there was still a long road ahead.

At some point along the way, when things between us were most difficult, when I felt her pushing me away with all her strength, perhaps that day in the library or the one down by the river, I understood that I'd become much more than her teacher; my role approached actual parenting. This realization hadn't scare me one bit. In fact, I welcomed it. Although I didn't know it at the time, this was exactly what I'd been looking for the day I first approached Rabbi Eliot.

The work I chose for Julie to read was particularly relevant to her own life. It had to do with how one deals with "boxes" imposed by others, situations not of their own design. I knew it was a risky choice, touching on so many issues relevant to her own life, but simultaneously understood that if Julie didn't connect to the words, if she couldn't relate, the reading would fall flat. What I didn't anticipate was the prickle of tears that sprang to my own eyes the first time I listened to her work her way through it.

> *Everything is upside-down at my house. People keep leaving when they shouldn't and not leaving when they should disappear. Nothing is the same day-to-day. Last week I went downstairs, and the furniture was gone.*

Julie had been startled by the words as well, her initial response to decline. "I can't do this." Her voice shook with emotion as she pushed the card with the text back toward me, across the table. "It's too close. Find something else."

I was gently insistent. "I knew you'd find it scary. I know you're feeling terrified. But, Julie, this is what everyone expects—your teacher, your classmates. They all expect you to freak out. It doesn't even matter what you read. You might as well make it count. In any case, that's the best way to ensure you'll do your very best. This is a challenge you need to accept—one I guarantee you'll be able to meet." Genuine and heartfelt was the only way to go.

Since that day, we'd read the piece together more times that I could count. I figured that its repetition would neutralize the emotional impact, enabling her to eventually get through the reading without breaking down or, God forbid, crying. But I couldn't help being moved with each and every reading. This girl, her story, her striving to be loved—it was one big continuing heartbreak. I didn't want her crushed before her classmates. This was where Belle came in.

"Julie? Are you ready?" I reached over and gave her hand a little tug. There was a sharp noise from the side. Belle had thrown her fork down on her plate. Hunched over, shoulders tense, mouth set in a straight line, her distress was obvious. It was clear she was put off by that sign of intimacy. Wanting to avoid making this more awkward than it already was, I quickly retreated, sitting back in my seat, placing my hands in my lap, and redirecting their attention. "Belle is your audience. She represents a whole classroom of students."

Julie laughed uneasily. "She doesn't look like a whole audience."

Belle smiled. Even better, the two smiled at one another. Maybe this would go well after all.

"All the more reason for this to be no big deal at all. It's just a dry run." I turned to Belle. "Your job is to keep your eyes on Julie. Don't flinch. You're a classmate. You're more likely to be judgmental than supportive. This is high school."

Now they both laughed. The ice was breaking.

"Maybe you should stand up." At my suggestion, Julie looked around at the other customers sitting and enjoying pie and openly grimaced. "Do I have to? In any case, it's not like it'll be at school. Not really. We're not in the auditorium."

"I want to pretend that we are. I don't want you to be *comfortable.* In fact, it's best if you're not." I looked around. A few kids were seated at tables, others clustered in front of the glass display case, checking out the options. "I wouldn't worry too much about the audience here. Everyone is far too involved in their pie to even notice you."

Julie cleared her throat, pushed her chair back, and stood. A quick peek around the place confirmed my hunch: not one person in the shop seemed to notice. I handed her the text and cast a sideways glance at Belle. She was slumped in her chair, exhibiting absolutely no interest whatsoever in whatever Julie was up to. She certainly was playing her part well. Looking back at Julie confirmed that this was going exactly as planned. She was anything but comfortable. In fact, she looked borderline catatonic, her eyes staring at the card before her as if she'd never seen it before. Whatever vibe had started to develop between the girls moments earlier wasn't helping her now. Julie was totally on her own. My heart ached. It was so unfair. No child should ever feel so alone.

"Now?" Her voice was feeble, her expression one of dejection. I began to second-guess this whole dress rehearsal. I hadn't intended for her to suffer. Maybe it wasn't a good idea after all.

Belle chimed in just as I was about to suggest we abort. "Now is good."

I cast her a sharp look. That had come out a bit too tough. She needed to be gentle. I'd told her that before we left the house. Julie wasn't cut of the same sturdy material as Belle's usual crowd. She ignored me and folded her arms in front of her chest, bad over good. She was quite obviously losing patience with this whole exercise.

Turning my gaze back to Julie, expecting to find her completely unhinged, I was surprised to see her looking steadier than before, even resolved. She cleared her throat. "So, um . . . 'Box,' by Lindsay Price." Her voice faded out at the end, the author's name coming across more as an addendum, less declared than aspirated.

There was silence. Her two-person audience waited. "And?" The impatience Belle had hinted at a minute earlier was now clear as day. My face reddened with anger, and I clamped my teeth together, trying not to chide her for being so rude. I'd planned a positive experience, not a humiliating one. I never anticipated that this exercise might do more damage than good.

"Listen. They're going to eat you alive. You know that, right?" Belle scooted her chair over to Julie's side of the table.

"Belle!" This was really too much. "This isn't helping!"

"It's the truth, Mom. She should know." Belle turned back to address Julie directly. "This is going to be painful. There's no way around it. They're all going to stare. The mean ones will snicker and whisper to their neighbors. Some might point and others might call you some nasty name. That's what teenagers do." She smiled widely. "It's our job."

Something was going on here. A vibe was developing, a teenager thing. Julie didn't look upset at all; instead, her face looked open and receptive. She knew what Belle was getting at. My initial concern ebbed, replaced by a heady mixture of excitement and pride. This was exactly what I'd hoped for and intended when I orchestrated this day. What I hadn't anticipated was that Belle would be the one to take the initiative, to direct its course; that I wouldn't have to drag her through the whole exercise.

"So! Let her rip." Belle stretched her bandaged hand out in a sweeping gesture meant to give the go-ahead. Startled by the sudden movement, Julie reflexively raised her arms in a blocking defense. The clash between the two was brief but agonizing to watch—Belle's face contorting in pain, her eyes immediately tearing up, Julie gasping, horror-stricken at her mistake. I leaped out of my seat to help, but Julie was already on it, grasping Belle firmly around the waist with one arm and using the other to gently hold her injured hand from beneath, raising it high in the air to relieve the pressure. She cooed softly, "Now, now, now . . . Come on. It's okay. You're okay."

Belle's twisted expression slowly returned to normal, the sudden, sharp onset of pain having obviously subsided. She seemed to be okay. I hesitantly lowered back into my chair and let out a sigh of relief. The girls, with the worst of that unexpected disturbance behind them, suddenly found themselves in a rather awkwardly intimate embrace. They carefully extracted themselves, both blushing, with a few half smiles, nervous pats, and mumbled apologies. This certainly wasn't how they expected things to end up when they'd been stiffly eating their pie. By the time they retreated to their original positions, I realized I was enjoying the whole scene. Observing two teenagers renegotiate their precious personal space was almost as good as theater.

"So." Belle was back to business, her voice sharp and unforgiving. She obviously intended to play this out to the end. "As I was saying." She cleared her throat loudly. "Just get to it. No hesitation. Don't show how you feel, even if you're dying inside. Teenagers aren't allowed to wear their emotions on their sleeves. No, no, no. Absolutely not. It's got to be all pomp and circumstance."

Finished having her say, she resettled into an all-too-familiar slump. I couldn't help smiling. This girl of mine truly was the epitome of a teenager, but this one time I could appreciate its charm. A teenager with a heart was a beautiful thing.

LILLIAN

"GRANDMA?"

The surge of relief upon hearing Belle's voice was indescribable. It blasted through me, leaving me woozy with pleasure. I collapsed into the chair beside me, assured that all was not lost. It had been so cold in my apartment lately. Since Belle left, taking her bluster, her dirty laundry, her infuriating little shrugs, and her multiple doodads, nothing had been the same. The space that had been my home for decades, the warm nest I'd occupied comfortably for as long as I could remember, felt icy and unfamiliar, the confirmation of everything that had gone wrong, everything I'd *done* wrong.

I closed my eyes a moment, offering up a small prayer of thanks, and wondered if this lovely moment had to do with what I'd arranged. I hoped so.

"Are you there? Grandma?"

"Yes, dear. I'm right here. How are you? I'm waiting for you back here in New York."

A soft chuckle came over the line. "I would figure you'd be happier there without me. No mess! No bother!" There was a little pause. She lowered her voice an octave. "No middle-of-the-night disturbances."

I was quick to correct her. "No, no, Belle. I loved your mess. And the rest? I could deal with that as well."

She didn't answer me, but I heard her breathing. It was so soft. I thought of the night she'd been brought home by her friends—the comfort I'd found in the regularity of her exhalations, the relief in knowing she was safe. Even then, when I should have been upset about her excessive drinking, I knew what meant more. I missed having Belle here with me despite the difficulties and challenges.

"Well, anyway. I wanted to let you know what's going on."

I restrained my usual instinct to jump in and commandeer the conversation. It was enough to just feel our connection over the line. I'd missed it so.

"You really won't believe it."

I couldn't wait. "I know all about it, dear. Your accident. It sounded horrible. But your father told me you're healing and you'll be just fine. I'm so relieved."

"Yes, it's going to be okay. My hand will heal. Thanks. No, Grandma. It's something else." Another pause. "It's something exciting. I just got a call from Julliard."

Sitting in the privacy of my kitchen, I took the liberty of smiling, inordinately satisfied at how I'd worked things out. But for Belle, I played dumb. "Really? Well, that makes sense. After all, you're such a wonderful addition to their class this year. I'm sure they were eager to hear about your recuperation and check up on when you'll be able to rejoin the program."

"Yes, yes. But that's not . . . I want to tell you the whole thing. So, I was so sure they were calling to say I'd have to leave the program, that I wasn't good enough. Or perhaps that I was good enough but not mature enough. The way I fell apart at the Easter concert, it made no sense for them to invest in me. You remember how badly I messed up. You were there—"

I cut her off. I didn't want to go back to that horrible event. "Oh, dear, you were just having a bad day. Everyone in that room, your professors, your friends—they all know you're better than that. You've got it all wrong. I'm sure they wouldn't—"

"Just listen. It's important for me to get this out. I want to own up here." I heard her swallow hard. "I messed up. I absolutely messed up. And not just there in that concert hall. That was just the last stroke in a whole line of . . . Well, anyway. They should have kicked me out. That would be fair. But that's not why they were calling. It was another reason completely."

I thought I heard a giggle. I smiled so widely it hurt. This was the first time I'd felt truly happy in a few weeks. It didn't matter that I already knew what was coming. Listening as Belle got to the punch line was just the best. I heard her inhale deeply as if preparing to jump into a swimming pool.

"Grandma! They were calling to tell me that I've been awarded a special scholarship for next year! I'll be able to do another year of the pre-college program, this time with full room and board!"

There was the distinct sound of huffing and puffing. Belle's exhilaration sounded much like that of a marathoner. It was time to come up with a convincing reaction of surprise. I dared not disappoint. "Oh, Belle!" I clapped my hands in delight, strong enough that the sound would cross the phone line. "That is absolutely the best news. I can't believe it. It's simply so exciting. I'm so happy for you, dear. And of course, well, you are so talented. It's not a surprise at all. Isn't it lovely to be acknowledged?"

"Yeah, yeah. Definitely. I guess. My head is still reeling. I was just so sure they were calling to explain why I couldn't continue. And then, well. Boom! This whole thing, these last few weeks, it's all been so overwhelming."

I felt as high as a kite, floating in the air above the kitchen table. *Who'd have thought that doing something so selfless could make me feel like the supreme empress?* I'd spent a lifetime convinced that nothing could be better than being the best, shining the brightest, having all eyes on me. But at this moment, having done something extraordinary for my beloved granddaughter, something for which I wasn't even receiving the credit, I absolutely soared.

"Mom." The change of voice was unexpected. I wasn't prepared. "Mom, it's me."

"Elizabeth? Belle and I were just speaking . . ." I crashed back to earth, trying to get my bearings and find solid footing. My dealings with Elizabeth had been so businesslike recently. The shift from gleeful to sober was difficult.

"I know, Mom. I took the phone. She's okay with my taking over the call. She's right here. In any case, as you can well imagine, she can barely sit still. She's absolutely bursting with excitement."

I shifted in my chair, trying to reorient, bracing myself. Our conversations so frequently disintegrated into unfortunate words and unpleasantness. I'd have been happy to hang up after sharing Belle's news and return to my own life, basking in the sunshine of my handiwork.

"So, you know what's up. Belle told you. We're all rather surprised. This wasn't what we were expecting, especially after what happened. We have a lot of questions, Mike and I."

I scooted forward to the edge of my chair, listening carefully. It was safest to let Elizabeth speak and stick to the simplest of responses. No matter what, I mustn't be myself and lead. It was imperative I didn't show my hand.

"I'm sure you do. It's quite something. She didn't give me any details, but I'd love to hear all about it."

I heard a shuffling noise, like she was pulling in a chair. "Mom, we have some things we want to ask."

I faked a laugh. "But why me? What does this have to do with me?"

"Well, frankly, that's what we want to know."

"How could this have anything to do with me? You know Belle. You know her promise. It's just lovely to have it confirmed in such an official way."

"Yes, well, that's true. But it doesn't really add up. Frankly, we were anticipating a completely different kind of call—"

I cut her off to stop this line of conversation. In a million years, I'd never confess to what I'd done. Unexpectedly, that had become part of the pleasure. "It's a wonderful opportunity for Belle, Elizabeth. I'm so happy for her."

"As are we, but it's not clear how—"

"And, of course, I'll be so happy to have her back in the city. This is a better solution for all of us, wouldn't you say?"

I knew she agreed with me. I also knew she'd never say it out loud. She was nothing if not the obedient daughter—to a fault. When she didn't respond, I continued, purposefully directing her elsewhere. "Elizabeth, it's quite a challenge being a good mother. You're doing a wonderful job."

I heard something that sounded like a sharp intake of breath, maybe even a sob. For a moment, I wasn't even sure of the source. It might have been me.

"Thank you, Mom. Thank you from all of us."

"I love you, Elizabeth. With all my heart."

ELIZABETH

MY HEART POUNDED HARD AS I pulled into the school parking lot. I was very late—in fact, too late. I anticipated what I'd find: the detritus of my inability to fulfill this most important commitment. Julie would be waiting on the front steps, probably hugging herself protectively, head lowered in resignation. The blow of my absence was too great, too surprising, and made absolutely no sense in consideration of the fact that I hadn't once, since we met, let her down. We'd rehearsed for this day incessantly, going over the part she'd be reading until she could have read it in her sleep, discussing how it would feel, standing in front of a large group of kids that weren't supportive, many of whom she wouldn't know. Belle even did her part. But nowhere along the way had either of us considered the remote possibility that I wouldn't be there to see her through it to the end.

Today was Open Day at Central High, a morning jam-packed with events intended to give potential students an impression of the opportunities available. Kids from the local middle schools were invited to walk around campus and attend classes, to take a good look at what they could expect next year. At first, Julie didn't want anything to do with the whole thing, insisting on staying back at the Center and steering clear of the kids who liked to make her miserable. But her lit teacher was conducting a reading marathon wherein students would read works nonstop, one after the other, in a seamless performance. Visitors were invited to come and go at will. This celebration of words appealed to me greatly. Why shouldn't she be involved? I knew she was up to it and saw this as the perfect opportunity to prove it.

Of course, I made clear that she'd have my complete and total support. I would pick her up that morning, bring her to school, and sit right there in the audience to guarantee a friendly face. At least, that was the plan. But things had gone differently. And the fact that I hadn't come through for her made pushing her into the whole situation against her will nothing less than cruel. In the final stretch of my bungled trip to school, I found minor comfort in the fact that this timid, fearful young girl who'd stumbled through most words on the printed page months ago could now read just about anything fluently. She was going to be just fine. It didn't matter that I wasn't going to deliver her signed, stamped, and sealed on this one day.

But those were only empty thoughts. It wasn't how I felt. Logic and facts didn't always make up for emotional baggage of the sort Julie carried. Nothing would make my failure okay.

Thankful to have finally arrived, I hurried through the main gate and the front green. The place was festooned with booths, many sporting balloons and colorful posters. A welcome desk was set up near the steps of the main building. I picked up my pace, certain I'd find Julie there, miserable, disappointed, and maybe even angry, refusing to go in alone. But she wasn't.

I continued up the front steps. From there I had a good view of the whole outdoor area. I scanned right and left. She had to be here somewhere. A quick call made while waiting by the side of the road with that blasted flat tire had confirmed that she'd left the Center with Rabbi Eliot. I had no idea how the rabbi came into the picture. The only explanation was that Julie herself called her when she realized I wasn't going to make it. That was a big deal. Trusting another adult and reaching out for help were signs that I'd done something right.

Of course, that didn't let me off the hook. Being where I was supposed to be in the first place would have been far better. On-site support was my job, my only job, and I'd blown it. My eyes shot to the side path that led around to the back of the school. Maybe she'd returned to that lovely spot by the river where she once, under great stress, found solace among the bulrushes. This was a reasonable possibility. I headed back down the steps and started along the path, berating myself out loud as I went. "How could this have happened? No one gets flat tires anymore. No one!"

The band of pain circling the crown of my head intensified dramatically. The pounding had begun a few hours earlier, the moment my car banked sharply toward the shoulder of the road and completely derailed my morning plan. In general, the flat shouldn't have been such a big deal, but I wasn't able to move those bolts and change the tire myself. I had to wait for help. And although I frantically tried to flag down cars, most zoomed by, ignoring the obvious fact of a woman in distress. So much for this being a "friendlier" part of the country where people had a bit more time and were more willing to step in and lend a hand. I'd gotten that wrong.

I was so relieved when the young man in the yellow Fiesta pulled up behind me, yanking his hand brake and bringing his car to a dramatic stop before leaping out and getting down to business. I wanted to hug him. Standing by the side of the road, I made some calls to make amends for my absence. I texted Belle to let her know where I was. There was no response. After the call to the Center, I dialed Rabbi Eliot herself. In this case, no answer was a good thing. They were probably on their way. Thank God for her. I laughed aloud at my own joke. The young man looked up from under the chassis and gave me a strange smile. He probably thought I was crazy.

Next, I called Belle. That was astonishing in and of itself. We almost never spoke on the phone, both of us more comfortable hiding behind the distance intrinsic to texts. Even more unusual was the request for help. Before prepping Julie, it was something I'd never done. I was sure she wouldn't comply. But that was before, and now things were different. Now there seemed a good chance that she'd step in if she could. There was no answer. Home recuperating and not participating in this Open Day, she should have picked up. I sighed. Maybe she was still screening my calls. *Old habits die hard.*

I looked at my watch. Mike had flown to Minneapolis that morning. He wouldn't check his phone for hours. I sent a battery of text messages to all the usual suspects: neighbors, a friend or two of Belle's—all part of my frenetic need to call in the troops. I received not one response. *Where is everyone when I need them?* Thankfully, my industrious young savior had me on my way quickly.

Arriving at the entrance to the riverside park, I made another about-face. This didn't feel right. Julie was somewhere inside the school—I just knew it. Trusting my instincts, I made my way back to campus and studied the easel by the welcome table where a huge whiteboard provided the timetable for the day's events in bold Day-Glo colors. I glanced at my watch. Right now, a few sample lessons were being held in the classrooms on the second floor and there was a tour of the science lab. The literature marathon in the main auditorium was ongoing. The pain in my head returned double strength, and I stretched my mouth into an expression somewhere between determined and at wit's end. "Just maybe . . ."

Elated by the sense that I was closing in, I took the steps two at a time. That's when it happened. There by the door, I was stricken by the strangest sensation. It came on quickly, a feeling of all-encompassing warmth, almost a caress. The pressure in my head eased up, and I picked up a distinct sweetness in the air, akin to jasmine. I didn't wonder at this at all. I knew what it meant, that it had something to do with Belle. Nothing quite compares with a mother's intuition: Belle was the key.

I paused on the landing and pulled out my cell phone, flipping through the texts. There was nothing new. She hadn't even answered the one I'd sent an hour earlier from the side of the road. It didn't matter. The clear sensation of her presence was fortifying. I headed through the front hall and along the locker-lined hallway toward the auditorium. I was astounded by the quiet. It was almost as if I were making this journey alone, the hordes of potential students touring the campus vanishing as I fulfilled my mission.

Just when I thought things couldn't get stranger, I stopped mid-stride. A very bright light was coming from under the double-door entrance of the auditorium, almost beckoning. So strange. As I renewed my approach, the light disappeared. I shook my head. I'd imagined it. This whole day was making me hallucinate, become unhinged. I said a little prayer as I grasped the door handle. Julie simply had to be here. Or maybe Belle—the feeling that she was nearby had become overwhelming.

Stepping inside, I was engulfed by darkness and a dense, overpowering silence broken by one clear voice. Seeking out its source, my eyes fell on a young man standing alone on the stage, illuminated by a single beam of light. Adjusting to the darkness, I took in the audience. It was packed, almost every seat occupied. A mixture of parents and teenage kids faced forward, their attention riveted on the boy reciting. Forgetting my own immediate objective for a moment, I listened to his gusty and enthusiastic rendering of what I immediately recognized as "Casey at the Bat."

> *Ten thousand eyes were on him as he rubbed his hands with dirt;*
> *five thousand tongues applauded when he wiped them on his shirt.*
> *Then while the writhing pitcher ground the ball into his hip,*
> *defiance gleamed in Casey's eye, a sneer curled Casey's lip.*

I almost forgot what I'd come for. This poem had always been a favorite of mine. My dad introduced it to me as a child. I reluctantly detached myself from the rest of Casey's tale and scanned the gathered crowd. I was here for a reason. I tried to discern the faces of the individuals seated, but the lighting was too dim. Reaching the back row, I began to despair. If Julie wasn't here, if I wasn't able to find her, I had no idea where to look next. This was the end of the road.

My eyes hopped around in a less systematic fashion, working their way back to the stage. I was desperate to find something familiar.

That's when it happened. My eyes fell upon the one silhouette I could never fail to pick out, no matter the size of the crowd. Belle was seated in the front row, just beneath the lectern. Although inordinately relieved, one mystery solved, my second sense proven right, I couldn't satisfy my confusion. She wasn't supposed to be here. She should have been back home. And what was she doing sitting in the front row? It was completely out of character. Belle was far more likely to opt for somewhere in the back, a spot from which she could fulfill her duty of attendance while still chatting with her friends. It seemed like a sign.

I frantically searched the seats nearby, convinced that Julie was there. She had to be. That would explain it. But she wasn't. And once again, I felt as if I'd come to an end. After searching the school grounds inside and out, I'd come no closer to discovering her whereabouts, let alone whether she'd screwed up the courage to come on her own and perform. She might have been here and then left. There was also the possibility that I'd gotten everything wrong. That she never even made it to school. That the message about Rabbi Eliot picking her up had been a miscommunication. I wondered whether I should run back to the car and head over to the Center. Maybe I'd find her there. We could talk. I'd make sure she knew that it was okay—that deciding to give this stressful experience a pass was just fine.

But something about Belle's presence held me fast. I couldn't leave just yet. Huddling close to the wall, I slid toward the front of the auditorium. I felt intensely remorseful. This whole day had been a fiasco of my own doing. I shouldn't have pushed Julie into participating in the first place; I should have fulfilled my promise to see her through it. In the end, I was the reason she couldn't find her way to a better place.

I numbly joined into the raucous applause for the boy who'd read "Casey," now taking a bow and exiting the back of the stage. The next act was announced. I didn't catch the words. I didn't even bother listening. There was absolutely no way this day could be saved. I was distracted by the shuffling of the audience, people getting up and moving on to other activities within the school, others coming in through the doors and taking a seat. A spotlight was directed at the waiting dais. My eyes idly moved toward it, more out of instinct than curiosity. A rustle of movement in the front row drew my attention, and before I knew it, Belle jumped onto the stage.

There was no time to try to make sense of what I was seeing. In any case, it instantly became clear. Standing there at the lectern was Julie, safe and sound, right where she was supposed to be. My heart skipped a beat, my eyes filled with tears, and my lips moved with a whispered exclamation of gratitude and relief. The scene before me, something I could never have dreamed up in a million years and one I would never forget, truly rocked my soul. It was Julie who'd been announced. It was her turn to recite, and Belle—my Belle? She was right there beside her.

It was obvious from the relaxed air between them that Belle had been with her for some time. Although I had no idea how this came about, one basic truth came shining through: Belle wasn't waiting for Julie to have a difficult moment of the kind we'd envisioned back in the pie shop. Instead, she swooped in from the start, playing at stage crew, tapping the microphone once or twice, moving the reading light a smidgen—all these insignificant gestures meant to assure Julie that she was there for her, that *someone* was there for her; to let her know she wasn't alone. And although I stood at a bit of a distance, I caught each detail of the scene playing out before me, those gorgeous minutiae that made the whole sparkle: the feeling of affirmation that passed between the two, Julie's trusting eyes, Belle's encouraging and confident movements; the way Belle gently squeezed Julie's arm, assuring her that she was on firm ground, before jumping back off the stage and taking her seat.

Belle had been right here helping Julie the whole time. As far as I was concerned, this was enough. In fact, it was everything. It was exactly what I would have wished for if I'd been given the chance to do so. I felt lighter than air, my spirit elevating as it burst with pleasure and a sense of fulfillment—motherly fulfillment. I'd done something right. With me missing in action precisely when I was most needed, Belle had seamlessly stepped in, filling the important role of chief support staff. My Belle, my uncooperative, recalcitrant, surly teenage daughter, the one who'd shut me out of her life completely just a year earlier, had gone out of her way to help a fragile girl she barely knew and, by extension, me. The thought alone made my head swim with vertiginous delight.

I plastered my back to the wall, completely absorbed, and barely noticed when someone took my hand. The insistent tugging eventually broke my trance, drawing my attention away from the glorious scene on the stage. At first, I tried to shake off whoever it was. I had no intention of leaving the auditorium, of ending this extraordinary moment, a true high point within the tumultuous annals of my life with Belle. But when I saw who was doing the leading, I couldn't help but follow. It was Rabbi Eliot.

I wasn't at all surprised. Everything fell into place. She'd brought Julie to school that morning. But her role in making this come about had been far bigger. It was she who had found a way for me to step out of my proscribed life, encouraging me to take the risks necessary to finding a new direction. Thanks to Rabbi Eliot, I'd become an anchor for this needy young girl, helping her get to this spectacular achievement: stepping on a stage before an audience of peers. I'd never be able to thank her enough for bringing together the disparate parts that enabled this picture.

Out in the hallway, blinking wildly to combat the sudden brightness of the fluorescent lights, the bigger picture receded, and I desperately sought the details. I wanted to hear everything, to know how this had all transpired. There were so many open questions.

"It was all Belle."

"I don't understand. What does that mean? You were the one who brought Julie to school. They told me so over at the Center when I called. Listen, I can't thank you enough." I babbled, speaking at double-pace. I couldn't rein in the rush of energy that this enormous shift in events had released. "I never would have made it in time." From inside the auditorium, I heard the words "The Box," and then a pause. I yearned to step back inside, sneak up onto the stage, stand in the murky shadows beyond the spotlight, and lay a comforting hand on Julie's back.

"That's technically the case. I did bring her. But I'm telling you, it was Belle. She called and asked me for help."

"I still don't understand."

She shook her head vigorously. "You don't really need to. What's important is that it happened. Belle recognized a situation that wasn't going how it was meant to—a circumstance in which both you and someone you cared about were going to be hurt. She knew Julie wouldn't take the stage without you and even getting her to school was going to be a major undertaking. When she got your text she went into action, calling me immediately. My part was easy; all I had to do was give both girls a ride over. Belle took over from there, stepping perfectly into your shoes."

Here she paused and smiled. "What you just saw was a true thing of beauty. I don't know a lot about all the steps in the middle, the moments that have passed since we first talked about your mentoring someone back in my office, since you met Julie. I don't even really know what's gone on between you and Belle. I know you weren't thrilled when she moved to New York. But back there at the retreat, before that awful accident . . ." She paused to look down at her feet, shaking her head. "I'm still so very sorry about that. But you know, right before it happened, I had a sense that she was in a different place: more centered, less angry. I hoped this calmer mode was spilling out into your relationship."

Rabbi Eliot reached toward me, grasping both my hands in hers. The gesture felt so wonderful, more of a blessing than an embrace. I didn't want her to let go. There was something so comforting about being held in just this way, by someone you respected; about being looked at with such an intoxicating mixture of warmth, understanding, and admiration. She couldn't have found a better way to express her confidence in my accomplishment, the fact that I'd managed to rediscover myself. All it took was turning my focus outward, toward the wider world, instead of dwelling on what was happening within not only the walls of my house but those of my mind.

"Elizabeth, this really is significant. All of this. And don't be so surprised by Belle. As I've tried to tell you before, she's a genuinely considerate young adult. I know that's been a challenge to accept—you've gotten the worst of it as the target of her growing pains, the bane of being a mother—but there's simply so much more. You're seeing that today. In the real world, out there"—and here she gestured down the long hallway of the high school toward the exit doors—"she's exactly who you've raised her to be."

I had the strong urge to give her a bear hug, swing her around the room, and sing out loud. I wanted to accept these rays of sun without question. But I still felt the burden of the long morning with its frustrating delays and maddening search, the questions and concerns of hours having left me depleted. I had to get back to Julie and do what I'd said I would from the start. I nodded back toward the door of the auditorium with a questioning face. "Should we—"

"I think not," Rabbi Eliot cut me off abruptly and, tucking her arm tightly in my own, spun me around toward the exit. "You've done your job. Beautifully. Now it's their turn."

I closed my eyes a moment, feeling as though I were melting from within, the tension that had gathered into a fierce headache earlier finally released by the true wonder I'd had a part in creating. I was in awe of the extent of my daughter's compassion, the significance of her actions, stepping up without hesitation, putting herself out for someone she barely knew—extending to her the same attention, care, and love she knew I would have provided if I'd been there. Belle's assumption of the roles of protector and mentor, essentially becoming a big sister, affirmed that she hadn't been ignoring me after all; in fact, she'd absorbed precisely what I'd hoped to convey through my devotion to her, to her father, to my work, and now to Julie. Her actions added up to a truer expression of love and compassion than any that could be uttered. This was as good as it got.

Walking out into the sunshine on Rabbi Eliot's arm I felt light, almost airborne. I could not have imagined a better ending to this day, a more satisfactory resolution to this period of renewal and self-discovery. The revelations and the ultimate truths discovered added up to larger gains than I could ever have foreseen. I paused on my way down the steps, feeling a pinch of dismay. It had taken so long to attain these insights. So much heartache might have been saved. But that was one of the lessons learned: time could never be manipulated, its pace forever beyond our reach. I accepted that and let go of what I couldn't undo, returning to the pleasure of the moment, the canopy of blue above, the lush trees of the school's campus soaking up the brightness of this beautiful spring day.

I happily embraced other findings. Mothering: it wasn't a science to be studied and conquered but rather a long and winding road to be followed with eyes and heart open wide. Being a daughter: much the same, both titles incorporating absolutely no givens, no promises. Eyes and heart open wide. Nature: it will have its way, spreading its magic, no matter our attempts to bend it to our will. And this: provided with enough nurturing sunshine and water, all flowers will eventually bloom, their petals spreading wide, their unique magnificence revealed to all.

Arriving at the parking lot, I had the most compelling and unexpected urge. I wanted to share this extraordinary day, my enlightenment, the euphoric feeling of discovery, and I knew precisely with whom. Although my long-standing default mechanism sought to fight this instinct, to snuff it out in order to protect myself, to avoid exposure, I did no such thing. There no longer seemed a need. I gave Rabbi Eliot another warm hug of gratitude and hurried to my car. It was time to call Mom.

THE END

ACKNOWLEDGMENTS

I HAVE BEEN PASSIONATELY INTERESTED in the subject of mothers and daughters for as long as I can remember, observing and experiencing both from the kitchen stool to bleachers, from the barbeque pit to the back seat of a station wagon. I have supplemented this fascination with literature, including classics that feature fabulous role models—Robert McCloskey's *Make Way for Ducklings*, Shel Silverstein's *The Giving Tree*, Louisa May Alcott's *Little Women*, and J. K. Rowling's Harry Potter series—as well as those featuring the types best avoided, Philip Roth's *Portnoy's Complaint*, Roald Dahl's *Matilda*, and Christina Crawford's *Mommie Dearest.*

My own mother set a high bar, tucking me in tight each night and reading to me until I fell asleep; faithfully attending every recital, concert, and game; chauffeuring me to more lessons than I could possibly ever count. Most significantly, she encouraged me to follow my dreams and showed me just how passionate one can be about one's children—fundamental elements of excellent mothering. I have tried to do the very same with my own.

My father, perhaps surprisingly, also contributed to the formation of the concept I've come to understand as mothering. He is—now was—the living proof of the significance of love and steadfast support, of assuring one's child of their parents' unwavering faith. Although having lost his own mother (and father) at a very young age, he was raised by a bevy of other loving women (grandmothers, aunts, and his mother's friends) who instilled within him the self-confidence and sense of security that enabled him to raise his own children in an atmosphere of love, encouragement, and support.

Of course, it takes a village, and I am enormously grateful to the many mothers who have come into my life—both before I became one myself and after, some met through family, some through synagogue and summer camp, some through school, some through work, and some through my best friends—for showing me just how many ways there are to mother and, just as significantly, why it counts.

My dearest friends—those who became mothers when I did, just as we were reaching adulthood—have had a large part in this journey. My experience has been extraordinarily enriched and improved by theirs, through the exchange of stories, laughter, and tears shared on the benches of playgrounds in both Israel and the United States; in deck chairs by the swimming pool at the Caesarea Country Club, and on towels spread on the sandy shores of Long Beach Island, New Jersey; next to the goat in Rittenhouse Square and on the sidewalk at the entrance to the kindergarten; at the end of a phone cord and, in these last few years, via text messages. My children have reaped the benefits of your advice, your warnings, your juicy tips, and your incredibly kind hearts.

I owe eternal gratitude to my husband for actually making me a mother—the very best thing that has ever happened to me, hands down—and continuing to stand by my side ever since with admiring eyes and infinite praise, even when it is entirely undeserved. My children, of course, have offered the very best crash course on motherhood possible, continuing, even as I write these words, to both challenge my efforts to get it right and affirm the occasional success—to assure me that no matter the result, it's all worthwhile. Witnessing all three currently wiggling into young adulthood is enough to remind me daily of the importance of simply letting them know I will always be in their corner.

www.ingramcontent.com/pod-product-compliance
Lightning Source LLC
Chambersburg PA
CBHW030354310726
48979CB00001B/302

* 9 7 8 1 6 4 6 6 3 5 5 2 8 *